The Inquiry

Will Caine

ONE PLACE. MANY STORIES

HQ
An imprint of HarperCollins*Publishers* Ltd
1 London Bridge Street
London SE1 9GF

This edition 2019

1
First published in Great Britain by
HQ, an imprint of HarperCollins*Publishers* Ltd 2019

ISBN: 978-0-00-832565-7

MIX
Paper from
responsible sources
FSC™ C007454

This book is produced from independently certified FSC™ paper
to ensure responsible forest management.

For more information visit: www.harpercollins.co.uk/green

Printed and bound in Great Britain by
CPI Group (UK) Ltd, Croydon, CR0 4YY

In memory of
my brother-in-law James
and his son Miles.

'There were one or two big ones. That's how we kept a lid on it for so long. But we were never fully sure about them. How could we be? They were from a different world.'

Ex-MI5 Officer, private conversation

2005

The ping of a phone. She jerks awake, grabs it, brings it close to her face, checks the time.

6.47 a.m.

Odd. No one messages her this early.

She lies back on her pillow, pulls up the duvet, clicks on 'view'.

Don't use the buses or tubes in London today.

She rubs sleep from her eyes. What the f— is this?

She scrolls down. Just a number. No name, no one in her contacts. She rechecks the number – nothing familiar about it.

She screws her eyes shut, kneads them with her knuckles, thinks. She hits reply, thumbs on keys.

Who is this?

She waits. After a few seconds, the phone pings again.

Message sending failed.

What *is* this? She clicks back on the message, hits 'options', adds the name as 'Anon' and the number to her contacts. She hits call. The ringtone is instantly interrupted by a woman's voice. 'The number you have dialled is unobtainable.'

Weird. Totally random. Has to be a mistake.

She gets up, washes, dresses, applies make-up, the everyday rhythms. The words still churn in her head. Butterflies jig in her stomach. She begins to realise she can't get rid of the nagging thought.

What if the text is for real? And the sender's chosen to vanish…

Stop imagining. It's a rogue message – people get them all the time from all sorts of weirdos. She wonders how many others must have had it. Thousands probably – some madman trying to create a scare. That's probably easy – a simple piece of code can do mass send-outs of texts.

Or just a sick joke from a sick mind.

She goes downstairs, makes her usual cup of coffee, toasts her usual slice of bread. She turns on the radio, volume low. All the chatter's about London's great victory the day before, winning the 2012 Olympics to be held in seven years' time. She feels better.

The nag's still there.

Should she show the text to her father? She goes back upstairs, creeps along the landing, peers in. Curtains drawn, no lights. He's still asleep, she shouldn't disturb him. Shouldn't worry him. In her bedroom, she straightens the duvet, puffs her pillow, goes to the mirror to brush her hair. She looks out of the window. The line of terrace roofs is the same as always. A dog barks. She jumps, her heart thumps. She shakes her head violently to shift the nag.

Down in the hallway, she grabs her coat and stands stock

still. The text is just… she comes back to the same word. Weird. What weirdo would send something like that?

Is there anyone *she* knows?

Just… just forget it. It's a prank, some fool's attempt to frighten.

Think. It must be nearly ten years since the last bomb went off in London, IRA, of course. Except for the nail bomber in Soho. Then there was 9/11 and the Madrid train last year. But whatever may happen in the rest of the world, this city, this country, is at peace. She's not going to take any notice of it.

Perhaps it's someone trying to organise a boycott, some kind of strike. Yes, her rational mind tells her, could well be that. Odd way to do it though.

She takes a deep breath, straightens her shoulders and, closing the front door behind her, strides out towards Tooting Bec underground station for the daily journey northwards to the Chambers where she's just starting the law career that will be her life.

On the tube, it's the same as always. Young couples chatting, eyes buried in books, ears plugged into Walkmans, mouths gaping with exhausted yawns. The carriage is filling to squeezing point. Drawing into Waterloo, she sees through the tube window a mass of faces waiting to crush her – a nightmarish canvas of every colour, scowling and grinning back at her.

The train jerks to a halt. Something hits her. She turns, sees a large rucksack on the back of a bearded young Asian. She catches his eye – he avoids hers. She goes on watching. His appearance – the neat haircut, trimmed beard – seems just like the photos of the 9/11 hijackers. She tries to remember if the Madrid train bombers used rucksacks to carry death. She has an overwhelming sense they did. Heat sears her face. She needs to get out.

The train stops, doors open. She pushes, the oncoming swarm miraculously divides to let her through. She pauses as the doors close and watches the carriages leave with their crammed human cargo. She walks, fighting for breath – the train grinds on towards King's Cross.

It was just a young man with a rucksack, for God's sake.

She crosses Hungerford Bridge and turns right along the river, the lightest of rain refreshing her. She looks around. Far to the west, beyond the pale grey hovering over the Thames, the sky is brighter. The day will clear. It will be the same as any other.

A bus on the opposite side of the Embankment, its passengers' faces like polka dots, heads towards the city.

'… buses or tubes…'

The buses and tubes are running normally. There's no sign of any strike action – or boycott. No demonstrators or posters.

The nag becomes a throb.

At Chambers she is greeted with smiles. It seems that, even if everyone else here is white and English, they like her and want her for the youth and difference she'll bring.

The clerk inspects her. 'Are you OK?' She detects his concern.

'Yeah, fine,' she smiles. What's he noticed? 'Just murder on the tube.'

What made her say that?

She wants to ask if anyone else got the same weird text that she did. But if none of them did, she can imagine them staring at her – who's the weirdo here?

She sits at her desk, fires up her computer and begins to study her case files. She can't concentrate, fingers sweating, slipping and sliding over keys. She feels the other three in her office watching her and looks up. Their heads are glued to screens. Instead, the face of that guy with the rucksack flashes before her.

It's no good. It won't go away. She looks at her watch – 9.21 am. Still most of the day to come. Surely loads of others must have got the text – the authorities probably know about it already. Even so, she should warn them, however nonsensical it might seem. But how? She's a young Muslim woman – might that not raise questions? Cast suspicion on her? Might they want to interview her father? Even her new colleagues in Chambers?

Best if there was some kind of anonymous helpline. She'll check for that on her computer. Head-down, concentrating on her search, she hears a distant sound. Sirens.

She hits a number for the Met's confidential line and dials it.

She hears more sirens. She looks up – her office colleagues are hurrying towards a window. She's seized by dread, stops dialling, puts the phone back. Is something happening?

She clicks on the BBC website. The 7th of July 2005. Nothing. The news is still all about the Olympics. The sirens are just an accident, a fire, usual thing, a day like any other, she repeats to herself.

She dials again. A recorded message tells her to hold on, someone will be with her very soon. 'Please don't hang up.'

Suddenly the BBC website flashes up 'breaking news'.

First reports of a massive disturbance on London's underground system

Slowly and silently, she puts down the phone and stares blankly ahead. A terror dawns.

Oh God. No. Surely not. Surely it couldn't have been him. Could it?

1

Shortly before lunch on a bright, late spring day, Sir Francis Morahan, Lord Justice of Appeal, and now chair of the Inquiry into the security services' record against terror attacks, handwrote a letter to Sara Shah, junior counsel at 14 Knightly Court Chambers, EC4. Despite the piercing sun, he took a grey woollen hat and matching gloves out of the bottom right drawer of his desk. Rather than his familiar grey coat, he then chose from the hooks behind his office door a waterproof yellow anorak, normally reserved for bad weather, and a broad white and red striped scarf. Carrying these under an arm, he turned right out of his office, avoiding the open-plan area housing the Inquiry's staff, and descended by the back stairs to the underground car park. He unchained his bicycle, put on the anorak, wrapped the scarf around his nose and mouth, pulled the hat down over his forehead and extracted sunglasses from a trouser pocket.

He pedalled out of the exit, which faced the new American Embassy in Vauxhall, then two hundred yards along Nine Elms Lane before joining the Thames Path. Feeling pinpricks of sweat on skin tightly covered by his chosen clothing, he cycled past the MI6 building, through the tunnel beneath Lambeth roundabout and carried his bike up the steps to Westminster Bridge, avoiding the crowds milling around the London Eye. Across the bridge he turned onto the Embankment and, after a few hundred yards, north into Carmelite Street, just east of the Inns of Court.

The heat now stifling, and anxiety flooding his body, he turned into Knightly Court, locked the bike on the black railings, rang the bell of number fourteen, climbed the stairs and, with a mumble of 'Letter for Miss Shah' in his best south London accent, dropped his envelope in front of a receptionist. She hardly looked up.

Morahan scurried back down the stairs and reclaimed his bicycle; only when he had reached the south side of the river did he remove the scarf, hat and jacket. He had paused, though not by design, opposite the Houses of Parliament. For the first time in years, decades even – perhaps right back to that moment when his brief spell as an MP and then Cabinet Minister had begun with the General Election victory of 1997 – Francis Morahan buzzed with excitement and anticipation.

She was the link; the one person able to make the connection he needed. And yet, if he told her that, she would surely run away. He had shaken the dice and dared to roll them. But, for the game to start, Sara Shah must agree to play.

Later that afternoon, the addressee of Morahan's envelope walked back from court to her Chambers with a senior QC.

'He's as bent as a coiled python,' said Ludo Temple.

'Hardly as deadly,' said Sara Shah.

'That's not the point, he's a crook.'

'Do I really care?' Striding side by side down Old Bailey, Sara turned sharply to the bulky, puffing figure on her right.

Her bright blue Chanel scarf flicked over a shoulder and her teasing eyes cast him a look of mischief.

He stopped, caught his breath and glared. 'A Ponzi scheme's a Ponzi scheme.'

'But a wine-selling Ponzi scheme…'

'Yes, and it's poor old buggers like… like what I'll end up as, conned into thinking they're buying bloody good claret without realising the pension's going straight into the man's pocket. And when they try to retrieve it, the whole lot's been sold to finance his floating palace on the Med.'

'So what? I don't drink.'

'I don't say prayers five times a day.'

'Ludovic!'

He knew that whenever she scolded him, he was near to overstepping the mark. But that was the fun of her – even if you did, she was quick to forgive; though he'd seen others shrivel under her silent raising of an eyebrow.

Over the past year, he had become ever more fond of Sara Shah – and ever more admiring. The greatest pleasure had been the change in his more cynical colleagues. 'Let me get this clear, Ludo,' Peter Alexander, Head of Chambers, had said at the chamber QCs' meeting, convened to discuss her. 'You want a Muslim human rights lawyer to join this criminal law chambers.'

'Yes, Peter.'

'And she wears a hijab.'

'Yes, Peter, rather nice and expensive scarves as it happens. Blue usually.'

'And you haven't forgotten that our principal earnings come from fraud, in which she has little or no experience.'

'No, Peter. She may have spent the last few years doing liberal luvvie stuff with Rainbow, but she began with criminal, including fraud, is well-grounded in all aspects of law, wants a change and is extremely clever. And extremely attractive too.'

'Aha,' piped up Percy Fairweather QC, rubbing his hands.

'Stop it, Percy,' said Amanda Fielding QC.

In fact, Amanda had been the main objector, saying she had no issue with either another woman – the more, the better – or a Muslim. But a Muslim woman covering up her hair was inappropriate for a chambers which should be seen as secular and progressive. 'Honestly, Ludo, will she insist on looking like that for the website photo?'

'Have a coffee with her,' he'd said. Which Amanda had. She waived her objection almost before taking a sip.

Sara herself knew there would be undercurrents. She also knew why even the stuffier members of 14 Knightly Court might see an advantage in bringing her on board. Briefs for Serious Fraud Office and HMRC cases were by far the most lucrative Crown Prosecution activity for a top criminal QC; as the law tried to move with the times, having a visibly observant female Muslim on the team ticked useful boxes. And how helpful it was that British justice still required barristers to turn out in black robes and a wig – to dress modestly and cover their hair. In a courtroom, the secular state and the dress choice she'd made for herself happily co-existed.

'You know me better than to expect an apology,' smiled Ludo as they turned into Ludgate Hill.

'I also know you well enough not to rise to it,' said Sara.

'But I *was* making a point,' he continued. 'I will never allow myself to feel sympathy for a man – or woman – I'm prosecuting. I couldn't care less if they're loveable old geezers, or if their victims deserved what was coming to them.'

'What about when you're defending them?'

His chuckle turned into a wheeze. 'When I'm prosecuting, he's a bad chap. When I'm defending, he's a good chap.' He paused to cough. 'Hell's bells, Sara, do you have to walk so darned fast?'

Knightly Court, at the eastern reaches of the Temple, lay equidistant between the Old Bailey and the Royal Courts, manageable walks even for Ludo. They entered No. 14 and climbed the gloomy, twisting stairs to the first floor, emerging into the broad light space of a modern reception. The receptionist stood to give Sara her envelope.

'Delivered by courier, Miss Shah.'

Sara glanced at her hand-scrawled name and '*PRIVATE AND CONFIDENTIAL*' written large on the top left corner.

'Expecting something?' asked Ludo with no attempt at hiding his curiosity.

'No,' said Sara. 'I've no idea.' He knew she was telling the truth.

She bypassed her office and headed for the ladies. The lengthening daylight hours made it easier for *Asr* – mid-afternoon prayer – as it followed the court rising. *Zuhr* – midday prayer – was more of an interruption and once again she had missed it. She would not leave court while it was in process and today's lunch had been earmarked for an update with the instructing Crown solicitor – an opportunity to impress a hand that fed both her and her chambers. She would try to make it up, resist the urge to flag.

She locked the door of a cubicle containing both toilet and basin and washed her hands the required three times, gargled, cleaned her nose and rinsed her face, clearing away displaced flecks of eyeshadow and liner. *Wudhu* offered a double soothing – the preparatory cleansing was also a relaxation of the courtroom tension. She cradled water in her left hand and washed her right arm three times up to the elbow. She repeated the actions on the other side. She passed water over her head, wetting the skin behind her ears and neck. '*Oh lord, make my face bright on the Day when the faces will turn dark.*' Finally, she removed her tights, sliding them below her three-quarter-length black skirt to bare her feet. One at a time, she raised each foot into the basin and submerged it, cleaning between her toes with her fingers.

She stood straight, inspected her eyes, saw the fatigue and sighed before heading back down the corridor into the chambers library. The rows of bound black volumes looked as untouched as ever – in these days of online research the room was a quiet retreat, and usually deserted when she wanted it for prayers; she suspected her new colleagues had been educated in the prayer calendar. The suspicion embarrassed her.

She thought of the exchange with Ludo and asked herself again if the switch from human rights campaigner to highly paid fraud specialist was corrupting her. The fact remained that she'd fallen out of love with too much of the human rights agenda – unable to repress an inner voice that Rainbow Chambers, and therefore she, had become prone to exploiting generously intended legislation. The sad truth was that rejected asylum seekers were often turned away for good reasons. She knew that in at least one case, perhaps more, she had represented 'victims' making false claims of British army brutality – and won. She'd come to worry that a realism about these sad people, born of too much experience, was chipping away at her humanity. She'd even started reading *The Times* ahead of the *Guardian*!

A move to fraud had been the right thing to do. If iron was entering her soul, better to direct it against hardened criminals, though she hadn't yet had to defend one. She remembered Ludo's 'good chap' and 'bad chap'. Cynic or wit?

Stop thinking and pray. She faced east; the slanting sun cast sienna rays above the opposite building. *'I intend to perform the four rakat fardh of the Salat Al-Asr for Allah.'* She paused, her mind cluttered, impossibly distracted, unable to slip into an automatic empathy with the words she was about to say. Perhaps if her father had drummed discipline into her in the way she'd seen with others, it would be easier. But Tariq Shah was not like that. For him it was cultural, not spiritual – something he and his family had always done. He occasionally looked in at mosque and, however sceptical he might be, wished no offence to Islam – nor any other religion. She had inherited the scepticism but not the temperament to relax with it; self-discipline was her only answer to both.

Ultimately, she told herself, emerging from the jumble of thoughts, it was her duty to her father that justified the professional move she'd made – the money to guarantee his comfort till the day he died. The comfort of this conclusion finally cleared her mind and she raised her arms over her chest. *'Audhu billahi min-ash-shaytan -hir-rajeem, bismillah-hir-Rahman-hir-raheem.'*

Ten minutes later, she was back in the room she shared at chambers with two other junior counsel. Marty Richards was out of London but Sheila Blackstone was there, make-up mirror angled towards full lips, to which she was applying copious layers of scarlet lipstick.

'Sara darling, you caught me at it! Good day in court?'

'Yes, fun,' said Sara. 'And utterly irresponsible. A wine fraudster. Who could care?'

'Half the QCs in this Chambers will care a very great deal about that,' said Sheila, eyes down on her mirror.

Sara hung her coat on a hook and looked at the hand-written envelope. She was tempted to chuck it in a bin – 'Private and Confidential' was probably shorthand for 'I need a free favour'. But there was an edginess in the scrawled writing that stoked her curiosity; anyone sending begging letters would write more neatly. She caught Sheila's inquisitive eye peering around the mirror, rose and left the room. She returned with the envelope to the ladies, the one guaranteed place of uninterrupted refuge, entered a cubicle and sat on the closed seat. She ripped it open. The printed heading was followed by the same scrawling hand-writing as on the envelope.

The Rt Hon Lord Justice Morahan
45 Chelsea Place Upper
London SW3 6BY

Monday evening

Dear Ms Shah

My apologies for writing to you in such an unusual way. You may remember that we met briefly in Cambridge two years ago at the 'Human Rights: A Judge's Role' conference. I was most impressed with your contribution to that and also by your formidable record in this area.

You will be aware of the government Inquiry into security service strategy against terror which the incoming administration appointed me to chair last year. There is a missing expertise in the Inquiry which I believe you are uniquely qualified to provide. Formally speaking, this approach should be coming not from me but from the Government Legal Department which administers such matters. However, I have overwhelming and powerful reasons for initially speaking to you alone.

I would therefore be most grateful if, in the first instance, you would meet me privately. I cannot impress upon you too strongly that it is vital for my sake, if not yours, that this meeting is confidential and unobserved. I leave it to you to arrange a time and place that would suit these criteria. I can travel anonymously by bicycle. Anywhere within reach of Vauxhall Cross would be suitable. The meeting would be purely exploratory and you would be making no commitment by agreeing to it. However, I do not exaggerate when I say that truly vital matters of state and possible wrong-doing are at stake.

I would ask you to deliver your reply hand-written to the address above. I hope very much to hear from you with your arrangement.

Yours most sincerely

Francis Morahan

Sara stood up with a jerk, blood rushing from her head. Both the author's identity and the fretfulness of the letter were a shock. She took a few deep breaths. Her thumping heart began to slow and the colour returned to her face. She wondered at how such perfect, concise sentences could emerge from such an apparently shaky hand. She didn't dare to step out of the cubicle until she'd calmed down. It was the most disconcerting letter she had ever received, prompting a scattergun of questions and images. Chambers was not the place to confront them.

She walked back to her room; for once she was relieved to find Sheila gone. She stuffed the next day's briefs and a sheaf of articles on cybercrime into her bag, grabbed her coat and headed for the exit. Ludo's door was open – deliberately, she suspected.

'Go on then,' he grinned. 'Something interesting?'

'Really, Ludo, is not a lady's privacy to be protected?'

He wasn't buying it. 'If it's an offer, tell them to sod off. It's my firm intention, Sara Shah, to clamp you in chains to 14 Knightly Court until my retiring day.'

She wandered over, gave him a pat on the shoulder, and headed out into the street, making for the Embankment. The sun was dipping beyond Big Ben and the skyscrapers of the new Vauxhall megacity. She crossed Waterloo Bridge, losing herself among the swathes of homeward-bound commuters. She found herself staring at the London Eye. The memory of that day – when it was still the new, exciting addition to the capital's skyline called the Millennium Wheel – struck her like a smack of iced water.

She must snap out of it. London, her logical mind told her, remained safe. For well over a decade after 7/7 only one fatality, that of Lee Rigby, the soldier drummer hacked to death outside Woolwich barracks, had been the result of terrorism. Not just in the city but in Britain itself. Then came the van and knife attacks in central London; the bombing of a pop concert at Manchester Arena, lethally shattering the calm; the reminder that terror had not, and would not, go away.

Compared with other death tolls – road accidents, fires, polluted air – the figures remained, it seemed to Sara, insignificant. The ultimate victims were ordinary Muslims, tainted by association, fearful of hate-fuelled revenge. Yet, unable to shift the strangeness of Morahan's scrawled letter from her mind, she found herself edgily inspecting the young Asian with the blue rucksack fidgeting in the corner of the underground carriage. When he stepped out of the train at Kennington, she was, despite herself, unable to prevent a flush of relief.

Back on Tooting Broadway, her mood changed. The Islamic Centre and halal butchers stood contentedly alongside trendy brunch cafés with eager central European waitresses and antipodean chefs. In this part of London few wore the full niqab and burka, but there were plenty of hijabis like herself. Some young Muslim women dressed in figure-hugging jeans and short-sleeved shirts; that was not her own choice now, but she never forgot the time when, all too briefly, she had also enjoyed that lifestyle.

She headed up the Broadway and into Webster Road with its terraces of small 1920s bow-fronted houses. A few sagged unloved, rotting window sills and yellowing streaks from overflowing pipes discolouring their whitewashed frontages. But most were spruced-up and clean, often with recently added porches and front doors proudly displaying their panelled multi-coloured glass. Her shrewd father had bought their house three years after she was born, during the heyday of Mrs Thatcher's right to buy, a nest for the family he'd once hoped to grow.

She had been just eight years old when her mother had died – how distant it seemed. Not old enough truly to know her; or to ask her what she really believed. Would her mother, with the conviction of a convert's faith, have seeded in her the certainty her father lacked? Whenever Sara occasionally referred to her, her father never seemed to want to engage; the answer was always a platitude. 'Yes, your mother was always a good woman.' 'Always true to God.' 'So beautiful.' 'I never stopped loving her.' It was territory he did not want to enter. After her death, the house had become father and daughter's sanctuary. She never thought of leaving him, whatever the pressures to marry from aunts and cousins. With him to look after, how could she? The truth was that, far from being her burden, he was her excuse.

She turned her key in the front door Yale lock and it opened. Noisily – a signal to her father that she was home – she wiped her feet, hung up her coat and after a few seconds called, 'Dad!' No answer; he must have forgotten to double lock on his way out. Despite such lapses, his brain was in good order and she remembered it was his bridge evening at the Working Men's Club up in Clapham. She smiled at the thought of him – his shortness, the little sticking-out tummy and the ever-present smile. A purist might have told him that card-play was un-Islamic; he would have joyously replied that it was a great Pakistani game, and Zia Mahmood the finest player the world had ever seen.

She went into the cramped kitchen, made herself tea and headed upstairs. After her mother's death, he had knocked through the two rooms at the back to give her a bedroom-cum-study with her own shower room. She later realised it was his way of saying he never would, nor could, remarry. No more wives, no more children. Just him and her.

She removed her scarf, jacket and tailored black skirt she

wore for work, replacing them with a loose blouse, cardigan and trousers. In the shower room she stared at herself in the mirror; the unblemished pale olive skin she was blessed with stared back. The odd line was forming on her forehead but the rest of her body from high cheekbones to slender ankles, was uncreased and lean – as photographs showed, the figure of her mother not her father. She rubbed her face with soap and warm water, patted it dry and returned to the bedroom. With half a sigh, she unstrapped her black holdall and lifted out the laptop and envelope containing Morahan's letter. From her desk she looked out at the row of neighbouring back gardens – neat flowerbeds and patches of lawn interrupted occasionally by messes of dumped detritus. She booted up her laptop and typed in the two words 'Morahan Inquiry'.

She clicked on the official website, then 'Chair and Panel', and found herself lingering over the portrait photograph of Morahan himself. She tried to remember him from that Cambridge conference. He'd certainly been on the panel at one session but she couldn't recall an actual meeting, seeing him close up, shaking his hand. It must have happened if he said so – and there'd been hundreds there.

Under the scrutiny of the camera, she detected an apprehension in the eyes, a trace of disappointment too perhaps. A figure that must be imposing peering down from the judicial bench under cover of the judge's wig seemed unsettled. Was he an unhappy – or disenchanted – man? His biography showed the bare bones of a personal life; married Iona Chesterfield 1977, two daughters. Otherwise it outlined a seamlessly upward legal career interrupted only by a five-year stint, 1997–2002, in Parliament, ending with his resignation both as Attorney General and MP.

Or was it a lack of fulfilment those eyes betrayed? His resignation seemed never to have been fully explained. Journalists and, later, historians writing about the Iraq war, assumed Morahan had seen it coming and got out ahead. She wondered if he himself had encouraged that narrative – whether those eyes hid another story.

Press coverage of the Inquiry was patchy. On the day of its announcement by the Prime Minister the *Guardian* had hailed it as a 'brave innovation to shine a chink of public light onto the security services'. *The Times* applauded the PM's initiative but warned that 'secret services must be allowed to keep secrets'.

She heard the front door lock click and footsteps below. She flinched. 'Is that you, Dad?' she shouted down.

''Course it's me, who else are you expecting?'

Who else indeed? She collected herself, went downstairs and bound him in a close hug, tucking her chin against his ear from her greater height. They broke away and he gave her a puzzled smile.

'Sara, you hug me tight. Are you OK?'

''Course I'm OK, just pleased to see you.'

He felt her relax. 'You looked agitated to me. That's not like my girl.'

'Pressure, I guess.'

'You gotta take it easy. Like me!'

'If only,' she laughed.

'Anyway, I got something to celebrate. I landed a better squeeze tonight even than that one you just gave me.'

She shook her head in mock disapproval of him and handed him the sheet of paper she'd been holding. 'You remember a while ago the government set up an Inquiry into the security services under a judge called Sir Francis Morahan?'

'Rings some kind of bell.' Tariq Shah was a news junkie, addicted to *Channel 4 News* and *Newsnight*. Sara was grateful for the short cuts it offered whenever she wanted to discuss something.

'Read.'

Her father read the letter once quickly, a second time slowly. 'I see why you're jumpy.'

'What should I do?'

'What do you want to do?'

'For once I'd like you to tell me.'

'You know I'd never stand in your way.'

'But would you approve?'

She could feel him trying to read her. 'You don't need that, Sara.' She looked silently down at the floor. 'See the man. Maybe he's in trouble, needs help. Maybe it'd be good for you. For your career.' He handed back the letter.

She raised her eyes. 'You'll promise never, ever even to hint about it to anyone. Anyone at all.'

'Why would I do that? Don't you trust me?'

'Sorry, Dad, 'course I trust you.' She felt a burn of shame. 'It's just that…'

'I know. It's… what's the word? It's peculiar.' He inspected her with an unfamiliar curiosity. 'You're afraid of something, aren't you?' he said.

It was the enduring sadness within the love she felt for her father – far greater than for any other human being – that made her, even eighteen years later, unable to answer him.

2

Two days later at 12.55 p.m., Sara Shah arrived at the Afghan restaurant on Farnwood Road, between Tooting High Street and the Common. She'd quickly replied to the letter after discussing it with her father; he'd driven to Chelsea Place Upper that night to put it through No. 45's front door. She'd ended the note by reminding Morahan, if he cycled, to wear a helmet; after her father set off, she wondered what on earth had possessed her to do so.

She'd proposed to Morahan a lunchtime meeting – somehow evening felt inappropriate. She was not in court that day and Ludo, as always, had happily agreed to her studying the next case files from home.

In one corner of the small restaurant, a young Asian family with two toddlers were faces down in a huge plate of sizzling mixed grill and chips. The mother and father showed traces of middle-aged bulge; she imagined the sweet slim little figures with their smooth cheeks and searching eyes going the same way. A jeans-clad boy and high-cheeked girl in a flowing red linen dress and cardigan, laced with a string of glass beads, were ordering; they must have sat down just before her. Pashtuns, she assumed. In the corner a Pakistani man sat alone munching, reading the *Mirror*.

Morahan had not replied to her letter; she understood that he must be nervous about communications. Her instincts told her that he would show up, even if it meant cancelling the Palace. They were correct; one minute after the designated time of 1 p.m., a tall figure strode past the window, turned through the door, and cast a wary eye over the restaurant. She rose, saying simply, 'Hello.'

'Hello,' he replied. He seemed unsure whether to offer a hand to shake, finally keeping it to himself. Culturally conflicted, she noted. He sat down across the Formica table and buried himself in the menu. He cast a further eye around and behind; none of the other diners caught it.

She hesitated, wondering whether to test his humour. 'It's hardly the Garrick or the Temple.'

'No.' Expressionless, he peered back down; she couldn't help noticing the thin prominence of the aquiline nose, with its near-perfect shallow curve. His skin was surprisingly smooth and unblemished for a man of his age; there was no sign of stray hairs emerging from nostrils or ears. His uniformly grey hair flopped elegantly over his collar edge. A good-looking man who had looked after himself. 'What will you eat?' he murmured.

'Just a salad, I think.'

'Yes, good.' He shot another glance at their fellow customers and out of the window. 'And then perhaps a walk. It seems too good a day to waste.'

As they made small talk, she tried to remember him as Attorney General but she had then been only in her early teens – try as she might, she couldn't place his face among the Cabinet of that time. He had a presence, but not that of a showman; she couldn't imagine him shouting and waving paper about in the Commons.

He rushed through his salad, a man on edge, itching for open spaces.

'Let me get the bill,' said Sara.

'No, please…'

'I insist. You have come to me. It's the least I can do.'

They stepped outside. 'I have my bicycle,' he said.

'Don't worry, it'll be here when you return. We're not the badlands.'

A few yards down the pavement, he spun abruptly. She followed his eye; the Pakistani man from the restaurant was scurrying into the street. As they turned, he halted and made to study the menu in the window.

He bent towards her ear, his voice a hiss of panic. 'It's not my imagination,' he said softly. 'That man is watching us.'

She grinned. 'That man is my father.'

He frowned, then smiled. 'Oh dear. I feel a fool.' For the first time, she felt him relax.

'It's all right, he's just a little over-protective.'

'I hope my presence is not too alarming.'

'I'll give him a wave to go home.' She looked back at her father, shooing him away. 'He'd make a terrible spy, wouldn't he?'

'I think perhaps if he wanted to achieve success in that profession, it might only be via the double-bluff.'

She looked at him; there was a twinkle in his eye. She tested him further. 'Shall we walk to the Common and find a park bench? Isn't that what spies do?'

They sat down, not at a park bench but an outdoor café. Morahan twisted around and, apparently satisfied they were out of ear-shot, leaned towards her.

'Before you begin,' said Sara, 'I must ask you a question. This is a public Inquiry. You said in your letter that normally it would be for the Government Legal Department to hire counsel, after discussing it with the Chair of course.' She lowered her eyes at him. 'Why the secrecy? Why you alone?' She paused. 'And why me?'

'If you allow me to tell you my story, Ms Shah, you will begin to understand.'

2018 – nine months earlier

Hooded brown eyes beneath heavy brown brows, familiar to him from television, bore in. 'I'm going to do this,' said the Prime Minister. 'I'm going to find out what went wrong.'

Francis Morahan had been mystified by both the summons and the secretiveness of the private secretary's phone call. 'All I can say, Sir Francis, is that it is to discuss a project close to the PM's heart, and one which he considers of great importance in advancing the government's agenda.' He could hardly refuse the summons but it was more than a decade since he had crossed the threshold of 10 Downing Street – an address he would happily have never returned to.

At 4 p.m. precisely the policeman stationed outside No. 10 opened the black door and Morahan was faced by a young man with floppy fair hair who seemed just out of school.

'Good afternoon, Sir Francis, I'm Andrew Lamb, assistant private secretary.' The schoolboy stretched out a hand. 'The PM is in the study if you'd like to follow me. Though of course you must know…'

'No, it's been many years.'

Robin Sandford, in charcoal grey suit trousers and a white shirt symmetrically divided by a crimson tie, rose from a stiff-backed armchair along with two other men. The sight of one sank Morahan's heart. 'Sir Francis, I don't think you and I have actually met…' the Prime Minister began.

'I think not, Prime Minister,' said Morahan, accepting the handshake.

Sandford turned to the fleshy figure to his right. 'But… er…'

The figure, grinning, stretched out bulbous fingers. 'Hello, Francis, long time.'

Morahan forced a smile. 'Hello, Geoff.' Feeling the same old revulsion, Morahan took in the drooping jowls, multiple chins, the roll of girth pushing into trousers held by braces, gold cuff-links glinting from a striped pink and white shirt and a purple tie. Steely hair in puffed-up waves and broad spectacles failed to mask the piggy eyes and calculating mind of Geoffrey Atkinson, Home Secretary – the enduring survivor from that distant era when the party had last been in government.

Sandford turned to the second man. 'I imagine you two have crossed paths?'

'Oh, I wouldn't quite put it like that,' said Sir Kevin Long, the Cabinet Secretary and most powerful civil servant in the land, upbeat in voice, rotund in shape, razor-edged in mind.

'Good,' said Sandford, waving them to seats. 'Francis – if I may…'

'Of course,' agreed Morahan lightly, distrusting the mutual courtesies.

'Some context first,' continued Sandford. 'On winning the election, I said this government would be different. We would be open and unafraid to confront ourselves as a nation, both the good and the bad. In my view – forget Europe, forget Russia, forget the economy – there's one bad that continues a year on to outstrip all others. And, in my time, will go on doing so. Extreme fanatical Islamism.'

For the second time, Morahan felt a sinking of the heart, a sense that he was being suborned into a morass of political game-playing.

'And yet,' said Sandford, 'for nearly twelve years, between 7/7 in July 2005 to Westminster Bridge in March 2017 and all that has followed since, we kept the lid on Islamist terror. I want to know what went right for so long. And what then went wrong.' He paused, locking eyes with Morahan. 'And may still be wrong.' He withdrew his gaze, eyes shifting to address a window. 'Secondly – and related to this – I want an independent examination of our security policy with regard to the hundreds of young Britons who went abroad to fight for Islamist terror and have now returned – many of whom seem to have disappeared or gone off our radar.'

'Are these not matters purely for the police and intelligence services?' said Morahan, calculating how to remain at one remove.

'You may think so, Francis,' replied Sandford. 'And, in different ways, over the year since we were elected, I've tried to ask them. I am not satisfied with their answers. There is no pattern, they say. We can't watch every sort of "lone wolf". At times, I have even sensed evasion. As if there's something they don't want to talk about. It's not enough. Therefore, I intend that the Home Secretary,' he nodded to Atkinson, 'should establish a public inquiry, deploying a range of expertise, to answer these questions.' He was edging ever closer to Morahan. 'I – and he – would like you to chair it.'

'Aren't you reaching for the unknowable?' asked Morahan softly. 'Indeed the impossible.'

Sandford grimaced. 'Nothing is ever unknowable. And in politics nothing should be impossible or undoable.'

'Have you consulted the chiefs?'

'You may recall – it was leaked to a newspaper – that the previous government attempted to have a judge inquire into the security services but they lobbied successfully against it. So no, I have not consulted the chiefs. And in anticipation of your next question, neither has this time attempted to stand in the way.'

'I think you'll find, Francis,' interjected Atkinson, 'that the Security Service – Dame Isobel in particular – understands this Prime Minister has a stiffer backbone than his predecessor.'

'And Six?' asked Morahan, repressing a rush of revulsion.

'Sir Malcolm,' replied Sandford, 'assures me of the Secret Intelligence Service's full co-operation. He is always keen to point out that SIS's involvement is restricted to its activities with regard to these people while they were, or are, out of the country.'

'You mean Five and Six are still...' Morahan hesitated, 'defecating on each other?'

'Not at all,' said Sir Kevin Long. 'Communications, I am delighted to report, are better than ever.' It was the Cabinet Secretary's first contribution; his beam spread broader than ever as he made it. 'The Cs meet once a week in my presence to iron out any turf issues. All most amicable.'

Morahan imagined the politely expressed arguments and precedents the Cabinet Secretary must have used to dissuade his headlong Prime Minister from unnecessarily opening potential cans of worms – and the gracefulness with which the civil servant would have accepted his defeat. Surrounded by these powerful figures and, despite himself, moved by Sandford's plea, he sensed the noose tightening.

'I can understand why you've come to me. I'm a senior judge. We sometimes have our uses, even for politicians. And, however briefly, I was once an MP and Cabinet member, so have an element of political understanding.'

'Precisely,' said Sandford. 'You are uniquely well-qualified.'

'There is the issue of my resignation.'

'I see no issue,' said Long.

'Nor me,' added Atkinson.

'Really, Geoff?' Morahan sighed.

'As I recall,' said Atkinson, 'Frank Morahan, as you were then generally known, resigned as Attorney General in the summer of 2002 to resume a highly successful career at the Bar and spend more time with his family.'

'Yes, that's what I said,' agreed Morahan. 'You may recall the timing. Six weeks after President George W Bush and Prime Minister Tony Blair agreed in Crawford, Texas to go to war with Iraq and remove Saddam Hussein. Come what may. As the government's senior law officer, I would be the one who would have to approve its legality. My view was that any such war would be illegal.'

'That's not what you said at the time,' said Atkinson. 'Not even in Cabinet.'

'It was less than a year after 9/11. I had no wish to be disruptive. I also believed the then Prime Minister to be an honourable man.'

'As we all did,' said Atkinson. 'As we all did.'

'I've never sought to justify myself publicly,' continued Morahan, ignoring the lie, 'but, as has been speculated, this was the real reason for my resignation. I also view that war as a prime cause of the very tragedy unfolding in our country which you are now asking me to investigate. I am therefore parti-pris.' Morahan stopped abruptly, stared down at his crossed hands. No one spoke. He raised his head in anguish at the three men around him.

'Hey,' said Sandford with youthful vigour, 'slow down. We're sixteen years on. That's hardly a partisan view, we all recognise it. All it means is that you got there first. We as a nation reaped the whirlwind you saw gathering.'

'Prime Minister,' said Morahan, 'sixteen years ago I left the world of politics to return to the law. I would prefer to stay there.'

'If you accept this role,' said Sandford, 'so you will. It may be enabled by government but it is a judicial inquiry. I'm asking you to both help me and perform a duty for your country.' With that, Sandford rose to his feet. The meeting was over.

Heavy-legged, Morahan pulled himself up, shook the three

proffered hands and, exchanging parting courtesies, headed for the door. The cherubic assistant private secretary magically appeared and escorted him out.

As the door clicked shut, Sandford turned to Atkinson. 'You knew him then. Will he do it?'

'He'll fall in line,' replied Atkinson roughly. 'Always a supine streak to him in my view.' Sir Kevin Long raised a discreet eyebrow.

'He had the guts to resign,' said Sandford.

'You're wrong. He didn't have the guts to see it through.'

'Will he see this through? I want it done properly.' He paused. 'Let's be clear, our secret friends need a bloody good kicking.'

'Your message was clear. We'll make sure he doesn't forget it.'

Sandford gave a conspiratorial smile. 'There's the politics of it too, isn't there?'

'What do you mean?' Atkinson's voice betrayed anxiety at missing a trick.

'We have four more years in power. During that time, there's bound to be a big one. Maybe several.'

'Yes, bound to be.'

'So when it happens, people'll never be able to say we didn't do everything to anticipate it – to think the unthinkable. That we didn't just leave it to the police and MI5. We shone a public light on them, we pulled together the wisest heads in the land to scrutinise them. No stone was left unturned.'

'That's good, Robbie.' Atkinson's admiration was genuine. 'Very good.'

'Thanks, Geoff. I'm surprised you hadn't seen it yourself.' Simultaneously they turned to the Cabinet Secretary but Sir Kevin Long was saying nothing.

'Well, let's hope that's all settled,' said Sandford, rubbing his hands. 'Kevin, perhaps I might have a minute with the Home Secretary.'

'Of course, Prime Minister.' The Cabinet Secretary eased gracefully from the room.

'What are you going to surprise me with now?' asked Atkinson.

'Think about it, Geoff. On whose watch did the terror return?'

'The last Prime Minister, of course.'

'And who was Home Secretary during the years the terror was being planned?'

Atkinson chuckled. 'The last Prime Minister.'

'Precisely,' said Sandford, triumph in his eye. 'Chilcot did for Blair. Morahan can do for her.'

'So...' concluded Morahan that evening, after explaining the Prime Minister's invitation to his wife, Lady Iona, at their Chelsea home. Like him, she was a public figure; née Chesterfield – which she'd kept as her professional name – she had risen to be Head Mistress of a prestigious London girls' school and one of the country's most formidable educationalists.

'So indeed,' she replied, looking beyond him.

He inspected the fine bone structure of her high-cheeked face, the still creamy glaze of her skin, the dark brown hair expensively laced with auburn tints – and, as so often, found it hard to interpret what was going on within. Was she even thinking about what he had told her? She might just as easily be hatching some new scheme in the compartmentalised lives they had become accustomed to living.

'Do you have a view?' he asked.

Her eyes shifted to engage his. 'The obvious one. If you scrutinise the security services, it may – probably will – bring their scrutiny onto you.'

'Yes.' He paused. 'That has been the main focus of my thoughts.' He stood and walked over to the drawing room triple window, resting against its ledge. 'Perhaps I've reached that stage of life when one can no longer be cowed.'

'In that case...'

'Put it this way,' he interrupted. 'I agree with the Prime Minister. It should be done. The intelligence services failed us in 2003—'

'Isn't that harsh?'

'They should have stood up to Blair instead of kowtowing. The blame was theirs too.'

'Some might say we've moved on from then,' she said softly.

Was she offering him, if at heart he needed it, a way out, an escape from the trap door? It steeled him. 'Sandford's right. We need to see inside them.'

'If they let you.' The softness had gone.

The next morning, Sir Francis Morahan wrote to the Prime Minister that it would be an honour to chair the Inquiry. A few weeks later he agreed its terms of reference with the Home Secretary:

1. To inquire, after twelve years countering of the terrorist threat, into the reasons for security failures and the lessons to be learnt in preventing future terror attacks in the UK.

2. To inquire into present security policy and strategy towards British Islamist extremists returned and returning from conflict zones.

Over the coming months premises were leased, a Secretary to the Inquiry appointed and supporting secretariat hired, a Government Legal Department solicitor seconded, a panel of independent experts assembled. Morahan gave a media conference at which he asked for submissions from interested parties. His secretariat found itself deluged by a torrent of paper, particularly from government departments apparently able to locate an unending supply of data and research with only limited relevance to his terms of reference, all of which had to be logged in, read and summarised for the panel of experts. Once this work was completed a senior QC and junior counsel would join the Inquiry to initiate its interrogative phase.

Occasionally, Morahan smelt the whiff of an unholy alliance between the likes of the Cabinet Secretary and the civil and intelligence services, to appear to be doing a naïve Prime Minister's will but all the while finding ways to thwart him.

'And then,' Morahan said, 'something happened.'

The Common had burst into tea-time life with the noise of mothers, toddlers just out of school, and bawling babies in prams. The café was filling up with ice-cream and sweet-hunters, the background noise forcing Morahan and Sara ever closer together.

Glancing around, he narrowed his gaze. 'You see, just as my envelope has dropped into your Chambers, a few weeks ago a similar envelope dropped through the front door of my house.' He peered from the café towards the green open spaces of the Common. 'It's become rather noisy here. Shall we take a walk?'

3

Three weeks earlier

As usual on weekdays except Thursdays, Sir Francis Morahan drew into Chelsea Park Upper promptly at 6 p.m. to allow time to change for whatever engagement his wife or his bar obligations had committed him to. He stowed his bicycle in the side passage hut and entered through the front door. An A4-size brown envelope lay on the mat – on it was stuck an address slip, typed only with his name.

A reading light was on in Iona's study ahead; if she was at home and had not picked the envelope up to leave it on the hall shelf – she disliked clutter – it must have been recently delivered. He wondered if the deliverer's timing was deliberate to ensure that it would go straight into his hands rather than hers.

He nudged open her study door. She raised her head and peered through light-blue titanium varifocals. 'Good, you're back.'

He hesitated. 'You didn't hear anyone at the front door just now, did you?'

'No.' She frowned. 'Should I have?'

'Nothing. Just wondering.'

'How strange you are sometimes.' She raised herself. 'Grosvenor House Hotel, 7 p.m., car booked for 6.30. Minnie Townsend's refugee charity do.'

She brushed past him and went upstairs. A dinner jacket was so much part of evening life that he could do the change in ten minutes. He retreated to his own study; he couldn't leave the letter until they returned – the label begged too many questions. He sat down, switched on his desk lamp, opened it with a paper knife and read. There was no letter heading and no date.

Dear Sir Francis

I write to you as a result of my involvement with a secret arm of government relevant to your Inquiry. Therefore I must remain anonymous.

It is within your remit to investigate certain activities by the state whose exposure will have devastating consequences. I can supply you with information, so far withheld from you, which will enable you to launch such an investigation.

I will deal only with you personally. Please understand that any communication by you via phone, email or any other electronic means may be being noted.

Neither my contact with you, nor my communications with you, nor any material I give you is to be logged into the Inquiry's database. They are for your eyes only. If you do log the material, I will know and contact will cease.

If you wish to proceed, please leave me a message saying simply Yes or No using the methodology in the accompanying note.

Please know me simply as 'Sayyid'.

It felt like a punch in the ribs; Francis Morahan had never received a communication that so startled him. He sat, eyes fixed, rereading it for a second and third time. He checked his watch; at the same time a cry came from above. 'Francis! It's twenty past six.'

He opened the middle right drawer of his desk, restored the letter to the envelope, placed it beneath a pile of other papers, stood to find a key concealed behind a particular book in a shelf above and locked the drawer with it. Beads of sweat formed on his cheeks – locking drawers was an unfamiliar act since he had left politics.

Upstairs in his dressing room, his cufflinks seemed to slide into their eyes less smoothly than usual; his hands tying the black bow were jittery. He sensed his wife watching through the door.

'Are you all right?'

'Yes, fine.' He completed the struggle with the tie. 'Don't know what's the matter with the bloody thing tonight.'

'I'll go down and tell the driver to wait.'

Their car turned onto the Embankment from Beaufort Street, the reddening sun casting shadows from the pillars of Battersea, then Albert Bridge. Morahan watched joggers evenly, rhythmically striding beside the river and fought for air against the seatbelt entrapping him. The accompanying note insisted that the 'simple yes or no' should be given by midnight. He tried to work out why 'Sayyid' was granting so little time. Did he know that Morahan would be occupied this evening in chit-chat with whatever members of the do-gooding plutocracy his wife had lined up at their table? That he would have no time to consult or discuss – even if he could have found anyone with whom to share? He flicked a look at Iona. They survived – and, in their ways, prospered – because they had decided at the crossroads in their lives that there would be no secrets in the alliance they would forge. But not tonight. Too soon. Too – how could he put it? – too baffling; too improbable that he, of all people, was entering into a secret world of 'dead letter boxes' and heaven knows what else.

'Sayyid' was asking him to act alone, to operate outside the system. The request flew in the face of the orderly due process by which, rightly in his view, he conducted his business. Yet, there was something about the letter which made him believe it was important. It felt not just cowardly but wrong to reject it – whether by logging it (he was sure Sayyid meant what he said and somehow had the means to know) or by failing to follow its instructions.

He considered the name 'Sayyid'. He'd had no time to check its meaning – perhaps it was just to indicate inside knowledge of the world he was entering. He would look it up later.

They were home by 11 p.m. He escorted his wife from car to front door and unlocked it to usher her in. Instead of following her upstairs, he headed towards the kitchen.

'Just remembered I've a letter to post,' he shouted up.

'Can't it wait till morning?'

'I rather need some air.'

'Well, try not to squeak that floorboard.'

He tore a strip off a cellophane roll, retreated along the passage to his study, found a sheet of paper and wrote 'Yes' on it. He folded it into an envelope and wrapped the cellophane around it. Back in the hall, he removed the bow tie and black jacket and put on an overcoat and his homburg, tucking the covered envelope in the inside coat pocket. The church was a brisk eight-minute walk away. He'd be there, leave the envelope and be back home within twenty minutes.

The roads seemed darker than usual, the traffic lighter. He found himself checking parked cars – for what? Men in sharp suits and trilbies smoking Camel cigarettes? He told himself to sharpen up. The gate to the churchyard was, as promised, unlocked – he hadn't been sure as he'd never had reason to enter it at this hour. As instructed, he took the path that led around the south transept, rows of graves standing grey in the half-moon light. He made for the right angle where the exterior of the transept joined the chancel. Counting out ten yard-long paces at forty-five degrees from that corner, he found the headstone.

GEORGE MANN
BORN 12 DECEMBER 1859
DIED 21 MARCH 1895
'PROUD OF HIS NATION, A NATION PROUD OF HIM'

He allowed himself a short smile and felt an unexpected surge of bravado. Seeing the gap between the head of the grave lid and bottom of the headstone, he slid the envelope between them.

Before heading upstairs, he googled 'Sayyid'. A leader, a master. A man who demands respect. Although, he reflected, it could just as easily be a cover – there was no reason to suppose it was either a man or a Muslim. The one thing he did know was that, for the moment, he must play by Sayyid's rules.

Forty-eight hours later, Morahan retraced his steps to the same gravestone. In place of the white envelope he'd left was a plastic sleeve containing a smaller brown one. He hurried home, shaking with anticipation, and slit it open. Inside was a curt message saying no more than 'Agreed', followed by an instruction to return to a different grave in a further forty-eight hours. He felt both wound-up and deflated.

Two nights later, as the hall clock chimed the three-quarter hour of 10.45 p.m., he called up that he was popping out again for a stroll. This time Iona emerged to glare down from the landing railings. 'It's becoming rather a habit.'

'Yes, I will explain soon enough. Nothing to worry about.'

The lid on the second gravestone was, as promised, unattached. It was also heavy – much heavier than he had anticipated. With his fingertips he could loosen but not lift it or ease it sideways. He had wondered whether Sayyid was a man or woman; now, a strong man seemed more likely. He himself was in his late sixties; while his legs adequately propelled his bicycle, his arms were used to no more than lifting legal submissions.

He looked at his watch. 11.05 p.m. Iona would be agitating. He needed a crow bar or something similar; he couldn't afford to delay and risk the morning light.

He stalked home, went upstairs and looked into her bedroom.

'I have to go out again.'

'It's all right, Francis.'

'No, truly.' His dry voice was urgent. 'There's a task I need to complete. I'll explain everything tomorrow morning.' He paused. 'Unless you have other plans.'

She eyed him quizzically and resumed her reading.

Out in the garden he scrambled among the clutter in the shed, opening his old wooden tool box for the first time, it seemed, in years; his days of DIY were long over. Perhaps the claw of the rubber-handled hammer might do it; he shoved it into a pocket. He had a better idea, but it meant re-entering the house yet again to fetch the car key. He had to tell her tomorrow. Edging open the front door and stepping on tiptoes he took the key from the hall shelf. The light was still on upstairs; he heard the pulling of a lavatory chain and padding of feet. He exited, opened the car boot, pulled away the bottom flap and saw that he'd remembered correctly; the wheel nut spanner had a lever on the end of the handle.

Weighed down, he set out again for the churchyard. He wondered how he would explain himself to a policeman. Caught in the act with an 'offensive weapon' – he imagined the headline, '69-year-old Government Inquiry Chair is Secret Grave Robber.' There seemed something fantastical about what he was doing. Yet he knew from the law courts just how easily chance, coincidence, or sheer misadventure could at a stroke change lives – and, sometimes, arbitrarily cut them short.

He managed to insert the hammer claw into the gap below one side of the lid and the lever on the car spanner beneath its head. Kneeling, he pressed down on both with the palms of his hand. He felt upward movement and with his knee eased the lid an inch to the right. One more shove and he should be able to slip his fingers beneath. He was sweating; he stood up and breathed deeply. How could this be necessary? Was his resolve being tested? He bent down again and repeated the process. The gap was now sufficient to show the edge of a slim brown plastic package, again A4 size. He forced his hand through, scraping the knuckles against the stone's sharp edge, far enough to grab the package between his second and third fingers. He stood up with it, back aching, heart thumping from the exertion, and concealed it in his coat.

On the walk home, he saw a dark-coloured Mercedes saloon parked ahead. Someone was in the driver's seat. He paused. Who? Why? Should he turn round, try to bypass it? No, stop being paranoid – too old for that. As he passed, he could make out the shape of a capped man, face burrowed down into a thick collar, sitting in the front, listening to the radio – Magic or Kiss or one of those other all-night stations churning out trans-generational beats. He glanced back at the rear window. It showed the round green disc of a licensed taxi. He relaxed.

At home, Iona's bedroom light was off. He sat down at his desk and gazed blankly for a few seconds at the package, lifted it and turned it through 360 degrees. No words, no markings on the brown beneath the plastic. He slid the envelope out and opened it with the paper knife. He extracted the small pile of contents. They were headed by a note in the same font.

Dear Sir Francis,

Thank you for your response.

This initial package contains personal files on five young British Muslims.

I have made two redactions.

The first is the KV2 serial number. This is information you do not need and would present an extra danger both to you and me.

The second is the name of the operation this was part of. Later I may give you this name, though not in writing. Knowledge of it is the most highly classified secret of British intelligence both now and since its inception. It is confined to very few.

Nothing else is blacked out (unlike the intelligence files your Inquiry has so far received where redactions render them effectively useless).

Of these five persons some are, or have been, combatants, others not. Some have disappeared. If you wish to fulfil your remit, you must attempt to trace these individuals or their families and take evidence. You must not use police or intelligence services to carry out this investigation. Those channels are compromised.

Knowing the potential consequences, I need your confirmation that you wish to continue. I will then advise you on obtaining the help you need.

These few files that I have been able to give you are the tip of a large iceberg. They are also its inception. From them a decade-long pattern follows.

A final warning. Once you knock on the first door, you must move fast.

Sayyid

Morahan lay the note aside, absorbed the accompanying instructions and began to leaf through the files. They contained print-outs of photographs; phone call intercepts; logs of suspects' movements. They were each headed by a brief biography containing a name, present suspected whereabouts, and previous addresses.

Who was this secret informant? Sayyid. Was he, or she, to be trusted? What position was he in to have access to raw classified files? If the operation he claimed to know of had really existed, how and why was he one of the few who knew of it? Were his warnings genuine or for effect?

Were the files themselves genuine? As a judge he was accustomed to recent police files, but his own experience of intelligence files on suspected terrorists went back to his brief time as Attorney General, mainly in the wake of 9/11, when the net was being cast far and wide. He tried to remember what these looked like; then realised it would be remarkable if the means of recording information in the digital age had not moved on. Did these print-outs have the ring of truth? Of authenticity? He stared at them again, working his way slowly through them, seeking out flaws or artificialities. If they were there, he could not see them.

If he could trust Sayyid it meant he must find an unusual kind of investigator. The memory of the Watergate 'Deep Throat', the prime cause of President Richard Nixon's downfall in 1974, flashed before him. 'Deep Throat' had passed his secrets to journalist investigators – the celebrity duo of Woodward and Bernstein. He could hardly imagine himself entrusting anything to the modern breed of British journalist. To maintain control, he must recruit an investigator to work within his team. Sayyid had already said he could not trust any part of the security or police services but indicated he might offer further pointers.

It was late. He could not do this alone. He needed to find someone he could trust with the know-how to track down and win the confidence of the men in this file – men who might be both frightened and frightening.

Over breakfast, Francis and Iona sat opposite each other in their usual seats, he with *The Times*, she with the *Guardian*. She lowered her paper and folded it with a crack; he followed suit.

'So…' she began in her customary way.

He told her a great deal; the first approach, the methodology – he needed to explain the late-night strolls – and the nature of the printed-out files Sayyid had given him.

The telling prompted him to reflect on the rigmarole of Sayyid's procedures. Surely there were simpler ways of doing this. It suddenly crossed his mind that Sayyid could be in some way playing him; deliberately conjuring him through a twisting chain of hoops. But why? To impress him? To whet his appetite? Even to compromise him? The idea that someone was setting a trap was monstrous; if he began to think that way, he was lost. He, part of an untouchable judiciary, was the independent chair of a government inquiry trying to seek out truth. What mattered was the information, not how it arrived.

'And that's it?' Iona said.

'So far.' He did not mention the grave tone or the warnings contained in the accompanying letters from Sayyid, not wishing to alarm her further. 'There will be more.'

'How much more?'

'I don't know.'

'How are you going to proceed?'

'I'm trying...' he began.

'You've not always been the strongest of men, Francis.'

'I know. You have been the strength in our... in our partnership.'

She sighed. 'The most important thing now is that you and I maintain the trust we've built. It hasn't been easy.'

'You know how much I appreciate it. And how much I rely on you and your judgement.'

'Thank you. It's not often said.'

'I hope I never give you reason to doubt it.'

'No.' She stared at him grimly. 'Are you truly set on pursuing this trail?'

'Yes, I think so.' He sensed the inner steel flexing. 'Yes,' he repeated curtly.

'I warned you that taking on this Inquiry might have consequences we couldn't anticipate.'

'I can face them. Now.' Saying the words, he forced himself to believe them.

'Yes, it's time. After what those bastards tried with you.' Her vehemence shook him, another punch in the ribs; his wife was a woman who hardly ever swore.

'That pretty much,' said Morahan to Sara, withholding just the final reference to his own past, 'is what has led us to being here today. I'm sorry it's taken so long to explain.'

Their circuit on the Common was drawing them back to the café, now becalmed in the lull between the afternoon mothers and children and the early evening mob of skateboarding teenagers.

'It's fine. Best for me to know everything,' Sara said. Morahan averted his gaze. Her instant trust reminded him of what he could not yet tell her.

'To put it bluntly, I need your help.'

'Why me in particular? I can see you need someone trusted by young Muslims to be your foot soldier. I can certainly give you suggestions.'

She was sharp. He had prepared his response. 'That's not enough. This person – or people – must be able to take affidavits. To unlock witnesses.'

'There are lots of Muslim solicitors. And it's the solicitor's job to provide evidence, counsel's job to interrogate it.'

'I realise that is the usual practice.'

'My career at the Bar has taken a new direction.'

'Yes.'

'This feels like a return to old territory.'

'For me, taking on the Inquiry feels like a return to a treacherous world of politics that I escaped fifteen years ago. But there's a tug of duty.'

'Duty?'

'It's an odd word these days, isn't it?' He paused and edged closer to her. She saw something different in his eyes; excitement, recklessness even. 'This is not just legal niceties. It's about the nature and the behaviour of the state – our nation. I need someone special. Trust me, I've looked around and, in discreet ways, asked around. There is no one better suited to the task than you. I am pleading with you to take on the role of junior counsel to my Inquiry.'

'And to be your investigator too. Your own private eye.'

'Yes, if you put it like that.'

'Snooping into my own community.' She paused. 'So some might say.'

He turned on her. 'Surely your intelligence would not allow you to say, or think, such a thing.'

For the first time she saw a force within – and a calculating mind intent on dissolving her objections. Even so, there was a desperation in his request. She remembered her father's words: 'Perhaps he's in trouble, he needs help.' None of that diminished the immensity of what he was asking her; to step aside from her career path and take a risk both personal and professional.

'Effectively, you're inviting me to go rogue.'

'Some might say that. But I am entitled to define my own legitimacy.' He sat back on the bench, disengaging eyes, peering blankly into the distance, trying to keep his shoulders straight. She saw a man battling to overcome his fears, confronting something he had never been faced with before, no more bolts to shoot.

He swivelled away from her towards the evening gloom. 'I could have turned him down, you know.'

'Who?' She was bemused; the remark seemed so out of context.

'Sayyid. The informant. Whoever it really is. He – she perhaps – gave me the option. I didn't have to. I could have let it go by. Perhaps I should have.' He suddenly seemed grieving over some loss or error; a fork in the road. This was something more than fear. Vulnerability – that's what it was. A man, once wounded, who might be wounded again.

'But you didn't turn him down,' she said softly.

'No. No, I didn't. You know why? I feel affronted. Personally affronted. It's not just their country to protect. It's my country too. All of ours.'

She wanted to do something alien to her – to place an arm around his shoulder, to comfort him. She leant towards him, then stopped herself. 'Are you afraid?'

He stirred. 'I'm not a conspiracy theorist. I don't believe our intelligence services shoot people in the head or drop them out of helicopters, or out of boats with lead in their boots. Or "disappear" them into cement mixers and car crushers or stuff them into suitcases or any of the other crude rubbish so beloved by the fantasists.' He paused; the late breeze rustled leaves and stroked the pond. 'My fear is different. It's not for me, I'm getting on. It's what there may be to find out. Not what may be about to happen, but what has happened. That there was some kind of more sophisticated… more invisible… evil.'

She had an overwhelming, even oppressive, sense that this was the most important conversation of both their lives.

'There was one other thing Sayyid indicated,' he said. 'If I move on what he's given me, it must be fast. In his words, I – we – have to stay ahead of them. It's immediate or not at all.'

He stood up, plea made, apparently no more to say. He made to leave, then halted, looking down on her.

'I know there's risk. Perhaps danger too. Terrorists and those who fight to contain them occupy another place. Albeit on opposing sides, they breathe the same air. The rest of us get occasional sightings – most of us through the distorting filter of the screens we watch and the newspapers we read. But I promise you, even if you and I must now breathe that air, I will look after you. Judges are a protected species.' A gentle smile softened him. 'My protection extends to you. I will always be there.' He turned and strode briskly away, allowing no reply.

Morahan was uncertain whether he had done enough for Sara Shah to bite. He couldn't remember the last time he had pushed so hard for something, surprising himself with the passion of his parting words. She was clearly perfect for the job. As she herself had said, there were other such young men, and women too, though very few, he suspected, to match her. But that was not the point.

That evening, returning briefly to the Inquiry office, he unlocked the desk drawer containing the Sayyid material and took out not one, but two folders. He had told Sara an incomplete story, one that deliberately missed its next chapter. Three days after the first delivery, a further note from Sayyid had dropped through his front door, instructing him to collect a second delivery from a different graveyard.

Morahan retrieved it without incident. This time the folder was thin, containing a single envelope. He'd wondered why Sayyid could not simply have dropped the envelope through his door. Perhaps, he reflected, it was because he was somewhere out there watching, making sure that he personally collected it.

Inside the envelope was a folded A4 print-out of a photograph and profile of a newly recruited barrister at Knightly Court chambers. Morahan vaguely recognised the face and name – perhaps he had seen her in court or at a conference. Stapled to it was a brief note.

> This is the person you must recruit as your investigator. She has special knowledge and a connection which I will make clear to you when I know that you have recruited her. At that time, I will also give you a final folder of material.
>
> Please trust me when I say that this investigation is vital for preserving this nation as a law-abiding accountable democracy.
> Sayyid

Sayyid's tone and his assertion of some poison at the heart of the state chilled Morahan. Even more chillingly, he was now being asked to embroil a young woman into a project with unknown consequences and dangers without, he felt, being able to give her the reason why. It was one thing to tell her that he had been approached by an apparent whistleblower calling himself 'Sayyid'; quite another to say that Sayyid had specifically pinpointed her as the route to whatever wrongdoing he wanted to expose.

Yet, however much he disliked himself for it, however much he had found Sara Shah a sympathetic, intelligent woman, he must resist the urge to come clean and tell her everything. For now anyway.

'What are you going to do, Sara?' her father finally asked, as he sipped his coffee and she her peppermint tea in the kitchen.

She'd explained the job offer but not the events described by Morahan that had led to it. She wished now that she had paraphrased his initial letter for her father, rather than allowed him to read it fully. If he ever knew the full circumstances, he would try to stop her.

'What would you do in my shoes?'

'How could I ever be in your shoes?' he spluttered. 'OK, let me ask this. Might it put you in danger?'

'No, Dad,' she smiled. It was her chance to row back. 'He was being alarmist.'

'I'm glad to hear that. So will it be good for your career? That's the main thing.'

She rose, walked round the table behind him, and gave the top of his shiny bald head a gentle kiss. 'I love you, Dad. Time to think.'

Two evenings later, mulling for the umpteenth time over the conversation on the Common, Sara sat at her desk staring out over the rooftops, sensing a door closing behind her. The question she'd raised at the very beginning lurked. Why her? Or rather, why only her? Yes, she did not underrate herself; yes, she could see how well-suited to it she must appear. But she was not the only one; to think that would not only be arrogant but untrue. Why was he so insistent?

Over those forty-eight hours memories dogged her with an uncontrollable viciousness. Was it to remind her that she'd once before had her chance to intervene, to save innocent lives? That time she'd failed. Was this her second chance? If she opted out or delayed for a second time now, would those memories ever fade away? Would she be consumed by guilt for the rest of her life?

She began to write the letter. Once it dropped through Morahan's front door, there would be no turning back. As the thought sank in, she felt a first tinge of fear.

She gathered herself and went downstairs.

'Dad, would you mind driving round with a second letter? Same address.'

He silenced the TV. 'What did you decide?'

'As you said, might be good for the career. So why not?'

What mattered was that he should never fully know what she was stepping into, nor Morahan's fear of where it might lead.

4

Within an hour of her arrival at Knightly Court the next morning, another envelope addressed to Sara Shah and marked 'Private and Confidential' was hand-delivered. This one contained a typed letter on Inquiry notepaper, signed by Sir Francis Morahan himself, offering an initial three-month engagement as junior counsel; a contract from the Government Legal Department would arrive within twenty-four hours, proposing a start on the upcoming Monday. All Sara now had to do was make her confession to Ludovic Temple. Fortunately, or not, he was in chambers, not court. She knocked on his door.

'Come!'

She entered. He rose with a giant grin. 'Sara, you don't need to knock, you know that.' She looked down at the letter in her hand and then her feet. He followed her eyes. 'What's wrong?'

'You remember that letter, Ludo?'

His face sagged like a collapsed soufflé. 'Hell, someone's made you a better offer. I bloody knew it.'

She looked up, the colour restored to her cheeks. 'It's not as bad as that.'

She gave him a broad brush picture of Morahan's initial

letter and her unorthodox dealings with him since, though she did not speak of his secret information, nor its source.

'Curious man, Francis Morahan,' said Temple. 'Something inscrutable, almost odd, about him. Never thought his resignation was what it seemed. Clever though. And affable enough. I wouldn't have imagined him as a doer. Not in the way you're now describing.'

'He seems determined.'

'Good for him. Give those rascals a kick up the posterior.' He frowned. 'But why you? Must be others he could get?'

'I've asked myself – and him – that. He's insistent.'

Temple sighed. 'Well, dammit, he's right. You're the best. But do you have to?'

She worried about sounding pretentious. 'I feel it's my duty. He needs a specific job done. I said I'd give him three months, no more.'

'Duty. Hmmm…' He affected to examine her. She silently held his eye. 'You mean it, don't you?'

'Yes, I think I do.'

He spoke with an unusual tenderness. 'Then you must do it. But stick to your guns and don't get bogged down. These inquiries go on for ever. Do the job he wants and then come back.'

'That's a deal.' She stuck her hand out and he formally shook it, both now at ease. 'I'm sorry to leave you in the lurch, Ludo.'

'It's fine. Next week's prep and I'm not back in court till the week after. I'll grab Sheila instead.'

'Not literally, I hope.'

'Ha! Funny girl.' He screwed up his eyes. 'Just as well you're the joker. We're not allowed to laugh at that sort of thing any more, are we?'

As instructed, Sara arrived the next Monday at the Inquiry offices at 9.15 a.m., having hung around to avoid being early.

The tube journey, Tooting Broadway to Vauxhall via Stockwell, was a breeze after the twists and turns to the Temple. She was met at reception by the PA to the Secretary, a squat, bespectacled young man with straggly black hair who announced himself as Clovis Hobbs-Fanshawe and managed nervously to stretch out a hand to shake while forgetting the accompanying smile.

Morahan, in a surprising and warm phone call over the weekend, had told Sara he'd chosen Pamela Bailly as the Inquiry Secretary – effectively its chief executive. She was a Treasury high-flier and therefore, he explained, not from a Department he might be investigating. He also said she was extraordinarily efficient. Sara wondered if Clovis had been terrorised by her. No doubt a bulging Oxbridge brain lurked behind his jumping eyes.

As she was ushered by Clovis into the Secretary's capacious office, Pamela Bailly sprang up and strode round her desk to offer a firm handshake. Brisk with an edge of brusqueness, tallish, trim, precise, a smart cut of auburn hair shaped to the neckline, she projected a force field of compressed energy. Sara suspected some of it was a cloak, though there was no obvious sign of brittleness on the sculpted red fingernails.

'Welcome, Ms Shah, delighted to meet you.'

'Do call me Sara.'

'I will. Pamela.' She paused. 'Not Pam. So… you're here to chivvy us along.'

Sara smiled, determined to forge some form of bond. 'I can see that no chivvying is needed.'

'In some ways not. A great deal of information, research and expertise has been gathered but we're still some way from formal hearings. Indeed, we've only just started the search for counsel. Now his Lordship appears to have pre-empted it.'

'I think it's more because he has some specific tasks in mind.'

'That would appear to be between you and him.' Was

there an edge in her tone? As if her own special access to her Chairman was being disarranged? She seemed a woman for whom control was important. 'At any rate,' continued Pamela, 'he seems to me a reinvigorated man and that is all to the good. We will all do everything we can to help you.'

Sara chided herself for the suspicion. 'I appreciate that.'

'Shall we do the tour?'

She led Sara out of her office, past Clovis's gate-keeping desk and into an open-plan space. From six desks, six heads peered noiselessly up. Four further desks were empty. 'This is the Secretariat,' said Pamela nodding briefly to the upturned faces without introducing them. 'Our junior counsel, Sara Shah.' The murmur of hellos was almost inaudible. Sara noticed that, despite the nature of the Inquiry, only one face was Asian – a woman, probably in her late twenties, wearing a knee-length skirt and long-sleeved blouse, head uncovered. 'The spare desks are for our distinguished panel members should they ever care to look in.'

A corridor led off the open-plan area; Pamela led Sara through the first door on the right. An older woman, full bosomed with long, steel-grey hair tied in an imprecise bun, looked up.

'Sylvia Labone, our archivist,' said Pamela. 'Meet Sara Shah, our new junior counsel.'

Sylvia rose with a cough – ex-smoker, Sara immediately assumed. Maybe still – there was a yellowness on her fingers. 'Good morning, Ms Shah.' Her voice was throaty, confirming first impressions.

'Sara, please.' She looked around at long shelves of files on rails. 'You're the keeper of the secrets.'

Sylvia scowled before degenerating into a further cough. 'If only.'

'We don't have a prayer room per se,' said Pamela, 'but there might be an appropriate corner here in the library. I mentioned it to Sylvia.'

You really are organised, thought Sara.

'Of course,' said Sylvia, 'whenever you wish. Never mind me, I've seen and heard it all.'

Sara followed Pamela along the corridor to an end door that revealed a large office with a broad walnut desk, leather chairs behind and in front, windows to left and right, and a long sofa running along the inside wall. To one side, the view was dominated by the four-square-mass of the American Embassy; to the other, across Nine Elms Road, stretches of the Thames were visible between designer riverside apartment blocks.

'Sir Francis's office,' said Pamela. 'It was his decision to base us here rather than Whitehall or anywhere near the Law courts. I think he felt across the river was more…' she searched for the word, 'appropriate for some of our potential witnesses.' She inspected the sofa and puffed up its row of cushions. 'He apologises. He'd wanted to be here in person for your arrival but the Home Secretary asked for a catch-up at the last minute.'

'Geoff Atkinson,' said Sara.

'Yes.' Her tone hinted at contempt. 'You'll find that Sir Francis has his own working pattern. He tends to stay late on Thursday evenings to catch up with the week. I believe he likes the undisturbed peace of a deserted office. I understand his wife shapes her social diary around that. As for everyone else, we're a nine to six operation and that's the way I prefer it. If you need to work late, we'll give you your own key and code.'

'I'd like that option.'

'As you will.'

Pamela guided her back along the corridor to a side door they had passed. 'Finally you. Legal.' She knocked and entered an office of similar size to Morahan's but with four desks, smaller windows and walls lined with book shelves. One desk was occupied.

'Morning, Pamela.'

'May I introduce Patrick Duke, Government Legal Department. In my view an inelegant change in terminology from Treasury Solicitors,' said Pamela, again with that edge. 'Patrick, this is Sara Shah. Sara, I'll leave you in his hands.' She bestowed a quick smile on them, turned on her heel and closed the door behind her.

Patrick grinned and shook Sara's hand. 'She's a piece of work.'

'I can imagine,' said Sara.

'Welcome.'

'Thank you.'

'Coffee?'

'Tea would be lovely if you have it.'

'I'm prepared. Builder's, Earl Grey, peppermint, chamomile.'

'Builder's is good.' His grin broadened and he strolled to a corner containing a kettle, cups and a mini-fridge. Though she was annoyed with herself for it, Sara couldn't help her surprise. He was tall and thin. And black. Unequivocally black. She followed him to the mini-kitchen corner.

'People tend to call me Paddy – rather a feeble joke from my days of incarceration at one of England's great schools, which I'm afraid has stuck.' He was well-spoken with a deep-voiced singer's projection. 'You know. A black paddy. Ha ha. You get a hit on two races in one. All terribly good-natured of course, old boy.' With only a small stretch of his own accent he escalated to an exaggerated upper-class honk.

'I think I'll unstick it and call you Patrick if that's all right.'

'Suits me. Sugar and milk?'

'Just as, please.'

He wandered over to a window. The view was dominated by one corner of the American Embassy which she had seen more fully from Morahan's window. 'Good to know our cousins watch over us,' said Patrick.

'What are those conical steel things hanging off the walls?' asked Sara.

'Secret anti-aircraft whizzbangs,' said Patrick. 'That's why it's such a monstrous mass of a building, not a nice slender spire. Packed full of rockets and helmeted men in black special forces suits ready to scale down the walls and occupy the streets shouting Delta and Zulu.'

Sara laughed. They sat down at neighbouring desks.

'Well...' he began. She tilted her head to the side, encouraging him. 'Our Chairman says he wants you to get out and about. Talk to people. He feels he's lacking actual, unmediated accounts from young Muslims themselves.'

'Yes.'

'Rather unusual? For counsel, I mean.'

'Not really, I did on-the-ground work for Rainbow.'

'But that's a campaigning chambers.'

'And we shouldn't be here?'

'There's no should or shouldn't. It's whatever Sir Francis wants. With one condition.'

'Oh?'

'I accompany you.'

She looked down at her hands. 'That might be awkward. It may be hard to win their confidence.'

'That's fine. You see them alone. Initially anyway. But you may need me to witness. Or for affidavits.'

'If I get any.'

'I'm sure you will.' He switched off the grin. 'And some of these characters won't be friendly. I'll stay out of the way but you can't be alone.'

'So you're to be my chaperone?'

'No, Sara, I'm just to be there. Even if all I am is your driver with a leather jacket, a Nigerian accent and a lucky zebra dangling from the rear-view mirror.' She couldn't help smiling and the grin reappeared.

Shortly before lunch, Morahan arrived and poked his head around the Legal department door. 'Sara. Welcome. Come and chat.' After the earlier conversation, she felt guilty about leaving Patrick; he gave her a friendly nod of the head.

Morahan guided her to one end of his brown leather office sofa while he sat down at the other. 'Coffee? Tea?'

'I'm fine, thanks. Patrick's been the perfect host.'

'Good. Decent chap.'

She hesitated. 'I hadn't realised he would be accompanying me on research trips.'

'Yes, I should have told you first thing. Would have but for our friend Atkinson's summons.'

'Oh, how was that?'

'He just wants it over. I suspect the appearance of enthusiasm in front of the Prime Minister was purely for show.' He gave a clipped chuckle, then frowned with what seemed to her embarrassment. 'Patrick persuaded me that you shouldn't be on your own. He is after all the instructing solicitor who would normally be running evidence gathering.'

'As long as he doesn't get in the way.'

'He won't.'

She hesitated. 'There's an issue.'

'Tell me.'

'Racism is not just white and black. It grieves me to say it, but there is often strong prejudice in my community against Africans and West Indians.'

'Yes, I know. It was one reason Patrick couldn't do the task I need you to do. Nor is he in your league.'

'I'm sure he—'

'No, he's not, Sara. You are an outstanding young lawyer

with the right credentials, both as a professional and as a human being.'

Sara saw him smiling at her with an almost paternal fondness and tried not to show her pleasure.

'I've no doubt you'll get on with him,' he continued.

'Oh yes,' she said enthusiastically. 'And there won't be any complications,' she added, immediately wishing she hadn't. She made to rise but he held up a hand to halt her and went to his desk. He opened the middle drawer, extracted a key and unlocked the bottom left pedestal drawer. He pulled out an unmarked white A4 envelope.

'This contains photocopies I've made from Sayyid's folder.' He handed the envelope to her. 'For Patrick, and anyone else, the story is that you are working initially from cases you came across at Rainbow which you hope will lead to others. It would appear that your first trip will be to the North.'

'Wherever it leads.'

They stood up together. 'Three people know about Sayyid. You and me. And my wife, Iona. I've put her in the picture and she understands the meaning of the word "secret". She also knows about you.' He ushered her to the door, then stopped. 'Of course there's a fourth person who knows too. Sayyid him- or herself. But once you start ringing doorbells, other ears and eyes may be alerted. For good or bad, we are a surveilled society.'

Sara returned to the Legal office. Patrick peered up, noticing the envelope under her arm. 'Secrets from the Chairman?' he asked teasingly.

Sara kicked herself for the carelessness and hoped she betrayed none of the thuds with which her heart had just rattled her ribcage. 'Chairman's induction,' she replied. 'He strikes me as a man who likes things done in a certain way.' She put it in her case. 'I honestly don't think I've the energy right now for house rules and regs. Might make my mark with Sylvia instead.'

'Good luck.' Patrick pulled a child-like grimace and returned to his screen.

Deliberately leaving the case by her desk to suggest nothing unusual, she went next door to the library.

Sylvia Labone looked up fiercely. 'You're back.'

'I thought I'd give you a rough idea of prayer times – though they keep changing, of course.'

'Would you like me to vacate?'

'Not at all, you won't be disrupted.'

She looked Sara up and down. 'Do you smoke?'

'No.'

'Of course not. Right, let me show you around.'

She walked Sara up and down the shelves, describing her colour coding for submissions, authors, reports and originally commissioned research. 'Of course, this material is all digitally stored too but our distinguished panel members often prefer to read hard copies. When they read anything at all.'

'It's impressive,' said Sara, trying to soothe a woman whom life seemed to have made congenitally angry. 'What about police and intelligence files?'

'Coming to that,' replied Sylvia irritably. 'Their research reports and general assessments are handled in the same way. However, since Snowden, anything classified, shall we say, is, frankly, fog and mist, subject to endless redactions. Most of them look like a sea of black waves.'

'Surely we can get more,' asked Sara brightly.

'You'd better get to work on our chairman,' she replied. 'Names. Names, places, times, addresses. It's all scrubbing brush without those, isn't it?'

At 5 p.m., Sara tapped on Morahan's half-open door.

'Come in, Sara, come in,' he beamed. His informality continued to surprise her.

'I've looked at those files,' she said. 'There's no guarantee of finding any of those five names or of them talking if we do.'

'Let's see. I trust your ingenuity.'

'And I've no idea anyway what story they have to tell.' She cast him a trenchant look. 'Do you?'

'No. Nor do I know whether Sayyid does or if he's leaving us to find out. And we have only his word that they lead to significant wrongdoing relevant to this Inquiry's remit.' He gave an encouraging smile. 'But at least there seems the one link, doesn't there?'

'Yes,' she said quietly. 'As you say, let's see.'

She hesitated, wondering whether or not to raise her nagging question. He read her. 'Is there something you want to ask?'

'I'm not sure.'

'Try me.'

'It's just – I know I've asked it before – why me? You've been so emphatic that it could be no one else.' She took the plunge. 'Is there anything you're not telling me?'

He rubbed his eyes and looked straight into hers. 'I promise you there is no one more suitable for this task. Every word I've exchanged with you since has confirmed that view.'

'And that's it?'

'Yes, that's it. We'll be a good team. You look after yourself. And have faith in me.' It seemed a strange choice of words from a senior figure more than thirty years older than her and with such greater experience. He was a likeable man but there remained something impenetrable about him. The niggle would not go away.

As she shut the door behind her, Morahan felt unease. The urge to confess the true reason for her recruitment had been almost irresistible. He tried to comfort himself; she would at least have Patrick's protection and he was thereby honouring his commitment to her – though he still didn't understand why the government solicitor had been so insistent on accompanying her.

Sara agreed arrangements with Patrick for an early train in the morning and he'd left for the day. Alone, she tried to work out why the Inquiry's office seemed somehow so unfamiliar, discomforting even. The only sound was the near inaudible hum of internal ventilation, breathing air into sealed units with sound-proofed windows and newly laid carpets. Not even the occasional click of shoe heels broke through. Nor voices.

That was it – the hush. In Knightly Court, there were interruptions of chatter, meetings along the corridors, the odd joke told in reception, a wheezing splutter from Ludo, the creaking of badly fitting doors. Here, in the open-plan office, there was silence; eyes glued to screens, only occasional murmured questions, overseen by the headmistressy figure of Pamela Bailly. Patrick, now she thought about it, bantered in their own office, not outside it; Sylvia, she suspected, gave up banter a while ago. Morahan himself, however forthcoming with her, was hardly gregarious. In this silence she detected not calmness, but tension.

Her phone sounded – a text. She clicked to view.

A colleague may not be what they seem.
Thought you should know. Take care.

Her heart racing, she checked the number. Not from her contacts. Not familiar. Her fingers burning, she hit reply and typed a single word.

Hello.

She awaited the ping, somehow sure of the worst.

Message sending failed.

5

Heading north out of King's Cross, they exchanged idle chit-chat before burying themselves behind laptops. Sara forced herself to act naturally with Patrick; the anonymous text preyed on her every waking moment, distorting the lens through which she grabbed occasional glances at him, in touching distance across the table, peering down at his screen.

She tried to convince herself there could be another explanation. It was more than a decade since that last text, sent in precisely the same form of language from an unknown number, had cast its shadow over her life. But people texted all the time, she told herself, without bothering with names. Except, as she well knew, the receiver would know the name from the number – or at least have a number that responded when they checked.

She'd repeatedly gone over the core words: '… A colleague may not be what they seem…' They were too vague to be meaningful. A nothing. Anyone could have made that up.

She needed to stop kidding herself – this was not a random coincidence. Either it was the same sender or someone who knew about, or once had some contact with that sender, and knew their modus operandi. But for what? To scare her? To help her? To undermine her?

She grabbed another look at Patrick, then found herself seeing those other faces in the Inquiry office floating by.

If only she could discuss it with someone. But she understood all too well the logic of her position. The text was a dagger only to her because of the message that July morning fourteen years ago. Unless she owned up to that, anyone looking at this message would simply tell her to ignore it. Some joker trying to wind her up, they'd say. Or the detritus of office politics and rivalries.

Perhaps, when she next saw Morahan, she might ask him whether he had reason to suspect that anyone on his staff was operating to a different agenda. He'd probably look at her with mystification. If he did, she could just about imagine herself showing him the text. She could already hear his reaction – don't worry, some idiot…

She was going round in circles. She could never, and would never, tell a single soul about the 2005 text. She had set that in concrete when the Met detective called on her a few weeks after 7/7. He knew only that she, like many others, had attended meetings where people now of interest to the police might have been present. She said she couldn't help him; she recognised none of the names he raised. He had no reason to doubt her.

The questions the text raised, the guilt it ignited were impossible, unthinkable to admit to anyone but herself. At that crucial moment, however much she could be forgiven for not instantly interpreting it, she had, as it turned out, failed in the most devastating possible way – a failure she'd carried like a death row prisoner's shackles ever since. The texts, past and present, were a weight she must bear alone. The only means of sidelining them was to focus single-mindedly on the task ahead.

Trying not to catch Patrick's eye she retrieved from her bag the Sayyid folder Morahan had given her. Wherever they now were – if they were even still alive – the five individuals named in the files all hailed from the town of Blackburn in East Lancashire. The files shared the same template, headings running vertically down the left column. The left heading was TOP SECRET, right side OPERATION with the following word blacked out. The next line began KV2 followed by a further redaction. The headings below ran: PICTURE; NAME; DOB; LOCATION; PHONE; HOME ADDRESS; FAMILY ADDRESS; FIRST CONTACT; CURRENT STATUS; NOTES; HUMINT; COMINT; LAST CONTACT; FILE STATUS.

One name was Samir Mohammed. His photograph showed a young Asian, probably taken in his late teens. Date of birth was 12 October 1987; home and family addresses the same number and street in Blackburn; current status 'inactive'; file status 'Closed 31 December 2006'. One entry withstood clear interpretation. Humint read 'Contacts not pursued after closure.'

Assuming he was alive – and had not since been involved in anything of interest to the police or intelligence services – Sara judged that he might be the easiest to approach. Whether or not he still lived in Blackburn was unknown. There was no hint of what story he, or any of the other four, might have to tell.

Announcing herself as a lawyer working for a government inquiry would guarantee doors slammed in her face. Tempting though it was – and even though she suspected it was the easiest way to get a foot in the door – she decided against presenting herself as an ambulance-chasing lawyer on the lookout for Muslim clients seeking financial redress against the police (a role she was all too familiar with). Instead she would introduce herself as a market researcher working on a project seeking to learn lessons on the past twenty years of governmental relationships with the young Muslim community.

She told Patrick her protocol. Despite that moment when

he'd seen her returning with the folder from Morahan's office, she stuck to the line that she was following up cases from Rainbow.

'Maybe when you arrive in the street of one of the addresses, you should knock on every tenth door,' suggested Patrick. 'Then if someone answers and is willing, do the survey with them. Just for show. It might protect not just you but your target.' He paused. 'Whoever they are.' He was grinning; there was no edge, just a hint of playfulness.

She smiled back. 'That's a great idea, thanks.' She'd already planned something similar but his helpfulness pleased her and she didn't want to discourage him. She'd been worried that their professional relationship, even without the anonymous text, would be uneasy after her show of resistance to him accompanying her. She had a further card up her sleeve but, for the moment, kept it to herself. She might not need to play it.

In the time left on the train, she checked websites on Blackburn and its environs, accumulating small details of local knowledge. At Preston, they picked up a hire car, Patrick easing into his promised role as driver.

'Do you sit in the back or the front?' he asked with the customary grin.

As they headed south out of Preston, she found herself glancing at him. Assuming, as she told herself she must, that things were as they seemed, she wondered what he was thinking about his role as bit-part player. She also noted his perfectly angled jaw-line and broad but straight nose. The edges of his black hair were touched with a few flecks of grey; otherwise there were no signs of age or sag and, even seated in the driving position, no bulge at the waist.

'You're inspecting me,' he said abruptly.

'Sorry,' she said. 'I do it to everyone.' She paused. 'Including Morahan. I can give you a precise facial description if you want.'

'I can manage without.' The grin returned.

'I know it's not easy, this,' she said.

'It's fine.'

'You're not a fool. You must want me to share.'

'It's OK. You'll tell me what you want when you want. Though I'd like you to know this: you can trust me. If you speak to me in confidence, it remains between you and me.' They turned off the motorway to a sign marked 'City Centre'. 'But there's one thing you do have to tell me right now. Where are we going?'

'Straight to the hotel, please. And if it's a dump, take me home.' Patrick set the SatNav for the out of town 'Savoy Inn' into which Clovis, with a blind loyalty to the name, had booked them. It turned out to border an industrial estate filled with garages and self-storage units. Ten minutes after checking in, Patrick opened the passenger door to a Sara dressed in a long broad black skirt which gathered by her ankles, dark brown jacket and marginally lighter brown hijab replacing the usual blue scarf. He cast a fleeting look of amusement and was reprimanded by a silent raise of her eyebrows.

Even if the Asian and white population split was similar, Blackburn seemed a different world from her part of south London. Though the people were the same, here there was just a distinct lack of bustle. She imagined the place in its Victorian prime; a boom town of the industrial revolution. Then it had been the weaving capital of the world; dotted with textile mills, over a hundred and forty of them according to her recent research, driving a massive churn of activity within the green fold of the hills where they lay. Granted, there had been little joy there for the sweating workers, lungs saturated by fine clouds of cotton dust, particularly the hand weavers who would eventually be overtaken by mechanisation. But there must have been a surge of energy. Now, except for civic relics like the museum, and one half of the town hall incongruously attached to its modern glass and steel extension, the great Victorian buildings had largely gone – except for the foul-smelling brewery – and the streets appeared lifeless, tinged with sadness. Shops and pubs were boarded up. People seemed to move more slowly, with less purpose.

The demarcation between the neighbourhoods housing the South Asian Muslims, and the two-thirds of the population who were white English, was stark and discomforting. Patrick, a black Briton, was out of place. He would have to maintain a low profile.

Samir Mohammed's home address in the twelve-year-old file was given as 59 Gent Street. Patrick dropped her at the low number end of the street and assured her that his watch would be discreet. She made her way up, knocking or ringing on numbers 9, 19, 29, 39, 49. Only one, number 29, answered. Her market research questionnaire was devised to last no more than ten minutes and she was soon sounding the bell of No. 59. A single chime responded, followed by a late middle-aged Asian woman still in the process of covering her head with a black scarf.

'Yes?'

Before Sara had time to answer, there was a shout from a male voice above. 'What is it, Mum?'

The woman looked at Sara with her clipboard and retreated to the bottom of the stairs. 'You come down, it's a lady wanting something.' Sara felt the excited flutter of the hunter closing on its potential prey.

She heard footsteps, then trainers and jeans appeared down the stairs followed by a tracksuit top and the face of a tall man a year or two either side of thirty. The age fitted.

'Yes?' His expression was sullen.

'Hello, my name's Sara Shah and I'm doing a survey of young Muslims' views of different government agencies–'

'Don't have time for that,' he interrupted.

She tried to engage him, her eyes enlarged with pleading. 'I know, I understand,' she said, 'but I've been walking up and down these streets all morning. There's no one who's in or will give me the time of day. If I don't do my numbers, I don't get paid.'

'You won't get paid?' He looked at her more closely, seeing the attractive face within the cotton surround.

'Yes, it's piecework.' She held up the questionnaires. 'No completed forms, no money.'

'Can't you make it up?'

'They'll find out. I'll be sacked.' He looked her up and down, his shoulders slumping, face peering up and down the street. Her chest tightened, cramped by his wavering. 'Please, I'm getting desperate. Won't take long.'

He hesitated. 'Nah, don't fancy it, to be honest.' She thought she had him but he wasn't shifting. He made to close the door. She had to play her last card.

'Wait a minute,' she said, keeping one foot over the threshold. 'There's a budget I'm allowed to use.'

Suspicion and interest competed in his eyes. He looked up and down the street. 'A budget?'

'Yes, I can offer you something. To help me reach my target.'

'What something?'

She took a purse out of her bag. 'A hundred. It'll only be a few minutes.' He was wavering; she crossed the fingers of her other hand.

'Nah. Not worth it.'

'Hundred and fifty?'

He eyed her closely. Until now, she hadn't decided how far she'd go. 'Nah.'

She couldn't lose him now. One final throw. 'I'm not really allowed to do this. Two hundred.'

His frown slowly turned to a smirk of victory. 'Go on then, come in.'

Sara made a mental note. There was something venal about Samir Mohammed.

He signalled to the front room. 'You wanna sit in there?' He disappeared into the kitchen. She overheard him telling his mother that it was something about a survey and his mother asking if the lady wanted a cup of tea. 'Yeah, she looks like she needs it.'

He came back with a tray holding a teapot, two china cups on saucers, and some biscuits. 'Mum likes it done proper,' he said.

'It's kind of her,' she said. He poured. 'As I said, it won't take long.'

'I'm not in a hurry,' he said. 'Not now anyway.'

'That's great. First up, I should ask you your name,' she smiled.

He hesitated, frowning. She held both smile and silence. 'Samir. That enough?' She said nothing. 'Most people call me Sami.'

'That's lovely, Sami, thank you. What's your line of work? Don't worry, nothing to do with this,' she said, glancing down at her clipboard, 'I'd just be interested.'

'Security. Down at the Rovers. Mainly evenings and nights. Match days too. That's why I'm home now.'

'Blackburn Rovers?'

His face spread into a broad, innocent smile. 'How d'you know that?'

'Well, they're a big team, aren't they?' Sara blessed the width of her research.

'Yeah, once.'

'The Championship's not a bad place to be.'

'Maybe we'll get back into the Premiership sometime.'

'Do you play?'

'Used to. Not much now. Tend to keep myself to myself.'

'Oh?'

'Yeah, easier, know what I mean?'

'Yes,' she said with soft sympathy, 'I know exactly what you mean, Sami.'

She sipped her cup of tea and looked happily at him, waiting. 'Well,' he said. 'What's this all about?'

'Just want to ask you a few questions for the survey,' she said.

'Survey?'

'Yes. Governments do them all the time. All anonymous. Just trying to find out what people think of their lives, what can be done to improve them, what their experiences have been.'

'Sounds all right.'

'Shall I start?' Sara laid the clipboard on her lap and began a list of questions with multiple choice answers. She'd designed it to be innocuous without sounding pointless – ranges of satisfaction or dissatisfaction over dealings with employers, council officials, education service and the like. Ten minutes or so in, she came to the final question. Omitting it would appear odd – it might also provide clues.

'OK, Sami, last one. The police.'

'Police?'

'Yes. Can't leave them out, can we?' Was there an anxious flicker of the eye or did she imagine it? If there was, it lasted just a millisecond. He was either sufficiently settled not to bridle further or cool enough not to react.

She went through the choices. Number of dealings over the past five years: 0, 1–5, 6–10...

'Can't say I've really had any,' he said shortly.

'OK. In that case, that's it,' she said.

'You mean we're done.'

'Yes.' She began to rise.

'No hurry. Have another cup of tea.'

She sank back and sighed. 'Are you sure? Your mum won't mind?'

'Nah.'

Sami disappeared with the tray into the kitchen. Sara wasn't sure whether he was lonely or looking for female company. Maybe, now that he appeared to trust her, she was a break from boredom. What, in any case, was she hoping to find? The trail that had led her to his door stemmed from something in his past twelve years ago. Without knowing what it was, she couldn't tell whether what had attracted the surveillance had even been noteworthy to Samir himself. He might simply have been an innocent link in a chain.

He swaggered in with a refilled teapot and, this time, cake.

'Mum insisted. She's always baking cakes. Watching too much Nadiya, I reckon.'

'I won't be able to move!'

'You'll need stamina.' He poured tea and looked at her awkwardly. 'You do this all the time?'

'No, just part-time,' she said. 'But it can be interesting. You get to know people. Sometimes they have stories to tell you wouldn't believe. You know, like, in this one we're looking at how Muslims are treated here and everything that's happened. 'Course, I treat everything in confidence but sometimes I can really help people.'

'Is that right? What sort of things?'

Sara looked at him as if she were in deep thought – buying time to calculate how far to push it. 'I can't say details of what people told me privately. But… you know… bad things happened. Sometimes there's a need to tell someone…'

He stared down at his hands, slowly rubbing them together. 'Yeah, suppose they did.' Maybe her prior knowledge was influencing her but she sensed a memory floating by him. She held the silence, hoping he would fill it. He looked up. 'Yeah well, stuff happens, don't it?' Then no more. Closure. Any further pushing could clam him up completely. She mustn't show disappointment. She quickly drained her cup of tea.

'That was lovely, Sami, thanks so much. And so nice to meet you.'

'You going?' She detected disappointment.

'Yes, better get back to it.' He rose too. 'I'll be here for another couple of days if you fancy another tea. My treat this time.'

'Dunno what I'm doing.'

Sara pulled a card from one of two sets in her handbag. It read, 'Sara Shah. Market researcher.' And a mobile number.

He read it quickly. 'Yeah, OK.'

'Give me a ring if you'd like to meet up.' She gave him the most intense look she dared. 'Be good to see you again.' Quickly she pulled back and smiled. 'Will you thank your mum for me?'

'Yeah.' He came to the door as she walked back onto the pavement. So great was the combination of expectation and frustration that she only remembered just in time that she was a market researcher knocking on every tenth number of Gent Street. He was still watching as she pressed the bell of No. 69. Reaching the end of the street, she chanced a final look-back. No sign of him. Or anyone else.

The car drew alongside as she turned the corner.

'Well?'

'Hang on a minute.' She settled herself in her seat, fastened the belt, and foraged in her bag for her make-up mirror as he moved off down the street. She removed it and checked her face, applying tiny pats of powder. Buying time again.

This was going to be impossible unless, to some extent

at least, she levelled with him, whatever the wariness now infecting her. What was there to lose anyway? He could see that she had case histories – it would be perverse not to share. To test trust, maybe you had to give it.

'OK. Morahan gave me some files.'

'That was pretty obvious, Sara.'

'Was it that bad?' She remembered his expression. 'Did you have a peek in the folder when I was with Sylvia?'

He slapped his foot on the brake and pulled in to the roadside. 'For f— Sorry, I'll start that again. What do you take me for?'

She was consumed by embarrassment, wanting to tell him about the text so that he'd understand. She mustn't. Not till she really knew him – if she ever did. And still that horrible, sinking feeling – what if he was the one she had to look out for?

'I'm sorry, Patrick.'

He softened. 'It's OK. Go on.'

'I don't know where they came from, MI5, Special Branch, your guess is as good as mine.' The half-truth was weak; she needed to be better at this. 'They relate to five young Muslims with family addresses in Blackburn. Two appear to have been closed by the end of 2006.'

'2006? Long time ago.'

'Yes. But the other three remained open.'

'And one of the five lived, or lives, in Gent Street.'

'I found him. He was at home. Still lives with his mum. I could hardly believe it. I finally got inside…'

'Well done.'

'I had to use a last resort.'

'Oh?'

'Used fivers.'

Patrick frowned. 'How many?'

'Actually, more like twenties. Ten of them.' Though he

said nothing, Patrick's eyebrows shot up. 'He's smart,' she continued. 'Greedy too. He'd never have done it for nothing.'

He was silent for a few seconds. 'Good call,' he finally said. 'I'll find a way of putting it through the books.'

She felt her shoulders sag with relief. 'I didn't feel especially proud of myself. Anyway, he warmed up, Mum was friendly, tea on saucers, he did the survey. I could see he liked the look of me.'

'Of course.'

She lowered her eyes. 'Didn't want me to go. We chatted more. Then I truly thought he might just be about to cough something.'

'But he didn't.'

'No. Don't know why he baulked. Or what I did.'

'Stop beating yourself. You did well to get that far.'

She winced. 'I left him my number. But I think he's slipped the hook. So onto the next.'

He was circling streets with no particular aim, listening. 'No,' he said. 'You've had a bite. These neighbourhoods are chatty. You carry on walking their streets and word will get around about you and your survey. Not bad words, just words. Give it twenty-four hours. Stay out of sight and mind.'

'Won't it be time wasted?'

'I've a better idea. Fancy climbing a hill?' Without awaiting her reply, he put his foot on the accelerator and sped without exceeding the limit too blatantly in the direction of the Savoy Inn.

She wondered why he hadn't asked to see the actual files – it was such an obvious request. The good manners to wait until she offered? Or a man who knew how to bide his time?

Sami Mohammed, concealed inside the porch, watched until she turned the corner. She reached the end of the street quickly.

Either there really was no one in at the further ten doors she'd approached or she hadn't bothered to ring any bells.

Who was she? Why had she seemed so desperate to get into *his* house? The old terror was creeping back. Was she part of them, testing him out? Or part of something else, wanting to rake over the coals? Perhaps embers still flickered and, even now, the fire hadn't gone out. He went inside, closed the door, and shot upstairs to his bedroom, bypassing the inquisitive stare of his mother.

He retrieved from its hiding place in his chest the card they'd left with him. Time froze as he stared at it – plain, three by two inches, now yellowed at the corners with a crease down the middle like the depression in an old man's back. On it a number, nothing more. The threat that came with it didn't need to be written down – he'd never forget it. 'If anyone ever starts asking questions, anyone at all, anytime at all, even years ahead, phone this. You don't, you're dead.'

He tried to work out the risks. If she'd been sent by them – what the reason might be this many years later he couldn't begin to fathom – he could end up dead meat if he didn't at least try to phone it. If she'd come from someone trying to go after them, he could still end up dead if he didn't warn them.

Or, if she was what she said she was, he'd do better to let things lie. Reflecting on it, he became ever more sure that she wasn't. It was as if she'd wanted him to suspect – know even – that she was more than she first seemed.

She'd wanted him to spill something.

Even thinking of those times – the times leading up to when he'd been given that little card and the lifetime warning – made his guts churn and his pulse quicken.

He picked up his phone.

He didn't expect the call to be answered so fast.

6

2006

Wherever they were headed, it wasn't Paradise.

5.30 a.m. He'd done morning prayers and lay in bed dozing. From his bedroom at the back of the house he heard a low whistle – his friend, Asif. He drew back the curtain and saw a familiar gesture of arms bidding him to the front. Asif up to some trick or other. Or in trouble, more likely. He had to go – couldn't let him down.

He sprayed deodorant all over, threw on jeans, T-shirt and a long-sleeved black sweater, put a comb through black hair and fledgling beard, salve on cracked lips, sports socks inside black trainers. He checked his watch. He stood up to his full six feet two inches, inspected himself in the mirror, clenched his mouth to examine uneven teeth, grabbed a brush to use later, felt wallet and small change in the left trouser pocket, stuffed brush and comb into the right, puffed out his chest.

He eased the bedroom door open, flicking a glance across the landing, and silently closed it. He tiptoed around the squeaky floorboard and, at the top of the stairs, heard the familiar rhythm of his father wheezing. He inched down, lifted his black leather coat from its peg in the hallway and touched his phone and house keys. Everything present and correct for whatever Asif had in store. Ready to go.

He slotted a key into the front door lock and turned it. A squeak from the floor above; he froze. No footsteps – perhaps it was a groan from the depths of sleep. It made him hesitate – ask himself why Asif needed him at this hour. In all the years they'd known each other, he'd never called this early. He'd have liked to turn round, to climb back to the warmth of his bed, to sleep and dream. He jettisoned the thought; it was a friend in need. He prised the door ajar and there was the grinning face, the arms outstretched.

'Hey, man,' he whispered, 'what's it about this time?'

'It's a summons,' his friend whispered back. They crept through the open front gate onto the pavement, the night still dark, a street lamp casting misty light on a whining milk cart further down the street.

'What you mean, a summons?' He looked at Asif; there was something not right, a glint of fear in his eyes.

Before there was time for an answer, his friend pulled away. Two figures in dark hoodies ranged alongside, clamping his arms and forcing him across the road.

'Hey, what the—'

'Shut it, brother, I'm just the escort,' snarled one, gagging his mouth with a black leather glove.

Sami turned his head and glimpsed Asif watching, the fear now tinged with regret. Did he hear his voice? 'Sorry, man.' Or did he just imagine it as his friend disappeared into the dawn gloom?

He was alone, outnumbered, unarmed, not even a knife. He thought of screaming. They saw it; the black-gloved fist slapped into his mouth. They pushed him into the windowless back of a small van; one leapt inside with him, the other locked the door. Imprisoned. Even if he overpowered his 'escort', there was no way out.

'What's this about, brother? I ain't done nothing,' he mumbled.

He heard the second man's footsteps circle the van, a door slam, the engine fire up, a jerk of acceleration pitching him against the carcass of steel.

The escort – his jailer, more like – pointed to his pocket and beckoned with a finger to hand over what was in it.

'What you want?'

The escort, staying silent, beckoned again. Sami feigned puzzlement. The response was a kick in the shin. Understanding, he handed over his mobile. He was allowed to keep his watch.

One hour gone.

It seemed unreal, a sick fantasy happening in a parallel universe. The silence became his oppressor, the unreality lifting like the misty dawn he imagined outside. He thought, rethought, re-rethought. What could they know about him? Sure, he'd talked stuff with the group – Ali, Farooq, Shay the glamour boy, Asif himself. They'd dreamed and schemed but it was never more than bravado. At least not from him. An ugly idea hit him – were any of them serious? Had they really meant it? Had he seemed to commit?

That night with the girl? There was some messing, sure… she was a bit young – but none of them actually did it with her. Nothing like some of the rumours he'd heard going around. After the foster mother complained, the police had them in but didn't even caution them. He'd wanted to apologise to her but the others told him to leave it. Surely it couldn't be that. If not, what else?

Three or so hours steady speed on flat roads – motorway, he assumed – then endless bends, falling and climbing, now the rattle of rutted lanes. Seated on the wheel-arch, he felt only the soreness in his behind and scraping in his bones. For the thousandth time he lifted an eye to the escort sitting opposite. For the thousandth time, there was no response.

He tried one gambit. 'I need to piss, brother.' Another. 'I can't say my prayers like this, brother.' A curl of the lip from the bleak figure facing him. A third. 'Which way's east?' The figure shook his head. 'Don't you speak, man?' A scowl.

The van juddered to a stop, swiftly followed by the crunch of boots on gravel and the shock of blinding daylight as the back doors were flung open. His escort shoved him out of the van and he managed not to stumble. They were on a rutted single-track road through the forest. There was no view, no contours in the land – no sense of height or terrain. He knew these men had been here before. One produced a bottle of water, filled a small basin, and gestured at him to wash and say his prayers. His heart raced as he wondered if they were to be his last. They watched and, when he'd finished, retrieved the basin.

'I need a piss, brothers.' They pointed to a bush and carried on watching. As he emptied his aching bladder, he stole a look to left and right but each direction led only to a canopy of forest. 'Where are we?'

'You're in the back of there, brother,' said the driver, opening the doors again.

'Hey, you speak.' Sami turned from driver to escort. 'He don't.'

The blow in the solar plexus doubled him up, arrows of agony tearing into his gut. 'Fuck!' was all he could say. They shoved him inside with a kick in the back of a knee. He looked down at the escort's hob-nailed boots and excruciating pain speared into his thigh. The grinding and spluttering of an abused engine drove them ever higher. He tried to imagine sky, sun, cloud, rain. Nothing came – just the implacable expression of the man opposite.

'You know what day it is, brother?' The escort's voice struck like a cymbal clash. He'd spoken. This time he'd be the one to say nothing.

'I asked you a question, brother. Do you know what day it is today?'

'What you mean, what day?'

'September the eleventh. Eleven nine. Nine eleven. Remember?' His voice leeched sarcasm. 'Fifth anniversary.'

'Yeah, fuck, sorry, brother.' Sami tried to stop the cowering in his mind from showing in his face. Nor the confusion, because he didn't know what he was supposed to say.

'And you call yourself a brother.'

'Fuck's sake, I'm confused. Wouldn't you be? Five years, yeah?'

'That's right. Never forget. Five years.'

The van slowed and snagged left, then immediately right. More footsteps, the tuneless squeal of a rusting gate, a door slam, then bouncing along... along what? The van stopped, turned and reversed, the doors opened. He emerged with head bowed; all he saw was a dark concrete passage, the van doors at right angles blocking right and left. He wondered what lay beyond and listened. A rustling, nothing more.

They dragged him along a ribbed concrete floor, a smell of hay and dung. Petrol fumes overtaken by shit. Stables, cows, horses? He'd hardly ever been outside the town or seen an animal beyond the halal butcher. They stopped, pushed open a door and hurled him through it. He heard the click of key in lock – his new prison. The floor was tiny squares of concrete, a bed of hay in one corner, a trough of water in another, a single tap and a bucket below. Soap and a roll of toilet paper. High up a small window, an inch or two ajar, too high and too small to escape through. Though he didn't know what he'd be escaping from. At least it offered some sense of light and time. Were they watching his observance? He should exaggerate to make sure, make a show of it. The stink of shit was overwhelming – he felt it seeping into his clothes and pores.

'Watch!' A voice from outside. The door half-opened, a hand stretched towards him. 'Gimme your watch.'

He tried to count the minutes and hours, washed and prayed according to his best guesses until, finally, the light through the window began to fade. The door opened; a new face appeared with a slice of bread and bowl of thin soup.

'Thank you, brother.'

The reply was a punch below the midriff. He recoiled. He looked at the food and tepid liquid and a tear trickled down his cheek. Angrily he brushed it away and began hungrily to eat and drink the meagre ration. When he finished, there remained an emptiness in the pit of his stomach.

Darkness. The sound of a dripping tap on the other side of the wall. He counted the gap – every three seconds without break. It stopped. He breathed deeply, forced himself to relax, closed his eyes and laid his head on the hay. Fatigue seized him and he waited for sleep to end the waking nightmare. As his eyes closed and peace descended, the drip restarted – a loud, metallic ping. He sat up with a jolt, nerves crushing him. Was the timing deliberate? Yet there was no noise, no sounds of other humans, no breathing beyond his now hurried exhalations. He looked up and around for cameras, both overt and concealed. Nothing. Some kind of lamp outside the window cast a shaft of light on the opposite wall. He tried to close his eyes to darken the reflection. Another drip. Then he woke up, cold and cramped.

After daybreak, more bread and a mug of black tea. He said nothing and it was delivered without violence. He was given a brush to clean his teeth and managed a small defecation in the bucket. When the plate and bowl were collected, the bucket was replaced. He didn't dare to speak words of gratitude.

On the third morning, after two more breaking, corroding days and nights, a different man looked in, less roughly dressed.

'Come.' Sami nodded, not opening his mouth. 'It's all right, brother, you may speak now.'

He felt exhausted, cramped, his legs like jelly. He forced his voice into action despite the dread of allowing the wrong words to escape. 'Thank you, brother,' he murmured.

'It is time for you to meet the Adviser.'

'It's everything I imagined,' said Patrick, turning the corner that brought the unique form of Pendle Hill into view. It was late afternoon – they had a couple of hours to get up and down before darkness would turn the great delineated mass visible in daylight into a brooding nocturnal shadow. 'You see photographs and don't think it could be like that. But it is. A blue whale. An enormous blue whale.'

'A whale?' Sara exclaimed with exaggerated alarm.

'Yes, don't you see the tail rising up from the valley and that smooth long back leading to the broad mouth feeding off the valley below?'

She turned to him. 'I think I see a man with an unexpected imagination.'

As the village of Barlow receded and they gained altitude, he in boots, jeans and anorak, she in trainers, jeans and hoodie, the north-west wind began to flap their jackets and flick their faces. The stony path on peat bog compressed by thousands of summer tramplings was dry and they skipped easily up it. Sara felt the tensions of the encounter with Sami ebb as her breaths deepened. Nearing the final crest, the wind strengthened and, once they were over it, was transformed into a roar, an invisible compression of sounds and waves ripping into their cheeks and rib cages. The summit plateau, Patrick's enormous whale-back, stretched into the distance.

'Let's get to the very top,' he yelled. In a few hundred yards they were standing by the cairn and trig point that marked the summit, the wind at its fiercest.

'I always wanted,' said Patrick, betraying for the first time a slight breathlessness, 'to see if it's possible to lean against wind.' He spread his arms and legs out. 'But until now I've never been in a wind strong enough to try it.' He slowly leant forward into its teeth until, finally, he was forced to put forward a leg to steady himself. 'Fantastic. It works. Try it!'

There was an edge in Patrick's challenge. Sara frowned at him, then grinned. 'OK.' She likewise spread her arms and legs. He was right; there was an invisible wall keeping her from falling. She leant further, and then, without warning, the wind relented a fraction and she went, the grass rushing towards her. She felt arms round her chest, pulling her back up and enfolding her, then releasing her.

'You went too far,' he said. 'Lucky I was here.'

'Yes, too far.' She felt suddenly embarrassed, foolish even, messing around on an isolated hilltop with a man she might instinctively trust but still hardly knew. 'Enough of the entertainment,' she said waspishly. 'Let's head down.'

As they reached the plateau's edge she paused before beginning the descent. The Ribble valley was alight in the late sun, arrows of reddening yellow bouncing off the Black Moss reservoirs below, a few farmhouses and cottages adrift like small boats in a calm sea of green. Remembering the modest streets of Muslim Blackburn, she was mesmerised by the peaceful spectacle below in the dying of the day. 'You can see why people might want to come to these parts,' she said, poise recovered. 'You'd have to travel hours out of London to see anything like this.'

'You can see why it spooked people too,' he said.

'Yes, the Witches of Pendle. I mugged up on them on the train. 1612. Twelve tried and executed. A land of superstition and fraudulence.'

'Nothing like now, then,' he said. There was no grin.

That night Sara went over the five files again. First contacts varied between the second half of 2005 and early 2006. There was wider variation in their outcomes.

1) Asif Hassan, closed in 2006.
2) Farooq Siddiqi, first contact 2003, 'exited 2007', file then closed.
3) Shayan al-Rehman, 'contact lost', file open.
4) Iqbal Jamal Wahab, 'returned 2014', file closed 2015.
5) Samir Mohammed, 'closed 2006'.

And there was the link. The one thing common to them all. Should she have bounced it on Sami? No. It would have been a huge risk, a shock tactic that could have deterred him irredeemably. No specific day was given but in June 2006 under 'Contacts' there was an entry in all five files. 'Interviewed by Blackburn CID. Released without charge.' It gave no hint of the content of the interview. It may not have been proof positive but it gave every sign of a connection.

If only Sami would get back to her, she might have gained enough trust to lure him into giving her the link; but she knew that bird might have flown. She would next try Asif Hassan's family address; as his file was also closed at the end of 2006, he, like Samir, might just have stayed in Blackburn. Or remained in touch with his family.

Who else was alive? Who, if any, was dead? And how?

What were the files designed to lead her to?

She washed, prayed and allowed herself a slow bath. Even

if the Savoy Inn's sanitary ware was peeling at the edges, the water was hot and she could stretch out her legs. She thought of Patrick's arms retrieving her. 'You went too far.' She tried to remember his expression at that moment; it wouldn't come.

A coded warning? 'Don't go too far again.'

7

'Move faster! You don't wanna keep the Adviser waiting.'

The end of the darkened passage emerged into a small courtyard. The sky was a clear blue, the sun hiding behind a slate roof to the east; below, greyish bricks and mullioned windows, a fanlight over a charcoal front door. As before, he could see no further – the courtyard walls were the screen now. He imagined hills and green fields, valleys and crystal streams, but there was no evidence of them, nor of where he might be. No people with accents or different-coloured skins, no road signs, no markings. No lights in the house.

They turned away to a carriage door opposite. It swung open, apparently of its own will; they entered a vaulted space, brightly illuminated with lamps hung high on thick oak beams. He shielded his eyes, adjusting from the days of dimmed solitude. On a platform at one end stood a long thin table, three figures looming over it. His guard gestured him to climb the steps and face them.

He took up his position and the seconds passed, perhaps even a minute – he'd lost all sense of time. He brought the three figures into focus. In the middle a tall, thin man with thick black hair unmarked by white or grey and a neatly trimmed beard was dressed in a flowing white robe, his cheek and jaw well-defined, neck and chin creaseless. A contrasting image of straggly-haired, grey-bearded, pot-bellied imams flashed before Sami and he felt ever more uncertain of what he was facing. To the left was a fair-skinned woman swathed in silky yellow, crowned by a light blue scarf; round the edges he could detect wisps of wavy blonde hair. Her azure eyes glistened like jewels and her straight delicate nose flowed seamlessly into full, unadorned lips. Even from where he stood, he smelt her sweetness. Starved of company for three eternal days, he thought they were the most beautiful couple he had ever seen. To the right, a different shape – burly and dressed in black, a rough bristled face, thick eyebrows hooding cold eyes and a flat nose with gaping nostrils.

The white-robed man stretched out his hands, palms faced upwards. '*Mashallah.* Welcome. Can I call you Sami?' His voice was soft, precise, clear; to Sami the tone and accent seemed in some way to belong to a rich and ancient civilisation; this man must be the Adviser. 'I know you have suffered.' He further stretched out his arms and Sami fell into his embrace. They hugged until the Adviser pulled away, yet without breaking his intense, powerful gaze.

'So, my brother Sami, now we must talk. Please sit.'

'Yes, Master.' He didn't know why he'd used that word rather than 'brother', only that this was a man he, in his weakened state, must submit to. He slumped into a hard wooden chair the guard placed behind him.

The woman spoke. 'Do you know why you have come here, Sami?' Her voice was soothing, enfolding him.

'No, sister.'

She stared at him with surprise. 'No?'

'They came for me. That's why.'

'Why did they come for you, brother?' It was the second man, his Pakistani accent rougher. He recognised a Lancastrian tinge.

'I dunno, brother.' He tried to read their three faces; nothing emerged. 'I ain't done nothing.'

'Is it good or bad to do nothing?' asked the Adviser.

'I dunno. What you want me to do?' he answered with the yearning of a starved dog.

'No, Sami, it is what you want to do.'

A tear trickled down his cheek. 'I dunno.'

'You must not tell us lies,' said the woman.

'That's right, Sami,' said the second man, walking around the end of the table to stand over him. He bent down, placing his mouth against Samir's right ear.

'We want to know whose fucking side you're on!'

His shout was so furious that Samir flinched wildly to his left, crashing off his chair onto the bare wood of the platform. The man hoicked him up.

'There is no need for unkindness or hurt,' said the Adviser. 'We must be friends. Return to your room and pray to Allah. You must think about your conscience and truth. We will pray for you too.'

The Adviser nodded once to the second man. He grabbed Sami by the shoulder, turned him and kneed him in the small of the back so violently that he crumpled.

Asif Hassan's family address of twelve years ago was 24 Pond Street. Obeying Patrick's rule of ten, Sara would only have to knock on two doors before arriving at the target house. No. 4 answered, detaining her for the ten minutes it took to speed through the questionnaire. Sara walked slowly by the next five doors. Her phone rang – Patrick, she assumed. Unhurriedly, she removed it from her bag; a number she didn't recognise. She felt that lurch in the stomach and took a deep breath.

'Yes?'

'Is that Sara?'

She punched the air, relief surging through her. 'Hey, is that you, Sami?'

'Yeah. You said I could call?'

'Yes, I did. It's good to hear from you.'

'Do you wanna meet again?'

She hesitated – don't appear too keen. 'OK, I could find time.'

'What about now?'

'Now? Where, Sami?'

'My house. It's OK, Mum'll be here.'

'I'll have to finish my street. Don't know how long it will take.'

'All right. But I gotta work later.'

'I'll be as quick as I can.'

'Yeah. OK.' He cut the call.

She phoned Patrick. 'He may have bitten.'

'Or he may want to see a pretty girl again.' She sensed there was no Patrick grin; he was managing her expectations.

'Should I finish the street? Even if it's just for show?'

'I'd get off it. Now.' It was the first time he'd spoken to her with any urgency.

Inside the car, he began to explain. 'Sami coming back to you might just be because he likes you. Or—'

'It could be the game changer,' she interrupted.

'Quite. You can't risk seeing anyone connected with the files till you're done with Sami.'

'OK. But Sami shouldn't think I've dropped everything for him.'

'Agreed. He needs to sweat with anticipation. Let it build.' He spoke with cold calculation. She looked at him and remembered that remark on Pendle Hill.

An hour later, he dropped her fifty yards from Gent Street. The predator's thrill resurfaced. She walked along the pavement at a measured pace, stopped outside No. 59, shook herself, stood tall, mounted the steps and, for some reason, tapped discreetly on the knocker rather than ring the bell.

The mother answered. 'Oh, *salam alaikum*.'

'Is Sami in, auntie?'

'I've been at the back, he said he was going out.'

Thoughts of intercepted phone calls, armed enforcers, police making arrests all flashed before her. His mother shouted up the stairs. 'Sami.' No answer. 'Yes, he must have gone out,' she said.

'Would you mind trying again?' asked Sara. 'It's something for the survey, I'm sure he said he was working late today.'

'Sami!' she yelled with a screech that made Sara jump.

A few seconds later, a pair of boots followed by jeans hurried down the stairs.

'I thought you wasn't coming,' he said. He inspected her in a way quite unlike their previous meeting. 'You go in the sitting room, I'll get tea.'

'I said it was my treat next time.'

'Nah, easier to have it here.' There was a new authority in his voice; he seemed to be setting the agenda, not her. He reappeared with tea and an uncut cake.

'A fresh cake,' Sara said.

'Yeah, I told you.' He poured tea, slowly cut a slice of cake, laid it on a plate and placed it on the stool by her chair. He sat down opposite.

'So there were a few things I forgot—'

'Nah.' He cut across her; she felt a frisson of alarm. 'So, Sara,' he put a heavy emphasis on her name, 'what you doing here?'

'I told you. The survey.'

'Nah.'

'What?' Nerves jangling, she gave him the most puzzled expression she could muster.

'What you really doing here?'

'What do you mean, "What am I really doing?"'

'Not hard to understand. I'm not an idiot.'

'Of course you're not an idiot.'

'The way you spoke to me, looked at me when you was leaving… there's something else.'

She put down her cup of tea and gazed at him imploringly. She hadn't begun to anticipate this. He might be her only chance of achieving something on this trip; she had seconds to stop him slipping through her fingers. He sat impassively, impossible to read, not giving her anything. She'd no idea whether he was operating from instinct or some kind of theorising he'd concocted overnight. Perhaps he'd talked to a workmate.

'Tell me, Sami,' she said, 'what is it that's been going through your mind?'

'That's not the point.' He sounded rougher. 'I wanna know what you're doing here.' He paused. 'It's all right. Mum's here. Ain't no harm gonna come to you. Just wanna know.'

She sensed his implacability and sighed, wanting to convey a sign of defeat while she worked out how much to give him. 'Can I trust you, Sami?'

'Depends, don't it? More like whether I can trust you.'

'I understand.' Now she needed to show submission. She picked up her workbag, took out the clipboard with the questionnaire and a folder beneath. She was on her own. She gambled. 'You're right, Sami.' She pulled out a tissue, blew her nose and wiped a non-existent tear from her eye.

'It's OK,' he said, softening. 'You can trust me.'

She buried the tissue inside her sleeve. 'It's true I'm researching the opinions and experiences of young Muslims. It's also true,' she spoke with intensity, 'that anything we discuss now is on the basis of total confidentiality. But yes, you're right.' She retrieved the tissue and sniffed again. 'I'm not a market researcher. I'm a lawyer working on behalf of an independent inquiry examining how the British government has treated young Muslims in recent years.'

'What's that?'

'The inquiry is chaired by a judge called Sir Francis Morahan.'

'Never heard of him.'

'I wouldn't expect you to have. The important point is that he's independent. Unbiased. And, Sami, at the heart of what he wants to understand is why some young British Muslims went off to fight. To be jihadists. How were they chosen? Who paid? And what's happened to them?'

A dark frown clouded his face. 'What the fuck's that got to do with me?' He looked around. 'Why you come to me anyway? I ain't done nothing.'

'It's OK, Sami, I know that.' She spoke softly, edging closer. 'Can I trust you with something? Really, really trust you?'

'I wanna see you properly. Under the scarf.'

'I can't do that.' Sara felt a cramping in her stomach.

'It's your choice,' he said. 'If I can't see you, I can't trust you.'

Why was he asking? Simple curiosity? Some kind of test of her sincerity – or devoutness? A darker thought flared. Did he think she was wired up? Perhaps he *had* talked – but to someone better informed than a workmate.

First try the obvious. 'Sami, I'm observing my religion – our religion – in the way I've chosen.'

'My religion's for me,' he said sourly.

She'd made a mistake. 'I'm sorry, I shouldn't have presumed.'

'Nah.'

'Why's this important to you?'

'I told you.' He stood up and crossed behind her chair to look out of the bay window. 'You're in my home. No one's looking in. My mum's in the back. You want me to trust you. But you deceived me. Now you gotta show trust in me.'

Was refusal or acquiescence the correct response? 'My religion's for me.' What had he meant? There were enough signs of some kind of observant upbringing. Or had he lapsed and become suspicious of zeal? She suspected that the story he had to tell – she was now sure that he had one – would provide the answer.

She hesitated. This was the wrong way to allow herself to behave, let alone think, whatever tactical advantage it might bring. 'Remember who you are,' she told herself. 'Remember the standards you've set yourself. Think of what you believe.'

She sensed him moving towards her and turned away. 'I'm sorry, Sami, I can't do that.'

He didn't bat an eyelid. 'Nah, thought you wouldn't.' She held her breath; was this it?

He sat down again. 'It's OK.'

She tried to withhold a sigh. There was nothing innocent now about Sami – but where lay his guilt? Slowly, saying nothing, she started leafing through the files on her lap. An instinct had told her at least to have them with her.

'You asked why I've come to you.' She picked out his file and handed it over.

He opened it and stared at the single sheet. 'What's this?'

'2006. It's probably police or Special Branch.' She wouldn't tell him it was MI5. 'Its existence suggests that, at one point, you were suspected of being involved in jihadist activity.'

'I never.'

'I know.' She stood up and crossed to his chair. 'May I?' She knelt down beside him and pointed to a column. 'It says "file closed". So nothing came of it.'

She fetched her workbag, judging she could give more. 'This is private, Sami, yes? Just between you and me.'

'Yeah.' He turned to her; she was just inches away. He could feel her breath. She handed him the other four files and his eyes roved slowly over them, one by one. 'I don't get it.'

'Do you know them?'

'Yeah. Then anyway.'

'Were they friends?'

'Yeah. Sort of.'

'In June 2006 you were all brought in for questioning by Blackburn police.'

'How do you know that?'

She pointed him to the common note on the five files. He looked at it silently, his face creasing in pain. 'It were nothing,' he said at last.

'What was nothing?'

'It were just a girl. Her foster mother reported us. They had us in, asked us what happened. Let us go. As I said, it were nothing.'

'Was there anything else they talked to you about?' He said nothing. 'Did they try to coerce any of you to do anything for them? Offer money perhaps?'

He was hesitating. Something had happened, she was sure. If not to Sami, then to one or more of the others. 'Nah, nothing else.'

She tried to lock eyes. 'Forget about the police. Your friends, Sami… were they doing something that could have got you into real trouble?'

He turned away, staring blankly at the window. 'I dunno, I never knew what it was.'

'Never knew what what was? What happened, Sami?'

He bowed his head and sat looking at his hands for what seemed an age.

'I never told anyone this before.'

8

2006

The fourth night was the worst because he could see no way out of it. What did they want? Some kind of confession or admission? To sacrifice himself for them in some way? To march into the Rovers' stadium and blow himself up? Those conversations with the other four kept coming back; he'd assumed at the time it was all bullshit, exchanges of fantasies. Had they been trying to draw him into something? Surely not Asif. That look he gave him as he was being led away was regret – and fear. Not a hungry, fighting look. No, not Asif – but the others… maybe.

The searchlight beaming into this cell – or whatever the space was – cast strips of brightness that seemed harsher than ever.

He thought of the real cell where the police questioned him after the foster mother complained.

Then one of the policemen – not the tough guy with the red beard, the other one with neatly cut fair hair and glasses, wearing a white shirt and grey tie – started asking him about the others. 'We know you have interesting conversations with your friends, Samir.' He'd asked what conversations and the tough guy just gave him a conspiratorial smile, tapping a finger on his nose. 'Come on, Sami,' said the smart one, 'you've even discussed targets with them. What you'd like to blow up. Who you'd like to kill.' It was just bragging, he protested, no one was serious. 'Maybe not you, Sami. But the others. Are you really so sure?'

And he was sure, then. Now, in the fourth night of this hell, perhaps he wasn't so sure. A drip from the tap outside. Count one, two, three. Another drip. A howling through the trees – a wind whipping up? He imagined a crying boy being led into the woods.

The smart policeman had shooed the red beard out of the room and come to sit close beside him. He leant in and whispered in his ear. Sami would never forget the heat of his breath.

'You could make some money, Sami.'

He recoiled. 'What you mean, money?'

'All you got to do is keep me posted on what your friends are talking about. What they're planning. Where they travel.'

'You wanna get me killed.'

'It'll just be between you and me. No one else will ever know. Every time you tell me something, there's three hundred quid for you. Once a week. Thirty tenners. Fifteen twenties, if you prefer. Make you a well-off boy.'

Next day they let him go but he couldn't shake off the suit with the grey tie. Almost every day, it seemed, he was there, lurking in invisible corners. 'Nice to see you again, Sami.'

The door squeaked open – he must have finally fallen asleep as its noise awakened him. Curled up against a straw bale, he forced his eyes open, the searchlight still flaring, the night behind still dark. He'd no idea what time it was. He heard a rustle and saw a yellow dress floating towards him and a figure sitting down beside him. He could see little more than a silhouette and scarf, but he instantly knew – the beautiful woman from the barn.

'It's all right, Sami.' As before, her voice soothed him. But back then it had been followed by the second man screaming in his ear.

'Is the other man coming?' he asked.

'No. Only you and me.'

'I wanna go home.' He felt tears welling.

'I know you do. But you must help us.' She paused, seeming puzzled. 'Do you like your friends, Sami?'

'Yeah, 'course I do.'

'Shayan, Farooq, Iqbal, Asif.'

'Yeah, they're mates.'

'Then why do you betray them?'

'I don't.' He began to cry. 'Never. Never have.'

'They paid you.'

'Who paid?'

'That policeman.'

Sami sat up and repressed the tears. 'Never. I promise. Never. I'll tell you. Yeah, he tried. Offered me money. I never took it. He kept following. I never let him. Never told him nothing. You gotta believe me.'

'Calm yourself, Sami. If you are true and loyal, then whose side are you really on?'

'I dunno. Our side, my mates'.'

'Do you want to be a soldier? Some of your friends do. We can give you money to go abroad. To build the Caliphate.'

'I dunno.' The tears returned. 'I'm not brave.' He buried his face in his hands. 'I just wanna go home.'

'Thank you, Sami. Is there anything more you want to say to me?'

He removed his hands, his eyes burning with fear. 'Please… will I be able to see…' He hesitated, wanting to use the word 'Master' but corrected himself. '… to see the Adviser again?'

She returned a look of profound sadness. 'That depends, Sami, on the Adviser's opinion.' She rose to leave the cell, her head rigid, not looking back. As the last swathe of her dress disappeared, the door slammed shut.

Two hours later, they came; the 'escort' and the driver. His hands cuffed and, this time, his eyes blindfolded, they led him through the entrance he'd first entered and onto gravel; he saw enough through the bottom edge of the blindfold to know it was still not light. He heard the van door open.

'Please,' he said, 'I need to see the Adviser. I gotta speak with him. Something to tell him.' The reply was a sickening blow crunching into the calf muscle of his right leg. They bundled him like a stiff-legged animal into the back and moved off in silence.

After half an hour or so, they stopped. This time, they yanked him out and grabbed him under his arms, dragging his body as his feet tried to keep up. Shafts of rising sunlight filtered through the gap under the blindfold. He felt himself sliding along leaves – and then the flash of yellow disappeared and he was in darkness.

They pressed him down on his knees. 'Kneel!' It was the first word he'd heard from either of them since they'd taken him from the cell. 'Look ahead. No turning.' The blindfold was pulled roughly from his head; now he understood why they'd applied it. Revealed inches in front of his terrified eyes was a gaping, recently dug hollow – a shallow grave. Though there was almost nothing left in his gut, he felt a sliver of slime dribbling around his crotch and buttocks. A rim of metal was jammed against his forehead. He heard a click.

No bang, still alive. 'Never, ever speak of this,' said the driver.

'You never came here. You never met no one. You just went for a little holiday on your own. Understand?'

'Yes,' he bleated. 'I understand.'

'You stink, you fucking coward. And if you ever blab, that grave stays. It's been dug specially for you.' He handed him a card. 'Keep this. Till your last breath. If anyone ever starts asking questions, anyone at all, anytime at all, even years ahead, the rest of your life, phone this. You don't, you're dead.'

A few hours later – he couldn't begin to guess how long – they pulled up in what he guessed was a lay-by. The van door opened, the handcuffs unlocked. They shoved keys, phone and a familiar wallet into his trousers. They dragged him out, slammed the door shut, sprinted to the front of the van and drove off. Even if he'd wanted to, he was too numbed with shock to note the number plate.

He looked around. He began to recognise where he was; by the main road leading off the motorway into Blackburn, a few hundred yards short of a bus stop. He climbed a gate into a field and tried to mop himself with grass. And then he walked.

Sami slumped back in his chair, his shoulders curled, his eyes closed. Watching him tell his story, Sara felt a witness to a terror relived – and a guilt that she had manoeuvred him into breaking a thirteen-year silence.

He stirred. 'Shouldn't have told you. Never tell anyone. But them four days…'

'It's OK, Sami. I would never, ever discuss it with another person unless you gave me your permission.'

He looked up at her, opening his eyes. 'I thought they was going to kill me. I thought I was dead.' She wanted to comfort him but restrained herself; she reminded herself that he harboured a guilt, whatever it might be.

'But you survived, Sami. And now you'll always be safe.'

'How do you know that?' He sounded almost hostile.

'I promise you.'

'No one can promise.'

'It was a long time ago.'

'Sometimes feels like yesterday to me.' The remark, a return to a sort of reality, seemed to restore him. Sara seized the moment.

'Did you keep in touch with the others after that? Your friends.'

He smiled ruefully. 'Nah. I never wanted to see them again. I kept looking for them on the streets so I could duck out of the way.' He reflected, as if reminding himself of something important. 'Actually, a few days after I did bump into Asif. Sort of. He was walking towards me on the pavement the other side of the road. It was too late to run or hide. He saw me and yelled, "Hey, Sami." I sort of waved at him and looked away. That was it. He didn't come after me. He knew something had happened. But he wasn't part of it. Not Asif. He was never serious.'

'Part of what?' She tried not to sound like an interrogator.

'I dunno. But it can't have been for nothing, can it? Not if they thought I was snitching on them.'

'After the woman left you and before they came to take you away, you said two more hours passed. Did anything else happen?'

'Nah.' His tone had changed, as if he was now bored.

'You're sure.'

'Yeah.'

'And you saw no one else.'

'Nah.'

'Do you know anything of what happened to the others?'

'Nah.' He paused, squinting his face. 'Not really anyway.' He seemed more interested again.

'Go on.'

'You don't give up, do you?'

She laughed. 'Sorry!'

'I did hear a few years ago Asif'd gone down to Birmingham and was training as a chef. Poisoning the customers probably.' He smiled with a tinge of fondness and regret. 'Dunno about the others. Never saw them.'

She had got all that would be of any use – time to move on. She stretched back her shoulders. 'I'd love to stay here talking, Sami, but I'd better go.'

'Yeah, suppose you had.' He stood up alongside her. 'I'll get your coat.' She'd expected him to want her to stay and chat more but it seemed he was drawing a line too. 'So what you do next?' he asked, handing her the coat.

'You mean after what you told me?'

'Yeah.'

'Nothing. I'll make a private note just for myself, no names or places or dates. It all sheds some light.' She locked eyes with him. 'I told you, Sami, I'd never do anything without your permission.'

'Yeah, but I was thinking something. If you had that file, why didn't you just come and knock on the door and ask to speak to me.'

'If I'd done that, do you honestly think you'd have let me in? Didn't we have to get to know each other first? To like each other the way I like you now? To trust each other?'

'Yeah, but what you did wasn't trusting, was it? How can I be sure?'

'You can be sure, I've given you my word.' As she put on the coat, he brushed past her to open the door. She turned onto the pavement, never looking back, niggled by the realisation that it hadn't gone the way she expected. She felt the heat of Sami's eyes on her back as she retreated up Gent Street.

Patrick was waiting around the corner. Sara checked behind, then joined him in the car.

'Productive?'

'Yes. After a sticky start.' She explained Sami's initial interrogation of her and gave him the headlines of his story. 'Quite a charge sheet,' she concluded, 'kidnapping, false imprisonment, actual bodily harm.'

'But just his account,' he said.

'Still, it doesn't feel like a one-off. There was a team. It was organised.'

'Sure. But what for? Why?'

Sara hesitated, reminding herself what was their shared knowledge and what was hers alone. Patrick now knew about the five Muslim files, Sami's story, and a deserted place with a man called 'the Adviser'. He did *not* know that the files were MI5 KV2 sourced, nor the existence of Sayyid, nor Sayyid's indication that they were the first step to revealing something cankerous within the secret state. And *neither* of them knew what that canker was, nor what lay further on the route towards it. Who was 'the Adviser'? Who was the woman? Above all, why the need now to rake over these coals?

'You're cogitating,' he said.

'Yes,' she smiled. For the moment, she would leave those pieces of knowledge where they stood. 'I was thinking I wished I knew the answer to your question.'

He was the one who now hesitated. 'Any suggestion – hint even – that it was more than threats and scares? That they actually did away with anyone?'

She detected an uncharacteristic anxiety – as if he'd rehearsed the question. She frowned. 'No. Not from him. Why?'

'Just wondering.' He paused. ''Cos that would be a different level.' As they stopped at red lights, he turned to her. 'You OK?'

'Yes, fine. Feels like you're the twitchy one.'

He grinned. 'No, not at all. Just drifting.' The lights changed, he accelerated decisively away. 'Would you mind something?'

'What?'

'It's my boy's football night and I always try to be there.'

'Your boy?'

'Yeah.' He grinned. 'Nathan, he just turned nine.'

'You never said.'

'Well, it's not part of this, is it?' He seemed uncertain whether to go on.

'You can't stop there.'

'It's my regular day of the week. And every other weekend.' He went silent; she waited. 'He lives with his mother. Well, mainly with the nanny as far as I can see.'

'She works?'

'When she feels like it.' Sara saw she'd scratched a sore. 'She went off a long time ago. No shortage of money her side.'

'I see.'

'You keep the car, I'll get a taxi to Preston station. Be back on the first train in the morning. Will you be all right?'

'Of course I'll be all right, Patrick.' The words came out more acerbically than intended.

His grin broadened. 'Someone said you don't tolerate idiotic remarks.'

'Only when they're made by clever people. I'll drive you to the station. You can sit in the back if you want and I'll wear a chauffeur's cap.'

After dropping Patrick off, Sara felt oddly irritated by her pleasure that he had no wife in tow – but, unless she'd misread him, puzzled by that trace of anxiety. It seemed a long way to come and go for a kid's football night.

This time Sami watched from the bay window. After she'd disappeared he went upstairs to his bedroom, slid down his jeans and unstrapped the miniature recorder taped to his right thigh. He switched off the record button and carefully placed the chrome rectangle inside the top drawer of his chest beneath the pile of underpants.

Task completed and the woman gone, he slumped with exhaustion. He felt faint and nauseous, and crossed the narrow landing to the bathroom. His mother below would be listening to his footsteps. He kneeled and leant over the bowl, trying to retch. Nothing came – the wave of sickness slowly passed and he gulped two mugs of water. A forced belch released air and his chest began to clear.

Had he saved his skin? Nine hours after the phone call he'd decided to make following her first visit, a man had been there waiting for him when he'd arrived for his shift at the Rovers. A man he'd never seen before – no resemblance, not even in colour, to the two men on that platform twelve years ago, let alone the beautiful blonde woman with the sweet smell and clean warm breath.

He could only hope, perhaps even pray for once, that when he met the man again, and they sat in his car while he listened to the recording – as he'd promised they most definitely would – the man would say he'd carried out the instructions right. With a reward to come. He thought of what might happen if he hadn't. The nausea returned.

9

The request from Sayyid threw Morahan; it had never occurred to him that he'd actually want to meet. Was it a trap? Might he reveal himself? Whatever the motive, he had to risk it and go. This time there was a difference in protocol. Instead of offering the opportunity to agree or decline a request, Sayyid had simply named a time and place.

11 p.m. Morahan waited in the appointed churchyard with an apprehension he again felt too old for. Nothing. The noises of the night seemed unnaturally loud. Breaths of wind rustling leaves, scurryings in the undergrowth, distant sirens. He looked around, half-expecting a black-coated man stalking him, awaiting the moment to stick a revolver in his back. Suddenly he was blinded by a flash of headlights. They went twice from full to dip – a summons. As he approached, there was something familiar about the shape of the car – and the circular green sticker it displayed. He understood; nerves dissolving, he opened the passenger door.

'Back seat,' said a muffled voice. It seemed to be coming through some sort of box. 'We will talk on the move.' The driver was sporting a cap, thick-framed glasses, a checked scarf wrapped round the face and a high black polo-neck sweater which rose above the collar of a black leather jacket. Morahan had imagined Sayyid in an office suit and tie, his natural habitat a corridor of power – or, at least, of information. 'It's better you cannot see what I look or sound like,' the distorted voice continued. 'For you, I mean.'

'I'm hardly experienced in these things,' said Morahan.

'I am not accustomed to giving senior judges classified documents.'

'You're acting in the public interest.'

'There are not many in your position who would see it that way. They would have reported the approach and been done with it.' Morahan noted the precision and lack of animation in his speech – more than just the product of the digital device. He was a man who chose his words carefully. 'They are the innocents,' Sayyid continued in his monotone, 'who put a cuckoo in the nest.'

He drove along the Embankment at a steady thirty miles an hour, waiting at Chelsea Bridge for the filter light to change. He turned right across the river, passed bikers stopping for coffee and burgers at the night stall, and turned right again into Battersea Park where he drew up in the shadow of a clump of trees.

'The young woman is on board, yes?' he said, his head making a quarter turn.

'Yes.' Morahan stopped, wondering what Sayyid knew or didn't know. One way to explore. 'She's gone North, following those files.'

No reaction, not a flicker. He passed a brown A4 envelope to the back. 'Now that she has arrived, I can give you a third folder. It contains a photograph and an audio cassette. It will replay on your dictaphone.' Morahan thought to ask how he knew what dictaphone he possessed but restrained himself. 'With this information,' continued Sayyid, 'you will detect a link. When you think the time is right, let her see it – the sooner the better.'

Morahan hesitated; he wished to appear neither stupid nor over-eager. 'A link that ends where?'

'That's for you and the woman to work out. As I told you, those files are the tip – and the beginning – of the iceberg.'

'Continuing the metaphor,' said Morahan languidly, trying to match Sayyid's tone, 'if the iceberg is man-made, who commissioned it? And controlled its size and temperature?'

'Let us cut the metaphor,' the voice snapped, ruffling the calm. 'That is why I wanted to see you in person.' Sayyid shuffled in his seat but didn't turn. 'Because that is what I do *not* know. There are people who think they know. But only one, possibly two, truly *does*.'

'I find that hard to interpret.'

'I understand.' The voice softened. 'They used to call it the wilderness of mirrors. Remember Golitsyn.'

'Remind me.'

'Our master spy, the double agent inside the KGB. Finally, he defects – they are onto him, he says. When he arrives, he tells us we are penetrated from top to bottom. The head of MI5 is a KGB mole – even a future British prime minister is a place man for the Russians. The head of CIA counter-intelligence believes him, as does a faction inside MI5. For the next decade we can hardly move because we are so scared of our own shadow. In a game of deception, how do you know whose side anyone is really on? How do you see into a conscience? Into a heart? And it matters because lives can depend on it. Thousands of lives.'

'What are you saying? There's some kind of traitor at the heart of MI5's operations against Islamist terror?'

'I am not saying anything. It is you who has just said that.'

'I'm sorry, Sayyid,' said Morahan gently, 'or whatever your name is – I can't play this game.'

'It is not a game.'

'Investigating these matters is not within my terms of reference.'

'It is. Look at them. Why did we once succeed? Why did we then fail? I do not know the answer. You raise the suggestion of treachery.'

'What else then?'

'Remember extraordinary rendition? What follows?'

'Tell me.'

'I cannot. You started your journey by hiring the woman. It is for you to decide whether to continue.'

Morahan looked through the car window from their darkened space across the broad tarmac of the park's concourse. A figure wearing a beret was stubbing out a cigarette underneath a lamp. He whistled; a dog came running. 'I think I should leave now.'

'Yes.' Sayyid turned on the ignition. 'I will drop you somewhere less isolated.'

He started the engine, turned round and headed down Chelsea Bridge Road. At the roundabout south-east of the park, he circled twice, satisfied himself no one was following and retraced his route across the river. 'Basic procedure,' he said, 'but better than nothing.' Instead of going left onto the Embankment he continued to Sloane Square and crisscrossed the Kings Road, heading all the while in the direction of Morahan's house. He stopped a few hundred yards short of it.

'We will not meet again.' He continued to look rigidly forwards. 'One final word. There is a destination. It is called Operation Pitchfork. I tell you this, but you must not allow any other to know you have heard this word. Not even the woman. At least not yet... if ever. That is too dangerous for you and her. And me. Take care of her. And of yourself.'

Morahan stepped out, easing the door shut; the car

accelerated smoothly out of sight. Tucking the envelope under his coat, he walked fast, pausing briefly to make a 360-degree sweep of the street. The only sign of life was the reflection of a foraging fox's eyes. He glared back and it scurried into undergrowth. Hunter and hunted.

Back home, he opened the front door and from the hall heard the sounds of Iona above stepping onto the landing. He looked up.

'All right?' she asked.

'Yes.' He forced a smile. 'Yes, of course.'

'I've an early start, so off to bed.'

'I think I might work on a while.'

'As you will. Don't stay up too late.' She retreated.

He went into his study, sat down and placed the envelope on the desk. He pulled out the contents. First was a single murky photograph. A table with a group of what looked like diners in the foreground, hints of more tables beyond. All unidentified. Was there something about one of the faces? He studied it. Probably not, must be his imagination. Too shadowy to make out anyway.

The second, and only other object in the envelope was a cassette tape. Remembering Sayyid's words, he took from the middle drawer of the desk the dictaphone on which he liked to record first drafts of judgements.

He inserted the cassette and pressed play. The tape revolved. After several seconds of hissing, he began to hear chatting against the background of what, assuming a connection with the photograph, had to be restaurant bustle. Whoever was recording must have been able to swing a directional microphone to eavesdrop on specific conversations. Some he could make out, others were inaudible or rendered unintelligible by background noise.

He settled himself to listen.

Initially, Sara was grateful for her solitary evening; time to relax, to think, to pray. Dinner at the Savoy Inn had been an unappetising prospect – not just the food but the stares of transient males freed of their wives. She'd bought a veggie wrap and a Coke from a petrol station on the road along from the hotel. Peeling off the plastic cover revealed a sogginess to the touch, and an affront to the nose like the distant whiff of a rubbish collecting lorry. She dumped it in the bathroom bin and washed her face and hands. The cure would have been the spiciest offering of Blackburn's hottest curry house but it hardly seemed the town for a stranger sitting alone and wearing a scarf.

She decided to go for a drive. The Blackburn of Samir's youth had, by all accounts, been a lively place attracting crowds of young people to once-famous nightclubs like The Cavendish – the 'Cav' – the entire top floor of a multi-storey car park where girls came down from the mills and danced around handbags dumped inside their circle while young men lounged against walls injecting pints of Thwaites beer for late-night courage. Later, the town had hosted nocturnal raves and no one seemed to mind too much. The clientele was solidly white; this place had also been a fertile breeding ground for the National Front.

Now the city centre was deserted – it was mid-week but hard to imagine what the attraction could be on any night. She drove past the occasional sad-looking pub with dimmed lights, and late-night stores with lonely faces slumped over motionless cash tills. On a whim, which she justified as a search for inspiration, she drove to Gent Street, parking a hundred yards down from Sami's house. The porch light was on and the sitting-room curtains left a sufficient gap to know that someone was inside. She looked in the off-side wing mirror. A figure was approaching at a fast walk – it could be him. Of course, if he was doing the evening shift, he'd be returning home around now. It was too late to start the car and attract attention; she slid down in her seat and pulled her scarf over her face. The figure walked on past without a beat. She peered up as it crossed the road and continued along the pavement, not even casting a glance at Samir's front door. She felt foolish, unable to conceive what enlightenment she had come in search of. Perhaps it was simply to check the reality of him; that he had lived through something that was not a fantasy.

Her phone buzzed. She recoiled, then forced herself to click on it.

Hope you're enjoying it up North.

An unfamiliar number, no name.

She turned away, staring blankly through the window at the dark street, frightened. A few seconds later, the phone, still in her hand, shuddered. This time it was ringing. With a name.

'Patrick!'

'Hey, sorry, is it too late? You sound startled.'

'No, no. It's fine. I was just in the middle of something.' She hoped he wasn't smelling her fear. 'It's kind of late to ring.'

'Yeah, sorry. Just wanted to be sure you're OK.'

'Of course I'm OK.'

'I didn't like leaving you.'

'I'm a big girl, Patrick.' She imagined the grin. 'How was the football?'

She sensed him hesitating. 'You know, Sara, I wasn't sure whether to tell you this. It was cancelled. Could have stayed up North.'

'Bad luck. But did you see him?'

'Not even that, he remained with the enemy. Sorry, the nanny.'

'What a waste.'

'I know. We could have been having dinner together at the Savoy.'

She forced a laugh. 'Goodnight, Patrick.'

'You too, Sara, and take care. See you in the morning.'

She clicked to view the anonymous message, telling herself not even to try to respond this time – and failing. She hit reply and typed.

Who are you?

Ping.

Message sent.

A new, different terror – someone was there. She waited for a reply. Five, ten, twenty, thirty seconds. A minute. Nothing. She took deep breaths, steeling herself. She dialled the number.

Half a ring, cut by a voice message. 'The number you have dialled is unobtainable.'

She put down the phone and buried her face in her hands. How was whoever this was doing it? How do you freeze a number just like that? Perhaps it was as simple as using a pay as you go phone – 'burners' she'd heard them called – and inserting and removing the SIM card. No trace – an anonymity switched on and off.

Gent Street felt like alien territory. She started the engine, drove to its end and turned right.

The figure who had walked past her stepped back into the shadows and watched her drive by.

Morahan checked his watch. 2.30 a.m. The tape had finally ended – just over two and three quarter hours. He wound back to the time-code he had marked. He'd listened to it twice over at the time, then played to the end to see if the voice reappeared. It did not.

He listened to the passage for a third time, just to make sure there was no mistake. As with all the conversations recorded, some parts could be made out, others not. The first voice was male, precise, clipped. He detected a vainness, a boastfulness perhaps, in it. The second voice was female, probably young, though, from both tone and expression, not a child or teenager.

M: *You were one person I had not expected to see.*

F: *Why?*

M: *I never forget what you said… INAUDIBLE…*

F: *If you're speaking of 9/11, my eyes have seen what followed… INAUDIBLE… INAUDIBLE… Of which you approve, I suppose.*

M: *Or perhaps of which I was prophetic… INAUDIBLE… INAUDIBLE… The Bush and Blair folly of Iraq… INAUDIBLE…*

F: *Our world?*

M: *Of course, our world of Islam.*

F: *INAUDIBLE… It may be yours… INAUDIBLE… INAUDIBLE… a world I want to share… INAUDIBLE…*

M: *… I want you to understand me… INAUDIBLE… INAUDIBLE…*

F: *INAUDIBLE… What are you talking about?*

M: *Can you not feel it all around you? Not just the Middle East… INAUDIBLE… INAUDIBLE… not just be part of the chorus…*

F: *What is your play?*

M: *Who can predict that?… INAUDIBLE… rain of death on our people… INAUDIBLE …*

F: *INAUDIBLE… INAUDIBLE… You even said it yourself. Time for me to leave.*

M: *No… INAUDIBLE… Do you think I would I ever want to frighten you?… INAUDIBLE… INAUDIBLE… INAUDIBLE*

F: *INAUDIBLE… I'm so sorry, I've lost track of the time. I promised to be home for my father.*

Those last sentences were clear as a bell – as if she'd been announcing it to the table. The accent may have slightly changed, but not the voice.

Morahan heard sounds above.

'It's late, Francis.'

'Yes, I know. Sorry. I've just finished.'

He packed the photograph and cassette back into the envelope, switched off the study light and climbed the stairs.

Iona was standing on the landing. 'I couldn't sleep.'

'That's unlike you.'

'I was worried.' She looked at the envelope. 'Did you get that from him?'

'Yes.'

'And it's kept you up this long?'

'Yes. I'll tell you in the morning.' He looked at her. 'It's more sensitive than anything I've had before. For some reason, I don't think locking it in my desk is a good idea. In fact I'm not sure having anything in my desk is a good idea.'

She stretched out a hand. 'Give it to me. I'll find a place for it.'

Morahan handed her the envelope. 'Thank you.' She looked into his eyes and sighed.

He went into the bathroom. He brushed his teeth and splashed water over his face, rubbing his eyes. He must hold his nerve. He told himself again that he was the independent chairman of a public inquiry lawfully established by the government of a democratic, constitutionally upright nation.

The mystery now was who she was – or had once been. Who had she known? What had she known?

10

A sharp Lancastrian morning brought a clear-mindedness which, Sara thought, had temporarily gone missing during the late-night trawl of the streets of Blackburn. Firstly, she must exert self-discipline over the anonymous texts – there was nothing to be gained from speculating about them and nothing in their words to alarm her. There seemed no way of tracing their origins.

She must not allow their mere existence to scare her. There might be an explanation for them one day – there might not. Back to the knowable.

Samir's story was, despite that misgiving about him she still couldn't pin down, a breakthrough. There had been some kind of significant operation which Morahan's source Sayyid was directing him to disinter – even if its exact nature remained unclear.

As for the other four names on the Blackburn files, at least she now fully understood that they were a group and why they had been hauled in by Blackburn CID. Their apparently easy release without any charge or even caution struck her as odd. It raised the further question of whether Special Branch, or even MI5, had smelt an opportunity. Sami's denial had not fully convinced her – even if he was covering for one of his former friends.

She decided there was no need to await Patrick's return before resuming her search. There was no answer at the file's addresses for Farooq Siddiqi and Shayan al-Rehman. One of the houses appeared to have been empty for a while.

Next was back to 24 Pond Street, the 2006 address of Sami's friend, Asif Hassan. Sara heard a shuffling and sensed an eye peering through the spy hole. Then a retreat, followed by heavier footsteps. A burly man around sixty looked down on her suspiciously. Right colour, right age to be Asif's father. Sara explained the Inquiry and her role; there seemed no further justification for subterfuge.

'We can't help you,' he said in a strong Lancastrian accent.

'I was hoping to contact a gentleman called Asif Hassan,' she said. 'I heard he was working as a chef in Birmingham.'

'Who said that?'

Sara kicked herself. Careless – she hadn't prepared for that question. 'I can't remember to be honest,' she said feebly, 'must have picked it up somewhere.'

He took a step nearer. 'All right, kid. Now hear this. He's not been seen nor heard of this thirteen year now. Since the morning he disappeared. With time, wounds heal. There's no giving false hope to his mother and sisters. So leave it. Understand?'

Sara saw the grief etched in the lines mapping his face. 'Yes, Mr Hassan, I understand.'

'And don't make that assumption neither.' With that, he closed the door. Sara kicked herself. Why hadn't she asked Sami the source of the rumour? How could he have heard something about Asif that was so clearly unknown to his family?

The final chance was 113 Medlar Street, home at one time of Iqbal Jamal Wahab. His files suggested that, after returning home, probably from Syria or Iraq, he had disappeared again. If he was known to have died in conflict, the British government or jihadists themselves would have told his parents. If he hadn't, where was he now?

This time the door opened – accompanied by an unfriendly reception from a young man she assumed to be his brother. Overhearing the doorstep conversation, an older man stepped in. Sara explained as before her role and its confidential nature.

'Yes, I'm Iqbal's dad and it sounds good what you're doing, love, but we can't help you.' His tone was polite but firm.

'I realise he's not here any longer,' she said, 'but could you just tell me when you last saw him?'

'As I said, we'd rather not and I'd ask you to leave us in peace. He came home briefly but we haven't seen or heard of him for four years now. We've not given up but we'd best not get involved.'

'I understand.' Sara shuffled her bag, began to turn and stopped mid-track. The father hadn't closed the door and was still watching her. She detected a yearning within him; it was worth a try. 'I don't want to intrude but might you consider taking my contacts?' This time, Sara picked out her card from Knightly Court. 'It's where I was working before I started this. You can always get me through them or on my mobile. No need to go near the Inquiry. Just me. Nothing official. You never know, you might need a lawyer sometime.'

He looked down from her eyes to the card she held. She felt her heart thumping.

'All right, love.' He took it, smiled and closed the door.

It was midday – Patrick's train was due at Preston in twenty minutes. Blackburn had for the moment yielded its secrets; there was no point in hanging around. She would meet him at the station, dump the hire car and jump on the next train south. She felt a touch of glee at the pointlessness of his journey wiping the grin off his face.

'You can turn round,' she said, stepping out of the car to greet him. 'We're done here. Time to go home.'

'Let's drive down!' beamed Patrick, not in the slightest put out. 'We can return the car in London.'

'What?'

'Point one. Cars are better for talking – you can't bury yourself in that laptop. Point two. As I say to my boy, once I've got you in the car, you can't get out. Point three. I didn't come all the way up here on one train to go straight back down. Point four. We have the pleasure of each other's company. Point five—'

'OK, Patrick,' she laughed despite herself, 'I'll accept point one. And you can do the driving.'

'Yes, ma'am.' He doffed the imaginary cap, chucked his bag in the back and glided into the driver's seat with apparently effortless elegance. Heading out of the town, she described her brief encounters with Iqbal Jamal Wahab's father and the man who must be Asif Hassan's father – unless his mother had remarried. She doubted it – the man's grief was too apparent.

'Strange,' he said.

'Yes, why would Sami hear something they didn't?'

'Probably trivial. A rumour's just a rumour.'

'Iqbal seems more tangible somehow. If he'd gone abroad to fight or been killed, I'm sure his family would know. What's odd is that he seems to have returned, been reunited with the family, and then gone off again without giving them any clue where.'

'Can't read much into that,' said Patrick.

'OK, what about Sami's story?'

'Yeah, I was thinking about that,' he said with an untypical lack of enthusiasm. 'Doesn't really fit, does it?'

'What do you mean?'

'Al Qaeda and ISIS recruiting in the UK was uncoordinated.

Young men initially, then women too, come under the spell of a shouty imam, sometimes get money, sometimes self-fund, then head abroad solo or in small groups. Maybe a bit of training in Pakistan or Afghanistan. Those who come back only attempt to operate in small independent cells. Or as loners. Since 7/7 that's always been the pattern.'

'I know. That's why Sami's story is significant. This so-called "Adviser" may be leading some kind of centralised operation in the UK.'

'But his account's a one-off.'

'We have more names than one.'

'Only a handful. And none of those have corroborated Sami's version.'

'Morahan told me the Blackburn files were the tip of an iceberg. The trigger. The inception. Everything, whatever it is, follows on.'

He shot her a caustic look. 'You didn't tell me that. How did he know?'

She searched for an answer. 'He didn't say.' She paused. 'I assume it came from his informant.'

A strained silence fell. 'I've said before you can trust me.' As he concentrated on the road ahead, she saw a smile forming. 'Know something, Sara? When you're caught on the hop, you're a rubbish liar.' He paused. 'That's a compliment, by the way.'

They were approaching the junction with the M40. 'Two and a half hours or so, Blackburn to here,' said Patrick. He was offering an olive branch. 'Say they'd headed south, another half an hour and they could be turning off the motorway towards some hills. Sami remembered a road winding up, didn't he?'

'Yes.'

'I can't imagine they'd have found the landed aristocracy of the Cotswolds too congenial so it's got to be south Wales.'

'Unless they were heading north to the Trossachs,' chipped in Sara.

'A fellow route bore!'

'Patrick, even I can circle a four-hour driving range around Blackburn. You hardly need to be in a car.'

'Then we wouldn't be having the fun of each other's company.' They passed a motorway services sign. 'Coffee?'

'Prayers first.'

Sara reappeared a quarter of an hour later. Patrick wondered how she found a place of calm – or whether that was even necessary. Maybe she had the skill of compartmentalising the mind and excluding the extraneous. Perhaps that was what regular daily prayer could do though. He thought of the regular Sunday services he'd been taken to as a child and the daily rituals in boarding school chapels. Even if his days of God, Paradise, Heaven and Hell were long gone, he felt a pang of envy.

She sat down opposite him and he slid a coffee and a couple of sachets of long-life milk across the tabletop.

'You're not vegan, are you?' he asked.

'Why on earth would I be vegan?'

'Your blooming complexion, I guess.'

'You can't wind me up, you know.'

'No, sorry. But I'm allowed to notice a beautiful woman when I see one, aren't I?'

She shook her head and tipped some milk into her polystyrene cup. 'What about your wife. Was she beautiful?'

He sipped and set down his coffee cup. 'Actually, the answer to that is yes. Blonde, slim and entirely gorgeous.'

'And you tall, handsome and exotic.'

'Ha ha, if you insist. In a weird way I was a trophy husband. A sort of exotica.'

'How?'

'I was a safe black boy. Son of a rich Ghanaian, educated at English public school, then Oxford. Her father was a Lloyds insurance broker. Bankrupted some of his clients but kept his own money. Country pile, London penthouse. She was into fashion, did some modelling...'

'How did you meet?'

'She came up for a Balliol ball. My last one. One of my law mates was in her circle, they were a pretty posh lot. Did drugs and lost their virginities at places like Marlborough.'

'And?'

'We were attracted. I mean I was gobsmacked, this goddess wanting me. I think she married me to show the world "I can do what the eff I want".'

'What did your parents say?'

'They swooned over her.'

'And hers?'

'Kept their mouths shut. Always civil to me. When it was falling apart, I once overheard her mother say "told you so."'

'What happened?'

'You *are* the inquisitor!' Sara gave a baleful shrug. 'We rubbed along for a while,' Patrick continued, 'then Nathan coming along changed it all, as I suppose kids tend to do. Within a year, she'd had fling number one. And then number two, who she went off with. He had a Ferrari then, I seem to remember. Still together though. Helps that he's loaded.'

'I'm sorry,' she said. 'I'll stop digging.'

'What about you?'

She laughed. 'Another time. Let's go. You can put your foot down, I want to put in an evening shift at the office.'

'You'll be on your own doing that.' A thought struck him. 'Although Morahan usually works late Thursday. Calls it his catch-up time.'

'In that case, I'll try not to disturb him.'

A couple of hours later, they drew up outside the Inquiry's Vauxhall office. She heard a clock strike the quarter hour – 6.15 p.m. Chronology was about to matter.

At that exact moment Sami Mohammed was nearing the main gates of the Rovers' ground at Ewood Park – not for work, but for the return meeting with the man. He'd walked all the way from home with his hand in his pocket wrapped around the device. Fifty yards short of the gates a car door opened to break his stride, followed by an arm waving him round to the front passenger seat. He got in, removed his hand from his pocket and dropped the recorder into an outstretched palm. Without a word, the man locked all doors and started the engine.

'Where we going?' asked Sami, failing to hide his fear.

'It's OK. Just you and me.'

He headed down the A666 from Ewood towards Darwen, left at the junction with the M65 but, rather than joining it, peeled off to the motorway services, parking amid a crowd of cars. 'This'll do, protection in numbers.' He swivelled. 'For you too, young man.' Sami saw a meanness in his face and the greased flat strands of dark hair, greying at the edges. He tried to make out the accent – it was unfamiliar, some sort of strong Irish maybe.

The man plugged the machine into a socket by the radio/CD player, thumbed a couple of markers and within seconds they were hearing a good quality recording of Sami's conversation with Sara. 'You can't get one of these commercially,' said the man. 'A fool couldn't fuck it up. Not that you are, are you, young man?'

For the next hour and a quarter they listened. Sami didn't see why the man needed to make him share the ordeal – couldn't he have done it alone through earphones? He hadn't dared suggest it.

At the click of the front door and echo of Sara's parting footfalls, the man cut the playback. 'You did well. Enjoy it?'

Sami, heart beating, stomach churning, could only murmur. 'I done my best.'

'You said it nicely about Asif.'

Sami didn't know how to respond. 'Thanks,' he tried.

'And you skated OK over the bit we can never tell.'

'Yeah.'

'Never ever.'

'Nah.'

The man took a wallet from his chest pocket. The movement gave Sami a moment of confidence. 'So what's it all about then?'

The man stared at him grimly as he extracted a bunch of notes. 'Not for you, young man. Not for you. You never fucking speak about this.'

Sami looked at the cash. Fifties, at least ten, maybe twenty – more than he'd hoped for. 'OK, yeah.'

'But you did well,' the man repeated. 'We could meet again if something else comes up.'

The cash was still in the man's hand. 'Dunno.' The hand didn't move. 'Maybe. Yeah. Could do.'

The hand moved and Sami took the cash. 'See you then,' said the man. 'Now, young man, you can fuck off.'

Sami frowned. 'You mean here.'

'It's your patch, isn't it? Use your feet.'

'Yeah. OK.'

'Now.'

Sami jumped out of the car and walked towards the car park exit as fast as he could. He still didn't understand why he'd been told to give the girl that story about Asif working down in Birmingham. Or to leave out that bit of the last night with the Adviser – the only bit that really mattered. Though he did wonder if he'd ever have been able to tell it to Sara – or anyone else – exactly the way it had happened.

2006

A few minutes after the woman left, two 'escorts' crashed open his cell door. 'Come!'

'Where we going?' he croaked.

'You said you wanna see the Adviser. Now's your chance.'

He hauled himself up, eyes liquid and jumping with fatigue, body smelling, hair itching. In the days he'd been there he'd barely eaten, but his guts were heavy and nervous. 'I need a shit.'

'No time.' They forced him on by the arms, one each side, crossing the courtyard, rain now falling, the muddy water splashing round his bare feet. He tried to stop and look up at the clouded skies; they tightened their grip. It felt like the dark heart of night.

Two small wooden chairs sat empty on the flood-lit platform. They pulled him up the steps and directed him towards one. He began to murmur. 'Why—'

'Shut it!'

The interior of the barn was airless, silent except for rain tapping on the slate roof. He sat; minutes passed. He tried again. 'I need to shit, man.' The tension within was building; he really did need to go.

'Stay!'

The escorts disappeared. He sat alone, not daring to move, understanding nothing except his own terror.

He heard a clanking. A figure in blue denim overalls, a canvas-like hood over his head, enchained around his ankles, his masculine feet bared, was dragged in by the escorts. They planted him on the seat opposite Sami. He flopped, his covered head bowed, bleats of sobbing. The only sounds as more minutes passed.

'We welcome you again, brother Sami.' The Adviser's rich voice, echoing through the vaulted barn.

Sami whipped his head around and saw, in the corner, the Adviser, sitting on a high-backed, throne-like chair. Standing beside him was the thick-set man. No sign of the woman.

Sami detected a movement of the head beneath the hood opposite. 'We have brought you to meet another brother,' said the Adviser. 'A friend of yours. He is in need of advice.'

The escorts loosened the rope holding down the hood so they could yank it off. The head was revealed – half-open eyes looked imploringly at him.

'Oh fuck,' whispered Sami. 'Asif. Is that really you, man? What the fuck are you doing here?' Asif's face was a blur of blood and bruises. His lips bled – or was it coming from smashed teeth? 'What they done to you, man?' Sami dreaded to think what might lie beneath the overalls.

'I dunno,' croaked Asif. 'I dunno what happened.'

The Adviser's soothing voice broke in. 'And we welcome you again, brother Asif, however much you have wronged us.'

'I ain't wronged anyone,' said Asif. He was hardly audible.

'Let me explain, Sami,' said the Adviser, 'so that you may gain understanding.' He rose from his chair, walked slowly across the flagstoned floor – his footsteps a regular, monotonous beat – stepped onto the platform and looked down at both of them. 'We have known for some months that one of your number, in your home town of Blackburn, has been having unwise conversations with a certain policeman. Conversations for which that person has been paid. Conversations which are an act of treachery to our people, to your brothers and sisters. We were sad when we had to conclude that the traitor was one or the other of you two. On our advice, one of the brothers raised this matter with you, Asif. You denied it most vehemently. When the brother suggested that, if this is so, the guilt could only lie with you, Sami, you, Asif, agreed. You suggested that more than once you had occasion to believe Sami was acting oddly. I therefore decided, Sami, that it was time for me to make your acquaintance – as I have now done.'

The Adviser circled the dais, inspecting them. The pressure inside Sami's bowels was unbearable. The Adviser's eyes fixed on him. 'After meeting you yesterday, Sami, I was in a position to give my opinion to the wise men above both you and me, who must cast judgement. Giving such advice is a heavy burden – in agreeing to shoulder it, I make my own sacrifice for our people. I must not act in a cowardly way and refuse such challenges.'

The Adviser dismounted the platform and returned to his throne in the corner.

'I will now give my opinion,' he said softly. He stood. 'Sami Mohammed.' His voice cut through the gentle beat of rain rebounding off the timbers of the barn. 'I have advised that you are telling me and the woman the truth. You, Asif Hassan, are guilty of treachery.'

Sami turned towards Asif. His shoulders heaved, tears pouring down his face, forming the blood into rivulets spattering the blue of his overalls. 'I never did, Sami, never did. I dunno who did. It weren't me, I swear on my life.'

The Adviser's voice lowered. 'Despite your treachery, Asif – towards your friend, Sami, as well – is there anything you, Sami, wish to say in mitigation for Asif?'

Sami looked at him. He realised too much sympathy might not sound good. 'I'm sorry for what you done to the brothers, Asif. And I forgive what you done to me.' He shifted to face in the Adviser's direction. 'He's been my friend. He won't do it again.'

'Thank you, Sami,' said the Adviser. 'Treachery is a sin. To forgive is to forget. But forget we must never do.' The Adviser retreated; the light in his corner faded to black.

The escorts leapt onto the platform, covered Asif's head and yanked him out of the barn. 'Don't you move!' one said to Sami.

He stayed seated, gut burbling, heart thumping, body sweating from head to toe. A minute passed, then another.

Then gunshots crashed in Sami's ears, ringing around the stone building. One. Two. A pause. Three. The dam broke and a stinking muddy brown river cascaded over the wooden seat and down its legs.

It was the smell of himself Sami never forgot. At the car park exit, as he threw a final glance behind, he could feel that same gurgling in his gut, just like all those years ago.

He broke into a jog on the roundabout and sprinted in the direction of Ewood Park. He wasn't on shift that night, but it was the nearest place of safety he knew. After a couple of hundred yards, he had to slow, lungs burning, heart pumping. He staggered to the gates and looked back down the road, half-expecting the man's car to draw alongside. If there was any sign, he'd enter the ground and find one of the guards on duty.

Nothing. No sign of the man or car. He hoped never to hear or see him again, but knew he couldn't ever, ever assume he was free of them.

Back home, he went straight upstairs, ignoring the light in the kitchen where his mother would be waiting for him. He counted the notes – fifteen. Seven hundred and fifty pounds.

Dirty money; money he'd sworn to himself he'd never take again, after those weekly bundles from the smart-suited policeman twelve years ago.

11

Sara let herself into the Inquiry office with her main entrance pass card – the reception area was deserted. An overnight commissionaire had been deemed an unnecessary spend; security was maintained by exterior CCTV cameras, burglar alarms, pass cards and individual code numbers on each floor. They were also beneficiaries of the round-the-clock monitoring of the neighbouring American Embassy, including guard patrols with dogs. Big Brother or Uncle Sam – depending on your viewpoint – on the doorstep.

She walked up the two flights of stairs to the second floor, entered her pass code and walked through the entrance corridor – toilets and kitchen to the left, the internal wall of Pamela Bailly's office to the right – and into the open-plan space of the secretariat. There was no Clovis at the desk guarding Pamela Bailly's door. A reading lamp hung over just one computer screen and keyboard. In front of them sat Rayah Yaseen, a research officer in the Inquiry secretariat, head bowed over flying fingers with turquoise nails. So far, Sara had hardly spoken to her, and took the chance.

'Hi, Rayah.'

She looked up. 'Oh, hi.'

'Working late?'

She stood up. 'Hardly late. I'm nearly done.'

'Are we the clichés?' asked Sara, trying to forge a bond. 'The Asian girls who put in the extra hours.' She sounded false to herself – it was a thought that normally would never enter her head.

'Before this, I was doing my first spell in private office,' said Rayah. 'We were all slaves there. Didn't matter who you were.'

Sara inspected her; she must be at least in her late twenties so perhaps had come up through the ranks rather than graduate fast stream. She was smartly dressed – tight-fitting red pullover, black knee-length skirt and highish-heeled black shoes.

'How are you finding it here?'

'Yeah, it's interesting. The panel members aren't always the easiest.'

'I've that pleasure to come,' said Sara. 'And how about Sir Francis himself? Actually, aren't Thursdays supposed to be his late night?' The question was innocent, but asking it provoked the thought – Rayah working late at her desk, also on a Thursday night.

'Why are you asking me?'

Sara again cursed her leap of imagination. 'Nothing. Nothing at all. Sorry if I was out of order.' The hole was getting deeper. 'I meant, he seems a nice man.'

'Sure, why wouldn't he be?'

'Absolutely.' Sara realised that not once had Rayah wanted to look her straight in the eye. 'Right, got to finish my stuff too.' She moved away towards the corridor leading off the open-plan area, puzzled by the tone of the conversation. Perhaps she should read nothing into it except the cautious reaction of a younger woman faced by a senior newcomer.

She tried the door of the archive room. Locked. Sylvia

Labone was long past any need to impress bosses with long hours. The door to the Legal office was open; she wondered if anyone had been nosing around. Surely they'd have locked it if they had – she couldn't remember how she and Patrick had left it. Morahan's door was shut. Part of her wanted to knock on it; she resisted the temptation and entered her own office.

What compulsion had made her even want to call by here? Patrick was all for going straight home and had encouraged her to do the same. Yet the journey felt somehow incomplete without returning to the surroundings she had committed herself to for the coming months. She had an urge to analyse, to theorise, to find from these first encounters a web which would form a structure; certainly to begin to build a chronology. The Blackburn group had attracted some kind of attention from late 2005 and through 2006 – the period after 7/7 when the security services, aware of their failings, were desperate to intercept new plots; to try new methods perhaps. Had they any inkling of the terrible experience Sami had suffered? Just say, after the questioning by Blackburn police about the girl, MI5 *had* succeeded in tapping up one of the group, why did none of the files contain any sign of it? Could it be that it was something too secret to be recorded on those files?

She was interrupted by a knock on the door, followed by Morahan poking half a head around. She looked up with pleased surprise. 'Sir Francis, hello.'

'Good evening, Sara, thought I heard footsteps but didn't know you were back.'

'We'd achieved what we could.'

'Come and tell me all about it,' he said with the warmth he always seemed to show her. There was the same sparkle too in his eye as when, during their first meeting, she'd suggested they were like spies talking on the Common.

He waved her to one end of the sofa and sat himself on the

other. She compressed Samir's story as concisely as she could, then the doorstep conversation with Iqbal Jamal Wahab's father. She omitted the inconsistencies about Asif Hassan's whereabouts.

'Did you come to any general conclusion?' he asked.

'It's sparse,' she replied, 'but I feel it indicates some element of central co-ordination that might challenge the received view of discrete cells or lone wolves being the sole MO of jihadis in the UK. Patrick is more sceptical.'

Morahan gazed out of the window beyond her into the gathering gloom and felt the back of his hair, stroking it down to the collar. She was unsure whether it was a mannerism or nervous gesture. Despite his friendliness, his experiences of sitting in a confined space with a young Muslim woman must be limited.

'And how was Patrick?' The question startled her; she'd assumed that he would follow the logic of the conversation and pursue the subject, not the person.

'He was fine.' She waited to see if he'd elaborate.

'Good. Decent chap.' The same words he had used before – no more.

If he wouldn't, she would. 'I can't help wondering why he was chosen for this job. Wouldn't a Muslim have been more suited?'

'I suspect there's no Muslim with the experience in the GLD. Plenty of younger ones coming up through the ranks – people are more aware of it now. So maybe there was an element of cack-handed "diversity". Remember that Patrick is not entirely typical. He had educational advantages and prospects not available to many other young black men at that time and has reached a senior level ahead of them.' He frowned. 'Has something come up?'

'No. Not really. It's just that I sensed once or twice he'd almost prefer we *didn't* find things than we did find them.'

'I'm surprised to hear that. He was extremely keen to do it. As I understand, he put his hand up almost the minute the Inquiry was announced. And came warmly recommended by his superiors.'

'Which superiors?'

He screwed up his eyes. 'What a curious question, Sara. GLD, of course.'

'Sorry, stupid of me.'

They exchanged smiles and fell silent. Despite her self-instruction to disregard them, she'd wondered whether to tell Morahan about the anonymous text messages; now that there'd been two, he should perhaps see them and there was no need to mention the 2005 text for him to take them seriously. Somehow, their exchange about Patrick made it the wrong moment. She would tell him next time.

He hoicked himself to his feet, at full stretch towering over her, and crossed the room to a window. 'I wasn't sure whether to confide something in you,' he began, 'and I'm afraid doing so may be more helpful to me than to you.'

She saw the other Morahan – the vulnerable man thrust into a strange unfamiliar world. 'Please do.'

'I have spoken with Sayyid.'

'You met him? Face to face?'

'Not quite.' Propping on the window ledge, he explained the circumstances of the encounter – the sighting limited to the back of a covered head, the voice distorted – and described Sayyid's mysterious remarks about the wilderness of mirrors. 'I've since reminded myself of the details, you may not know them. It happened in the early 1960s. The Prime Minister Golitsyn pointed to as a Soviet sleeper was Harold Wilson. He was nothing of the sort, of course, but it didn't stop his name being blackened and the intelligence services allowing suspicion and accusation to eat away at them.'

'I don't see how that could relate to Islamist terror,' she said.

'I know,' he replied uneasily. 'My curiosity about Sayyid's arcane methods is leading to a sixth sense that somehow he is playing me. I'm the trout on the end of his fly as he slowly pulls me in.'

'We can only deal in facts,' she said softly. 'Files, documents, witnesses, statements. Physical evidence if we ever find it.'

'Yes, you're right. That's what I tell myself too.' He hesitated; she wondered if it was her cue to leave. Instead he walked back to the sofa and sat down. 'There's something else I've hesitated to ask you,' he said softly.

'You must feel free to ask anything you want.'

'Yes, I thought you'd say that.' She felt him squirming. 'It's just this. Sara, have you ever been the subject of a security service investigation?'

'No,' she said vehemently.

'Good, good. I was sure not.'

'Why are you asking?' She felt the blood rushing to her cheeks. 'Has something come up?'

'No, not at all.'

Whatever had prompted him, she knew he wouldn't own up to it. Perhaps she could throw him a bone. 'Look, I was interviewed post 7/7 by a Met detective. I'd attended one or two meetings organised by characters who might not have been as nice as they appeared. They asked me about them. They weren't people I knew so I couldn't help them. I imagine lots of us – if you see what I mean – were interviewed. But that was it.'

'Yes, of course,' he said. 'Thank you for easing my mind.' Smiling again, he stood up. 'Not that it was ever uneasy – I'm sorry now even to have raised it. Never have any doubt, Sara, that I think you are a very remarkable woman and there's no one I'd rather have by my side.'

'Thank you,' she said, shyly. 'Now… time for me to go home, I guess.'

'Of course, you've had two long days.'

'Just Rayah left, I think.' He gave not a flicker of reaction; she felt tarnished by her earlier speculation and strode back to the Legal office with an urge to escape into fresher air. She stuffed the folder in her travel bag, gathered her coat and headed towards the open-plan area. Rayah was still there, staring at her screen. Sara noticed her quickly change the image.

'That's me done. Good night.'

'Me too in a mo.' She looked up at Sara, engaging her eyes for the first time. 'An old school friend's having a party tonight. Do you wanna come, he's always short of women?'

'That's sweet of you but I'm heading home – I'm afraid our Chairman requires me to do some reading. He who must be obeyed.' She tapped a finger to her nose in what she instantly knew must seem an idiotic attempt at togetherness. Why had Rayah asked? She must have known what the answer would be. Once again, the loneliness of the Inquiry – and the loneliness she detected in Morahan – hit her like a lead weight.

At 7.20 p.m., the same time that Sara left the Inquiry office, Patrick, having dropped off the hire car in Victoria, approached the front door of a three-storey Victorian house five minutes' walk from Brixton underground station. After his divorce he'd bought the maisonette on the top two floors as his London home. It was convenient, low maintenance and a neighbourhood he liked – cultured, progressive and fun, a transformation from the riots and roughness of thirty years before that never ceased to amaze him. On his way home he'd been unable, to his irritation, to stop thinking about Sara – it was a long time since he'd enjoyed a woman's company so much. However hard he tried to discard the image of her smooth skin and shining eyes – and that occasional raised eyebrow – he continued to be thwarted. Taking the front door key out of his pocket, he told himself to wise up.

'Hey, Patrick!'

A voice nearby. Were they talking to him?

'Patrick!' The voice was louder, the accent a hint of Scottish. He turned in the direction it came from. A suited man stood in the half-light on the pavement a few yards to his right; a second man, wearing a blue denim jacket and jeans, muscular, shaven-headed, lounged to his left. There was something familiar about the first man – fair, almost blond, wavy hair, chunky and, yes, the accent. It took just a few seconds for the memory to click in. What was the name? John? John something – he couldn't remember. Maybe he'd never been given it. Thirteen years were compressed into a split second. It was definitely him – the man who'd hovered in the background while he inked his signature on that piece of paper. The error they'd suckered him into – the greatest single mistake of his life. His heart thumping, he told himself to stay cool.

'Hello?' asked Patrick.

'Yes, hello.' The Scottish accent was more pronounced.

'I'm sorry, do I know you?'

'Oh, come on, Patrick, you remember.'

'I'm very sorry,' Patrick replied, straining for politeness despite his agitation, 'I'm afraid I don't.'

'It'll come to you, laddie.'

Patrick made to slot the key into his front door. The shaven-headed man was beside him before he'd even raised it to the lock.

'I just wanted to say hello,' said the first man, coming closer. 'For old times' sake.'

'I truly don't know what you're on about.'

'We won't worry about that. It's OK, we're keeping an eye out. Watching your back.'

'If you don't mind, I'd prefer you to leave me alone.'

'Yes, of course,' he said cheerfully. He nodded to the second man. Patrick felt a precise, savage finger punch into his kidneys.

'Jesus!' he couldn't help crying out.

The fair-haired man's mouth pushed against his ear. 'We know how much you wanted this gig,' he hissed, his accent now in full Glaswegian flow. 'And why. So, boy, just in case you haven't got this yet, we let you have it. Because we're on the same side, aren't we? And don't you ever fucking forget it.' A knee crashed into Patrick's groin; he buckled, silent tears of pain clouding his vision. The two men sauntered off, one of them softly singing the chorus of 'You'll Never Walk Alone'. Patrick raised the key to the front door lock. He was shaking so violently that it was only on the eighth attempt that he managed to slot it in. He crawled up the staircase, hesitantly turned the Yale into his flat and collapsed onto a sofa.

Slowly, he felt his brain cells getting back to work. Until Morahan had given Sara the files, the jeopardy seemed to have been avoided – there *were* no sides. Now, with the intervention of his source – whoever that might be – and Morahan's recruitment of Sara, there were signs of the situation unravelling. And if two sides did emerge – as his visitors were clearly anticipating – he'd have to decide which one he was on.

Sara took her case and a meagre tray of food upstairs to her room. Her phone pinged. It was a message from Morahan. What... why...?

Found something extremely significant which, if at all possible, I'd like to discuss face to face ahead of the morning. Can you be here in an hour? Morahan

A range of thoughts bombarded her; one she felt disgust with herself for imagining. No, he was not that sort of man; her suspicions of Rayah had been misjudged. He might show fondness, but that would be it. She suspected, despite an unexpected onset of fatigue, that sheer curiosity would end up rendering her unable to resist going back in. Still, leave the option open; don't reply yet.

She sat down, chomped at an apple and, almost by rote, fired up her computer. She checked her emails; there was one from Patrick. 'Trust you're now home safe and sound. Was fun and interesting. Not too bad a team, eh? P.' She was pleased it did not end with 'x'. Perhaps there was nothing more behind his apparent lack of investigative spirit than a wish for a relaxed life.

She tried to apply herself but her eyes wandered. Morahan's text hung over her. She checked her watch. 9 p.m. It was too intriguing and, if she hung on until morning, curiosity would only keep her awake. She texted back to say she was on her way.

Half an hour later she was re-entering the office – card pass, floor code, door open. A couple of ceiling lights – left on overnight for security, she assumed – guided her through the open-plan area to the passage leading to Morahan's door. It was slightly ajar, a streak of light escaping onto the wood-effect floor. An old man working through the night on his unexpected adventure. What had he discovered? She assumed it was connected to Sayyid; perhaps he had revealed himself, was even behind that door, unmasked. She listened for voices or whispers. Nothing.

She knocked gently and eased the door part-way open. The desk was empty, illuminated by an anglepoise light and a lamp beyond in the far corner. Blinds were drawn over the picture window. He must have popped out for a breath of air.

She closed the door and retreated to the open-plan office to await his return.

She reminded herself that at the end of the passage beyond Morahan's door were the emergency stairs which also led down to the car park. As it was the exit and entrance nearest his office, she guessed that he might use them. She went to check. The emergency exit door was firmly in place. For fear of setting off an alarm, she decided not to test it by pushing the bar. Turning round, she thought she'd better check his office again.

A squeak – something moving behind her? She whipped round. Nothing.

Unnerved, she silently retreated, trying to conceal herself by hugging the corridor wall. She scanned her own office – no one, no sign of movement, no spirit of the night. Pamela's office door locked tight. No movement beyond, no other doors open. It must be her imagination. A door hinge creaking, wind beating against a window, a water pipe gurgling, a building emitting a groan.

She returned to Morahan's office and pushed the door further open – no change. She entered and did a visual sweep right to left ending on the sofa, now in shadow, where she had been talking to him just a couple of hours before.

In that shadow lay a prone figure.

12

The head lolled over the sofa's arm, the body sprawled across its breadth. In the dimness she could make out two legs stretched wide apart. One lay on the sofa cushions, the other dangled down to the floor, the foot still in a dark grey sock resting on the carpet. The shape gave no sound or movement. Creeping closer, she saw that the trousers, still loosely belted, were lowered down to mid-thigh, a flaccid penis extending back from just above the belt.

Sara stretched out an arm and with the back of her hand lightly brushed his forehead. It was cold; no movement or reaction. Withdrawing the hand, her skin touched strands of lifeless hair. She recoiled..

Her first sharp intakes of breath, and a repressed shriek of 'Oh God!', multiplied into a violent thumping of the heart and bile rising in her throat. Her stomach seemed literally to be dropping, her bowels involuntarily loosening. She turned and sprinted for the toilet, some trick of memory recalling the impact of a soldier's fear before going into battle. Afterwards she removed her scarf, washed her hands and face, checking in the mirror that this was still her true self – intact, unaltered, survived. She tied the scarf back on, breathed deeply and regularly, telling her heart and brain to calm.

She walked back into the open-plan area and sat down. What mattered was not to panic. First, she must steel herself to go back into his office, switch on the main light to confirm what had happened, then remember to switch it off again. She'd been sure when the first outline of the figure came into view that it had to be Morahan; it was there in the shape and length of the body and legs. But, even as she touched him, she'd only managed the most fleeting look at him before retreating.

Back in his office, under the main light, she inspected his face. It hung backwards and upright from the sofa arm on which his neck rested, staring blankly at the ceiling. Around the neck was a tightly buckled belt. She felt an urge to release it, to unshackle him. But she knew enough not to touch anything; there was no doubt he was lifeless.

The back of Morahan's hair dangled limply like loose tassels from a damp mop, the angle of his head allowing the strands to fall separately in slim branches from his collar. His eyes were open and blank, his cheeks and forehead pallid. She could see purple around the base of the neck. She had a sense that he had not been dead for long; the timing of his text meant it must have happened within the last hour and a half. Her eyes ranged briefly over his body to confirm the partial lowering of his trousers and pants. The penis lay surprisingly long between his legs. She caught a strange whiff... like paraffin.

She should phone an ambulance and the police without delay. She withdrew to the door, switched off the main light and made a quick tour of the floor. The Legal office was untouched and the Archive door remained locked. There was no sign of disturbance in the open-plan area. Pamela Bailly's office door was still locked. She scanned the ground from the windows on both sides of the open-plan area. No evidence of people or movement or cars or bikes. She moved a hand towards a phone, then hesitated. She was alone, no spectators inside or out. She sat down to think.

As reason and calm, insofar as they were possible, returned, an overwhelming instinct told her that, with nothing to be done for Morahan himself, the priority, whatever the reason for his death, was to protect the original of the Sayyid folder. She assumed that, along with the Blackburn files, it must contain some sort of communication – a note or a letter – from Sayyid to Morahan. In the unexplained circumstances of his death, the police were bound to cordon off his office and conduct a search. Should they come across the Sayyid material, they would take possession of it – with unknowable consequences. This might be her only chance to secure it.

A second instinct was that the phone call to the emergency services should not be delayed too long.

Morahan was clearly dead; she could allow herself a few minutes. She recalled the moment he'd handed her the envelope with the photocopies. She approached the front of his desk and looked down. He'd taken a key from the middle drawer. It was closed. She mustn't leave evidence that she'd opened it. She looked around for a cloth or handkerchief – anything to cover her hands. Of course, she realised, there was an easier solution. She removed her hijab and wound its silk material through her fingers so that each one could move individually. She opened the drawer. Two set of keys, probably his house and car. She pulled further – a single key lay at the right back corner. She grabbed it – it felt smooth and slithery in her silken hands. She leant down to the left pedestal and tried the key in the bottom drawer. It fitted. She began to turn it; it moved. She slid the door out.

Empty. Nothing. Bare wood.

She looked at her watch; that operation had taken nearly five minutes. How much longer could she give herself? She must remove the evidence of her tampering. Fingers sweating inside the silk, she closed the bottom left drawer. No need to re-lock it as they wouldn't know it ever had been.

Had he moved the folder? Perhaps the original had never been there. Unless someone had already taken it.

Where else in his office could he have hidden it? She retreated to the position from where she'd had her last conversation with him and surveyed the room. Apart from the desk, there were no obvious secure places. Chair, sofa, open shelves, glass cabinets. She remembered him getting up and addressing her from the window, leaning back on the ledge. She sensed it was a place he liked to stand, whether to look outside or to talk from. Below it was a boxed in radiator with a brass grille. She approached it.

She examined the grille; rather than being screwed in, it appeared to rest on slots. She shook it gently. Movement. Her fingers were sliding in the silk – too hard to grip. She unwound the scarf – they'd hardly check a radiator grille for prints, would they? She lifted; the grille came loose. Behind it a radiator running the length of the window. Again, nothing. Her eyes were drawn to the thin gap between the radiator and the wall. She checked the right side, could just get her fingers behind and slide them from bottom to top, searching for some kind of contact. She moved to the left, repeating the process. Two thirds of the way up she hit something – an edge of paper or envelope. She tugged. It stuck. She pulled harder and heard ripping. It came away, sellotape dangling from one side, a tear on the other.

Had he anticipated that someone out there would want to invade his desk?

She wiped her brow with the scarf and rubbed the sweat from her fingers on her shirt. Don't touch anything else. She walked back to the desk, lifted the phone and dialled 999. No need to avoid her prints on that handset.

She guessed she could count on another three or four minutes. She ran her eye over Morahan's office. No sign that she'd disturbed anything – no reason she hadn't gone straight from discovering him to the nearest phone... and then, as she now did, to the bathroom.

She put the envelope beside the basin, washed and dried her face and hands, wiped her shirt, replaced the scarf on her head. Now more composed, she picked up the envelope – feeling it again, it seemed surprisingly thin and light. She peeped inside. It didn't look like the Blackburn files. What else? Did she have time to read or take it in? She removed the contents – a one-sheet print-out of a corporate-style profile and a short note.

The profile was all too familiar. She read the note. Her heart hammered, her legs wanted to give way. This was not the moment to try to understand all the implications.

What did Morahan really know? What game had he been playing? Playing with her.

A tornado of thoughts crashed in from every direction. There was a design to her being here, thrust into a perfect scenario for scandal and conspiracy theories. One of the country's most senior judges – a man engaged in an inquiry of supreme national importance – found half-naked with his trousers down, asphyxiated by a leather belt. And, as and when it came out, discovered by an attractive young lawyer working with him.

Still quiet. She had an overwhelming urge for a final look inside the office. A scene of morbid stillness. She went to stand over him; the purple around the neck might have sunk a little, perhaps the nose and cheeks were even paler, almost white. How could this beached shape have been having that animated conversation with her less than four hours before?

She heard sirens, growing louder with every second. She

put the contents back in the envelope, folded it into quarters and stuffed it down the back of her shirt. She returned to the open-plan office and switched on more lights.

The intercom buzzed.

13

It could have been a seance in a mortuary waiting room. An ambulance and two paramedics had arrived half an hour before and death was confirmed. Sara had phoned her father, saying she'd be late and would explain when she saw him, then Pamela Bailly and Patrick Duke; the three of them now hovered silently in the open-plan area. A police sergeant and constable were with the paramedics in Morahan's office.

Pamela spoke. 'We need a list and a plan.' Sara and Patrick looked up, waiting for her to pronounce. 'Lists first. Those to be immediately informed. The Prime Minister's and Home Secretary's private offices. No. 10 and Home Office Heads of Press. Office of the Lord Chief Justice. The Inquiry's panel members.'

'What exactly is to be said?' asked Patrick.

'Oh,' replied Pamela with an untypical airiness, 'I think simply that Sir Francis Morahan tragically and suddenly died in his office, cause of death is being confirmed.'

'There'll be more questions.'

'Then they will have to wait for answers.'

'Should the Inquiry staff come in tomorrow or be stood down?' asked Sara.

'Come in. A common understanding will be more easily achieved if we gather together.' Patrick and Sara exchanged looks at her choice of words.

A scruffily suited man entered the open-plan area and directed himself to Sara. 'Miss Shah?'

'Yes.'

'I'm Detective Sergeant Buttler. Two Ts.' He smiled cursorily. 'I understand you discovered the body.'

'Yes.' She quickly registered him; a stocky figure, receding brown hair curling at the edge, twinkling eyes and loosely pulled tie which suggested a man confident in his role.

'Perhaps we could have a quiet word.'

Sara turned to Pamela for guidance though without understanding quite why. 'Feel free to use my office.'

'Thank you,' said Buttler, 'and you are…'

Pamela rose and offered her hand to shake. 'Pamela Bailly, Secretary to the Inquiry. I should be your main point of contact here.'

'As you will.' He followed Sara inside the office; they sat down facing each other at the Secretary's small conference table.

'This is purely informal at this point, Miss Shah. Just to get myself up to speed on the basics.'

'I understand.'

'What is your role here?'

'I'm junior counsel to the Inquiry. I work for the Government Legal Department.'

'You're a lawyer. Good.' The twinkling in the eyes spread to form a grin.

'Not every policeman would agree,' said Sara, trying to respond in kind.

'My favourite profession.' The grin settled into sympathy. 'It must have been a nasty shock.'

'Yes.'

'Would you mind going over the timings?'

Sara felt a prickle of sweat beneath her armpits. She went through the evening; her return to the office, Morahan looking in, briefing him.

'His mood?' asked Buttler.

'Same as always. Polite. Clear. Positive.'

'And then?'

'I went home and soon after received a text from Sir Francis – around 8.30, I think – asking if I could come back in an hour or so if I was able to. I was surprised but assumed he wanted to go through some papers.'

'Do you have that text?'

'Yes, of course.'

'Could I see it, please?'

'It was sent confidentially.'

'I understand but it might help.'

'I suppose it can do no harm now.'

Sara took her phone from a pocket and went to the inbox. She felt a sudden panic. She looked again, scrolled up and down. The text wasn't there. Did she delete it? She hardly ever did – phones could store millions. A rash of sweat spread to her neck and chest – she hoped it wasn't showing. Perhaps, with everything that was going on, she'd somehow deleted it on autopilot? Yet her memory was usually faultless.

Feeling the heat in her cheeks, she looked up at Buttler. 'I'm sorry, the text appears to have been deleted. I don't understand it as I don't remember doing that. Perhaps I did – seeing the body put me in rather a spin.'

He eyed her for a few seconds. 'You mean seeing the Chairman's body half-naked and dead may have impelled you to delete his text?'

'Yes. No. I mean there was nothing unusual about the text. Just saying he wanted to discuss something in the paperwork.'

'I see.' He paused. 'Never mind,' he continued brightly, 'we should be able to retrieve it. And it'll be on Sir Francis's phone too.'

She looked down at her phone to check the 'Sent' box and breathed a sigh of relief. 'Look, here's my text replying to him, saying I'm coming in. That shows I must have got his.'

Buttler, expressionless, inspected her for a split-second. 'Perhaps you could continue.'

'I got the tube – it's an easy journey for me which he knew so perhaps that's why he felt able to make the suggestion. I arrived soon after 9.30. His door was shut, so I poked my head through it but there was no sign of him. I returned to my office and waited, assuming he was taking a break. I was bemused. I wondered if I'd misunderstood something and he'd wanted me to come to his home.'

'You had his address?'

'Yes, he'd given it to me.'

'Were you a frequent visitor to his house?'

'No, not at all. I'd only just met him.'

'Oh,' said Buttler, sounding surprised. 'But he'd given you his address.'

'Yes.'

'Go on.'

'When he hadn't reappeared after another fifteen minutes or so, I decided to check again. I didn't want to interrupt so I just edged the door open. I was still bemused so I decided to look further in. Then I saw it.'

'It?'

Sara patted an eye with a handkerchief. 'The shape. The shape on the sofa.'

'I'm sorry to take you through it,' said Buttler. 'Were there any lights on?'

Sara, recovering, put on a tiny show of straining to recollect. 'No, I don't think so. The curtains were open so there was some light coming in from the American Embassy lights and construction sites.'

'Then?'

'I went closer. You've seen it. I'd rather not describe it in detail.'

'No need.'

'I touched it… him. There was no movement. I tried to find his pulse. Then I phoned 999. From his desk phone.'

Simultaneously, they looked round – there was movement outside. A woman had entered the open-plan area, accompanied by a policeman. Sara knew it could only be Lady Morahan. She turned back to Buttler.

'We can resume tomorrow,' he said, understanding too what he was seeing. 'If there's anything more.'

They entered the open-plan area; Iona Morahan was heading towards the corridor leading into her husband's office. Buttler followed to join her. Sara sat down beside Patrick and Pamela, all holding their silence till she disappeared.

'I just can't imagine…' said Patrick.

'No,' said Sara. More silence.

Iona and the two policemen reappeared within a couple of minutes. She broke away from them to join the Inquiry staffers.

Pamela stood to offer a hand, 'Lady Morahan… a tragedy… we are all so sorry.'

Iona turned to Patrick and Sara. 'Mr Duke and Miss Shah, I presume.'

'Yes,' they answered in unison.

'My husband spoke highly of both of you.'

'He was a great man,' said Patrick.

'Yes,' echoed Sara. 'I wish I'd known him longer.'

'I suspect he would have thought the same about you,' she smiled bleakly. Sara caught the eye of Buttler listening in.

Iona looked across at the policeman who had escorted her. 'I think perhaps I will go straight home now.' He moved towards her offering an arm; she rejected it, instead striding alone toward the stairs.

'It's late,' Buttler said. 'There's no need for any of you three to stay. A police guard will be posted overnight – Miss Bailly, perhaps we could run through security and entrance procedures here.'

'Of course,' said Pamela.

'Because of the nature of the death, a scene of crime officer will attend as soon as possible and also a pathologist. There may be biological evidence still intact.'

'Evidence of what, Mr Buttler?' asked Pamela abruptly.

'Simply confirmation of timings and causes,' he replied with the expression of a benign assassin. 'In a case involving a prominent person, you'll appreciate that police conduct will be under scrutiny and all procedures and avenues must be followed.' Sara suspected that, for once, Pamela Bailly knew she'd overplayed her authority.

Patrick stood. 'I drove in. Any south Londoners want a lift home?' No replies. 'Sara?'

'If you're sure.'

The second they closed the car doors and he'd started the engine, he pounced.

'So what really happened to Morahan?'

'God, Patrick, you're not allowing much time.'

'We may not have much time.'

'OK. The appearance is that he died from auto-erotic asphyxiation.'

'Except that you and I know he didn't.'

She turned fiercely to him. 'Actually, it just could be.'

'No. It all smells wrong.' He accelerated angrily. She watched him as he concentrated on driving.

'Patrick?'

'Yes.'

'Are you OK?'

''Course I'm OK.'

'It's like you're sitting on hot coals. It's not like you.'

'Aren't we all?'

She didn't answer, sure there was something else. Speeding through the empty streets of south London in the small hours, they reached the junction of Tooting Broadway with Webster Road.

'Where's your copy of the Blackburn files?' he asked.

'At my house.'

'I'll take them. We don't have the original so we need to make a further copy. And put both copies in safe storage.'

'I can't do that.'

'You've got to.'

'Morahan gave them to me to keep.'

'Sara,' he said urgently, 'if you get caught with those files – even being in possession of them, you'd be breaking the Official Secrets Act. That would be it. Operation over. And think what would have happened if Morahan hadn't given them to you. It wouldn't just be him dead – the evidence would have died with him.'

'OK,' she said weakly.

'Another thing. When you were talking earlier, did Morahan finally tell you his source?' Patrick asked. ''Cos knowing that puts you in danger too.'

'No,' she lied. Morahan, from the outset, had sworn her to secrecy about Sayyid. With the changed circumstances, she suspected she would have to tell Patrick soon enough – but not yet. It was certainly too early to tell him about the envelope behind the radiator – she had first to come to terms with it herself. But if they were both holding things back, she knew that either they must engineer a means of declaring their full hands together or their joint pursuit was over.

They drew up outside her home. The lights were on, Tariq still up. Patrick parked, switched off the engine and made no movement to get out. He turned to her and waited.

'You've hardened since we drove down from Blackburn,' she finally said. 'And I don't think it's just Morahan.'

'If it's not, it doesn't matter. It's not relevant anyway.'

'Patrick, if we're carrying on with this, we'll have to go all in, both of us.' Her voice was low, her eyes liquid with intensity. 'No holding back.'

Face to face, just inches from each other, their breaths audible in the silence of the night, he felt transfixed by her. He mustn't allow that. He turned away and opened his door. Still in his seat, he looked rigidly ahead, cutting the moment. 'And you're saying you're holding nothing back?' he murmured.

He jumped out of the car, not awaiting or wanting a reply, and strode around the bonnet as she opened her door and jumped out. They walked in silence to the front door. She waved him inside, introduced him to Tariq and explained his role in the Inquiry. She left the two of them together, wondering what her father would think of her new colleague.

She went up to her room to retrieve her photocopies from the Blackburn folder and handed it to Patrick.

'Thank you,' he said quietly.

She waited for his car to start and the engine noise to die away.

On the way back to his Brixton flat, Patrick stopped in the Waitrose car park on Balham High Road. He checked the files. There were no other documents. For the moment the threat, it seemed, was contained. The unknown was what else would emerge – and whether Morahan's source would dry up now that he was dead. If there was more to come, he assumed it would be routed to Sara.

She was right. To keep going, they would have to tell each other everything – almost. That was the catch – if no further evidence or documents *did* emerge, there was no need, from his point of view, to open the can. It might all blow over. The question, after the two events of the past seven hours, was whether that was the outcome he now wanted – or they should be allowed to have.

'What's happened?' asked Tariq as Patrick shut the front door.

Sara gave her father the headlines in as brief and understated a way as she could. He asked no questions, seeing she just needed to bury herself away. Blessing him for it and hugging him goodnight, she rushed up to her bedroom.

She sat down at her desk, retrieved the envelope, unfolded it and took out the contents. She placed Sayyid's note beside the print-out of her profile and stared at it.

> This is the person you must recruit as your investigator. She has special knowledge and a connection which I will make clear to you when I know that you have recruited her. At that time, I will also give you a final folder of material.
>
> Please trust me when I say that this investigation is vital for preserving this nation as a law-abiding, accountable democracy.
>
> Sayyid.

Whatever the motives for Morahan's delay in telling her, if he wasn't a half-naked spread-eagled corpse straddling a sofa, she'd be silently cursing him. Instead she was the inheritor of his baleful legacy. And Sayyid was the bacillus that had evolved to confuse and devour them all, beginning with Morahan himself.

Nor was this second offering his ending. '...a final folder of material...'

Had he delivered it? If so, where had Morahan concealed it? At least, she told herself it would not be his office – he'd surely run out of hiding places there.

The texts, the files, Sayyid… someone who knew about her past was tracking her. She sensed ever more vividly the long tail of the secret she had kept hidden for so many years.

Events and her history were ensnaring her. She had to break out.

14

The night, at this moment, might feel unreal but it was pregnant with momentous, unknowable consequences. It would be just hours until the outburst of TV and radio reports, soon followed by the scream of tabloid headlines.

The story would run and run. Was Morahan always a flawed character subject to unusual passions and desires? If so, the chorus of media and online chatter would demand, what on earth was he doing in such a prominent position of trust? Or was it murder by sinister forces of some sort, mocked up to look like a sex game? She remembered the storm and speculation when that GCHQ operative was discovered trussed up in a suitcase. They would be as nothing compared with the fireball Morahan's death would ignite.

Awful times lay ahead for Iona Morahan: the sheer humiliation; the scurrilous ripping apart – in the name of psychoanalysis – of their marriage and relationship; the titillating questions of what could drive a man of such stature and respectability to an end like this.

Sara went to her window and looked down on the back gardens and roofs beyond; how many sordid secrets were housed within those walls? Who knew what their closed curtains concealed?

She needed air. She went downstairs, let herself out and looked upwards. Nothing, no stars, no moon, no outlines of clouds. She walked fast in the direction of the high street, imagining even its nocturnal murmurs might comfort her.

Pointless. She turned round – had to find sleep to prepare for the horrors of the morning. A few yards from home, she saw a car on the other side of the street, its sidelights on, inside the outlines of two figures. She thought she caught a head turning towards her.

She let herself back in, double-locked the front door and attached the security chain.

A marked police car was outside the Inquiry's office, along with a couple of unfamiliar vans. Inside, the staff were grouped in the open-plan area. Patrick beckoned her over.

'Sorry I'm late,' she said. 'Hardly slept.'

'How could you have?' He smiled weakly. 'Forensics are in Morahan's office and they want to go through Legal and Archive too.' Sylvia Labone had parked herself in a corner, peering, as far as Sara could see, over half-moon spectacles at *The Times* crossword.

'They'll do a sweep through Pamela's office too,' he said, quietly enough for the words to drift no further.

'Why bother with that?' asked Sara with the same caution.

'Every stone will be turned, I guess,' said Patrick. 'As our friendly copper warned last night.'

'Where is Pamela?'

'Home Office. They must be hopping around like crickets. Chirruping away.'

'What's been said to the staff?'

'The bare bones. They've been asked to stick around so a note can be taken of names, roles and their movements yesterday.'

'What are the police saying?'

'I saw Buttler briefly – thought I should get in early – they'll be calling it an "unexplained death". I said why not "accidental" and he gave me a world-weary look. He's gone back to Kennington.'

'So we sit and wait.'

The main office phone rang, startling her. 'For you, Sara,' said Clovis.

'Who?'

'Didn't say.'

'Didn't you ask?'

'She sounded trembly.'

'Oh for—' Sara stopped herself and walked over. 'Hello, who is this?' She cupped her hand over the mouthpiece and frowned at Patrick. 'Yes, I'm sure that will be fine. I can't see why not… Yes, right away.'

She put the phone down, Patrick now at her side with raised eyes. 'Lady Morahan. She asked me if I could possibly pop over.'

'Interesting,' he said. 'I'll drive you if you like.'

'No. I'll walk out and hail a cab. No footprint. If I'm careful.'

'I'll see you out.' She frowned. 'It's oppressive in there,' he finally said as they walked down the stairs.

'Sure.'

He noticed her distance. 'It's OK, I won't linger.' She cast him a half-smile as he swung open the main door.

A second police car was drawing up to the entrance. Forensics, Sara assumed. Suddenly she was half-blinded by three quick flashes coming from a single direction. She turned to Patrick, a question in her eyes.

'Shit,' he said. 'First of the paparazzi. Never thought it would be this quick.'

'Must have been a leak,' she said.

'More likely a sharp-eyed security guard. All the comings and goings. Easy way to make a few quid.'

'Can you distract the photographer while I get away?'

'I'll try.' He paused. 'But just in case, don't get caught smiling.'

She swivelled and marched off, detecting the heat of more flashes behind her.

Sara hadn't seen the house in daylight before; the double-fronted, lead-windowed, dark brick houses set in their calm, tree-lined backwater spoke of a traditional English bourgeois affluence when the very idea of living the other side of the river would have appalled its well-heeled residents. She wondered what Lady Morahan might have made of her husband trekking to the far reaches of south London to meet a young Pakistani woman wearing a hijab.

She rang the front doorbell and looked around. Thirty or so yards up the road, a police car was parked on a double yellow line, inside it a uniformed man and woman.

The door opened, revealing a Lady Morahan whose composure seemed to Sara remarkable. Her night must have been agonising, yet she was smartly dressed in black trousers and a red shirt, make-up concealing any sign of distress, offering a quick smile.

'Miss Shah, how kind of you to come.'

'It's no trouble at all, Lady Morahan.' Sara cast a glance up the street.

'Yes, they've called in,' said Iona, following her eyes. 'Pleasant young man and woman. Said they're here to keep an eye on things just in case.'

'In case of what?' Sara asked, instantly realising what a stupid question it was.

Iona shot her a beady look. 'Come on, in you come,' she

said briskly. 'Shall we dispense with "Miss" and "Lady"? I'm Iona, you're Sara. All right with you?'

'Of course,' smiled Sara.

'Coffee?'

'Thank you. Only if it's no trouble.'

'Not at all. Why don't you go into the drawing room? Make yourself comfortable.'

The large square room smelt of polished walnut side tables and the residue of dying embers in the fireplace. Above the mantelpiece hung a large portrait of a seated woman swathed in shawls drawing a landscape in a sketch book.

Sara surveyed the room, unable to stop herself imagining hiding places. She walked over to a baby grand piano in the corner; a book of Bach preludes was open on the music stand. The closed top was a display of framed family photographs: Francis and Iona ducking confetti as they emerged through a church porch on their wedding day, he in a grey frock coat, she in a white dress, the apogee of English traditionalism; two daughters, the older raven-haired, the younger auburn, at different ages from toddlers' dresses to child bridesmaids to school uniform and adulthood; the wedding of the younger to a smiling young man with neatly cut fair hair and a sheen of money and breeding; what she thought might be a fortieth wedding anniversary formal portrait of the Morahans. All far removed from a skinny old man with his trousers halfway down his legs.

She heard a rustle in the passage and swiftly moved from the photographs to the portrait.

'Searching for something?' asked Iona with that same beadiness.

Sara smiled ruefully. 'Examining your family, I'm afraid.'

'Well, that one's my great-great-aunt Dorothea,' said Iona, wheeling in a trolley. 'She went down the Nile in 1895.'

'How amazing!' said Sara.

'I have her sketch books. She never married so they've ended up with me.' She carefully lifted a cafétière and poured coffee into two china cups on saucers. 'Milk and sugar?'

'Just milk, please.' Sara took the cup and they sat down on the sofa. Its proportions and her distance from Iona felt identical to her conversation with Morahan the previous evening.

'You've come from the office,' said Iona.

'Yes.'

'Of course you have. That's where I phoned you.' Iona slumped a notch, for the first time creases dusting her face. 'How was it there?'

'Quiet.'

'Waiting for the dam to burst, I suppose.' Sara allowed her a moment. 'I don't know how to say it to the girls.'

'Have you spoken to them?'

'I waited till this morning. I couldn't really bear to. I said it seemed to be a heart attack. They're on the way up.'

'I'm sure that will be a comfort.'

'Will it?'

Sara had a powerful sense of her striving to say something. She tried to radiate empathy, hoping whatever it was would emerge without prompting.

'You see…' continued Iona. She stopped again.

'Nothing you say will go beyond this room,' said Sara.

'You and I share certain knowledge. Of some recent events.'

'Yes.'

'Though he knew you only briefly, Francis's trust in you was clearly unreserved.'

'It seemed so. I appreciated it.'

Iona straightened herself, summoning energy. 'To fully understand him, I have decided to share knowledge with you of certain *past* events. Just possibly they may have relevance.'

'I see,' said, Sara, waiting, trying not to betray the breathlessness of her anticipation.

'Francis had a predilection.' Iona took a tissue from a slit in a bronze box on the side table and patted her face. 'It was the real reason he resigned as Attorney General. It turned out he had formed a friendship with a young man. A relationship. But it turned sour and Francis felt threatened. And wounded. Of course, I was shocked when he confessed to me. I hadn't suspected at all.' She had been looking down at her hands and now raised her head. 'Though there was always a feminine side to him. It made him a kind person. But that doesn't have to mean homosexual.'

'No, of course not,' said Sara.

'Or gay. Or whatever you like to call it. But it didn't make me feel for one minute that I wanted to part from him. Our lives together were never dominated by that side of things. We had too much in common, too much to gain from each other at home and professionally. I said it shouldn't change us and if he wanted to have such relationships, I was happy to be deaf and blind.'

'That was generous of you.'

'Some might say cowardly. But it worked. Over the years, Thursday nights, like last night, became his work late night. To this day, to this hour, I honestly don't know whether it really was work that he stayed for or the physical needs he may have had.'

'I take it you don't want the police to know of this,' said Sara.

'That's something I need to think about. And whether the girls should know too.'

Sara studied the woman just an arm's length from her, hair scraped back into a simple bun. Agony was now etched in the creases of her skin. If it helped to explain the circumstances of her husband's death, Sara should try to persuade her to tell the police. But her own powerful instinct was that it did not; if so, there was nothing to be gained by making a public confession of it. Whether or not she told their children could only be a matter for her.

'Thank you for telling me,' said Sara. 'I understand how difficult it must be.'

'Yes.' It was no more than a murmur. There was something further this woman wanted to share, Sara was sure of it. Another long-buried secret. Iona raised herself, walked over to a window, peered out as if she was checking for some observer, and turned. 'There was an added element to his resignation.' She paused, still hesitant. 'Francis was visited by two gentlemen, from what it soon became clear were the intelligence services. They had detailed knowledge of his proclivities and relationships. They said that, if he wished to stay in office, they could protect him from any form of public exposure. But...'

'There was a but...'

'Yes, they would like to have occasional meetings and briefings with him about the political world he inhabited. About individuals. About their private discussions, their private habits.'

'Bastards,' said Sara with quiet fury.

'Yes,' said Iona, resuming her seat. 'Bastards.'

'What did he do?'

'He declined their offer, to put it that way. He told me it was a slippery slope; he'd prefer to resign and return to the law. Which he did. They never contacted him again. Even though he rose high in that world, I suppose you could say they had the decency to leave him alone.'

Sara perceived more sharply than ever that what she'd become embroiled in was far more than an investigation of the past; it was a collision of past and present that had turned toxic. 'I don't think decency applies,' she said. 'Then or now.

I was with your husband just an hour or two before he died. He was excited, yes, but not about some sexual encounter he had in store. I'm sure of it. The excitement was in what he was reading.'

'The files?'

'Yes. And no doubt other material he was matching it with. Understanding where the trail might lead.'

'You do realise, Sara, that excitement of one form can lead to excitement of another. I imagine it would only take him a phone call to summon it.'

'It's possible but I don't believe that's what happened.'

'Just suppose it was that, bad as it is,' said Iona. 'Might it not be better than the alternatives?'

The doorbell rang, making Iona jump. Sara felt a surge of relief at not having to address the question the widow had left hanging in the air. She returned with the dark-haired daughter, the one with no evidence of marriage from the photographs on the piano.

'Jennifer, my eldest,' said Iona. Sara noticed all too easily the split second during which Jennifer was wondering what an Asian woman wearing a scarf was doing in her parental home.

'I should be leaving,' said Sara.

'Yes,' said Iona, 'there must be much to do.' She turned to her daughter. 'Give me a moment, darling, I'll see Miss Shah out.'

She led Sara into the hall. 'Hold on a minute, could you?'

Before Sara had time to answer, Iona was skipping up the stairs. Within a minute she was back, carrying a slim rectangular package wrapped in birthday paper. 'I'm sure he'd think you must have it,' said Iona, handing it over. 'In any case, there's no one else.'

'Thank you,' said Sara. She crammed the package into her bag, shook Iona's hand and turned towards the front door. As she closed it behind her she saw the widow retreating, relieved of at least one of her burdens.

It had to be.

'… a final folder of material…'

How had it arrived? Where had she been keeping it? Irrelevant questions. All that mattered was what was in it. Peering up the street at the waiting police car, this was not the time or place to open it and find out.

She felt more exposed and alone than ever. As if to fight it, she walked fast, willing herself to take sharp, deep breaths – to build a flow of oxygen to dispel the smog of doubts and suspicions. She realised the dangers of frenzy and paranoia fuelling conspiracy theories against what had become known as the 'deep state'. The case of the MI6 man stuffed in a holdall endured so long that it even formed the plot of a television drama where the city lived only by night and an assassin might be waiting around any corner. It was the currency of the age; nothing was allowed to be simple. The problem in the case of Sir Francis Morahan was that nothing *was* simple. What was it he had said to her when they first met? 'I'm not a conspiracy theorist. I don't believe our intelligence services shoot people in the head or drop them out of helicopters.' Was that because they didn't need to?

Crossing the Kings Road, she saw a news stand and picked up the *Standard*. Morahan's face dominated the front page. 'MYSTERY DEATH OF JUDGE,' screeched the headline. The vultures had moved rapaciously. She turned the first page. Inside was a double spread – night pictures of the Inquiry offices and ambulance outside. Sensing the worst, she turned the next page. Daylight, more photographs. There it was – herself and Patrick leaving the building, police car alongside. There was even a byline: 'Morahan Inquiry solicitor, Patrick Duke, and junior counsel, Sara Shah.'

Information in the accompanying article was scarce, speculation fevered. A brief torrent of words thrown together in minutes. The wildness of some of the guesswork suggested that, at least, nothing concrete had emerged from anyone at the heart of the Inquiry or its staff. Journalistic phrase-making was now reframing the Morahan Inquiry as 'highly controversial' and 'at the heart of the Prime Minister's drive to open up Britain's security services'. The judge himself had become a 'fiercely independent and committed delver into truth'. The writer who invented that last line might, thought Sara, have unwittingly created his own truth.

Her phone rang. The number showed private, triggering a quiver of agitation. 'Hello, who's this?'

'Sorry to bother you, Miss Shah, it's DS Buttler from Kennington CID.'

Relief merged into dread. 'I thought you'd done with me.'

'Yes, just about. One or two loose ends. Could you pop down to the station to help me sort them out? Informally, of course. The Inquiry office is under siege so not a place for a quiet chat right now.'

'I can see that. When?'

'Might now suit?'

'Now?'

'The quicker we can put it to bed, the better. The media are crawling all over it.'

Sara looked at her watch. 1.15 p.m. 'An hour or two be all right?'

'Whatever time suits you, Ms Shah, I'll be here all afternoon.' She cut the call, distrusting the detective's friendliness and claim of informality.

She hailed a taxi, unsure where she wanted it to take her. The words 'Webster Road, Tooting, please,' came out of her mouth. The cabbie sighed as she opened the door and stepped inside.

She opened her bag, felt the package and rummaged beyond it for her phone. She hit on Patrick's number and relayed Buttler's call.

'I'll come with you,' he said instantly.

'I'll be fine.'

'He's devious. I'm coming. Where are you?'

'I'm going home, have lunch with my dad. Find some sanity.'

'You're a good daughter, Sara, see you there 2.30.'

She told the driver to drop her at the turn into Webster Road. She walked warily up the pavement, eyes constantly swivelling through 360 degrees. No thing, no person seemed out of place. No car resembled the one with the two men during the night. The house was empty – it was her father's lunch day with the group from the depot.

She went up to her bedroom, drew the blinds, sat down at her desk and pulled the package from her bag. Angrily she unfolded it and removed the wrapping paper to reveal an envelope. She slit it open. Inside was a photograph – no note or message accompanying it. She felt further inside and retrieved two small objects – an audio cassette and dictaphone.

Yes – the final delivery.

The photograph was grainy, the expressions unreadable – a photograph that had been taken without the knowledge – or consent – of those in it. Despite its murkiness, she recognised it and the restaurant setting instantly. She inserted the cassette into the player and began to listen. Not that she needed to – the memory of that evening was clear as forked lightning. An icy foreboding was beginning to give way to the dawning of a terrible comprehension.

She checked her watch – time to leave for Kennington. She was in no state to answer questions – whether from Patrick or the detective. Should she phone to cancel? No. It would only raise alarms. She must tough it out. She went into her bathroom, roughly splashed and rubbed her face, reapplied make-up. She brushed her hair, glared at the mirror and forced her face to enact the shape of a cynical lawyer's smile.

She returned the photograph, tape and player to the envelope, folded it back into four and selected a location for it during her absence.

At Kennington Buttler led them into a scruffy office within CID; the detective was taking pains to avoid any suggestion of a formal police interview. When Sara had arrived with Patrick without any forewarning, Buttler had even greeted him as an old friend – perhaps he was canny enough to anticipate it.

There hadn't been time for Sara to brief Patrick on her conversation with Iona Morahan. She had no intention yet – and until she'd worked out the possible consequences – of telling him about Sayyid's second and third offerings.

Buttler sat them down around a scratched wooden table. 'Apologies, I should have offered. Tea? Coffee? Biscuits have probably run out.' His twinkling eyes were in full dance.

'We're fine,' said Sara. Patrick cast her a quick look for her reply on his behalf. She lowered her eyes back at him.

'Right,' said Buttler. 'I've got a note of the timings you gave me. Just one question. You said it was 8.30 p.m. that you received the text message from Sir Francis asking you to come back.'

'Yes, around then.'

'And it's gone missing from your phone.'

'Yes. As I said last night, perhaps I did delete it in all the chaos.'

'It's an odd one.' He paused, apparently stumbling over a puzzle. 'That sent message isn't on Sir Francis's phone either.'

'What?' The pinpricks of sweat returned. 'He must have deleted it.'

'Yes, you'd think that would be the explanation. But our first examination of the metadata to try to retrieve it contains no indication that such a message was sent.'

'That's crazy,' said Sara. 'I read it.'

'So you said.'

'There are circumstances—' began Patrick.

'If you could just bear to hold on a minute, Mr Duke,' said Buttler, showing for the first time a touch of steel. 'I'm just trying to get the facts and chronology straight. Would you object, Miss Shah, if we borrowed your phone for a few hours at your convenience to make sure the message was there? We should be able to retrieve it.'

Sara turned to Patrick. She knew she'd read the message – why else would she have returned to the office? – but had a sickening feeling of some insidious trap closing on her. 'I told you I texted my reply to say I was coming in. That's still there. So I could only have been replying to his text.'

'Are you trying to imply,' interrupted Patrick, 'that in some way Ms Shah is inventing this text? And for some bizarre reason wrote her own text in reply just for the sake of it?'

'No, sir, I'm implying nothing.'

'Because if so, you may need to move on to more formal ground.'

'At this point,' said Buttler amicably, 'I feel it's best for all our sakes to continue to proceed on an informal basis.'

'I understand,' said Patrick, 'that certain applications of smart phones allow a user not just to eliminate traces of sent messages from their own phone but also all traces, including metadata, from the receiver's phone.'

'You're ahead of me on that one, Mr Duke. Here it's the geeks in their funny rooms who look after all that.' He smiled sweetly. 'But I'll take your word for it.'

'I have no problem whatsoever with you inspecting my

phone,' declared Sara abruptly. Patrick glared at her. 'I've nothing to hide. If a third party has intervened to delete this message from Sir Francis's phone and, in that case I suspect, my own phone, that will require further investigation.'

'What third party, Ms Shah?' asked Buttler. 'And for what motive?'

'That is your job to establish, Mr Buttler,' said Sara, faking her lawyerly smile.

'Indeed,' said Buttler, acknowledging it. 'Moving on, you gave me the timings of your comings and goings at the Inquiry office.'

'Yes. CCTV will confirm the exact timings if there's any need for that.'

'Unfortunately not,' said Buttler. 'CCTV appears to have been out of action last night.'

'What?' burst in Patrick.

'Yes,' he mused. 'Ms Bailly didn't seem too surprised. She told me it was often "on the blink" – to use her exact words.'

'Why the hell didn't she get it sorted?' said Patrick.

'She didn't seem to view it as a priority,' said Buttler.

Sara looked over to Patrick. 'Rayah will be able to confirm the timings, she was in the office when I got back.'

'You mean Ms Yaseen,' said Buttler.

'Yes.'

'Ms Yaseen,' said Buttler smoothly, Sara smelling another unwelcome surprise, 'has stated that you returned to the office around 6.30 p.m. and then left sometime around 7.15, 7.20 p.m., shortly before she herself departed for the evening.'

'Then at least you have that,' said Sara frostily.

'She was, however, unable to confirm that you had actually left the building.'

'What else would I have been doing?'

'Ms Shah, I am only laying out what we know for sure and what we don't.'

'How do you know Rayah herself left?' said Sara.

'Fair point.' Buttler made a show of an agreeable concession. 'And we will be checking her phone records too and her friends' confirmation of her arrival time.' He smiled, as if none of the three of them should be in the slightest bit worried at the direction his train of thought was taking. 'There is one final curiosity,' he resumed. 'Miss Shah, did you notice any particular smell when you discovered the body.'

That whiff of paraffin hit her like a dart. She wasn't prepared for the question or where it could lead. 'I'd just stumbled across the dead, half-naked body of a man I had been having a professional conversation with some four hours earlier. I hope you'll forgive me if my senses were numbed.'

'I quite understand. Perhaps you could answer my question.'

'Mr Buttler,' interrupted Patrick, 'you're going over a certain mark of which you're well aware and I must ask you again either to desist or move to a formal procedure.'

Buttler turned to him, all twinkles and humour banished. 'No more questions after this, Mr Duke. I assure you again it's in all our interests to get to the end of this.'

'It's OK, Patrick,' said Sara. 'Whatever track he's on, it's wrong.'

'Thank you, Ms Shah. So?'

'I'm sure there were smells of different sorts but I was too shocked by what I was seeing to notice any.'

'The reason I ask is that clear evidence has been found of a medical cleanser, perhaps some form of paraffin-based wipes, on the bared skin of the naked man, mainly around his private parts, pubic hair and lower belly.' Sara began to see the trap – and how neatly it must have been laid. 'The obvious explanation is that another person was with Sir Francis and cleaned that skin in order to avoid the possibility of any residual DNA evidence of their presence.' Buttler paused; Sara and Patrick watched him silently. 'The implication is that the other person or persons present feared residues of their body fluids may have been present and wished to eliminate them.'

'Unless Morahan cleaned himself before expiring,' said Patrick.

Buttler displayed the world-weariness Patrick had seen before. 'I don't think that would be a likely order of events, Mr Duke.'

'No,' said Patrick flatly. 'I can see the potential significance of that evidence. It does indeed point to a second party being present during the events that preceded the death. What I cannot see is why you have dragged Ms Shah down here to follow a line of detection which has absolutely nothing to do with her.' He paused for emphasis. 'And without providing an iota of credible evidence for it.'

'Ms Shah,' continued Buttler, ignoring him, 'saw Sir Francis early that evening. She says she was summoned back to his office though we can find no corroboration of that. Then she became the person who found him.' Buttler turned to Sara, adopting his most sympathetic expression. 'I'm a simple person, Ms Shah, with what you might think is a simple mind. But in my experience it's the simple explanation that is often right. So let me suggest one that has the advantage of chiming with the known facts. After you left the office around 7.20 p.m., you waited in the local area until Ms Yaseen departed. You returned to the office, as you and Sir Francis had arranged. You had a sexual encounter which eventually led to his accidental and unfortunate death. Understandably frightened by this, you fabricated a text with the aim of showing you only returned to the office later in the evening for work reasons. If this, in outline, is what happened, now is the time to tell me. There will be no legal consequence, no charges. You will have committed no offence. The only offence you're in danger of committing is if you withhold evidence which would assist us in resolving the cause of death.'

Sara raised her eyes at Buttler, engaging him with ferocious intent. 'Look at me, Mr Buttler,' she said. 'Who do you see?'

'I see an attractive, intelligent young woman, Ms Shah.'

'You're wrong. You see someone who is committed to their work and who lives their life according to a certain set of ethical and religious rules.'

'I can't allow appearances to stand in the way of resolving this tragic event.'

'You've a job to do. I understand the suspicions you must allow yourself to have. But you must understand that, being the person I am, your theory is wholly impossible.' The flatness of her words was laced with a quiet fury.

'Thank you, Miss Shah,' said Buttler, brushing off the anger he perceived and now breezy again. 'I'm grateful to you and Mr Duke for allowing me this conversation.' He stood up and they followed suit. 'If you have any reason to change your mind or your memory produces any further recollections, just give me a ring.' He took out two cards and gave one to each of them. 'You know where to find me.' He ushered them out of the room, through the CID office and shook hands at the front lobby. 'As I say, I'm always here.'

Sara and Patrick left the station in silence, neither wanting to speak first.

'I try not to see wickedness,' she finally said, 'but sometimes I despise this world.'

'Coffee,' said Patrick, nodding to a café over the road. They wove their way between stationary traffic to the opposite pavement. 'I'll get.' She sat down on a plastic-cushioned chair at an unwashed melamine table. 'The waitress will bring them.' He sat opposite and forced a smile; she didn't return it.

She gave him the headlines of her conversation with Iona

Morahan. 'I always had this feeling,' she said, 'there was something buried within Sir Francis. Even though I could never have imagined what it was.'

'God,' said Patrick. 'What bastards they were. It was pure blackmail.'

'Yes. Illegal and unforgivable.' She paused. 'Iona's confession to me was in confidence. I suppose I'm breaking it telling you. But it means I can't use it to refute Buttler. Mind you, he'd probably say his Lordship liked it both ways.'

Patrick frowned. 'Yes, he probably would.'

'So...' she said. 'I've been set up.'

'Maybe. But, if so, it's a frightener. In the end, the evidence would never hold.'

'You're being too imprecise.' She was curt, almost hostile.

'Let's work it out. Forget paranoia and all that. Explore every angle.'

She looked down at her coffee, warming her hands on the cup. Though the day was balmy, she shivered. 'Go on.'

'Someone has to have been with Morahan for whatever sex act took place.'

'Assuming there was one. The medical cleanser could be a feint.'

'That's smart.' He paused. 'A suffocation dressed up as an auto-erotic accident.'

'Yes. Another tack. I hate myself for asking this. How well do you know Rayah?'

'If you're hinting at that, I never picked anything up over the past months.'

'She's full-on,' said Sara. 'Say he did go both ways – she might not think twice about giving an influential man what he wanted in exchange for a favour.'

'Not like you then,' said Patrick with the familiar grin. He intended it lightly but she remained stony-faced. 'Sorry, Sara, I was just trying—'

'You don't need to "try" with me.' The silence returned.

'I'm just a bloody idiot sometimes.'

She relaxed and stretched a hand across the table, placing it on the back of his hand. 'It's OK. You were trying to lighten up. Just don't bother.' She withdrew the hand.

'Understood,' he murmured. 'So... I guess our friend Buttler could build the same scenario with Rayah as he's done for you. Probably already has.'

'Let's hope one of her friends checked their watch when she arrived at her party.'

'Then there's the text message.'

'I did get it,' said Sara with untypical emphasis.

'Of course you got it.' He edged nearer. 'You don't think for one minute I—'

'No. It's just that I feel I'm living through some kind of madness. You begin to mistrust yourself.'

'You mustn't,' said Patrick sharply.

'No.' She shook her head. 'What have you done with the files?'

'There's a copy in safe storage. It's better you don't know where.'

'What about the originals? The original photocopies, I mean. I'll need them.'

'I reckoned the safest place for them is my desk in the office. They won't go there again.'

For the first time, Sara managed a smile. 'Well, if they do, at least we'll know for sure, won't we?' She drained her coffee. 'Back to the office?'

'No, home. Who needs the media gauntlet?'

They walked into the street, simultaneously looking around and behind. They caught each other in the act and exchanged rueful grins.

'What was it we were to get shot of?' she asked gently. 'Paranoia?'

'As a man once said, just because you're paranoid, it doesn't mean they're not out to get you. I'm heading for the tube.'

'Think I may walk for a while. I need to blow off some steam.'

'OK.' He grabbed her by the wrist. 'Sara, if there's anything you know, anything you're not telling me, any tiny bit of info, any strangenesses, weird calls, whatever, you've got to tell me.' He released his grip and she stood back from him.

'Where did that come from?'

'You're right. Things have changed. I'm going to look after you.'

'I can look after myself, Patrick.'

'How did I know you were going to say just that?'

He turned smartly on his heel and strode off in the direction of Kennington tube. Sara wished she'd known him for years, not just a few days. She still could not fully read him – and he seemed to send different signals at different times.

One thing she felt sure of – she was safe with him. He was a good man; the issue was whether he was a strong or a weak man.

Clouds swelling with menace were gathering as she turned back for the second time that day into Webster Road. Head down, she upped her pace to beat the imminent burst of rain.

As she put her key in the lock and began to turn, the front door flew open. Behind it stood her father, glaring.

'Dad?'

'See that car?' He was pointing at a black Ford Galaxy a few spaces along the street.

She followed the line of his finger. Inside were two men, sitting side by side, doing nothing. One of their heads turned towards them. She glared back, determined not to show alarm. 'What about it?'

'Reckon I've seen it here before. See those men inside?'

Sara affected to look more thoroughly. Should she tell him? 'Maybe I did. Last night. But nothing to worry about. Probably just minicab drivers waiting for a hire.'

'They're not local,' said Tariq. 'I don't like it. I'm going to check it out.'

'No, Dad, leave it,' she said with force. But he was away, too late to stop him.

She watched as he neared the car and tapped on the driver's window. It was lowered and words exchanged; she knew her father's would be querulous. She should somehow have stopped him. The passenger got out, came round and approached Tariq. He was big and broad, the playground bully standing over his prey. He bent down, whispered briefly in Tariq's ear and straightened, holding his ground. Tariq took a step back, appeared to say a few words, put his hands together, bowed and withdrew. The window slid back up; the passenger returned to his seat. The car remained silent and still.

The cloudburst broke as he retraced his steps. 'Let's get inside,' he said, rejoining her, rain flattening his hair, fear creasing his face. 'What's going on, Sara?'

'What did they say, Dad? Who were they?'

'Not sure. One was a Scottish-sounding gentleman, the other rougher, London rough. They told me to be careful what I said, all they were doing was keeping an eye on you for your own safety. For your protection. I said I was quite capable of protecting you. Then the big fellow who got out whispered in my ear, "You just keep out of it, little man. This is way, way above your pay grade. Now you just fucking get inside that house of yours and stop asking questions." I tell you, Sara, he frightened me. He was scary.'

She put her arms on his shoulders. 'I'm so sorry, Dad. You should never be near any of this.'

'Of what, for heaven's sake? It's that Morahan. His letter to you. Him dying so strangely. You should not have got involved. I should never have encouraged you.'

She hugged him and drew back. 'It's fine, I promise. I too don't know what it's all about yet but it will blow over. His death was an accident. Some people get a little over-excited, that's all.'

He frowned. 'I wish I could be sure. For God's sake, take care.'

'I will. But there's nothing to fear for me. Maybe it's for the best. Now I must go up and work. I'll get something from the fridge to eat.'

She walked into the kitchen, opened the door and stooped to the crisper at the bottom. From it, she retrieved the envelope she'd concealed there. Grabbing an apple she had no desire to eat, she turned angrily and headed for the stairs. The secret state could try scaring *her* off – but she wouldn't let it touch her father.

Shadowy figures sitting at a table in the foreground. Three facing front-on in a diagonal line of the camera's sight – a thick-set man, outline of a rough beard, wearing a dark jacket, maybe leather. Two other males, hard to make out more. Opposite, nearest to the camera, just the sides and backs of their heads showing, three more figures. Furthest right a woman, wearing a scarf, its colour undefined; in the middle a second woman with long hair in black silhouette and jacket; on the left, sitting upright and gesticulating, wearing a collarless tunic, a jet-haired man with a trim beard running from sideburns round the point of his chin.

She inserted the cassette into the dictaphone and pressed replay. She continued her listening of the recorded fragmentary conversation. The majority of the time, it appeared to be picking up the voice of the jet-haired man. She assumed he was the main target of the surveillance. The assumption, and its possible implications, appalled her. The tape hissed on; she forced herself to stay alert, to try to disentangle words and sentences that signified anything.

M: You were one person I had not expected to see.
F: Why?
M: I never forget what you said… INAUDIBLE…
F: If you're speaking of 9/11, my eyes have seen what followed…
INAUDIBLE… INAUDIBLE… Of which you approve, I suppose.
M: Or perhaps of which I was prophetic… INAUDIBLE.

She stopped, wound back and replayed. The final proof – as if it were needed by now. She recalled those words from the note Sayyid had pinned to her corporate profile.

… This is the person you must recruit as your investigator. She has special knowledge and a connection…

She finally had the completed answer to that initial and recurring question. This was why Morahan had wanted only her and no one else – the secret he had held back from her until, finally, it was revealed as his deathbed bequest. She, Sara Shah, was the long-haired woman in silhouette in the photograph – the connection the jet-haired man sitting beside her.

Should she feel abused by Morahan; that his manipulation had been wrong, even immoral? Or had he felt he had no choice; that she was the person he must have to arrive at whatever truth Sayyid was driving at – and his means justified that end.

Could she, should she, have guessed what might be in store from Sami's account of the Adviser and the beautiful woman alongside him? No, she told herself, her time with the man had been spent four summers before – the night of that restaurant dinner was the first time she'd seen him since that ordeal. As for the woman – she'd been told about her but never set eyes on her till that evening. There was nothing from what she'd known or experienced of the man – or woman – for such scant strands to make that connection so many years later. Even if, now that she'd seen the photograph and Sayyid's letters, and heard Sami's story, the strands were joining up.

A further implication was chillingly clear. Whoever had recorded and photographed that evening would have made it their business to find out more about each person who was there – including her.

Were they tracking her now? Damn them. She crept downstairs, trying not to disturb her father – there was a weak light from the sitting room – and eased open the front door. The evening was clearing, broken clouds making patterns in the sky, the first pale show of moon flitting in and out of their animal-like shapes.

She walked into the middle of the road, stretched her arms upwards, beginning a circle to the clouds' rhythm, as if to say, 'I am free no matter what happens here on earth.' Halfway round she stopped. They were still there. She stood, staring. No reaction.

As she neared the front door, headlights flashed on and off and an engine started. She quickened, closed and locked the door and heard a car accelerating fiercely past.

Back in her room, she picked up the photograph and held it close to her eyes. Something was nagging her about it. She tried to remember the exact date, then realised it could be on the photograph itself. There was a tiny white scratching on the bottom right corner. 23rd June. No year; she didn't need to be told that.

She looked again at the three faces front on to the camera but furthest away from it. She didn't recall being introduced to the man on the far right – she'd hardly noticed him as all her attention and conversation was focused on the man beside her. But now looking closely at that face, there was a familiarity – a connection lodged deep in her memory. She googled to check, hoping it was only a resemblance; the consequence of it not being was too horrible.

A photograph came up on Wikipedia. She linked to two news sites which also had photographs. She manoeuvred the three photographs into three corners of the screen, isolating the face from the restaurant photograph into the fourth corner.

There was no doubt. Mohammad Sidique Khan, the leader in July 2005 of what became known as 7/7. The man who, in blowing himself up on the Circle line, had taken six other lives with him; who had led three other suicide bombers to their deaths along with a further forty-six innocent victims.

Two weeks before, unknown to her until now, she had sat at his table and been recorded in the act.

15

Sara Shah was a rational being. Since settling into her legal career, she slept well at night. She wasn't prone to detecting conspiracies; she didn't allow suspicion or paranoia to affect her judgement. Yet, from the moment she woke after a second fretful night, she couldn't prevent her brain and eyes wanting to assess threats from every angle.

Her first act was to put on loose-fitting pocketed trousers and a shirt and jacket. She needed to get the contents of Sayyid's second and third deliveries out of the house. The office might be under some scrutiny but it was safer than home. Her choice of dress gave her options.

Her second act was to inspect the street. No sign of the car or its occupants.

Her third act was to vary her journey to work, hailing a cab from the high street rather than summoning one to her house.

With Morahan dead, only one other person, Sayyid, knew that her presence at a restaurant table, next to the man on her right in the surveillance photograph, was the link to a deep morass of illegal activity of which Sami's story was only the tip. Although the audiotape indicated that she and that person had some familiarity with each other, she could not know whether Sayyid – or Morahan – had any detailed knowledge of its extent.

Sayyid was responsible for drawing her into this, but he, or she, was an opaque mystery. Pressing the code to enter the Inquiry's offices – with a smart of irritation that no one had yet thought to change it – and then climbing the stairs and inserting her second-floor pass – which should also have been reconfigured – she entered the open-plan area feeling a wave of irritation towards Sayyid. He was the visiting sprite who'd fired the starting gun and then retreated into some far undergrowth, invisible from the field of play but, from safe cover, watching the game unfold. Why?

The office was silent. Rayah's and Clovis's eyes were fixed to their screens, refusing to be distracted by her appearance; Pamela Bailly's office door ajar with no sign of life beyond. It still felt as lifeless as the mortuary in which Morahan's stiff body must now be lying. The Inquiry had been an organic living being; now it was decapitated. She murmured a faint 'Good morning' and quickened her stride towards the corridor and the Legal office.

Patrick stood to greet her, grin restored. 'Coffee?' he asked, just like that first time she'd walked over to join him by the espresso machine.

'Still as the dead, isn't it?' he said.

'My thoughts exactly.' She watched him place the cup and push the button, the grinding and gurgling emitting reassuring sounds and smells. 'Anything happened?'

'No. Though I hope one thing that's happened is our friend Buttler thinking better of his crazy theory.'

She took the cup and saucer he was holding for her and they walked together to his desk. She sat down opposite and slowly sipped, trying to arrange her proliferation of thoughts into an orderly list. 'His theory isn't crazy. It fits the known chronology.'

'But not true.'

She narrowed her eyes. 'No, Patrick, not true.'

'Sara, it wasn't a question, it was a statement.'

She shook her head. 'Sorry. I guess this is what it does to you.'

He drained his cup and walked over to the expanse of window, staring at the American Embassy, its strange conical ornaments reflecting the sky, and the muddle of blocks and towers beyond. She ranged alongside. 'Buildings,' he said. 'Great slabs of concrete, steel and glass bolted into the ground. At the centre that enormous mass of the Embassy – the central event, if you like. The death. It stands out but around it there's no clear pattern. Structures of different heights made of different materials. Brick façades, huge plasticky panels – red, green, grey, silver, blue – smooth concrete, windows of all shapes and sizes. But let's imagine we change the colour of one of those giant panels.'

'Metaphor over?'

He turned to her. 'What if it wasn't Morahan who texted you?'

'I don't follow…'

'What if the person Morahan was with texted you from Morahan's phone? And he was already lying dead on the sofa.'

'You mean… you mean I was summoned to be the patsy.' She closed her eyes, turning over the vileness of it. 'The fall guy. Girl, rather.'

'Or, as I said, it was done to scare you. Either way, it explains why your text was remotely deleted. It also shows a certain expertise – but one an amateur might possess. I was bluffing that with Buttler but I've checked since. You can even get gizmos to do it on the net though it might depend on the phone you have.'

'Keep going.'

'It means one very simple thing. Because of the chronology the medics were given, no one made an issue about the exact time of his death. And it rapidly becomes too late to revisit once the body's beyond a certain stage.'

'I'm seeing it.'

'Quite. Morahan could have died any time after you left the office. From 7.15 p.m. onwards.'

Sara recalled that parting conversation when she left for home. 'Rayah.'

'No.' Patrick almost raised his voice. 'By which I mean that in the same way there's no concrete evidence to link you, there's none to link her either.'

'She could have let someone else in,' said Sara.

'Yes, she could have.' He shot her a hang-dog grin. 'And many other things could have happened too.' Patrick stared out again. 'That's the point. This is the perfect death to induce speculation. One piece of evidence, the remnants of cleanser, shows someone was with him before, during or after his death. If there *was* a sex act after which the cleanser was used, he may have died later, alone and innocently. So the cleanser itself does not prove a crime. Any hare can run. Russian crime syndicate, MI5 cover-up, the blackmailer he was refusing to pay. It will be unsolvable.' He paused. 'Let's sit. Let's really look at each other.'

She frowned for a second. 'OK.'

He went back to his desk. They locked eyes. 'It will be unsolvable,' he repeated, 'unless there's something someone knows that they're not letting on. That might begin to explain it. We don't have that something yet. A few Muslims being taken for interrogation to a mysterious guy they only know as the Adviser or whatever doesn't do it. A few Muslims going missing—'

'More than a few if it's the tip of the iceberg—'

'Doesn't matter how many. Not on its own. Lists of missing people in the Sayyid files, whoever they might be, don't mean anything unless there's a pattern. A uniting factor. Some kind of agent – individual, organisation, force, whatever – which is so significant – or has done something so out of order – that it has to remain buried for ever.'

He drew his chair even closer, the strength of his eyes and soft urgency of his voice beginning to alarm her. 'Unless there's something more – something that some big fish's whole being, whatever side they're on, depends on concealing – it stops here. Morahan's death is just a sad accident that happened to an old man who liked the odd moment of excitement. We can't take it any further.'

'Yes, we could stop it here,' she murmured.

'Look inside yourself,' he said. 'Is that what you want? Be truthful.'

'I could ask you the same question.'

'Two days ago my answer would have been different to now.'

'So something did change.'

'Yes.'

'What?'

'It's not relevant.'

'I have to know.'

He cupped his face in his hands. Motionless on her seat, she waited. 'All right. I had a visit.'

He turned away; she wondered if he was aware of his intensity. She rose and took up his former position by the window, her back to him. 'Tell.'

'After I dropped you off at the office, I was hailed by two men as I approached the front door of my flat. I recognised one of them from an episode twelve years ago both visually and from his Scottish accent.' Sara almost buckled, thinking of her father's description of the driver in the parked car. 'He reminded me whose side I was on,' continued Patrick. 'The second man, it turned out, had an expertise in knuckle blows which he used to reinforce the message. The one who spoke addressed me as "boy".'

She stood at an angle, her profile silhouetted by the morning light flooding in. Despite the long skirt and scarf wound over her head and shoulders, her svelteness and a frailty he saw for the first time stirred him.

'I'm sorry, Patrick. Not just bastards, racist bastards too.'

'It was premeditated. To get under my skin.'

She hesitated, wondering whether to tell him about the men waiting outside her house. No. This was not the moment – not what this conversation was for.

She turned. 'So, whatever it is their "side" is protecting, wherever it might lead, you don't want to let them get away with it.'

'I don't know. Because I don't know what's buried there.'

'Is that why you're doing this? Because you think there's a buried reason that explains why Morahan wanted me? And it may be linked to his death?'

He rubbed his eyes and squinted, feeling wrong-footed, assailed by a confusion of emotions. It was safer for both of them if she knew nothing more. If he provoked her into making some revelation, he couldn't foretell the outcome. And for him, if not her – yet or ever – it was personal. Would the door between them, that he'd believed she was allowing slowly to open, now slam shut?

'It's your decision,' he finally said.

Sara too understood the moment with a devastating clarity. Morahan's death would almost certainly mean Sayyid drying up as a source – he was most unlikely to start giving classified information to anyone more junior. In fact, she recalled Morahan saying Sayyid had told him in their strange car trip that there would be no more.

There was no need to embroil herself further; no need to be propelled on a journey whose direction she could not control. Morahan's death would be consigned to history as an unsolved oddity, beloved of conspiracy theorists but otherwise forgotten. She could go back to Ludo. Men in parked cars would fade away. Maybe that would be for the best.

It was not a decision she had the right or strength to make alone; she had to find a way of sharing it. There was no one else.

'There are two things I've held back,' she said at last. 'In doing so, I've had to lie to you. I apologise. Firstly, Morahan did, by the end, tell me everything about his source.' Evenly and without emotion, she gave Patrick the account Morahan had given her of his dealings with Sayyid; his summary of the contents of the note that accompanied the Blackburn files; and Morahan's description of his conversation with Sayyid in the car.

Patrick listened in silence. He fixed his gaze on her as she gathered her thoughts, composing herself for the further revelation.

'The second thing is this,' she resumed quietly. 'After I discovered Morahan's body, I did a quick search of his office.' He eyed her sharply. 'Don't worry, I found a way of leaving no trail. Behind the radiator covered by the grille below the main window, an envelope was sellotaped. It turned out to be a second delivery from Sayyid.' She described the corporate profile of her and the words of Sayyid's accompanying note. Patrick was slowly shaking his head. 'What have you done with the note?'

'I hand-wrote a copy, then flushed it down the toilet.'

'OK, but—'

'There's more,' she interrupted. 'Just as I was about to leave Iona Morahan's house, she stopped me. She went upstairs and returned with a small package. She'd wrapped it in birthday paper. I went straight home, not to have lunch with my father but to explore that package. I didn't dare open it until I was on my own, out of sight. It turned out to contain the further delivery Sayyid had promised Morahan if he succeeded in recruiting me to the Inquiry.'

'I realised you weren't telling me everything,' he said. 'But I never imagined how much you weren't.'

She sagged, her head drooping. 'I couldn't tell you yesterday, Patrick. Not before the interview with Buttler because it was better I carried the strain of it alone. And not after because too much was swirling around. I had to let it settle. To work out where I stood.'

'It's all right. You've had so little time to see into me.'

'It's only in the last few minutes that I've come to be sure of where I stand.' She said it flatly, oppressed by the weight of the secrets she'd been forced to carry and the lies she'd been forced to tell. 'Look away for a minute.'

He frowned, but did as she bade. She removed her jacket, raised her shirt and pulled down an envelope wedged between the shirt and skin of her back. 'You can turn round.' She approached him. 'Inside this is a photograph of a group of people taken fourteen years ago.' She handed him the envelope and then pulled one small package out of one trouser pocket, and a second from another. 'One of these contains an audiocassette, the other a recorder to play it back on.'

Patrick prised the photograph from the envelope. As he held it up, she moved to stand over his shoulder. 'That woman,' she said, touching the back of the head with her fingernail, 'is me.' She moved her finger to the right. 'That man is the connection I have that Sayyid referred to.' She removed her finger. 'That person lies at the heart of whatever it is we're trying to reveal.'

Patrick was staring rigidly at the photograph, apparently

dumbstruck. He removed his spectacles, rubbed his eyes, and looked at it again, this time for longer. He was shaking, searching for words.

'I've seen this photograph.'

She was electrified. 'What?'

'This must be what they're scared of. Perhaps they lost control of it. Of him.'

'You recognise him?'

'If I'd thought for one second you'd ever set eyes on him, let alone known him, I'd never have pushed. It's not safe, we don't go any further.'

'No, Patrick, that's a decision we make together. First of all, you have to explain.'

'You see, I was there at the beginning.'

16

A moment frozen in time, senses dulled, sounds stopped.

A world tipping.

Patrick saw it in her eyes. 'Let's get out,' he said, jumping up. He glanced out of the window. A low blanket of grey. 'Grab your coat.' He snatched his own off a hook. 'This is no place to talk, can't see through the walls.'

Without waiting for her reply, he was on his way. She gathered her bag, took her red mackintosh, and followed. As she passed the open Archives door, she peeped in, catching Sylvia Labone's eye and the glare of her frown – should have kept her eyes ahead. She caught up with Patrick at the stairs, racing to match him. Once outside, he inhaled deeply. If they'd looked up and round, they'd have seen Sylvia watching them from her office window.

'Where now?' she asked.

'Where's the safest place to drive if you're speeding?' he asked.

'Don't know.'

'Past a police station.'

Heading in the direction of Vauxhall Bridge, traffic noise covering, he began to speak.

'There's someone who wants to meet you,' said Keith Barron, head of the Treasury Solicitors.

'Someone, sir?' said Patrick.

'It's all right, Patrick, you don't need to do "sir". This someone is one of our friends from Thames House.'

'The Security Service.'

'Correct. MI5.' Barron peered up at the ceiling and addressed himself to it. 'It appears they are engaged in a negotiation with an individual who is asking for certain guarantees.' He bore back down on Patrick. 'They gave me a profile of this person and asked for an in-house solicitor who might be able to strike up a relationship with him. I know you've only just joined us but you're the man for the job.'

'I know nothing about that world,' said Patrick, bemused.

'That's a plus, you can play the innocent. Are you up for it?'

Patrick thought of the dull prospect of his next departmental visit. 'Yes. Thank you.'

'I'd been there literally two weeks,' said Patrick, striding down Nine Elms. 'Just finished my compulsory two years at the City law firm slave drivers who'd put me through articles. There was a job ad at the Treasury Solicitors. It's the Government Legal Department now. I applied and got it. They were sending me round the departments. As I remember the next visit was to the Driver and Vehicle Licensing Agency in Wales.' His grin had been absent for the longest Sara could remember. Now he shot her one. 'MI5 sounded more exciting.' The grin didn't last long. 'Idiot that I was.'

'Doesn't sound like you were being given a choice,' said Sara.

'You don't say no two weeks in, do you?' He paused as they stopped at the pedestrian lights to cross towards the river. 'The someone's name was Walter Thompson. Barron gave me his number and said he was expecting my call. He said hello, gave me a time – 12.45 – and a place. That was it.'

'Where?'

Patrick pointed airily towards Millbank Tower. 'Over there. Not exactly St James's, is it? They don't do pizza in the clubs there. I arrived five minutes early – wanted to be sure – told a waitress the table was booked in the name of Thompson. She led me to a corner. There he was, reading *The Times*. Fifties, I guessed, roughly parted sandy hair, mud-brown corduroy jacket with brown leather patches covering the elbows. Oh… and a dark red cravat dangling down over a check shirt.'

'Patrick Duke.' The voice was gravelly – an actor's voice, Patrick thought.

'Yes, that's me, Mr Thompson.'

'J. Call me J. Everyone does.' Patrick was bemused. 'Walter Thompson. J Walter Thompson. Geddit?'

'You mean the ad agency—'

'Of course. Our organisation, adoration of initials.' He leaned across, lowering his voice. 'C, M, Q… so they decided to call me J. Company humour, I'm afraid. Sit down. I'm having an American Hot. I've asked for tap water.' He peered over small brown-rimmed half-moon glasses. 'Tell me about yourself. No need to hold back. This hidey-hole is the most discreet spot in London. Try bugging a conversation in the clatter of this place.' Patrick could see that J, his back to the corner wall, had in his sights the full swathe of the restaurant and pavements lying beyond. Patrick's only view was of J.

He laid out the bare bones of his life: son of a rich Ghanaian; educated at English public school; law degree; City solicitor intern; now learning the ropes at the Treasury Solicitors.

'That tells me nothing,' said J brusquely. Patrick sagged,

slicing slowly through his pizza. 'Attitudes, culture, conscience, thoughts, prejudices. That's what I want to know. Let's start with the last.'

'Prejudices?'

'Yes. What are yours?'

Patrick slapped down his knife and fork. 'I don't do prejudice.'

''Course you do. We all do.'

'All right, if you insist. Bad-mannered, middle-aged men asking rude and intrusive questions for a start.'

J reddened with what seemed a flush of anger, then exploded into a thunderous chuckle which subsided into a fading splutter. 'Good chap! What else?'

'Rich public school arseholes.'

'Go on.'

'Arrogant overpaid city lawyers, weasel wordsmiths, puffed-up politicians—'

'Pakis?'

'I beg your pardon,' said Patrick softly.

'Arabs?'

Patrick's voice was laced with a quiet contempt. 'Is this some kind of sick game? Whatever's been said to me in the course of my life, I've never given a fuck about the colour of another man's skin. Or his race or culture for that matter.'

'Religion?' continued J, unabashed.

'Or his religion.' In another place at another time, Patrick felt he might have punched him in the face.

'Me neither,' said J, taking a sip of water. 'Sorry, always good to take a fellow's temperature. Particularly given the task in hand.'

It was a test; he'd passed. 'What task?'

'Not for here. Let's enjoy our lunch and find out more about each other. Are you a cricket or soccer man?'

An hour later, pass issued, bag scanned and through the security pods, Patrick found himself closeted with J in a small barely furnished ante-room at Thames House. He had sometimes wondered whether the dull uniform grey exterior matched what was inside; so far, the answer was resoundingly yes.

'How did you react to the events of July the 7th?' began J. They sat at opposite corners of a brown leather sofa – Patrick had a mounting sense of that colour becoming his abiding memory of the day.

'I was shocked. Like everyone.'

'Why? Something was bound to blow, wasn't it?'

'It doesn't soften it. The luck and arbitrariness of life. And death.'

'How about the bombers? Sacrificing themselves for their God.'

Patrick hesitated, unsure whether this was another of J's tests. 'I didn't bother myself thinking about them,' he replied.

'Fair enough. But I'm asking you now.'

'You're putting me on a spot where I don't want to be.'

'Tough. Speak.'

'They weren't mad. Or sick. Or evil. Or any of the other tabloid epithets. They were sort of blinded. Blind-alley idealists.'

'You can understand how they arrived at their destination.'

'"Understand" may be putting it too strongly. I've felt anger. Destructive urges even, as a black boy at a British public school. But I could never graduate to the deed of killing.'

'What about on the battlefield?'

'Never been there.'

'As a soldier in uniform,' said J, ignoring his answer.

'That's different.'

'Isn't that what the bombers were? Soldiers in uniform fighting for Allah.'

Patrick frowned. 'Where's this leading?'

J ignored him. 'Enough of 7/7. What about 9/11? Rather bigger deal. Deaths in the thousands.'

'What the hell do you want me to say, J? That at least it had a bit of style about it?'

'That'll do,' said J cheerfully. 'You'll get along with our friend splendidly.'

J jumped up from the sofa with surprising agility to remove two files from his bag, which, Patrick noted, was, for variety's sake, a light tan rather than dreary brown. 'I realise some of this may seem like an interrogation,' he said mildly, 'but the thing about working in intelligence is that it does pay to be intelligent. It's all about the ability to get inside the other fellow's head.'

From the first slender file, J fished out three photographs, cropped to show head and shoulders. Two were fuzzy, the third in perfect focus; together, they composed not just a face but the beginnings of an expression. 'He's called Kareem,' said J. 'Full name Kareem Abdullah bin-Jilani. Well-off Gulf State family, English public school educated, good degree.' He bowed his head to peer over his glasses at Patrick. 'Bit like you. But somewhere along the line, the similarities end.' J retrieved the photographs and made a show of examining them. 'A couple of days ago we invited Kareem for a chat.'

'You invited him?'

'If you'll allow an elastic interpretation,' he replied.

'Kareem,' repeated Sara, slowly shaking her head. 'It seems impossible. And yet...' She left the thought unfinished.

They'd stopped in the middle of Vauxhall Bridge on the Westminster side – to the right MI5's cruise-liner frontage, to the left Millbank and Thames House beyond.

'Yes,' said Patrick, 'Kareem. The man you sat next to in

the restaurant. The man you already knew. Your turn to say something?'

'No,' she replied abruptly. 'We'll get to the end of your story first.'

He screwed his eyes at her, his disappointment obvious. Or was it dissatisfaction? Either way, she had to download him first; only then would she know what she needed to give back.

He sighed, turning from her to the river. 'OK. J gave me some background. How, since 9/11, whatever happened elsewhere in the world, they'd been successful at home. Plots were intercepted, plotters imprisoned. But then came 7/7…'

'You spoke of shock and the luck of life and death,' said J. 'My reaction to the 7th of July was anger. A fury that we didn't stop it. That we didn't know enough. Or, rather, that we had much of the knowledge but we didn't know how to prioritise it. Or make the right connections. We were an army bristling with rockets and guns but without a spotter behind enemy lines. We at MI5, MI6, Special Branch, NCIS – that's the National Criminal Intelligence Service, Patrick—'

'Yes, J, I know what NCIS is—'

'We all vowed better co-ordination. "Dare to share" became the new motto. Kareem was one of its first opportunities.'

J handed the photographs to Patrick. 'Look at him. Get to know him. Try to understand what's inside.'

'Don't I get to meet him?'

'Oh yes. You'll meet him all right.' J took a breath while Patrick obediently stared at the photographs. 'In fact it began well before 7/7. Back in late 2003. During the Christmas holidays, some Pakistani post-grads from Queen Victoria College, London, boarded an Air South Asia Express flight to Islamabad. One was called Kareem Abdullah bin-Jilani, twenty-six years old and writing a thesis on the mathematics of aerodynamics. Rather than turning right into the plane and heading for economy like the other five, he turned left into first. A stewardess noted how the group had separated and thought it unusual enough to inform the captain.'

He paused; Patrick, looking up from the photographs, was paying full attention. 'You've got to remember – it was less than two years since 9/11. And there had been the attempt by the "shoe bomber" to blow up an American plane in mid-air. The captain took an informal stroll through the first-class and economy cabins, eyeing them up. He saw nothing amiss but took two precautions. He ordered a manual check of the group's hold baggage and rearranged the seating plan to allow his two plain-clothes armed marshals to be in close sight of them.

'But the single PhD student sitting in first class kept niggling at him. He radio'd ahead to the airport to suggest that passport and customs might like to take a look. This request itself was so out of the ordinary that the airport authorities passed it on to ISI.'

'ISI?'

'The Pakistani intelligence service. You don't know everything, do you?' he said sharply. 'They in turn asked the local MI6 head of station if Kareem's name was on their files. He wasn't. From then on, he was.'

J rose, stretching his shoulders and neck. 'Ever been to Islamabad, Patrick?'

'No.'

'Wouldn't bother. Kareem lands, the MI6 man puts a cheap tail on him. Leaving the airport, he splits from the other five and takes a taxi to a four-star hotel. Day one, he doesn't emerge from his room. Day two, he visits the HSBC bank's local headquarters and the offices of a shipping and construction company. In the evening he stays in his hotel, ordering room service. Day three, he exits the hotel ground-floor lift – he's carrying a packed suitcase and wearing weather-beaten jeans, hiking boots and a khaki jacket. He pays his bill and strides out with purpose. The tail notes he rudely brushes aside a commissionaire offering to summon a taxi. He walks along the main street and an earth-spattered Range Rover draws up. He jumps in. The local watcher reports the car heads north-west out of the city in the rough direction of Shangla province. The number plate's obscured by baked mud but he says it's far from new and has a noticeable dent in the exterior of the front passenger door. The watcher doesn't have a car and there the tail ends. Limited intelligence which the station head sits on.

'But of course,' said J, now circling the small room, 'what the station head does have is the time and date of Kareem's return flight. Something intriguing happens. Again it's a first-class ticket but Kareem doesn't show up at the airport. The ticket's never cancelled or changed. That means two things. First, there's enough cash flowing around for the money to be waived. Second, it turns out after further checking that Kareem booked a completely new return flight with a different airline a week earlier than the original.'

'That could have been a decision on a whim by a spoilt rich boy,' said Patrick.

'Yes,' agreed J, eyes shining. 'However, the flight was to Amsterdam where Kareem hung out for a couple of days before changing to a domestic European flight to London.'

'Perhaps he was interested in marijuana cafés.'

'Indeed. Or Rembrandt.' They exchanged a quick grimace, a mutual understanding that the possible excuses were ceasing to add up. 'Put it this way. A series of mild, possibly meaningless actions but, pooled together, an indication at the very least of a man who did not wish to be intercepted on his way home.'

'Or, perhaps, a man who thought he was being watched

already,' said Patrick. 'Maybe the station head asked the tail not to be so invisible for once.'

'Smart, Patrick,' said J. 'I wondered if he did too. If so, he was too modest – or too cautious – to admit he rolled that particular dice.' J snatched a look at his watch. 'Good heavens, tea-time.'

J slid out of the room, pulling the door to with a gentle click. After two or three minutes, it struck Patrick that either J was summoning something more than a cup of tea or he was using the intermission for other purposes. He had a sense of being observed; presumably no room in this building was a private space. Or if not watched, at least listened to. His 'test' had simply shifted location from the restaurant to home base. Perhaps someone's ears had also been flapping while they had eaten their pizzas.

The door edged open and a face appeared around it. Not J but a middle-aged, bespectacled, long-skirted woman with fair hair, greying at the edges and tied into a loose bun. She looked surprised.

'Oh sorry,' she said throatily with a friendly smile. 'Didn't know it was occupied.' She paused, inspecting him. 'Can I help?'

'I'm fine, thank you,' said Patrick. 'He said he'll be back in a minute.' He sensed it would be wrong to mention that he was with J.

'Good.' She disappeared, shutting him in, without further questions.

A foot kicked open the door to reveal J carrying a tray with a china teapot, two cups and saucers, milk jug, sugar bowl and a small round chocolate cake. 'Supermarket fare, I'm afraid, best I could find in the kitchen. Our standards are slipping.' Not for the first time, Patrick felt wrong-footed. 'Milk before or after?'

'Is that another of your tests, J?' replied Patrick, recovering.

J gave a short chuckle. 'To continue. Kareem finally lands

in London after his circuitous journey and we take an interest. Not heavy – too much manpower for a tentative lead. But we go fishing in the cash river, have a gander at bank accounts – he had two in his own name and another three via nominees which we tracked back to him. Another small indicator – why would he need them? Payments are going to three imams who are on our radar and two charities organising rural UK "adventure" holidays for young Muslims. There are irregular but significant payments to two airlines flying to the Middle East and south Asia.'

'All of which could be genuine charitable and educational causes,' said Patrick.

'And there's his own charity too,' continued J, not answering. 'Islam in the Community. Discreet but a means of giving Kareem a presence. Here he now is, back in Britain – a good-looking, articulate young Muslim, charismatic even – with a network of contacts. But a different creature altogether from the rabid preachers. There's something sophisticated about him – agile, supple, lithe. And inscrutable.'

'You still had nothing concrete.'

'He begins to work the student Islamic Society circuit, initially in the Midlands and the North. One-day trips, innocent enough stuff, no apparently significant meetings. Then we hear he's on the bill in London at Queen Vic's. We decide to attend in person.'

'We?' said Patrick, eyebrows raised.

'Yes, a young lady there who's occasionally helpful to us.'

'Muslim?'

'Of course.'

'Name?'

'Really, Patrick, the questions you ask. More tea?' With a hint of ceremony, J topped up their cups, helped himself to a splash of milk and dropped in two lumps of sugar which he stirred in with great deliberation as if the circling stew of pale brown might contain unsuspected secrets of its own. 'We're logging the phone numbers Kareem's calling – cheap surveillance tool and surprisingly productive – it shows a call that morning to a red velvet-lined restaurant in W2 – London's little Arabia. We send along a girl and boy team, camera in his tie-pin, microphone and recorder in her handbag.' J took the second, thicker file from below the first and extracted a document and a single photograph. 'Pay dirt.'

Patrick examined the photograph; one face was just recognisable from the saturation press coverage of the 7/7 bombings, the profile of a second from the photographs J had already shown him. The backs of two female heads were in silhouette, impossible to identify. The document was a verbatim transcript of a multi-party conversation. 'Wow,' he said. 'Mohammad Sidique Khan dining with Kareem bin-Jilani.'

'Yes,' said J, 'wow, as you put it. The oddity is that this was taken because we were monitoring Kareem. Not Sidique Khan. His name had come up but he was never considered a serious threat. That was the tragedy.' He pointed to the transcript. 'When you plough through this, you can see that Kareem was unfamiliar with Sidique Khan. It was this other chap – turned out he's called Aaqil – who'd brought him along.'

'What about the others?'

'The girl with the hijab was – is – called Maryam Saeed Britaniyah, once upon a time the rather less exotic Marion Green. Middle-class family, wellish-heeled, she was working as a PA at a city hedge fund. Where, by coincidence, the bin-Jilani family had investments which Kareem, as the London presence, kept an eye on. She apparently fell in his thrall.'

'The other girl?'

'We put a tracker on her but she ended up clear. Not part

of the picture now. He tended to whisper to her so we didn't get much.'

'A tracker?'

'Yes, soft tail, not a combined op. Just two of ours. Girls, of course. Show respect and all that.'

'For how long?'

'Couple of months. I seem to recall she spent rather an uneventful summer.'

'You're saying I was under surveillance for two months,' said Sara dully. Up till now, she'd been listening in silence. 'Just because once at a restaurant I sat next to a man they suspected.'

The grey sky was blackening, promising rain. 'Let's move,' said Patrick, 'we'll go back and cross the road. There's a Pret we can take cover in.'

The skies opened as the pedestrian lights turned green to allow them over the bus lanes and carriageways, Sara protecting her head and scarf with her coat. Inside they dumped their bags and coats on a corner table at the back, furthest away from the counter. Sara settled, watching the onslaught of rain.

'Not as good as mine at the office,' said Patrick, returning with coffees. He forced a smile as he set plastic cups on the table.

She didn't move, eyes apparently magnetised by the downpour. 'He gave you a transcript,' she murmured.

'Yes.'

'Sayyid gave Morahan just the recording.'

'Less bulky. Or he couldn't access it.'

She thought. 'Or because what mattered was that he listened to the voices.' Silence as the depth of Sayyid's manipulation of Morahan sank in ever further.

'Shall we go back to the photograph?' Patrick asked softly. She nodded her head. 'I'd no idea it was you. I was never given a name. I didn't even know of you till now. But yes, according to J, the second woman in the photograph – you – was under surveillance for two months.'

'No wonder some of us hated them.'

'But wouldn't they have asked themselves the obvious question?' She turned. 'As I ask myself that question now.'

'Ask it.'

'What were you doing there?'

'Yes. It's the obvious question. But they could have come and asked me instead of watching me.'

'Perhaps. But you must see they might have thought you could lead them somewhere.'

She sipped her coffee and moved closer to him.

'It was a coincidence,' she said softly. 'The meeting sounded interesting. I'd no idea he'd be there. He recognised me and I thought it would be rude to refuse the invitation to join him and his friends for dinner.'

'He recognised you?'

'Yes.'

'What about the woman? The one J said was called Maryam, previously Marion.'

'I hadn't met her before.' She paused. 'I'd heard the name. When she was just Marion.' She paused. 'If this part of it ever becomes significant for what we're doing, I'll tell you. Right now it isn't. OK?'

Part of him wanted to test her – how could it possibly not be significant? – but he felt he'd touched some buried grief. It would come in time. 'Look…' he said, as if searching for consolation, 'I was never entirely sure I could believe every word J's big rich voice uttered. At least it's better than if you'd been the young Muslim woman helping MI5.'

'Could you have believed that of me?'

'Some might see it as patriotic.'

She inspected him, her eyes narrowing harshly. 'Perhaps you really could.'

'We were all younger then. Perhaps we all did things.' He breathed in deeply, a bead of sweat on his normally cool brow. 'I know I did.'

17

'Good morning, Patrick,' J bellowed, jumping up from a leather sofa in the back lounge of a rotunda style hotel on Cromwell Road and offering his hand. 'How extraordinarily nice to see you.'

He greeted Patrick with a delighted but puzzled smile, as if the last thing he expected was to bump into him at this place at this time. A grey-suited man and pink-skirted woman sitting in the opposite corner and dressed for executive action whipped round with pained disapproval. 'Just in case they might be interested,' said J *sotto voce*, gesturing Patrick to sit alongside. 'But happily that reaction says not. Coffee?' They sat, looking out upon a narrow stretch of green lawn, two floor-to-ceiling aluminium-framed windows lending the room an ugly functionality. 'Right. There's stuff you need to know and stuff you don't.'

J made a visual sweep, then produced a small silver rectangular object. In a tiny hole he plugged in the needle-like jack of a single earphone, handed it to Patrick, indicated to pop it in his ear, and switched on. Patrick found himself listening to a conversation; one voice, well-spoken and deep, was clear; the second presumably was at the end of a scratchy telephone line.

'It was a failure,' said the first voice.

'I don't understand…'

'Too inelegant. Too unfocused. Too indiscriminate.'

'It's not easy.'

'It was wrong.'

The conversation cut out, replaced by a hiss. 'That was friend Kareem,' said J, 'apparently showing some remorse.'

Patrick himself checked the room, removed the ear phone and returned it to J. 'He could have been putting it on.'

'Yes. But not in my – our – view to the person we think he was speaking to.'

'Our?'

'To come,' replied J sharply. 'He's been caught dining out a month before with the lead bomber of 7/7, it shows he's implicated. We've also now got a financial trail a criminal mile long. That's why we decided it was time to bring him in for a chat.' J took a final gulp of coffee and crashed the cup back onto its saucer. 'He's going to be your new friend.'

He grabbed his brown coat off the sofa arm, jumped nimbly up and strode out of the room. In the hotel lobby, without stopping, he stretched out a hand for a brown trilby on a hatstand and skipped down the front steps, Patrick trailing in his wake. A sharp shower, filtered through arrows of sunlight, was bouncing shiny pellets of water off the pavement. J put on the trilby and turned to Patrick. 'Important lesson of life, never be caught without a hat.' A hundred yards or so down Cromwell Road, he made the diagonal turn into Lexham Gardens. Patrick peered up through the rain to the tall terraces of stucco-fronted Victorian houses. Perhaps it was J's presence that moved him to see them as a box-set of anonymous hidey-holes for the affluent; the sort of place where a certain sort of gentleman might house his mistress – or an intelligence agency its spy.

J stopped at the seventh house on the south-east side of the street and descended the basement steps. The external door opened before him; he entered, waving Patrick in with uncharacteristic energy. A lean-faced, wiry figure dressed in a chauffeur's uniform, his black hair greased down to preserve a crisp parting, glanced out and closed the door.

'Good morning, Len,' said J.

'Good morning, Mr J,' came the reply in a strong Ulster accent. For some reason, Patrick instantly imagined him as J's one-time silent assassin.

'This young man is called Patrick, we'll be seeing more of him.'

Len stuck out a hand. 'Pleased to meet you, sir.'

Patrick read the 'sir' as the gnarled sergeant-major's nod to the raw officer cadet. He realised he hadn't asked J the obvious question. 'You never said why you're bringing me here.'

'Didn't I?' he replied ingenuously. 'Kareem's asked to see a solicitor.'

'A solicitor?'

'Yes, thought you'd have figured that out.'

'Whose side am I on?'

The reply was raised eyebrows. 'You're about to meet the person in charge of this little operation,' said J. 'Ask her if you want.'

'Aren't you?'

'Good lord, no, I'm a mere outrider these days with the occasional idea.'

'Anyway, what operation?'

J grinned. 'Stuff you don't need to know, Patrick. She's called Isobel Le Marchant, rising star of the service. If she gets this right, she'll be headed straight for the top.'

They walked down a passage past a study-like room – Len's domain, Patrick assumed – then an opening into a kitchen, followed by a closed door. J opened it, switched on the light and peered in, Patrick at his shoulder. It was a large bedroom, no window, two abstract paintings on stone-coloured walls, an en-suite bathroom leading off. The bath, shower and basin taps were gold; a scent of lavender sweetened the enclosed air. 'Gloriously vulgar,' said J. He scanned both rooms. 'Just want to make sure someone's bleaching the loo.'

They continued to a wider wood-panelled door at the end of the passage. J knocked and entered without waiting for a reply. A spacious room stretched out, the end glass panels revealing a small basement courtyard with high whitewashed brick walls. At the room's centre was a rectangular table, also glass, with two mounds of magazines and catalogues; among them Patrick could see copies of *Country Life* and a catalogue for a recent Old Masters' auction at Christie's. Between them lay a tray containing a large cafétière full to the brim, white china milk jug and sugar bowl, four piled saucers and four cups. Two white-leather sofas at ninety degrees to each other were grouped around the table, separated at the corner by an oversize television. The natural subterranean darkness was relieved by a dazzling montage of sunken ceiling spotlights, a slender serpentine trail of smoke from a resting cigarette curling its way through their shafts of illumination.

Two figures rose from a sofa. The taller one was wearing brushed blue jeans and a crisp white linen shirt. His jet-black hair was neatly cut, allowed at the back to fall to the base of his neck. A cropped, shaped beard and moustache enhanced the symmetry and angularity of a starkly defined face, straight nose and almost black eyes, topped by brooding lashes and brows. The beardless spaces of skin and neck were of a spotless purity, unusual in such a masculine face.

The other figure was also tall and slim, a tight-fitting cream skirt stopping at the knee, below which were incongruously stocky legs. Her pale hair was on the turn to grey, but delayed in its progress by blonde highlights creating tiny waves on layers descending to a taper on the shoulders. A pink shirt outlined slim breasts and upper body but the face itself was plainish, neither ugly nor alluring, hazel eyes sunken, nose just too thin and long, lips falling short of generous.

J stopped short of the glass table which separated them. 'Isobel. Kareem.' He glanced at Patrick. 'May I introduce Patrick Duke. He's come in response to your request, Kareem.'

'My request?' said Kareem. A man, Patrick instantly suspected, more used to delivering orders than asking questions.

'You wanted a solicitor,' said J.

Kareem looked Patrick up and down. They were both tall, lean, athletic men; the contrast was the colour of their skins, black and tan. Patrick, in a charcoal grey suit, striped shirt and blue tie was the more formally dressed but, somehow, less elegant. Kareem presented a gliding, harmonious flow from top to bottom; it appeared to be attracting the rapt attention of the woman standing beside him.

'So,' said Kareem, with an audible hiss, 'you are a solicitor.'

'Yes, sir,' said Patrick, adopting a suitably deferential relationship to his 'client'.

'At least you have manners. You may call me Kareem.' He looked across to J. 'Others were not always so courteous. Is my relationship with my solicitor confidential?'

'Of course, Kareem,' said Isobel. Patrick noticed that J did not react at her assumption of command. The voice was deep, the accent classless; he wondered whether she had changed it upwards to match the clubbiness of the intelligence services at the time, well over two decades before, when she would have been recruited. Or perhaps, when the organisations themselves changed to be open to all, she adapted – a posh girl from a well-connected family assimilating to the new egalitarianism.

'Thank you, Isobel,' said Kareem, enveloping her in a radiant smile.

She smiled back and turned to J, reshaping the creases as a frown. 'Shall we make ourselves scarce?' J cast a regretful glance at the undrunk cafétière and followed her out of the room.

'Come, Patrick,' said Kareem, waving him towards the sofa. 'Now you can tell me why they selected you.'

'I've no idea.'

'Perhaps it is because you are black and I am brown. The Nigger and the Arab.'

'Why would they do that?'

'Because they misunderstand the racism that might divide you and me – or because they understand it all too well.'

'You overestimate them.'

'In any case, neither you nor I would fall for it as we do not share their own racial misconceptions.'

'Correct. I was just the next cab on the rank.'

'The rank of Her Majesty's Government's Treasury Solicitors.'

'Why do you make that assumption?'

'Because it is true, of course. There is no need to embarrass yourself by confirming or denying it. You also are a young and inexperienced lawyer who might do as he is told.'

'You're my client, Kareem,' said Patrick. The taunting liberated him. However many secret cameras and buried microphones were being watched and listened to by Len, whoever he was, no doubt with Isobel and J alongside, he would play the role they'd allotted him under his own rules. 'I take my instructions only from you.'

Kareem shrugged. 'No matter. Let us start with how I come to be here.'

'They'll be monitoring,' said Patrick.

'Of course they will be.' Patrick hoped the admission would build confidence but it cut no ice. He needed to be smarter. The speech patterns of the man beside him were an indication of a precise mind, perhaps also a need to show perfect mastery of a second language. No contractions, every word delineated, all in the same modulated, clipped pitch. A man who had learnt not to raise his voice, whatever might seethe inside.

'However,' continued Kareem, 'this part of the story is about their actions, not mine.' He stood and peered at the ceiling, addressing it in the same monotone. 'Why does one of you not come and retrieve the coffee you left behind? Let us not be the cause of waste.' He turned to Patrick. 'Unless you would like to pour yourself a cup first.'

Patrick attempted a conspiratorial smile. 'I'll leave it for them. J is always thirsty.'

'Yes, J. A fluid, slippery character.' He moved closer, lowering his voice. 'The woman is more to be trusted. Not unattractive, do you think?' The voice was not low enough to evade the invisible listeners – deliberately so, Patrick assumed. A small move in whatever game Kareem was playing. 'They brought me here illegally.'

'How?'

'I believe the correct word is kidnap. I was walking near my flat. It is a quiet residential street. A large black car with tinted windows drew up. Three men jumped out and bundled me inside, placing me on the back seat between two of them. They were fast and professional.'

'Did you try to resist?'

'I do not deploy personal violence.'

Kareem leant towards the table and extracted a cigarette from a pack of black Russian Sobranies. Beside it was a gold Dunhill lighter. He drew lightly from the filter-tip and exhaled a gentle plume of smoke. 'They supplied the cigarettes. It is good when people do their research. The lighter, however, is mine. Perhaps their budget could not match it.' Taking another draw, he gazed at the bricked courtyard through the window panels; Patrick detected in him a satisfaction, pride even.

He rested the cigarette on a glass ashtray sitting on the sofa arm. 'After twenty minutes or so we arrived. I had the impression that a space in front of the house had been vacated. The man who spoke in the car showed me the rooms, invited me to make myself at home and inquired whether I would like any refreshment. He said a visitor would soon arrive.' He looked up again at the ceiling. 'This was J.'

'What were your first impressions of him?'

'I thought he was somewhat scruffy. I was initially more interested that he was carrying a case from my flat, neatly packed with clothing, a washbag, an assembly of necessities from my bathroom.' He smiled fleetingly. 'Perhaps that was cheaper too – saved them buying new.'

'They entered your flat.'

'Yes, burglary. Add that to the charge sheet.' Patrick produced a slim notepad and pencil from his chest pocket. 'Put it away, there is no need.' He paused. 'I realise this will get me nowhere – I understand what they call deniability.'

'We have laws in this country.'

Kareem shook his head with a dismissive smile. 'We will not debate that. J introduced himself, told me his position at MI5, and declared how delighted he was to meet me in person after observing me for so long. I assured him that the pleasure was entirely mine. Then he dangled his bait – I remember the words verbatim. "You are free to leave this flat any time you wish," he began. "However, should you do so, you will be immediately arrested by the Special Branch of the Metropolitan Police. There is sufficient evidence, legally obtained through the correct warrants, for you to be given a double-digit prison sentence for money-laundering and conspiracy to finance and commit terrorist acts. I am here to suggest that we spend a little time discussing an alternative. From something you recently said to one of your colleagues, I think that you might be interested."'

Kareem stood up abruptly, grabbed the pack of cigarettes even though the first one was still burning in the ashtray and walked over to the glass doors. He stared out, reflecting, it seemed, on the immensity of his predicament. For a moment the veneer of pride dulled briefly with a dropping of his shoulders. He straightened and swivelled.

'Join me,' he commanded. Patrick moved alongside him by the glass. 'These panels open. If I ask, we can step outside, the rain has stopped. What do you see there?'

Patrick decided not to play clever. 'A table. Metal fretwork. Matching chairs. Brick walls. A wisteria that's shed its flowers.'

'I meant – what do you *see*?' repeated Kareem.

'If you insist. There's no apparent way out.'

'Well done, Patrick.'

'Unless J's bluffing.'

Kareem smiled gently. 'Are you even allowed to suggest that?'

'I told you, I'm here for you.'

'He was not bluffing.'

'Do you have regrets?' asked Patrick.

'That's enough,' said Kareem. 'Be careful where you tread.'

The guard was back up; Patrick understood this man had no desire for friendship. Any relationship was professional only. 'You want legal help. What can I do for you?'

'Further conversations have taken place. It turns out that they are, in effect, offering me a job.'

'What job?'

'That is not for you.'

'What is for me?'

'I want you to arrange a contract. A proper legal contract.'

'He wanted a contract!' Sara exclaimed, allowing herself to shout against the noise of splashing and passing buses and lorries.

As soon as the rain had ceased, Patrick had insisted they move on; they were now on the Albert Embankment riverside pavement heading towards Lambeth Bridge where, he said, they would cross the river and complete the circuit. Sara was unsure whether Patrick's 'passing the police station' theory was invention, convenience or learnt expertise. As his route took in MI6, the approaches to the Houses of Parliament and MI5, it was certainly thorough. Perhaps the real reason, which he'd left unstated for her sake, was that safety was best found in high-profile public places. None of this stopped her regularly looking around and behind; nor, she noted, did it stop him.

'A contract,' she repeated more softly. 'For a man who, by his own admission, would be found guilty of terrorist conspiracy in a court of law.'

'Yes,' said Patrick. 'But he was canny. He must have seen how much they wanted him. J would have played it cool, but I wondered at the time whether Isobel Le Marchant had betrayed desperation.'

'To beat the bombers or get herself to the top?'

'That's unusually cynical of you, Sara. She's a woman in a man's world and she's made it. Dame Isobel Le Marchant, Director General of MI5.'

'Not the first one though,' said Sara. 'Or even the second.'

'Quite so. After they'd allowed it twice, how much harder it must have been for her to complete the hat-trick. She would have needed constant success.'

'But we don't know what that "success" was. Or what Kareem's job was to be.'

'No.'

'We have to assume that all Sayyid's clues and information connect,' said Sara. 'So he's operating out of some kind of interrogation base as "the Adviser". And the Blackburn files are a window into it.'

'Yes,' agreed Patrick. 'Glimpses. But no more. No sense of the scale Sayyid's suggesting. Or where his activities – whatever they precisely were – end up.'

'No. We've lost Morahan, we've almost certainly lost Sayyid too. Maybe we've lost ourselves.'

Before Patrick had time to respond, her mobile rang. 'Hello… Are you there? Who is this?'

She shot a puzzled look at Patrick, shaking her head. She jerked up, on instant alert, marching forward in excitement, Patrick the one now keeping up. 'Yes, Mrs Green… She really does, does she?… You think straightaway… tomorrow, yes, I'll come, I'll change plans… Thank you, I'll jot it down…' She gestured to Patrick to pass her pen and paper and began frantically to write. 'Yes, I understand, I'll try not to… Midday tomorrow then… Thank you so much, Mrs Green, goodbye.'

She put the phone away, buried her face in her hands and stopped in her tracks, leaning against the railings overlooking the river. Patrick waited for the seconds to pass. 'I heard breathing. It felt like a woman. Then her mother took the receiver.'

'Hold on, Sara. Who?'

'Marion. Maryam.'

'The other woman in the photograph?'

His question went unanswered. 'Why?' she murmured. 'How?' He'd never seen her eyes wild like this. 'The paparazzi. She must have seen the photo of me… of me and you. I guess it was in papers everywhere. Then all the TV coverage.' She paused. 'But she's got my mobile number. What does she want from me?'

He moved close to her. She seemed brittle, a twig on the verge of snapping.

'Does it connect to whatever you haven't told me about Kareem?' he asked gently.

She stayed silent, thinking back to that one time they'd met – the subdued, fragile young woman in Kareem's thrall. Yes, of course. It had to be. The girl who became the epitome of beauty Sami once beheld. Now she could imagine how he must have been stirred – and terrified. She harked back again to the dinner. A faint memory of passing a scrap of paper with her number on it. Her phones had changed… but her number always stayed the same.

Her moment of reverie was interrupted. 'Remember,' said Patrick, 'all you've said is that you once had a dinner conversation with Kareem, purely by coincidence, and that he recognised you.' He hesitated. 'You must know the tape suggests you weren't total strangers.'

They locked eyes. 'Let me see her first.'

'I should come with you.'

'No. This time, I'm going alone.'

18

'I'll drive you there and back,' said Tariq Shah.

'Dad, it's miles,' replied Sara. 'You can take me to Clapham Junction.'

'You shouldn't be on your own. Not after those men in the car.'

Tariq fiddled with a shortbread biscuit, dunking it in and out of his evening mug of tea, unsure how inquisitive his daughter might allow him to be. 'What's the truth of it all, Sara?'

'Dad, I honestly don't know. It was probably just a heart attack.'

'Was he found the way they're saying? Horrible thing for you to witness. Disgusting.'

'We can't always see into the minds and bodies of others.' She laid a hand on his palm. 'It will soon calm down. Those men haven't been back, have they?'

'Maybe not,' he said forlornly. 'But how do we know?' He jumped up from this seat, as if to deliver a speech to her. 'I still don't think you should be travelling alone to all ends of the country interviewing people you've never met. How do you know there won't be an axe-man in the cellar waiting to pounce?'

She laughed, putting her hands on his shoulders. 'At least you haven't lost your sense of humour. It's a sleepy village in Devon, not downtown Kabul.'

'They may be inbred. You don't know what these English country bumpkins get up to when the moon is out.'

She gave him a kiss. 'The train leaves at 8.10. A lift to the station would be lovely.' The kiss became a quick hug and, as she broke away and headed upstairs, he stirred his tea gloomily and munched the biscuit.

The taxi took her through Honiton's picture-book high street, lined with olde-worlde antique shops and whole-food cafés, into the beginnings of a long, wide valley. It was enfolded by gently rising, luxuriantly green fields, divided by orderly hedgerows and dotted with copses of beech and birch. A comforting landscape, the hills of Devon not too intimidating, the horizon open without being endless, the ridges tapering harmoniously into a serene blue sky. On this bright day, it was an arm of England extending an affectionate hug. A place where a fractured mind might come to heal.

A tiny doubt seized her. Could she be heading into some kind of trap? Surely not – Mrs Green's voice and accent matched this gentle patch of conformity. Yet how had she known... the taxi, slowing down to go through a small gate, arrested the thought.

Sara stepped out onto a short gravel driveway leading to a perfectly white bungalow, its flawless paintwork reflecting the sun. She walked up the drive, stopping at a window to adjust her blue scarf to reveal just the front fold of her hair and rang the doorbell. Though its ding-dong was loud and clear, there was no answer. She counted the seconds, then, more as a nervous tic, took her phone from her handbag and checked her diary. There was no false memory of place, date or time. She rang the bell again. A flurry of footsteps on gravel followed immediately.

A shortish figure, grey hair, spectacles hanging over a check shirt, appeared breathlessly from around the side of the house. 'I'm so sorry, I've kept you waiting.'

Sara recognised the voice from the phone call. 'Not at all. Mrs Green?'

'Yes.' She raised the glasses and gave her a quick look up and down. 'And you're Sara, of course.' She did not offer a hand to shake, appearing in too much of a hurry to retrace her steps. 'I've been trying to get Marion to sit outside. She probably won't.'

Sara's expression spelt a silent question.

'Agoraphobia. At least that's what the diagnosis became. Though it might have been given several names as it's so unpredictable. One consultant said she was suffering post-traumatic stress disorder. It was part of the reason to find this place for her – the hope that if any surrounding wouldn't frighten her, this might be it. No noise or cars, no endless sea or expanses, but not too enclosed either.'

'I didn't know...' began Sara.

'Why would you?' Her response sounded severe; Sara suspected it was just her manner, aggravated by the suffering and frustration of dealing with a damaged daughter. Mrs Green offered a handshake. 'Sorry, it takes me over. I don't like formality. Call me Elizabeth.'

'How long has Marion... Maryam...'

'Stick to Marion – though it can change.'

'How long has she had this?'

'Since we got her back. Off and on.' Elizabeth Green sighed. 'Over ten years now. Almost eleven, in fact.'

'You got her back?'

Elizabeth did not elaborate. 'Come and ask her yourself. I don't know what you'll get out of her. It goes up and down.'

They stepped through French windows into a sitting room. Sara itched to ask how they'd known where to find her but she sensed that Mrs Green wanted to get straight back to her daughter; it would be a mistake to interrupt her. She must bide her time; maybe it would emerge naturally.

A wispy figure, holding one hand to the side of her face, sat on an armchair at right angles to the invading shafts of sunlight. Elizabeth headed for a sofa opposite and gestured Sara to sit down beside her. The woman in the chair was skeletally thin, wearing a pale cotton blouse which drooped over small breasts and a loose-fitting white skirt. Though the day was fine and the sun strong, Sara could feel the artificial warmth of radiators. She stole a look at Elizabeth, seeking her guidance; it was returned with a nod.

'Hello, Marion,' Sara said quietly. The face opposite raised itself and the hand moved from the right cheek to rub both eyes. She squinted, trying to focus. 'I'm Sara. We met once. You… your mother… phoned me.'

'Yes, of course, of course.' The face was suddenly animated, eyes blinking rapidly. 'Sara. Sara Shah. You came.' She turned to her mother. 'Mama, it's Sara Shah, have you met her?'

'Yes, darling, we introduced ourselves. When I mentioned her name to you, you said you wanted to see her.'

'Did I? Yes, I think I did.'

'Why did you want to see me, Marion?' asked Sara.

'Don't you know? You must know. My Kareem. He talked about you sometimes.'

'He talked about me?'

'Oh yes, all the time.' Marion stretched out her left hand to a photograph in a silver frame on a side table and handed it to Sara. 'Shareef. Our son.'

Sara stared at the photograph of a boy around ten or eleven years old, she guessed, with the unmistakable features of his father; the straight lines of jaw, chin and nose, the full head of wavy black hair and dark brown eyes staring soulfully into the camera. Only his skin was different, a tone or two lighter.

'He's a beautiful boy, Marion.' She handed the photo back; Marion held it close to her face, her eyes relaxing as she silently and absently gazed at it.

Sara saw that the true child was Marion. She wondered whether to break into the reverie or let it pass and again looked to Elizabeth for instruction. This time the response was a shrug. Sara told herself there was no point in coming here if she did not at least try.

'Did you live with Kareem, Marion?'

Marion stared into the middle distance. Using Sami's information, Sara risked a further hunch. 'Do you remember the place where you lived? Was it like a farm?'

'A farm.' Marion paused – it seemed she was now making a rational effort to remember. Her eyes lit up. 'Yes. A big farm. Down in the dark valley. Hills all around. Our high table in the big hall.'

'What was your high table for?'

'It was exciting. He said it was our new mission. I would be his queen.'

'What was the mission?'

Marion's face distorted into an ugly combination of menace and thrill. 'To find traitors. We were hunting traitors.'

'Traitors to what?'

'Traitors, traitors, traitors.' Her eyes whipped past Sara and Elizabeth onto the interior wall opposite. 'I went to see them in the cells. When he told me to.'

'Was one of them called Sami?'

Marion concentrated ever more fiercely on the wall. Sara wondered whether she was hiding in its blank space or some kind of vision was appearing on it.

'Yes, Sami. And others. I don't know what happened.'

'What did Kareem tell you to do?'

'He wanted them to confess.'

'Confess to what?'

'Confess,' she repeated, her voice draining away. Her face dropped, both hands closed over it, and a frantic nodding overwhelmed her. 'There was screaming, the animals screaming,' she wailed.

'Enough,' said Elizabeth quietly. She went over to her daughter, wrapped her arms around her body and pulled her close. 'It's all right, Marion.' She stroked the back of her rocking head. 'You don't need to do this. You're safe now.' The agitation subsided; Marion sunk into her chair, reverting to the drooping figure Sara had seen when she'd entered the room.

Elizabeth pulled herself away. 'Come into the kitchen, I'll make coffee.'

'Will she be all right?'

'Yes, it's not unusual. It used to be panic attacks, sweats, dizziness, racing heartbeats, yelling that she's going to die. Now she tends to do this. Her way of coping, not as bad as it looks.' She smiled weakly. 'Sometimes I think she might mend.'

Elizabeth shut the kitchen door behind them – its top half was a broad pane of glass with Marion's chair in its line of sight. 'We'll never know exactly what happened. The psychiatrists rather enjoy the mystery of the different causes of agoraphobia. And the different effects it can have. A sudden shock, violence, living under the constant oppression of a man like him—'

'Did you believe he was violent?'

Elizabeth, busying herself with setting cups and saucers on a tray, did not immediately reply. She stopped fiddling, put hands on hips and looked severely at Sara. 'I think I should know what you're really in search of, young lady.'

'Yes, you have every right to. But first, would you mind

telling me how and why you got in touch with me? I assume it must have been that photograph in the newspapers.'

'Photograph?' Elizabeth, puzzled, picked up a mobile from a shelf. 'It's Marion's. I keep it with me when she's like this.' She clicked, scrolled and clicked again. 'Read this.'

Dear Marion. Sara Shah would like to get in touch and meet up with you. You may remember seeing her some years ago at a dinner. And I expect Kareem talked to you about her. She's now a lawyer. I think it may be helpful for you to see her. It will give you a greater understanding. I will text you her mobile number separately.

'Do you know anything about this?' Elizabeth demanded.

'No,' said Sara, hoping her surprise – and shock – didn't show. 'It's extremely odd.'

'It certainly is. I thought you may be able to throw light on it.'

'No… I'll try to think who it might be…' She detected a trace of anger in her interrogator and knew the inadequacy of her response. 'Did you try to reply to it?'

'Yes. But the message didn't get through for some reason. I tried again but no good. Not that it mattered,' said Elizabeth, checking on Marion through the glass. 'I googled your name and "lawyer" and found your Chambers' website. There was a short announcement saying that you were being seconded for three months to the Morahan Inquiry.'

'I didn't realise my Chambers had done that,' said Sara. Not that that mattered now either – the press photograph had destroyed any attempt at discretion. Still stunned by the anonymous text, she was grateful that Elizabeth seemed to be taking charge.

'Be that as it may,' continued Elizabeth. 'I felt perhaps that enabling Marion to speak to you might unlock something that could help her. I fear it hasn't.'

Sara told herself to concentrate only on Elizabeth. 'At least she talked. And coherently…'

'Until the animal screams came.'

'The screams may have been real.'

'What do you mean?' Elizabeth asked sharply. 'Does Marion have anything to fear?' Elizabeth Green could be intimidating, thought Sara, wondering whether that might once have affected her daughter. 'I promise you, Marion will never be drawn into this.'

'Drawn into what exactly? That's my point.' She hesitated. 'After locating you, I read up on the Morahan Inquiry. To be honest, I was the one who really wanted to meet you. Selfish of me perhaps.'

'Why selfish?'

'Because Marion's interest should be paramount. And I may not have allowed it to be.'

'I'm glad you made contact, Mrs Green—'

'Elizabeth. Please.'

'Sorry.' Elizabeth allowed a reconciliatory smile and took the tray to a kitchen table. From there too, the reclined figure of Marion remained visible. 'I said you have every right to know what I'm doing,' continued Sara. 'It seems that Kareem may be relevant to the Inquiry. He may have had some kind of involvement with extremist imams, vetting potential recruits for their so-called jihad. But it's hazy and there's no such thing as a reliable witness when one tries to probe.'

Elizabeth took a sip of coffee and a quick glance at her daughter. 'I don't know,' she said.

Sara's antennae went on red alert. 'Don't know what, Elizabeth?'

'Whether to tell you.'

'I beg you to. You have my promise that what you tell me will be treated in confidence.'

'You see, we went there.'

'Where?' Sara asked softly, hiding her excitement.

'It was June 2007. Marion had drifted away from us – we'd heard nothing from her for two years. About 5.30 a.m. one day the phone went. Normally we'd have ignored it but for some reason my husband, Denis – he's died since...'

'I'm sorry...'

'Yes, I always feel it's what killed him... anyway he must have been awake – always rose with the lark – and went downstairs to answer it. It was a short call. He came up and simply said, "She needs rescuing." That's all, he was so shaken. He said, "I'm going now." I said, "I'm coming with you." He tried to stop me. "I know it's that man and I might kill him," he said. "That's exactly why I'm coming," I said.'

'"That man" meaning Kareem,' suggested Sara.

'Yes. We'd only met him twice. He came to stay with us once here in Devon. It was August 2001. We had rather a nice country house but I sold it after Denis died to find something more practical for Marion and the boy. And me, as it's turned out...'

'August 2001? Are you sure?' Sara chided herself for allowing any consternation to slip.

'Of course, why shouldn't I be?'

'Nothing. Nothing at all,' she said, trying to recover. 'Just seems so long ago.'

'Not to me. He was unforgettable. Charming, polite, extraordinarily handsome. But a skin and soul of polished armour. You had no idea what might lie beneath. You could see she was hanging on his every word, obeying every command. Because command is what it felt like when he addressed her.' Elizabeth was in thrall to a remembered image that seemed to burst into life before her.

'And the second time?'

'We'd come up to London, staying in Denis's club as usual. We'd phoned ahead – normally Marion was busy but this time she accepted our offer of dinner and asked if she could bring him. Of course, we said. It was autumn 2003. Apart from the beard – at least it was neatly trimmed – his appearance hadn't changed. He was courteous, but aloof. No small talk. The only time he became engaged was to give us a lecture on the folly of British and American foreign policy. As it happened, we found little to disagree with but he delivered it with an air of superiority that Denis found insufferable. "I've got to get her away from that man," he said later. I told him there was nothing to do but lie low and wait, she'd have to see through him for herself.'

'Was Marion working?' asked Sara. She calculated the time-line of Kareem's progress, fitting it into Patrick's chronology. The simultaneities of the summer of 2001 would have to wait.

'She'd given up at the hedge fund and I think she just trailed after him. She had a little money of her own but he clearly had plenty, though I never gathered what he actually did to earn it.'

'I suspect he didn't need to.'

Elizabeth peeped through the door glass and went into the sitting room. Sara watched her raise Marion in her seat and puff up the cushion behind her. She placed a book, a marker inserted a few pages in, onto her lap, took her right hand and lay it on the cover. A mother who was not ready to give up the quest to repair her daughter's mind.

She returned to the kitchen with a quizzical expression. 'Did you know Kareem?' she asked.

The question came from nowhere; Sara felt it like an arrow to the heart. 'No,' she smartly replied. 'No, I didn't.'

'You seem awfully well-informed about him.'

Sara raised her eyebrows. 'Do I? I hope so. Certain things have come to light. It's my job to pull them together.'

'I'm not sure I should be telling you any of this. This kitchen's becoming a confessional.'

'If so, I am the priest. It all stays between you and me.'

'All?'

Sara found herself unable to lie. 'All except one thing. The location of this so-called farm. I will never say how I got the information.'

'And today never happened.'

'Yes.'

'All right.' Elizabeth allowed herself to relax, her mind made up, and paused to summon the energy and memory for her story. 'Marion did one clever thing. She'd remembered the postcode. I assume she got it from his SatNav – they were a relative rarity then but that young man always equipped himself with the latest gadgets.' Realising she must allow the flow, Sara stopped herself asking if she still had the postcode. 'All she'd said to Denis was, "I've got to get out". He asked her, "Where, Marion, where are you?" She gave him the postcode, whispered, "I can hear him coming," and the phone went dead. We chucked a few things in a case, he drove far too fast up the M5, onto the M4 and across the River Severn. I remember the low sun behind us lighting the gateway into Wales. Denis liked toys too so he also had a SatNav. By 8 a.m. we were past Abergavenny and Brecon, imagining her captive somewhere in that mass of green. I couldn't get death out of my mind and kept imagining those rounded mountain tops as giant burial mounds.'

Elizabeth broke off, still, eleven years later, shivering with the dread that had beset her that morning. She walked over to the window, staring out at the postage stamp of front lawn for a few seconds and then returned to refill the kettle. 'God, I think I might need something stronger to get through all this.'

'Please do,' said Sara.

'What about you?'

'I don't drink but don't let me stand in your way.'

Elizabeth inspected her again and smiled weakly. 'No, you wouldn't. I'm afraid I find it helps.' She went into the sitting room, reappeared with a bottle of gin and took a cold can of tonic from the fridge.

Watching her pour, Sara decided the moment was right. 'Do you still have the postcode?'

Elizabeth pinged open the tonic. 'Yes, you're bound to ask that. The answer is no but I can show you near enough on a map.' She brought her drink to the table and sat down. 'Now you know where, do you need more?'

'It all helps. So much is about understanding him.'

'It must have been around nine that we found ourselves crawling down a narrow lane. The SatNav got us this far but they can't have had the precision of today – so we were following instinct. We passed one or two single barns and sheds but they didn't feel big or cared-for enough for someone like Kareem. I remember Denis saying it must also be secured; we should look for locked gates. We travelled up and down a couple of times – one wonders now whether he had spotters watching us – and then off a track and just beyond a stone pillar, we saw a possibility. Denis turned down it and there it was. A solid double gate with two CCTV cameras at each corner and an entry phone. He got out of the car and pushed the buzzer. No answer. He tried again. Still no answer. He pushed a third time; when there was still no answer he yelled into the speaker phone that if no one came to the gate he would ram it with the car and force entry himself.'

'Would he have?'

'He might have, his blood was up. I kept quiet. Any interference from me would have made it worse. The gate began to swing open. And there was Kareem, dressed in a sweater and jeans. It was hard to say if he was smiling or smirking.'

'Not wearing anything more ceremonial?' asked Sara. 'Like a robe or tunic.'

'I don't remember anything like that. Denis said, "I want my daughter back." Didn't even bother with a hello. Kareem – he was as cool and urbane as ever – replied, "Your daughter chooses to stay here with me." "That's not what she told me four hours ago," said Denis. Kareem claimed she'd just had a scare in the night and was fine now. Denis marched towards what looked like the front door. "I would rather you did not go there, Mr Green," warned Kareem. "You would be trespassing." "If you don't allow me to see my daughter within the next thirty seconds," Denis said, "I'll summon the police and report you for kidnapping." I remember Kareem gave him the strangest smile. "That will be difficult as your mobile phone will receive no signal here." He seemed remarkably confident – as if he was untouchable. Then, unaccountably, he changed tack. "Of course you may see your daughter, Mr Green. But may I remind you that we are here for calm retreat, which you are interrupting."'

'What sort of place was it?' asked Sara.

'I could only judge from the outside. What seemed the main house was dark stone, leaded windows, coal-coloured slate roof. Then at right angles there was a sort of barn but again stone-built, each end whitewashed. A series of outbuildings stretched off, piggeries and stabling, I imagine. It was a decent-sized complex. If it wasn't for the idea of Kareem as a working farmer being absurd, it would have been just a farm in the middle of nowhere. But his demeanour and the security made it seem like some sort of cult centre.'

'Yes, I can imagine. Sorry, I interrupted.'

'It was odd. After all the bravado, it fizzled out. Kareem said he would fetch Maryam – as he called her – and asked us to wait outside. His greatest anxiety was that we shouldn't go inside. I felt he'd made a quick decision. He wouldn't fight to keep her. When he reappeared through the front door with her a few minutes later, she was carrying a suitcase. He turned to her almost off-handedly; "Here is your father, Maryam, he has come to collect you." As if she wasn't worth the fuss and he didn't care too much. She'd served her purpose and he'd wrung her dry.'

Elizabeth raised her glass with an unsteady hand and drank. 'You're the first person I've described it to in such detail. There was never a reason to. Marion was just another of life's casualties.'

'Did she speak about it?' asked Sara. 'At the time, I mean. Before the shock fully set in.'

'No. That was the sadness. On that four-hour journey home, she didn't say a word. Not one. I sat in the back trying to engage her. She let me put an arm round her but that was it. I noticed her wrists were heavily bruised and asked her why. She didn't reply. Then, just as we turned into the drive at home, she looked up at me, said, "I'm going to have a baby," and started to cry.'

Elizabeth's eyes glistened and a single tear crept down a cheek. She reached for a tissue, wiped it off and blew her nose. 'I'm so sorry,' said Sara.

'Don't be. He's a nice boy. She just hasn't been able to be a mother to him. He's at boarding school now and I look after him here during holidays. So I've got to stay alive till he's grown-up.' She smiled at Sara through shining, wet eyes.

'Did Kareem ever get in touch about the boy?'

'Never. If you're thinking he might not have realised, I know damn well he did.' It was the first time Elizabeth had shown anger.

'Yes,' said Sara with a certainty that surprised her; she shouldn't have let it escape. 'And there was no thought of

going after him to take responsibility as a father?' she continued quickly.

'No, we just wanted never to see him again. However much
Denis might have liked him punished.'

'He had money.'

'May he rot in hell with it.' She glanced at Marion. 'I always
assumed he tried to force her to have an abortion and that's
why she made the phone call. I never felt for one minute that
callous young man's religiousness was for real, it was just
his recruiting dress. It must have taken an immense act of
will – and courage – to ring us. God knows what would have
happened to her if she hadn't.'

Sara, understanding that there was to be no happy ending,
allowed silence to fall. The initial gruffness of the older woman
was no more than a lifelong pain etched throughout her whole
being. Perhaps some relief might come through her grandson
if she survived to see it – though every day she must fear signs
of him growing into his father. 'I've kept you too long,' she
said. 'I'll ring for a taxi.' She removed the card she'd taken
from the driver and dialled the number on her mobile.

Elizabeth watched. 'I'd drop you at the station but I can't
leave Marion.'

The phone answered; Sara broke off to summon the taxi.
She replaced the phone in her bag. 'Did Marion ever tell you,
or hint at anything more than what you've just said?'

Elizabeth reflected for several seconds. 'It was usually just
the "mission" and "traitors". But just once she opened her eyes
wide to me and said a single sentence with great intensity. It
probably means nothing – just her fantasising, or retreating
into some sort of weird mysticism.'

'Can you tell me?'

'If you really want. Let me remember the exact words. She
said, "When I feel the smell of life inside me, I must leave the

smell of death." It's not evidence of anything and she spoke it like that, in the present tense. If it meant anything, she was probably talking about sheep. Or rats.'

They stood up and Sara followed Elizabeth into the sitting room. Marion appeared to be sleeping so she murmured a goodbye and they stepped through the French windows into the garden. The sky had darkened and the first raindrops of a gathering storm spattered on the patio. The valley's welcome of friendship now held a grey foreboding. Sara heard the crunch of wheels on gravel; she felt relief at the taxi's arrival and a sadness for the two women she was leaving behind.

'I knew him,' she said.

'I know,' said Elizabeth.

'But you didn't—'

'Why would I? It's none of my business. Each one of us must decide what secrets to bury.'

'Even with a lie?'

'Best not with that. And you're no good at it.' Sara looked down ruefully at her shoes. 'Don't take it amiss, that's a compliment.'

'How did you know?'

'I'm a psychologist. I peer into people's souls.' Sara looked up and Elizabeth's gentler smile was fading. 'When you have a minute,' she continued, 'look up the word "sociopath". See if it summons any ghosts.'

Elizabeth turned on her heel. After a few seconds she stopped and turned back. 'It's that he might come for her – that's what scares me.' Without a further word, she disappeared round the side of the house. A woman, thought Sara, who has come to dislike saying goodbye.

On the train back to London, her attempts to read notes, papers, anything were disrupted by memories and thoughts.

She submitted and, staring through a window at the passing fields, allowed them to flow.

The anonymous text message to Marion had shaken her to the core. Even though the tone differed from the curt anonymity of the texts to herself, the sender surely must be the same. She recalled those messages. It was true that one colleague, Patrick, was not what he seemed. Could the text when she was in Blackburn just be saying: *I'm here, I'm with you, keeping an eye on you, keeping you safe?* And now the apparently helpful text to Marion's phone. Who was pulling her strings? What was their motive? Both questions unnerved her. It was more than that. She was frightened – because she understood she was no longer in control, and perhaps never had been.

An unsought image of the pregnant Marion's bruised wrists led to images of charred limbs – and then back to a sublime, innocent moment of her life before all of this. The evening of July the 6th 2005 when she, her cousin Salman, his wife Nusrat, and their new baby – with the baby's two-year-old brother fast asleep along the passage – were finishing a celebratory supper at the couple's basement flat in north London.

The surprise was sprung over ice cream and a chocolate sauce that matched the baby's eyes.

'We're naming her after you,' said Nusrat.

'What?' Sara replied, incredulity giving way to delight. The baby's parents were paying her the greatest possible compliment.

Sara.

'You never had a brother or sister,' said Salman. 'So we thought you could be special to each other.'

'Thank you,' she replied. 'That means so much to me.'

She examined the tiny, two-week-old ball of new life; creased cheeks, half-opened eyes, wisps of dark brown hair.

Earlier she'd watched the mouth feeding greedily from her mother; how could a being so fragile pulsate with such energy and hunger?

There was a further reason to smile. That morning, in Singapore, it had been announced that London had beaten Paris to host the 2012 Olympics – billions of pounds of investment, a new Olympic city, new stadiums; the greatest show on earth would be coming to the home city of the small group supping around that kitchen table. The baby would be a seven-year-old girl when the games arrived.

As they cleared plates, Sara saw that the parents were near to dropping with a happy fatigue. Just after 9.30 p.m. she rose to leave, embracing them both and planting a gentle kiss, the tickle of a daisy, on the baby's forehead. She walked to Holloway Road tube station, taking the Piccadilly line to King's Cross to change for the rest of the journey home to Tooting. It brought another reminder of the contented family she'd just left. Salman had recently started a new job at Cambridge Science Park; despite the commute – tube to King's Cross, train to Cambridge North, then all the way back each evening – it was an opportunity he couldn't turn down. If it worked out, they were already talking of moving out of London to a different life of country markets, green fields and space for a growing family.

It was an exciting time for Sara too. She'd just finished her articles and in a few weeks was to begin her pupillage at a forward-looking Chambers in the Temple.

She was home by 10.40 p.m., her father still up, watching, as was his custom, the first half of *Newsnight*. She told him about the baby and the honour they'd bestowed on her. He beamed.

'Amazing about the Olympics,' she said.

'Hey, I'll be retired by then! I'll get booking my seats.' The beam broadened even further and he gave her a big hug. 'Off to bed now. Can't all be on holiday.'

Happily tired in a world that seemed calm and beautiful, she had a night of dreamless sleep.

And then, at 6.47 a.m., her mobile had sounded.

The horrors of memory.

The memory of how on the next day, July the 7th, when it was too late, she stayed safely in the confines of her own home and watched the burnt-out bus above ground and the white-suited helmeted figures heading below ground working to retrieve the blackened fried bodies of the dead.

Of never being able to live with herself if her cousin, Salman, heading into King's Cross for his daily commute to work, was caught in it.

Of her shame that Salman living would be, to her, more important than others dying.

Of the baby girl called Sara.

The memory of 2005. The year of birth and death.

Without realising it, staring out of the window, she'd slumped against the side of her seat. Fields and trees had been replaced by London's suburbia slicing through her reflections. She straightened. She remembered Elizabeth's parting words and typed 'sociopath' into her phone. The phrases and adjectives brought bile to her throat. Superficial charm; lack of shame; promiscuous sexual behaviour with a tendency to violence; changes image to avoid being caught out; needs stimulation; authoritarian; desire to enslave victim; callousness; may state goal is to rule the world.

A chill ran through her. She told herself to return to the practical task of planning the next moves. While the Inquiry was headless, she and Patrick must pursue Morahan's remit, inspired by the Sayyid documents. Their window of opportunity might be short; in these circumstances no government could allow such a high-profile Inquiry to meander. It was still only late afternoon as she drew into Waterloo.

Half an hour later, she was turning into Webster Road, a briskness in her stride and mind. Outlines of a picture of Kareem and the ugly project that might be the darkness at the end of Sayyid's arrow were beginning to emerge. There was no time to waste. She would get straight to work. Files, chronology, connections, coincidences.

She glanced up and down the street – no sign of unexplained cars or visitors. She fished the front door keys out of her bag. The mortice was unlocked; her father was at home – after the sadness of a distant Devon valley, the welcome of a smiling, chubby man who, not once in his life, had harboured a malicious thought.

She turned the Yale lock, opened the door, and, with a broad smile, entered the hall.

'No,' she cried out. 'No, no, no!'

19

Looking at him, she felt a love and a dread incomparable to anything she'd felt before.

He was sprawled unconscious at the bottom of the stairs. She put a hand to his mouth and nose; he was breathing, but the rise and falls in his chest were weak, almost imperceptible. An ugly purple bruise spread around his right eye; she guessed he must have fallen down the stairs and hit his head against the bottom newel post. There were signs and smells of vomiting; reporting that injected urgency into the woman's voice on the other end of the 999 line.

The paramedics came quickly; it seemed more like seconds than minutes – the shock must have been distorting all her senses. A specialist resuscitation doctor, they said, was on the way. They checked the exact time she'd discovered him. Was there any regular pattern of behaviour to indicate when he might have returned home? That, at least, might give them an outer window for the time of the injury. She nervously asked whether he would be all right; they said, with a possible brain injury like this, it was best to wait until the CT scan. Fortunately, the local hospital just minutes away had a state-of-the-art neurological unit, one of the best in the country.

The resuscitation doctor arrived and told her simply that it looked like a severe injury; but 'your father is still breathing and his heart is still beating'. There was no reason yet not to be hopeful, though she might wish to pack a small bag for the night. They suggested she took her time to allow the scan to be done, and her father settled in his bed, supported by the stimulants and pain relief that would make him comfortable. She was not to worry if they kept him in an induced coma – there was nothing unusual about that.

Their every word terrified her.

Tenderly they slid his body, their arms cradled around his head and neck, onto a stretcher and strapped his chest and legs. A drip was set up over him and clear liquid began to sink through a tube to a needle planted in his wrist. They carried his still, prone body into the ambulance; she stayed by the front door, watching, not wanting to be in their way. For someone whose life was so often about problem-solving, she felt useless. As the ambulance door slammed shut and its rear end receded and disappeared at the junction with the high street, she felt bereft too.

She turned back inside, pushed the door shut, went to sit at the kitchen table and stared blankly ahead at the dresser holding cups and saucers, seeing nothing. Her thoughts were the flotsam and jetsam of a pilotless ship adrift at sea. Would he need a toothbrush, washing and shaving things? Would he ever be able to use them again? Maybe it was just a sort of concussion. Maybe he was subsiding in the ambulance. Was he dead already? She told herself not to be ridiculous. Like thousands of other old men and women, he'd fallen down the stairs, taken a bash on the head, and would recover soon enough.

Who should she phone? Uncles, cousins, aunts? The prospect of their fussing and worrying, the drama it would instantly become, was intolerable. She would wait till she was at the hospital and had more certainty to impart. For now, she would face it alone – as she had faced so much of her life.

She would give it an hour; the hospital was no more than a few minutes by Uber, the one stroke of luck. What if they had been in that sleepy Devon village, hours away from anywhere that could cope? How often must Elizabeth Green live on her nerves, awaiting her daughter's next crisis?

She needed to rid herself of disorderly thoughts. There were fifty minutes to prepare for whatever ordeal lay ahead. She went up to her bedroom and laid out a small travel case on her bed. It smelt fusty. Other smells floated at her. An after-scent of unfamiliar sweat disguised by deodorant, perhaps cologne? She went to open the back window overlooking the garden to breathe the evening's freshness. It was ajar, the latch in place on the second slot. She was sure she'd closed it before setting off in the morning; she always did unless she knew her father was at home all day. But this was a Thursday, his regular lunchtime club, a fixture in his diary.

Perhaps, in the rush of anticipation as she'd left for the journey to Devon, she had, for once, overlooked it. Unless her father had opened it when he returned after the lunch club. Was that why he was upstairs – and had then fallen on the way down? It didn't fit. He never entered her room – it was her private space which he honoured.

She packed her computer, the Qur'an and a novel into the case. She imagined that hours of sleepless waiting might lie ahead, and went to her desk to retrieve the charger. It seemed somehow tidier than usual; she must have done a quick sort before she left – she couldn't remember. She checked the drawers – nothing had changed. Not that there was anything to find – Patrick had the Blackburn file copies and she'd left him with the photograph and tape. She hardly needed to see or hear those again.

The evening sun shafted across the leather inset on which her computer sat. There was something missing; she couldn't think what. She suddenly realised – the motes of dust on the leather usually illuminated by the rays, or caught by shafts cutting through the casement window, were absent. Perhaps the cleaner had called in today – her fortnightly three-hour visits had become irregular and they'd given her a key to come and go. That could explain the window too. She felt a surge of relief – this was not the time to start imagining things. Though the after-scent was not of a woman. Maybe the cleaner was ill and sent her husband instead. None of it added up. Stop thinking…

She put a change of clothes, nightgown, slippers, washbag and make-up bag into the case. Forget the taxi, she needed air – if she cut through by the footpaths, the hospital was close enough to walk to. She googled the hospital map to locate the neurology unit. Her father would be there by now. There'd been no phone call; she assumed that was good.

Night had fallen as she reached the hospital; inside, it buzzed with the electricity of artificial light and air-conditioning. The duty sister in the neurological unit tried to give her a comforting smile which she found dismaying, and led her to the intensive care unit. Her father was on his own in a separated corner of the recovery ward with its own entrance, bordered by glass and blinds. She was shown into a small ante-space; a nurse sat there alone in front of a computer and shelves of medical supplies.

Sara introduced herself.

'Hello, Sara. My name's Bridget and I'm looking after your father.' The nurse had curly red hair and chubby cheeks. A soft Irish accent. Like the ward sister, she offered a smile of sympathy. 'We'll be doing our very best for him.'

'How is he? Can I see him?'

'Of course you can.'

Sara entered – 'room' was too domestic a word but it was his own unit and gave him privacy and quiet. She felt grateful to them for it.

His appearance was ghastly – her chest and stomach tightened; she had a momentary breathlessness. Bridget noticed. 'Don't be put off by what you see, it's all there for a reason.' Tariq was lying on his back, two, if not three, drips fed into him from different sources and a metal tube hung out of his mouth, like the hook from a caught fish, gasping for air. Sara felt the direction of her gaze being watched by the nurse. 'We're pleased with his breathing but that there in his mouth is the artificial respirator. So we can give him a helping hand if he's faltering.' Sara looked at her, noting the choice of language, and then back to the bank of monitors. 'Heartbeat, breathing, blood pressure, temperature,' said Bridget.

Sara peered more closely and tried to remember the last time she'd had her blood pressure taken and what sort of figures they showed. These seemed much lower. Again, Bridget needed no prompting. 'The blood pressure's a little low but we're pumping in stimulants to raise it. You can see from his vital signs that he's giving it a good fight.' Sara saw nothing but felt too overwhelmed to ask for further explanation. She sat down on a chair beside the bed and laid her hand on the back of his right hand.

'So what happened, Dad? What on earth were you up to?'

She sat silently for half an hour, hoping for the instant miracle that would open his eyes and animate his face into its familiar smile. Nothing was going to happen quickly.

Bridget hovered at the door. 'We have a small room with a

sofa for families,' she said. 'There's no one else there tonight so you might find it comfortable. Room for a few others if you want too.'

'Thank you,' said Sara, 'yes, I'll need to make some calls.'

'The senior registrar's just called to say he'll be down in five minutes to explain everything. Maybe best you see him in the family room. Then make your calls after that.'

'Yes, good idea.' For once in her life, Sara was pleased to be told what to do.

'Your father has sustained a severe brain injury,' said the senior neurological registrar, who had introduced himself as Azhar Mahmoud. He seemed young to Sara, as young as herself – though she quickly realised there was no reason why he shouldn't be. He was tall, bespectacled, and closely and elegantly bearded; his blue surgeon's smocks anointed him with a halo of authority.

'I see,' said Sara feebly.

'The CT scan shows considerable bleeding inside the brain and what we call a subdural haematoma. Our first priority is to stabilise him and very carefully drain some of the excess blood from his brain. When that's done, we'll consider operating.'

'How bad is it?'

He smiled and shrugged. 'I don't believe in holding out false hopes – or false dangers for that matter. The good thing is that we don't consider from the CT scan that your father's injury is what we call "un-survivable". If that were so, we could do nothing but make him comfortable and allow him to slip away in peace.'

'This all sounds so bad,' said Sara, unable, for the first time, to restrain a tear.

'I'm sorry, Miss Shah, I truly am.'

'Please call me Sara.'

'Of course. There's a reasonable chance that he can pull through this.'

'How reasonable?'

'Please don't ask me to give odds, I'm not a betting man.'

'I think he was sometimes,' said Sara, smiling through the tears.

'Well, let's hope he fancies his chances. In the meantime, for the next few hours, perhaps a day or two, just allow the time to pass. If he gets through that and we can operate, I think we can give him back to you.'

'In what state?'

'Again, I give no guarantees.'

She could see that, while he had finished delivering his verdict, there was something left hanging. 'So is that it for the moment?' she asked.

'There was one other thing. This was a very considerable blow to the head from a fall down the stairs. Do you have particularly steep or long stairs? Might he even have fallen over more than one flight of stairs through gaps if the staircase was wide?'

'Not at all,' said Sara. 'It's a modest terrace house. Not very high ceilings. Just ordinary stairs.'

'Oh well. If he'd had a heart attack or stroke and fell without being able to protect himself in any way, that could explain it more. But there's no sign of that. Possibly he was rushing and tripped and his momentum took him into a hard object.'

'It must have been the newel post. But he never rushed.'

'Well, it doesn't matter now. If I may advise you, don't put your own life on hold while we're waiting.'

He stood up, Sara followed suit. 'Thank you.'

He locked eyes with hers. 'I won't let him down.'

It was past 10 p.m.; she wouldn't yet start the family phone calls and ignite a nocturnal panic. She'd be in trouble if he died during the night, but the surgeon would have said if he thought it at all likely.

She wanted to be alone with him. She was fond of her aunts, uncles and cousins, particularly of Salman, after the honour he and Nusrat had given her – but she'd never confided in them. Nor they in her. She'd wondered sometimes if they saw her as too much of an 'achiever', breathing the Everest-high air of the Inns of Court. Or perhaps her adult seriousness towards her religion – and her choice to wear the hijab – had created a distance. The same went for her friends – she had plenty, the majority these days from her work – but never that one close, life-long friend to turn to in distress. It had always been her father – except when it would have agonised him too much. In the end, that's perhaps who she was – or had become. A woman alone. Currently, the only person she could imagine sharing her despair with was the one who'd understand the meaning and consequence of the moment.

She checked her watch. 10.20 p.m. Would he mind? Particularly after the peremptory way she'd rejected his wish to come with her to Devon. Would she be sending a signal she might regret?

She dialled his number. There was not a second of hesitation. 'I'm on my way,' said Patrick.

She was beside her father when he arrived, creeping shyly into the room, silently pulling up a chair. 'I'm so sorry.'

She briefly rested the hand that was not attached to her father on his arm. 'I'm OK. Thanks for coming.'

They sat silently, watching him, listening to the bleeps, trying to make sense of the various graphs' interminable repetitive progress. A repetition whose interruption spelt danger. The one thing he understood was that she, not he, should break the silence.

Instead, it was the nurse. 'Can I bring you tea – or coffee?'

she asked brightly. Sara turned and shook her head. Patrick followed her lead. 'You must rest,' said Bridget, 'nothing will change tonight.' Patrick tried to catch Sara's eye, to give her the energy to move and convey the understanding that it was her father's will, not hers, that would save him.

Eventually – time was relative and unmeasured – she rose and left, Patrick following. Only when they reached the family room, she flopping on the sofa, he sitting opposite on a hard-backed chair, did she say something meaningful to him.

'The accident doesn't add up.'

'You're ahead of me,' he said. 'A universe ahead.'

'I can't think properly. I'm hungry.'

'I'll check the place out.' Within a few minutes, he was back. 'They keep a corner of one of the canteens open overnight.'

They sat at a Formica table opposite each other on plastic chairs. Patrick stirred sugar into coffee, not wanting to tell her that he'd been drinking at a club when she phoned, and then sucked peppermints as he drove. She sipped from a can of Diet Coke and munched monotonously on a plastic-looking sandwich and a banana. Around them were the quiet stirrings of bleary-eyed night life in a hospital that never slept; the anaesthetist telling a joke to the theatre nurse; the three generations of black-scarved, black-robed women – grandmother, wife, daughter – waiting for news of their male loved one; the curly-haired West Indian cleaner rhythmically swishing her mop over the linoleum floor; the cashier flopped on her elbows, forcing her eyes to stay open for the next customer.

Sara leant back and poured the final dregs of Coke down her throat, Patrick trying not to watch her too closely.

'Do you want to talk?' he asked.

'I don't know if I'm inventing things,' she said. 'The shock is probably distorting it all.'

'Take me through your day. Yesterday you had that phone

call. I saw your excitement. It was all you could think about.'
He paused, a regretful kindness in his eyes. 'You hardly said
goodbye.'

She stretched a hand across the table. 'I'm sorry.'

With one hand, he took it, with the other he stroked the
back. 'What for?'

She described the train journey; the valley; Elizabeth Green;
Marion; the deserted Welsh farm; the rescue; the tragedy of
destroyed lives. Arriving home, opening the door, his body
by the stairs, the voices of the paramedics still echoing in her
mind. The kind nurse. The gentle registrar. The fight for life.
The last question.

'What was he implying?' asked Patrick.

'I don't think he was implying anything. He just couldn't
understand it.'

'And you?'

She allowed a moment to pass. Yes, he had to know. She
withdrew her hand and sat up straight. 'We had visitors in
our street.' Patrick screwed up his eyes, concentrating hard.
'Parked in a black car. Watching. When they came a second
time, my dad went over to ask who they were and what they
were doing. One had a Scottish accent, the other was big and
burly. They told him it was way above his pay grade, they were
there to protect me, f— off back into the house.'

Patrick took a deep breath. 'I see,' he said calmly.

'Sounds like your visitors.'

'Undoubtedly.' He thought for a few seconds. 'It's interesting
it was the same two men.'

She frowned, puzzled. 'Why?'

'It suggests that whatever is or isn't happening, this is a very
tight operation. It may be authorised, known just to a handful.
Or it may be off the books.'

'Meaning?'

'I still have that tiny element of faith,' he said, 'that official would be better.'

'He could just have tripped at the top.' Patrick stayed silent, waiting for her. 'Or someone hurled him down, smashing his head against the post.' She peered down, hands circling the Coke can, the canteen seeming to go eerily quiet.

'I imagine you never read James Bond,' said Patrick, breaking the moment.

She looked up and smiled. 'It's hardly a feminist tract.'

'I did. As a disobedient boy under the bedclothes with a torch.' He'd injected a thrill into his voice which relaxed her. 'So you won't remember Goldfinger's three card trick. "They have a saying in Chicago, Mr Bond. Once is happenstance. Twice is coincidence. The third time it's enemy action." That's fiction, we have the reality. Happenstance is the Sayyid files, coincidence is Morahan's death, third time... your father. Enemy action.' Any trace of humour vanished.

'Who's the enemy?' she asked.

'Ask another question. What secret is the enemy after? Or trying to cover up?'

He was trying to tell her something; she reminded herself of their interrupted conversation. 'A piece of paper, perhaps?'

He half-closed his eyes. 'I never finished the story, did I?'

20

2005

His distaste slowly turned to a certain admiration. Kareem – a man being held in a pseudo-cell by senior MI5 officers with whom he was negotiating his freedom – should have been the one making pleas. But cool, calculating, bold, he had turned the tables. It was he who was deciding whether or not to grant them his favour, he who was laying down the conditions.

'What makes you think they'll give you a contract in any meaningful, enforceable sense of that word?' asked Patrick.

'Because they need me,' replied Kareem. 'They're clueless. They have no inside knowledge.' They had moved outside and he was looking over Patrick's shoulder to the empty sitting room behind the glass. A growl was building in the sky; they craned necks and saw a jumbo jet lumbering on its midday approach towards Heathrow.

'An ugly beast,' declared Kareem. 'How sad that we no longer see Concorde. My degree was aeronautical engineering. Perhaps instead of ending up here,' he gestured to the walls around them, 'I might have trained as a pilot and sat in the cockpit of that beautiful creation. It restored one's faith in the genius of British design and creativity.'

Patrick couldn't tell whether he was genuine or dripping irony. 'Why didn't you?'

'Perhaps you may not have noticed, Patrick. The world changed.'

I will not react to the arrogance, the superciliousness, Patrick told himself. He wondered whether Kareem ever raised his voice; whether it was possible to goad him, to breach him. He suspected not. 'So, your contract – what do you want it to contain?'

'Standard elements for civil service and government employment. Salary with increments. Holiday. Pension scheme. Time off in lieu for weekend work.'

'You want MI5 to give you a staff job.'

'Why not?'

'Have you raised it with them yourself?'

'No. I prefer to use my lawyer.' He gave Patrick a condescending nod of approval.

'I'll convey your terms to them.'

'There is one other condition,' added Kareem airily.

'Yes?'

'I require indemnities.'

'Indemnities for what?'

'The job they are offering me will expose me to situations where I may personally have to make unpalatable decisions. I require indemnities against any risk of prosecution as a result of any such decisions or actions by me.'

'What job? What decisions and actions?'

'Not relevant to you.'

'Then how can I negotiate indemnities for you?' asked Patrick.

'Ask them. They are the intelligence services. I suggest they use their intelligence.'

Patrick recalled J's similar play on the word – two peas from the same pod. 'I will convey that request too.'

'Please understand, Patrick,' the tone remained calm but a steeliness had emerged, 'this is not a request, it is a requirement. I am not going to hang for them.'

'And if they refuse it?'

'I have no desire to appear in a court or go to prison but there will be no deal without it.'

'What can you offer them in return?'

Kareem answered without hesitation. 'Loyalty. I appreciate their offer, which will give my life a new purpose. As I think they understand, my reflections on these matters since the events of July have brought a change.'

'Are you saying you positively want this job? Whatever it might be.'

'It will give me the mission I need.'

His choice of words was so curious that Patrick, though he knew it would displease his 'client', tried again to probe. 'Could you explain?'

'Explain what?' Kareem exhibited a faint contempt.

'What your mission is. After all, you'll be changing sides, betraying your own.'

'My own, Patrick?' The condescension was now deliberate and unconcealed.

'You know what I mean.'

'How little you understand of the world.'

Kareem was giving no more. 'Let's go back inside,' said Patrick, 'I'll talk to them.'

'Thank you. If you do not mind, I prefer to stay out here. It can become a little enclosed.' Patrick turned to leave. 'Perhaps you could ask someone to bring me a cup of mint tea. In addition to the cigarettes, their research was sufficiently professional to have some in the kitchen.'

Lowering the brass handle of the garden door, Patrick was interrupted in mid-action. 'One final thing...' He stopped to look back. Kareem was a picture of insouciance. 'As I will be devoting my life to your Majesty's Service, I would like the honour of an invitation to a Buckingham Palace garden party so that I may shake the hand of the reigning monarch.'

Patrick gave an acquiescent nod. 'Of course.' Restraining himself from kicking the door open, he went inside.

J and Isobel Le Marchant walked in through the internal door opposite. They were accompanied by a newcomer, a blond-haired man in his thirties.

'May I introduce you to John, Patrick?' said Isobel. 'He'll be joining us on this.'

'Pleased to meet you, Patrick. John Donald.' He stretched out a hand; Patrick noticed a hint of Scottish burr. 'I've heard a lot about you.'

Patrick assumed the three of them had been watching.

'He's biting,' said J.

'We're biting,' said Patrick gloomily.

'Wise up, Patrick,' said Isobel sternly, 'it has to be a two-way deal.'

'He's got some nerve.'

'It's bravado,' she replied. 'His reaction to being cornered. He can't afford to show weakness.'

Patrick turned to J. 'How do you know you can trust him?'

'That's Isobel's call. She's the boss, I'm the gofer.'

'Hardly, J,' she said without smiling. There was something of the schoolmistress about her, thought Patrick, wondering what hidden depths had allowed her to rise so fast in such a traditionally patrician organisation. Perhaps that itself was the reason. A diverse MI5, 'fit for purpose' in New Labour's twenty-first century. Perhaps they looked at him and thought the same.

'The decision will go to the top,' said Isobel, 'but this is a unique opportunity. I've brought John in as our third pair of eyes. He agrees that we've never before had a chance to recruit such a high-quality asset from this particular world.'

Patrick, after his initial experience of Kareem's slipperiness – not to mention his priggishness – wondered how they could possibly be sure of him.

Sensing his hesitancy, Isobel continued. 'You see, Patrick, I personally have spent time with Kareem. I can see inside him. That is my job. Particularly as I will be his handler; I would not contemplate it unless I was sure.'

Patrick hoped J would interrogate her further. He didn't. The show was moving on. 'This contract,' said J.

'Yes,' said Patrick. 'It's ridiculous.'

J smiled gently. 'Is this the way to represent your client?'

'Precisely,' agreed Isobel without sharing the smile. 'If he wants this so-called contract, I have no issue with that.'

'He won't accept it unless it's a genuine contract of employ-ment. And he didn't seem amenable to negotiation on the terms.'

'That's better,' said J, 'your client would be proud of you.'

'It will have to be signed by a senior officer of MI5. Including his so-called indemnities.'

'It cannot be with MI5,' said Isobel. 'For reasons of security.'

Patrick asked himself what reasons but, again, judged it best not to question her. 'Then with whom?' he asked instead.

'That's really a matter for government lawyers,' she replied. 'I'd imagine you'd want to oversee any employment contract in circumstances as unusual as this.'

'Perhaps I should speak to my boss,' suggested Patrick.

'Perhaps you should.' She turned to J, smiling sweetly. 'Shall we leave Patrick to make his call?'

'What did you do?' asked Sara. She had finished the banana but a rubbery remnant of the sandwich remained on her plate, curling slightly at the edges.

'I phoned Keith Barron,' said Patrick.

'Remind me—'

'Head of the Treasury Solicitors, as they were then. He answered immediately. I had a sense this was all pre-arranged. I was just a cog in an engine that was purring smoothly towards an agreed destination.'

'What did he say?'

'I reported my conversation with Kareem and his various demands. Barron chuckled and said "cheeky bastard" or something. I think I said, yes, he's some piece of work. Then I asked him about the contract. He said, "Well, Five seem very keen on it so I guess we should oblige them." I couldn't believe he was so nonchalant. Presumably he didn't think it worth the paper it was written on. "Who's going to draw it up?" I asked. "You're our man on the spot, Patrick." "What about signing it?" "Same goes. You have my unqualified approval."'

'What?' Sara's interruption cut through the canteen's buzz of refrigeration and strip lights. A couple of mournful faces looked round. She lowered her voice. 'Sorry, it just seems so – what's the word? – cavalier.'

'I guess lies were just one of the currencies in play,' said Patrick. 'Those imaginary Saddam Hussein weapons of mass destruction hadn't been finally exposed. I didn't know what to say, it all seemed so surreal.'

'What next?'

'I used a standard template. J filled in the main figures – Isobel had left the room, I got the impression she didn't want to dirty her hands any further. I added Kareem's indemnities as an appendix. Tried to make it read like a bureaucratic formality.'

'Did you get Barron's approval in writing?'

Patrick looked crestfallen. 'I hinted that would make me more comfortable. He just laughed. Told me not to be a muppet.'

'It gets worse and worse.' She paused, recalling again the final words of Elizabeth Green. 'Did they do tests on him?'

'What tests?'

'Psychometric, for example. Didn't they think of bringing in a psychiatrist or psychologist?'

'It was never raised.'

'I don't understand their confidence.'

'It was Isobel more than J. She'd made her decision and that seemed to be it. J wasn't being modest, he really was just the sidekick.'

'Kareem charmed her, overwhelmed her,' said Sara. 'Just like with Marion...'

'Yes?'

'Nothing. I was wandering.'

She was baulking at something; he tried not to show he'd seen it. 'Maybe so, but it wasn't just that. I got the impression that Kareem was excited.'

'Because it pandered to his self-regard?' She was staring down at her hands.

'Yes. That's exactly how it felt.' How much more did she know, or understand, about Kareem?

She raised her eyes. 'Finish the story.'

'Len the "driver" had facilities in his little front office. Computer, printer, photocopier, scanner. We made three copies of the contract, signature page at the back. I took it out to Kareem. He read it silently and slowly, far more slowly than was needed to take it in. I could feel him celebrating within but his face didn't even twitch. Finally, he signed all three, handed them back to me and said, "I'll wait out here for my counter-signed and witnessed copy." Not a further word, let alone a thank you. I went back inside—'

'Who ended up as the counter-signatory?' asked Sara. He wearily rubbed his eyes. 'I don't need to ask, do I?' He shook his head once. 'Oh, Patrick. And the witness?'

'Len. Isobel and John – I forget his surname – had disappeared, J just looked at the ceiling. Len Rogerson, it said on the page. That certainly wasn't his name. I later discovered that the address he gave was a block of council flats that had been demolished several months before.'

'But your name and address were genuine.'

'Yes.' He slapped both palms on the table and looked beseechingly at her. 'I was still in my twenties – just – for God's sake,' he whispered fiercely. 'It was my first real government job. I felt… corralled. As if this was my big initiation test and my whole career might depend on it.'

'Who kept the three signed copies?'

'Kareem himself, a second was taken by J. I took the third.'

'What did you do with it?'

'You're interrogating me, Sara.'

'I, we, need to know. Because what if happenstance is Morahan's death and coincidence is my father's fall? And the third stage – what converts the whole pattern into enemy action – is still to come.'

'Are you telling me you know what that will be?'

'No. If only I did. But the farm that terrorised Marion Green and Sami Mohammed has the smell of death. The very words Marion used. The files contain cases of unexplained disappearances. The tips of icebergs, our source says.'

'We still only have those tips,' said Patrick. 'They prove nothing. A dead end.'

'No!' She'd raised her voice; realising it, she glanced around the canteen. There was no one in earshot. 'We now have

Morahan. My father. We have the threat to you. Above all, now you've told me, we have the contract. I don't think you truly understand what it might be.'

'What do you mean, it might be?'

She moved to within inches of him. 'For God's sake, Patrick, you must have suspected,' she whispered. 'Kareem's licence to kill. In some form or other. To murder. Say that's what it was. Imagine the consequences if Sir Frances Morahan had ever begun to suspect that and then succeeded in proving it.' She paused. 'Imagine the consequences if you and I prove it now.'

Death. The black-scarved women had disappeared and the anaesthetist and nurse returned to their work; in their places a blonde-haired, tear-stained girl in her late teens comforted by an older woman, perhaps waiting for a young lover's fate to be decided. The arbitrariness of the night; a motorcycle crash, drug overdose, stabbing, an old man's heart finally giving out.

'Did I suspect that?' said Patrick softly. 'I'm not sure I had the imagination. But, yes, I knew it was all wrong. I was too weak. Or too scared.'

'As you said, you were corralled, manoeuvred, whatever you want to call it.'

'It's always haunted me. It's the reason I wanted to be on the Inquiry. When I first heard about it, the terms of reference felt like a pistol shot – if that contract with my name on it ever came out. I thought I could control things from the inside.'

'But then Sayyid came along. And Morahan. And me.'

He bowed his head. 'Yes.'

'And now?'

'I have to be able to live with myself.'

Sara rose. 'Come on, back to Dad.'

He felt – and looked – beaten. 'Do you want me to stay?'

She moved towards him, kneeled, and held his face in her hands. 'Of course I want you to stay.'

There seemed no change – the expressionless face, soft breathing, barely rising and falling chest, the light show of the monitors, the depth and colour of the bruising.

'How's he doing?' Sara asked Bridget, knowing, as soon as she'd asked, that the question was unanswerable.

'The blood pressure's only down a tiny bit,' she replied chirpily. 'He's still doing most of his own breathing. The heartbeat's strong. Now why don't you try to get some sleep?'

'I'd rather be with him.'

'OK, love, I'll be behind the door if you need me.'

Patrick sat on a plastic chair beside her. She turned to him. 'You've told me your story. And you kept your word, you didn't pursue your question.'

'It's not important now,' he said.

'It's become important to me. I think it may be relevant too.' She spoke quietly, her words covered by the hospital whirr. She looked back at her father. 'It's the one thing I never told him. The only secret between us. So if I tell you now, in this place, perhaps he too will hear my words. Or perhaps he won't. That will be for God to decide.'

'Sara,' said Patrick quietly, 'that's not rational. He's unconscious.'

'On this night I don't like the word "rational". Nor the word "unconscious". What is "rational" about him lying there and you and me watching him? What control do you think reason – or even medicine – have? How do we know what's happening inside his head, his mind? I told you what the surgeon said. The doctors too can only wait. So, through my God, this is where I can deliver myself to the judgement of a greater being.'

He stayed silent, numbed by the clarity of her words and the softness of their delivery.

'Let me go back to my beginning. Or should I say the time of my fall?' He watched her gazing into her father's eyes, and sensed a horror returning. 'I first met Kareem eighteen years ago. 2001. Do you remember that summer? The world, our country at least, was becoming a better, happier place…'

21

She'd just turned eighteen, A-levels were over and her cousin Salman was marrying a girl called Nusrat. At a distracted moment during the *mehndi*, where she was among the giggling girls hennaing the bride, she glanced at the circle of young men – Salman's university friends – jigging away, blasting out tracks from Panjabi MC's *Legalised*.

He stood aloof, part of them but not taking part, neither dancing nor singing, tall, slim, a sheen of jet hair settling on the nape of his neck. He seemed older than the others, graver, more intense. His brown eyes, dark as the thickest forest, were so fiercely locked on her that he might have been piercing into her very soul. She stared back, her mouth ajar, eyes wide open. Boiling with embarrassment, she felt her face reddening and imagined mascara melting down her cheeks.

The wedding was two days later, the venue a white stucco-fronted Victorian hotel off Wimbledon Common. White linen-covered tables lined a huge reception room, bride and groom enthroned beyond them on a dais beneath a vast gold-framed mirror strung from a picture rail. On one side, three floor-to-ceiling sash windows flanked by furled red velvet curtains looked out onto a lawn mown in criss-crossing diagonal lines. It was the grandest event Sara Shah had ever attended; her cousin and his bride had even made a table plan.

She had to avoid him, mustn't embarrass herself again. She worked out the seat she'd grab to ensure she faced away from the table of Salman's uni friends, where he'd be placed. Once, just once, she turned for a glimpse. His eyes were still honed in on her like a heat-seeking missile. For a nanosecond she locked on.

'Seen a ghost?' asked the cousin sitting beside her.

'Who is he?' whispered Sara.

'Don't you know? That's Kareem. Kareem Abdullah bin-Jilani.' The cousin lowered her eyes. 'Loaded, apparently.'

Towards the end of June, she was sauntering in jeans and a pink blouse along Tooting Broadway. A clear mid-afternoon sun warmed her bare head and arms; she'd never felt such a bursting sense of liberation, of the ripening of a fuller life. Except for a few ugly race riots in the North, the country itself, particularly her bubble of south London, seemed to share her optimism. New Labour under smiling Tony Blair had just won their second general election. Conservatism and its innate pessimism were crushed. There would be money for health and schools, employment for young people, opportunity for everyone.

As she turned off Tooting Broadway in the direction of home, a low-slung red sports car pulled in beside her. A tall, lean figure jumped out.

'It is Sara Shah, is it not?' She tried to frown; but her face couldn't help spreading itself into a smile. Don't stare again, match him...

'And if it is?'

He was disconcerted. 'I am Kareem.'

'Yes, I know.'

He returned the smile. 'Ah, you are playing with me. Can I offer you a lift anywhere?' There was already something about his tone and speech pattern. A voice with deep resonance but soft, not loud. The precise English of a foreigner seeking perfection.

'I'm on my way home, thanks. It's just a few hundred yards.'

'I wanted to approach your father at the wedding for a formal introduction. But you kept disappearing.'

'I'm sorry.'

'It is OK. Now we have introduced ourselves. Perhaps you would like to go for a short drive?'

She knew she shouldn't. Her father trusted her – that's why he'd felt able to devote himself to work and achieve his promotions. She'd be breaching that trust. But, after all, this man was a friend of her cousin... almost family, well-behaved and educated. She looked around. No one was watching. She hesitated – he watched and waited, making no move himself to return to his driver's seat. He *was* extraordinarily attractive. What were a few minutes in a lifetime? What harm was there in it?

'OK. Just a short one.'

He whisked round the front of the car and opened the passenger door. She jumped in and slammed it shut, ducking her face. As he walked round the back of the car, she craned her neck to see his midriff flashing across the rear window. He slid into his seat, started up and revved the engine.

'I shouldn't really,' she said.

He snatched a quick look at her. 'Please, it is your decision. You can get out if you prefer.'

She didn't answer; he'd said it so considerately that it felt OK. He accelerated away. Guilt competed with an overwhelming sense of triumph. Butterflies danced in the pit of her stomach.

'We could go to Wandsworth Common. White yummy-mummy land. None of our people will be there.'

She laughed. 'How did you meet Salman?'

'At Queen Victoria's. I am just finishing my Masters there. He is a fine chap. I hope he and his bride will be happy even though it is an arranged marriage.'

At the mention of weddings, she fell silent, feeling that little tap on the shoulder of what her father would think.

'Salman's area is mechanical engineering, mine is aerospace,' Kareem continued.

'Sounds interesting.'

'Yes, I am also taking my pilot's licence.'

'Isn't that expensive?'

They were stopped at lights; he swivelled towards her. 'Fortunately the family firm pays. You may think this is unfair privilege. I would.agree with you.'

Rather than pursue the point, as he turned back to the road she chose to make a more detailed inspection of his profile. A silence fell – she wanted to fill it. No, what she wanted was just to look at him, to touch his arm, to feel his skin. She knew that couldn't be and tried to discard the thought. Had he noticed?

'What are your future educational plans?' It seemed he hadn't.

'Starting my law degree in the autumn. Queen Vic's too.'

'Did you ever wish to go to uni outside London?'

'Sometimes.' She hesitated. 'I think my dad still needs me.'

'What about your mother?'

'She passed away when I was nine.'

'I am sorry, Sara. I was not aware of this.' He allowed her a moment – no pressing. A sensitive man.

They turned into a short road of double-fronted Victorian houses. 'The gardens of these houses back onto the Common,' said Kareem. 'I understand they sell for three million pounds.' He paused. 'To bankers.'

He stopped and looked at his watch. 'Perhaps this is already the short drive you suggested?'

'It's OK.' No way did she want this to end yet. 'We can go for a quick walk.'

A path took them diagonally across the Common, past young mothers with blonde hair wearing pastel shades and pushing double buggies. They reached a copse by a pond and sat on a bench, streams of sunlight dappling the water and casting dancing flickers on their faces.

'What are your summer plans?' she asked.

'I must first finish my dissertation.'

'And then?'

'I would like to travel a little to understand my origins better. The Gulf in particular. There is family pressure to join the business but I am not sure what this will achieve for me.'

'What do you want to achieve?'

He considered her question as if it were the first time he'd been asked. 'Change the world maybe. There are many bad things.'

She frowned, unsure of his meaning, of how serious he was. He seemed to be revolving something in his mind, unsure whether to speak it. This time, she looked at her watch. 'Perhaps you should drop me back.'

'Of course. It has been a delight to meet you properly.' He rose, gesturing her to come alongside him, but he did not reach out for her hand. 'I would love to spend some more time with you, Sara,' he said walking back to the car. 'Perhaps we could do some outings?'

She didn't know what to say.

'It would be in the cause of education. For both of us.'

She certainly didn't want to say a flat no. 'Maybe I should ask my dad.'

'Of course, if you feel you need to.'

She knew with cast-iron certainty that she should. So must he. 'He's very busy,' she replied. 'I hate to disturb him.' The double meaning of the word struck her.

'It is entirely up to you, Sara.' They reached the car and he opened the passenger door. 'Perhaps in daytime it is permitted.'

She slid in. 'Yes, perhaps it is.' He shut the door on her.

She wondered what his 'outings' might be. The way he spoke of travelling made her see the limits of her own horizon: a life spent in the same neighbourhood, no money for the foreign or exotic. He was from a different, more expansive world.

They began with matinées of two musicals: *Peggy Sue Got Married* with Ruthie Henshall, *My Fair Lady* with the *EastEnders* star Martine McCutcheon, in her first stage role. They had prime seats in the front of the dress circle; she remembered what her cousin had said. 'Loaded.' The shows offered interesting things to talk about.

'So,' he asked, 'what is your verdict on a soap opera actress trying to perform one of the great musical roles?'

'I thought she was wonderful,' she replied eagerly. 'She has that lovely round moon face and sparkling eyes.'

'Her voice?'

'She sang nicely.' She hesitated. 'Didn't she?'

'Yes. Nicely.' He smiled at her over the coffee they had afterwards. 'A correct and generous verdict. But perhaps not one of the great voices.'

'I wouldn't know.' She thought of young Eliza Doolittle and old Professor Higgins, introducing her to a new world of glamour and intellect. Kareem was a lot younger than Henry Higgins.

'In fact,' he continued, 'Audrey Hepburn's voice in the film with Rex Harrison had to be covered by a proper singer as she was not up to it.'

'Oh...'

'And this is why, for the film of *The Sound of Music*, Audrey Hepburn did not take up the role and opened the door to Julie Andrews who could sing properly.'

'I never knew that.'

'Even if she was not as beautiful.' His grin as he spoke the word, his eyes staring fiercely into hers, was electric. 'What movies would you like to go to?'

They went to matinées of *Lara Croft: Tomb Raider* with Angelina Jolie and *Planet of the Apes* with Helena Bonham Carter. And exhibitions – the one she most enjoyed was at the British Museum, about Cleopatra. She was overwhelmed by the space and beauty of the newly opened Great Court.

'So, Sara, was Cleopatra a *femme fatale*, unlucky, or destroyed by her own hubris?'

'Hubris?' she asked.

'Yes, the pride before the fall.'

'Oh, right.'

'Might it be fun to take tea at the Ritz hotel?' he asked one afternoon. She looked alarmed; the idea seemed so alien. 'After all, it is the height of British afternoon sophistication.'

'What will I wear?'

She found a smart enough skirt and blouse.

The tea arrived, stacked on a multi-layered china dish: sandwiches, cakes, biscuits. She reached with her right hand to put a selection on a plate and placed her left hand on the table, stretching it slowly and by tiny degrees in his direction. Would he spread his towards hers?

He kept his hands to himself, sipping and eating with a rare elegance for a man. His fingers were long and artistic, unencumbered by black hairs. The perfect gentleman.

One afternoon, as he dropped her near home, he proposed a picnic on the South Downs and described the beauty of its hills and views. They could visit Bignor Roman Villa and take in the mosaics.

'It will be a cultural visit.'

She hesitated. It felt like a new step. 'As long as we're back in good time,' she said.

He collected her from the usual rendezvous. Past South Wimbledon tube, out of range of anyone spotting them, he pulled up in a lay-by and opened up the hood of his car. She'd once idly asked what it was, though it interested her little; 'Mazda MX-5 convertible,' came his contemptuous reply. 'This car is nothing special. One day I will drive you in a real car.'

'Isn't this a real car?' she'd asked.

He'd laughed. 'It's hardly a Lamborghini.'

Travelling through places like Chiddingfold, Northchapel, and Petworth was a revelation, though she had the impression it was familiar to him. Village greens lined with thatched cottages and wisteria-clad, rose-bricked square houses; Norman churches with solid naves and neat square towers; at Chiddingfold itself a grander church with flying buttresses and decorative crenellations; pub signs with names like 'The Green Man' swinging gently in the slight breeze.

'I've never been to places like these,' she said. She had to raise her voice as the late summer air beat into their faces and ruffled through their hair.

They stopped at Bignor where she was captivated by the jewel-like sheen of the mosaics. 'Two thousand years old,' she said in near disbelief.

'That is the point,' he said. 'The Romans made themselves at home in these parts so why should not we?' She looked around – there were no other non-white faces.

He parked and they climbed up Bignor Hill onto the South Downs Way. She had warmed up and taken off the sweater she'd worn in the car, revealing a sleeveless T-shirt; even though it was early September, it was all she needed as the midday sun burned, beads of sweat glistening around her neck.

'Let us find some shade for the picnic,' he said, stretching out a hand. She took it and entwined her fingers through his. It was the first time, beyond mere courtesy or accident, that they had touched.

There was a knock on the door from the ante-space; Bridget walked through carrying a clipboard and charts. Sara stopped talking and they both looked up at her.

'Sorry, am I interrupting?' asked the nurse.

'Not at all,' replied Sara. 'We were just reminiscing.'

'I won't be a second.'

'It's fine,' said Patrick. 'Hardly a place for hurrying.'

'You should see us when it's all going off.' Bridget turned up the lighting and looked down at Tariq. 'He's calm enough, isn't he? I wonder what he's thinking?'

Sara and Patrick exchanged raised eyebrows while she noted readings from the monitors and checked the intravenous flow. 'Not a lot changing. That's good enough for me. I'll leave you in peace.' Dimming the lights, she quietly closed the door behind her.

'So then…?' said Patrick.

'Yes, I'll never forget that moment. The warmth, the beauty of the day, the contours of the hills. The touch of his hand. As if I was being set alight.'

Her expression darkened.

22

He led her by their enfolded hands off the track, down and across a field to a copse. There in a clearing, he dumped his rucksack and hamper, and laid out a rug and two cushions.

'Wherever I am, I like to have my creature comforts,' he said.

Shafts of sun drove through leaves and branches to warm her. She sat on the rug, cross-legged, watching him. Even the simplest of his movements was beguiling. The clasping of their hands confirmed at last that perhaps they were more than friends; not that she had doubted it but, over the days and weeks spent together when he would never give her a physical hint, not even a peck on the cheek, she had occasionally wondered. She could, of course, never allow him to go beyond the most chaste of touches. Though, if his lips were to approach hers...

He unpacked the picnic, and offered her a smoked salmon sandwich, crisps and tomatoes, and lemonade which he removed from a cold bag. When she'd finished these, he pulled out a small box with two slices of cheesecake which he placed on paper plates.

'I wasn't expecting all this,' she exclaimed. The walk had made her thirsty and she stretched out her plastic glass. 'This lemonade's delicious. What did you put in it?'

He smiled. 'I am glad you are enjoying it.'

He watched her drink and eat hungrily; she felt his eyes on her. 'You're not eating much,' she said.

'I prefer to watch you,' he said. He edged closer and put an arm round her, kissing her on a cheek as she chewed – his lips had touched her skin almost without her knowing. She light-heartedly affected to ease him away but liked the close-ness. He accepted the hint, took a sandwich for himself and fastidiously nibbled it.

'This is a place I could stay for ever,' he said.

She turned to him, beaming with pleasure. 'So could I.' The sensations coursing through her body and thoughts churning in her head were unlike any she'd felt or known before. Until now, 'love' had been a dutiful, unquestioned affection for her father and a few of her favourite relatives. There'd been the odd boy she'd had a crush on but this was wholly different; she was sure she'd discovered what the word 'love' could really mean. Did he feel the same?

After the picnic, they lay down on the rug and pillows and she felt sleepy, almost in a trance, serenaded by the soft rustling of leaves and cries of birdsong.

She thought she heard a stirring in the undergrowth. 'What was that?' She opened her eyes to find him leaning over her.

'Just a fox coming to get you.' He grinned and stroked her cheek, slowly moving his hand down to intrude beneath her T-shirt.

'What are you doing?' Whatever her mind told her to say, her body was relaxed, at ease. His fingers now stroking her breast, a fluttering of goosebumps gave a thrilling shiver. He gently removed his hand. She felt relief and disappointment.

He raised his head over hers, looking down on her. 'You are a beautiful woman,' he said. 'I have never seen a beauty like yours.' She frowned and shook her head at him. 'I mean it.'

He cradled her head in his arm and moved their faces closer together. He kissed her, his tongue travelling around her mouth and teeth in a way she had never imagined. She reacted unsurely and he drew back. 'Have you kissed a man like this before?'

'No.'

'It is good, yes.'

'Yes, it's good.' She turned her face. 'But we shouldn't.'

'Do you not love me, Sara?'

She gazed into his eyes, so close that they seemed to go in and out of focus. 'I think so, yes.'

'Love, yes. I believe this is our love. It is all right, we will do nothing you do not want to.' He looked deeply into her, with the gentlest of smiles. 'But does it not mean the time has come when we must know each other properly?' His hand moved more eagerly down to her trouser belt and she felt him undoing her buckle. She wanted to say no but her throat was dry; words wouldn't come out. Her belt opened and he pulled down the zip of her jeans, his fingers creeping beneath her pants.

'No,' she gasped, 'this is wrong.' Among the forces assailing her, an intruder sneaked in: fear. She hoped he saw her fright because then he would know he must stop.

'Allow a man to judge what is right and what is wrong,' he said. 'We will do no more than we should.' He straightened, now seeming to tower over her. 'Let me just see you. All of you.' She was feeble, woozy, her mind felt separate from her limp body. She closed her eyes – trying to ignore what was happening. She felt his hands slide her jeans down; a breeze passed between her sweating legs. He removed her boots and socks and slid the jeans over ankles and feet. She put a hand on her pants, but still lay inert, eyes closed.

'Your skin seems so pale,' he said.

'My English mother,' she murmured.

'You never told me that.'

She breathed softly, his voice echoing, her sleepiness over-whelming.

'Perhaps this explains why there is something so special about you.' He eased away from her and she heard tiny, muted sounds of undressing, a zip opening and a brushing of clothes. She half-opened her eyes; he was crouched over her, his shirt still on but trousers and pants down to his knees. She saw the pinkness large and straight.

'We mustn't,' she whimpered.

'I will be careful,' he said. It was happening, she must move. She tried to raise her shoulders but his hands were on them, pinning her. His body was over her, blocking her escape. He yanked down her pants, put his knees between her legs and pried them apart. His breath came heavily and urgently.

'Stop,' she whispered. 'Please stop.' She raised her voice. 'No. Please no. I'm not ready. Not yet.'

He clamped his hand over her mouth. 'Shush.' She felt breathless. 'It is too late, Sara. It will be beautiful. This is our love.' He pushed himself hard into her: for reasons she did not understand – maybe a fear of suffocation – she instinctively put her arms around his back and pulled him up and against her so tightly that his head dropped over her shoulder and the oven-like fierceness of his breathing passed beyond her.

He forced hard, further and further into her, hurting her more than when he had entered, then, with a shudder, flopped on top of her, motionless. For a second she wondered if he'd died. Suddenly he raised himself, pulled himself out of her, still stiff, the most painful seconds of all. She felt trickles dripping on her pubic hair and thighs. He turned and slumped on his back. Freed of his weight, she could breathe more easily. A prickling burned deep within her eyes. She couldn't bear him to see and rolled away onto her side where she could brush escaping tears away. He'd put her jeans to the side of the rug and she stretched a hand to grab tissues from a pocket. She wiped herself where he had been and retrieved the tissue. It was smeared with small streaks of fresh blood.

She heard sounds of him cleaning and tidying himself and then felt his body closing once more against hers.

'It was good, yes,' he said.

She didn't want to reply but somehow – instinctively and without thought – a tiny voice murmured, 'It hurt a little.'

They drove home in silence. Occasionally he turned to look at her and smiled; her eyes stayed fixed on the road ahead. Her body was sore, her head clouded with shame. There was no one she would be able to tell what had just happened. It was inconceivable to say anything – anything at all – to her father. Perhaps if her mother had been around things would have been different…

She thought of friends with mothers and sisters, all on hand to advise and confide in. If only she'd been able to discuss Kareem with such a sister, none of this would ever have happened; right at the start they'd have said, 'No!' She'd never have found herself with a man, unaccompanied, in a deserted wood, miles from home. Now, after this, she was more alone than ever. She would always be alone; always have to work it out herself.

'He raped you,' said Patrick. 'Violently. Sounds like he drugged you as well. It was an assault.'

Sara's eyes were on her father, motionless except for the chest, slowly expanding and contracting. 'We shouldn't use such words,' she whispered. 'It might upset him.'

The memory was making her shaky, buffeted by a swirl of emotions. Fear, anger, guilt, the sense of violation that had never left her. She had one hand on the bed; Patrick took the other and gently held it between both of his. 'If your father was listening, he'd use the same words as me.'

'I didn't understand it at the time,' she forced on, appearing not to hear him. 'I couldn't tell anyone.' She stared at her father. 'Least of all him. Certainly not the police. The disgrace. My first thought was that I'd have to marry him. It seems absurd now to think that was the only solution for the person I then was.'

'To think how careless he was.'

'Care was not in his vocabulary. You only realise that later.'

'No,' said Patrick. 'Except for himself.'

'The ridiculous thing was that I didn't end it there and then. He and I were the only ones who knew what had happened – there was no one else to talk to. I had to try to work it out. I might be pregnant. He said he had tickets for a trip on the Millennium Wheel. It wasn't one of my study or work experience days so I said yes. And among the crowds, nothing could happen. There was a part of me that still ached to see him – to understand better, to know answers. To look at him.'

They agreed to meet at the entrance to the Wheel at 2 p.m.

She arrived early and hid behind a tree, watching, waiting. Ten minutes later he showed up. He looked around, searching, a puzzled expression in his eyes. The anxiety on his face momentarily pleased her – until she started wondering how long he'd stay before giving up. Maybe he'd approach another girl and offer her the ticket to accompany him. She jumped up from her seat and ran, exaggerating her breathlessness so she could say she'd sprinted from the slow-running tube.

'Hello, Sara.' He was as controlled as ever. 'Did you not think I would wait? Have I ever been impatient with you?'

The heat of summer had worn off and the day was cool enough for her to need a cardigan over her cream blouse and jeans. Kareem wore a brown leather jacket she hadn't seen before; it enhanced his lean figure and the flat stomach beneath. She tried to ignore it. She gave him a peck on the cheek and resisted when he tried to pull her into his arms.

'It is time for our ride,' he said, affecting not to notice.

The wheel inched its way up until they could take in the sweep from Tower Bridge to Vauxhall and beyond. The day was cloudy, compressing the city more intimately than a clearer sky. From this angle the epicentre drawing the eye could only be Westminster and Whitehall: the glass walls of City towers were too immersed in greyness, the flatlands in the far east and west too undefined. London's skyscraper boom stood smeary in the murk.

Sara leant on the rail by the curved window, awe-struck by the street patterns below and the tiny figures scurrying through their day. It was her city, whatever her family roots and culture – and she was a modern woman of contemporary London with all its opportunities and temptations. Her eyes swivelled right to Lincoln's Inn – her future, taking on the white, male supremacy. Had she now ruined it all?

She felt his hands gliding from behind over her hip bones and joining at the front of her waist. Unthinkingly, she leant back into him and felt his hardness against the top of her buttocks. She froze, scared of both her modernity and of him – and of where it had led her. She pulled away and turned to face him.

'It's stunning,' she said, forcing a smile.

'Yes.' He didn't return it. 'What do you see when you look below?'

'I see the city I live in.'

'And when you look at Big Ben and those Houses of Parliament?'

She frowned. 'What do you mean?'

'Just say.'

'Tradition, I guess. British democracy. Pretty pinnacles.'

'That is not what I see,' he said with unusual coldness.

She saw the same change in his expression as when he had silenced her in that dappled copse. The same intruder, fear, returned. He looked around – the other two couples in their pod were a few yards away with their backs to them, out of earshot. He moved closer to her and whispered harshly into her ear.

'What I see are centuries of false superiority. Empire, financial exploitation, colonialism, snobbery, the takeover of lands and culture. Oppression is the word vulgarly used but commonly understood.'

She squinted at him. Where was all this coming from? 'You don't look like an oppressed person to me, Kareem,' she murmured back.

'How do you know, Sara, what beats within me?'

'Do you want to explain?'

'Anger. The hurt of our people. I sometimes burn with the desire for revenge.'

'Why? It's history. It's over.'

'No. It is never over.'

'We live in a different world now. It's becoming more equal. Yes, it's slow and there's a way to go, but we'll get there.'

'My God, I might wish I had your innocence, your illusions. But when I look down at this so-called Palace of Westminster,' he hissed, 'all I want is to see it explode into the air and spew out flames. And for those inside to fry and their souls to rot.'

She looked down and away from him, surprise turning to shock and, then, mystification. In the seconds he spoke those words, a potential and fearful truth flared. The man she had seen as one person was, stage by stage, act by act, revealing himself as quite another. 'I can't believe you mean that, Kareem.'

His shoulders slumped, the fire diminished. 'Yes,' he said dully. 'I mean it. I mean it when I say it.'

'If it's just words, don't speak them.'

'Every revolution begins with "just words".'

Their pod was now past the Wheel's zenith and, as it crept back towards ground, they stared out in a subdued, uncomfortable silence, emerging into the dampness of a gathering drizzle. She wanted to get away. More than want, it was desperation. To hasten her escape, she tried to display a gratitude she did not feel. 'It was great, thank you, I really appreciate you getting the tickets. But I said I'd meet someone for tea.'

'Oh, who is that?'

She frowned, shook her head at him and, as the pod came to a rest, turned to go. Did he seem momentarily ashamed? Was he capable of feeling shame?

'I would very much like to see you again so that we may discuss any issues that have arisen between us.'

'Maybe.' She spoke into the distance.

'I will wait in the car in the usual place on Thursday.'

'Maybe,' she repeated.

She turned on her heel and headed towards Westminster Bridge. As she sped up, she glanced back to check he wasn't following, her heart thumping so hard that it was painful. She looked up to the top of the Wheel – thank God she hadn't been alone with him in that pod.

The date was Monday 10 September 2001.

'Can you remember where you were on 9/11?' she asked Patrick.

'Of course. Sitting in the law library. One or two people started leaving. You could detect an atmosphere. Within minutes we were all out watching the TV in the bar next door.'

'Impossible to forget, yes?'

'Totally. And you?' he asked.

'It was one of my work experience days at the solicitors' – I didn't know then which branch of law I wanted to do. It was the end of the lunch break. Like you, we all crowded round. In our case it was in reception. It was the only place with a telly.'

She stood and peered through the glass partition to the ante-space. The nurse was seated in front of the computer, the small ward beyond as silent as the night except for the occasional siren from the streets below. No signs of consciousness in her father – she must stop looking for them.

She sat down again beside Patrick, moving both her hands around one of her father's. 'And yet,' she said, 'unforgettable, appalling, catastrophic, tragic, out of the blue – whatever you might want to call it – Kareem didn't even phone or text me. Nothing. Even after what he'd said on the Wheel. I thought he might feel ashamed, want to apologise without delay.'

'Perhaps, for once in his life, he was too embarrassed,' said Patrick.

'I don't think so. I can imagine him sitting on his own, watching it all unfold. But I still can't fully imagine what was going on in his mind.'

She took a book out of her bag. 'That night of 9/11 I stood on a chair in my room to fetch my copy of the Qur'an from a top shelf. It had been gathering dust for years.' She laid it on the bed and opened it at a marker. 'This was the page it fell open at. Must have been the last time I'd read it. Chapter 33, Verse 35. I've no idea what girlish thoughts I'd been having. Read it.' She paused. 'Read it to me aloud.'

Patrick gingerly took the book. '"For Muslim men and women, for believing men and women, for true men and women, for men and women who are patient and for men and women who guard their chastity, and for men and women who engage much in Allah's praise, for them has Allah prepared forgiveness and great reward."'

'I hadn't guarded my chastity, had I? But what seemed a miracle happened – my period came. I thought pregnancy would be my punishment. When it wasn't, something changed. The fear went. I knew where I stood. I thought hard. I decided to see him one last time.'

23

The red Mazda sports car, hood down, drew up; she glanced around and got in.

'Where would you like me to drive you?' he asked, as courteously as when he'd first exchanged words with her.

'Let's go back to white yummy-mummy land.' Her tone was even; she determined to keep it that way.

They drove in silence, he glaring at the road and tut-tutting at straying pedestrians while she stared ahead.

'Do you wish to walk?' he asked, parking neatly and switching off the engine.

'No, we'll talk here.' She whipped round. 'I expected to hear from you after what happened on Tuesday. I don't know what. Even a word of comfort.'

He tapped his fingers on the steering wheel; she waited. 'I did not see it as entirely necessary. Further, I would not have known what words to say.'

'You always have something to say. You certainly had enough to say when we were looking down on Parliament.'

'That is true.' He sounded subdued.

'Didn't you think at least that it was a weird coincidence?'

'I truly have no idea of what you mean.'

'One day you talk about Parliament exploding, the next day three thousand people are killed in the Twin Towers.'

His eyes narrowed. 'If you are trying to find some sort of connection, Sara, I suggest that you analyse such events more rationally.'

She sensed the rage within him but still did not understand what was driving it. Whatever it was, she was going to confront it. 'It made me feel I don't know you. Don't understand you.'

'I do not take it back,' he said. 'What was done on Tuesday was justified.'

'What?'

'I told you. Our people are entitled to payback.'

'Killing all those innocent victims.'

'Those towers were not innocent. They were symbols of domination. Imperialism. Exploitation. Like the Pentagon. Like the White House if the fourth plane had got through.'

'Do you truly believe that, Kareem?' She no longer felt eighteen; in the past two days she had grown up and was now an adult trying to drum sense into a wayward fool. 'Because I hope you're just in some muddled way theorising. Philosophising. Whatever you want to call it. And you'll grow out of it.'

He softened. 'I hope one day you might grow into it.'

She fought back tears – she refused to release them – welling up from an indefinable sense of betrayal. That, somehow, he had cheated her, not just sexually but by not presenting his full self from the outset; and that she had betrayed herself by not having the intelligence or insight, before he engulfed her, to probe beyond the outer sheath of the civilised and romantic gentleman.

'An action like this,' he continued, 'will have a counter-reaction, then a counter-counter-reaction which will show up the West for what it is.'

'What do you want, Kareem? War? Chaos? You're someone who can do so much good if you choose to.'

'This *will* be good. If you had spent as much time as I have among the West's upper classes, you would agree with me.'

'Is that where this is all coming from?'

'No, they are only a symptom. We have suffered centuries of rapacity and aggression. Now we can begin to redress the balance of history.'

She looked away. He spoke with a cold aloofness – as if he were an automaton repeating a drilled-in slogan. Had there always been something of that about him? The way, as she now reinterpreted it, that he gave his opinions – as if he'd always rehearsed? There was the same handsomeness but a dullness in the eyes. No joy. A dead stare.

'I don't believe this is the real you,' she said at last. 'Not the person I've been spending all this time with.'

He took time to answer. 'Look at me, Sara. You are beautiful. I have never felt for anyone what I have felt – what I feel – for you. Such a wanting. Such desire.'

'And I've allowed you to have it.' Tears threatened again and she wiped one angrily away.

'No, we have had each other. And we must continue to. It is our fate.'

'Not like this. Not after what you did.'

'You must not regret it. It was a wonderful thing that we were joined.'

His perception was so one-sided that part of her wanted him to know the truth. But what was the point in trying to reverse or recapture what might have been? Now it was no more than a wrongly imagined dream. She gathered her bag and moved her left hand towards the door lever. He grabbed both her hands with his.

'Do not leave. We have to be together now. It is our destiny. It is God's will.'

'Don't give me your pretence of God, Kareem.' For the first

time, her tone changed – not a shout but a low hiss. 'I thought your God says sex is prohibited outside marriage. What God's will do you dare to claim after what you've done to me?'

She tried to free her hands but he tightened his grip and began to twist. 'Let me go.'

'I will never release you.'

'Let me go.' This time she shouted. A mother with a pram was walking past the car. She beat her face against the door, screaming. He crunched and turned the skin of her wrist ever tighter. She screamed again, catching the woman's eye. Kareem saw it. He let go. She opened the door and rushed towards the pram.

'Are you all right, love?'

'No. Yes. I'm fine, thank you.'

She ran, not daring to look behind to see if he were pursuing her. After a hundred yards or so she slowed to check: there was no one in sight, just the sound of a reedy-voiced car starting up and accelerating harshly into the distance. She looked down at her wrists, turning bright red and fiery with pain.

'The flash of anger,' said Patrick, 'is something I never saw. We were courting him, flattering him.' He suspected she had never told anyone the story before; certainly not the real story. 'But I can imagine it inside him.'

Sara moved within inches of her father's becalmed face, watching him silently.

'I think your father,' said Patrick, 'would want to ask you why you never went to him at the time.'

'I'd answer that, even if it was partly because I feared his shame, it was mostly because I couldn't hurt him.' She paused. 'What I'd have done if I got pregnant doesn't bear thinking about.'

Patrick allowed the flicker of fear, still kindled by the remembered dread, a moment to ebb. 'And then?'

'A couple of months later, I was chatting with Salman, my cousin who got married. "Your friend, Kareem, was a handsome chap. What's he like?" I asked lightly. "Didn't know him that well," Salman replied, "he was only on the edge of our group. He always paid for things so I thought I should invite him." Then he gave me a look. "Why, Sara, do you fancy him?" "'Course not," I said. "He's probably got a girlfriend anyway." "Yeah," he said, "I've mostly lost touch with him since the wedding, but he did have a girl hanging around. Called Marion. English. Quite posh. Sorry if you fancied your chances, kid," he said.'

'Oh, Sara,' said Patrick.

'I know,' she said. 'Among everything else, what a fool. But my main thought was different. I escaped. Marion would become the abused.'

A moment passed, then Patrick spoke with hot intensity. 'They must have been mad.'

'Who?'

'MI5 in the form of Isobel Le Marchant, now Dame Isobel... if, in some way, they were giving this man no one properly knew the power of life and death over other human beings.' He looked as if he wanted to flagellate himself. 'And a signed contract saying that he'd never be brought to book.'

'Yes,' said Sara calmly. 'Though it's still only our assumption.' She laid her arms on the edge of her father's bed and rested her head on them. 'Imagine being Sami, brought before him, being told he's called the Adviser. Whatever the name, he can see he's the one who decides fates. Imagine being Marion, or Maryam, so terrified that she has to escape from him.' She paused and rubbed her nose along the sleeve of her sweater. 'Imagine being me, an eighteen-year-old virgin lying beneath him, overwhelmed and pinned down, about to be raped. And him loving it all.' The confusion of emotions was resolving to a cold, enduring anger.

'Power,' said Patrick. 'The love of power.'

'And what was he doing to you?'

'Again trying to exert his power, I guess.'

'He had no power over you. Or Isobel or J.'

'The power of manipulation, then. They were desperate.'

'And no underlying principle. It's all about himself. It doesn't matter whose side he's on. Politics, ideology, religion all irrelevant.'

'What about Islam?'

'It would never have been more than a means. Causes were handy tools, nothing more.'

'You can't be sure of that.'

'Yes, we can. You saw for yourself it didn't matter to him that he was switching sides. He just had to preserve a dominance. My question is whether Isobel fully saw it. Maybe she did. Maybe she deliberately gave him a role that fulfilled what he needed. Maybe, with that same deliberation, she stroked and massaged him. "It's you the world is depending on, Kareem." Can't you imagine it? "One day, Kareem, your greatness will emerge for those in a position to see it." Maybe it went like that.'

Patrick sighed. 'Or, you're wanting to say, maybe it didn't.'

She sat bolt upright. 'Precisely. Who was manipulating who? Who really was in control?'

'There's one simple indicator,' said Patrick, eyes aching from fatigue and the alcohol in his system that he'd been disguising. 'She got to be Head of MI5.'

'Indicators are not enough.'

'It's late, Sara, you should sleep.'

'No,' she whispered harshly. The anger, now overt and visible to him, overwhelmed any sense of exhaustion. Anger with herself, with her father and himself, with fate – a moral anger he'd never seen before. 'Kareem needed a victim. Always.

He lined them up. That's what gave him the kick. I was one. Marion, Sami, how many others we may never know. Each time his appetite was whetted more. You, Patrick, you were a victim, you signed that contract.' He stayed silent, closing his eyes again. The storm had to blow itself out. 'Was Isobel a victim too? That's what we need to know.' She put her lips to her father's ear. 'Come on, Dad,' she whispered urgently, 'I'm asking you too. Wake up and tell me the answer.'

The nurse entered and knelt by Sara, putting an arm round her. Patrick could tell she'd been watching. 'Let him rest.'

Sara stretched out a hand; he took it and led her away. Bridget nodded to him and he nodded back in agreement. She went peacefully with him to the family room and lay herself on the sofa, curling up like a small child. He returned to the intensive care unit and asked Bridget if there was a blanket. By the time she had found one and he was laying it over, her eyes were closed. He watched her for a few minutes and left.

Around 5 a.m. she stirred, wondering briefly where she was and why she seemed alone. She checked her watch – it would soon be time for prayers. As the events of the night and the image of her immobile father were replayed, she found no inclination for them. Her mouth tasted sour and bitter; her breath must be foul. She tried to recall what she'd eaten or drunk; the attempt made her hungry and thirsty. She rose, turned on a light, and inspected herself in a mirror. There was a door ajar in the corner; she remembered there was a washroom. A toothbrush, toothpaste and unpacked bar of soap were on the basin. For a moment she was puzzled, and then, for a second, even though she'd already packed a toothbrush and paste in her bag, felt a tiny joy. She removed her scarf, brushed her teeth and soaped her face, dabbing it lightly with paper towels.

Rather than turn right towards the intensive care unit, she remembered the nurse's instructions and turned left to the canteen. There was increased shuffling and pacing of smocked men and women along corridors, trolleys being wheeled, a hospital waking up. She pushed open the double doors; two porters were closing and shifting a partition in the canteen. Its disappearance revealed a single figure sitting at a table, back bowed, shoulders hunched, head flopped on arms. She crept slowly opposite and murmured, 'Thank you, Patrick.'

A blurry-eyed face raised itself. 'What for?'

'The things you got for me. Being here.' The face shook itself and forced its eyes open. She hesitated. 'You could have stayed in the room.'

'You might have thought it disrespectful.' She smiled at him, saying nothing. 'Coffee?'

'This time I'll get it,' she said.

She returned with steaming cups and biscuits. 'I never got to the photograph. The reason you and I are here.'

24

The audience drifted through swing doors in their ones and twos to the bare lecture room. It was a smallish gathering; Sara did not count precisely but certainly fewer than thirty. Murmurings of 'Hello, brother' and 'Hello, sister' were interrupted by occasional cries of recognition.

The dramatically changed world after 9/11 had brought both vengefulness and soul-searching. She had marched against the Iraq war in the great London demonstration of 2003, rubbing shoulders with all colours and creeds. But in the warp and weft of daily life, that good-natured togetherness was a mirage. Once you might have been called 'Paki bastard' or 'bloody Arab'; after 9/11 you were a 'fucking Muslim' whether or not you'd ever set foot inside a mosque.

She had gradually made herself less visible, wearing modest, fuller clothes. It had been an almost subconscious process; when she occasionally analysed it, she wasn't sure whether it was more the consequence of her individual violation by Kareem or of the violation of the world beyond. She was unresolved about Islam as a religion, still lacking a deep-seated faith and sceptical of the afterlife, but admiring its discipline and calming prayers. She was on a journey of discovery, and when she saw that the Queen Vic's Islamic Society was hosting an evening with leaders from the 'Islam in the Community' campaign, she went along.

The President of the Society led prayers: '*Bismillah hiram maan niraheem…*' Then two figures walked on to the platform.

She wanted to flee but in this close-knit group it was impossible without making a scene. He was as tall and lean as ever, the black hair wavy and lustrous but longer, hanging down over his collar, his fine-boned face now supplemented by a shortish, groomed beard running in a neat line from one ear and around his chin to the other. He was dressed in a free-flowing white robe. The handsomeness aimed at saintliness, a prophet for the contemporary world. He spotted her instantly and smiled. She was trapped.

The woman alongside him she did not recognise. She was also tall, a sky-blue silk scarf over her head, strands of blonde hair pushing through its edges like tiny shoots in cracks of paving. Her face was roundish, her skin pale and unblemished, with a prettily snubbed nose and cupid lips. Together they looked ethereal.

'Brothers and sisters,' began the president, 'we're privileged to have with us this evening Kareem and Maryam from Islam in the Community…' Sara remembered her conversation with Salman four years before. The girl he'd called Marion had become Kareem's convert and adornment.

Kareem related with his customary precision of speech how the post 9/11 world had awakened the visceral prejudices of the Christian and Jewish West against Islam. 'So what are we to do? What does Islam in our community now mean?' Sara scanned his listeners, a few eagerly attentive, others blank-faced or looking down at their hands, perhaps wary.

'What is our own personal struggle – our jihad – to be? Do we – as in the bad joke of Christians, who aim cluster bombs at innocent families and children in Afghanistan and Iraq, while claiming allegiance to their prophet's instruction to turn the other cheek – do we accept and submit? Or do we fight? And what are to be our weapons? Words only? Or must there now be more than words?'

When he finished, the few who'd shown rapt attention clapped loudly; beyond them the applause was lip service. One or two kept their hands to themselves, ignoring the disapproving looks.

Sara searched for an escape route but the geography of the room was against her. The exit was at its lower level; she would have to walk directly past Kareem to reach it. Instead it was he who made the first gesture, moving up and beside her before she had time to think.

'Sara!' He smiled, stretching out his arms.

'Kareem.' The magnetism was still there, the beam of energy from those brown eyes. She looked at him, avoiding any animation, keeping her hands by her side.

Maryam joined them. 'Did you ever meet Sara?' asked Kareem innocently; he must have known she had not.

'I would never forget if I had,' said Maryam with gushing flattery.

'We're going to eat,' said Kareem, 'you must join us.'

Sara wished she had a prepared excuse that would have stopped him. 'No really, I must—'

'Of course you will come. We have room in the car. We are meeting a friend or two who will interest you.'

The president of the society loomed alongside. 'Yes, you must come.' She felt locked between them, their prisoner. But there was a tiny flicker of curiosity too.

The sports car had been replaced by something much larger

with tinted windows. Kareem and the president sat in the front, Maryam and Sara in the back.

'How did you know it would be Kareem speaking?' asked Maryam.

'I didn't,' replied Sara. 'No names were given.' She paused, catching sight of him glancing at her in his rear-view mirror. 'It was a surprise.'

'A good one, I hope.' Sara did not answer. 'How long have you known Kareem?' asked Maryam.

'Oh, we go back a while.'

'Did you meet at university?'

'Yes. His third year, I think. And you?'

'I was doing jobs here and there,' Maryam answered vaguely. 'There was no university for me.' Sara detected bitterness and the shutters rising. There was a waspishness and also a fragility about her.

In silence, they pretended to listen to the two men in front. Through the tinted window, Sara saw the lights of King's Cross and St Pancras struggling against the evening sun as they headed west, finally turning into Edgware Road and towards Marble Arch. Mothers on pavements in black burqas wheeling babies in smart new buggies, and the occasional open-topped Ferrari or Lamborghini with Kuwaiti or Qatari number plates, driven by white-shirted young men wearing gold neck chains, revealed the oil-enriched tip of England's inverted pyramid of Islam. It wasn't like that in the suburbs of Bradford and Birmingham.

Stopped at traffic lights, Kareem turned round. 'Bayswater. Full of Arabs like me. And the best Lebanese restaurant in London.' The funds continued to flow.

There were six of them gathered round the table, the four who had arrived in Kareem's car and two other men out of her direct eyeline – Asians in their late twenties from Pakistan or

Bangladesh, Sara guessed, hardly making them out in the dim lighting of the restaurant. Sara and Maryam automatically sat down next to each other, Kareem placing himself to Sara's left.

'You were one person I had not expected to see,' he said.

'Why?'

He lowered his voice. 'I never forget what you said. Perhaps your eyes have since been opened.' She felt the charge in his use of the word 'eyes' as his burned into hers. She winced, fearful of his ability to beguile her and flushed with irritation at his assumption of superior knowledge.

'If you're speaking of 9/11, my eyes have seen what followed,' she said. 'Of course I've had to rethink. Hasn't everyone?'

'In that case it has had its effect.'

'Of which you approve, I suppose.'

He stared inscrutably at her. 'Or perhaps of which I was prophetic. The war of the West against the East, reaction and counter-reaction. The Bush and Blair folly of Iraq. My God, can you imagine a surer way of arousing our world against theirs?'

'Our world?'

'Of course, our world of Islam.'

'No, that is not our world of Islam. It may be yours. But if I manage to find my world of Islam, it will be a world I want to share, not one I want to dominate others.'

'Sara, you are still too young. Too blind.' She felt herself warming, anger building at the condescension, the arrogance that was now insufferable. Why had she not seen that early enough? He moved closer, whispering. 'Great things have happened in the world. Great deeds. There will be more to come. Believe me.'

'What do you mean, Kareem?' He watched her silently, adopting his most mystical expression. 'What are you talking about?'

'Can you not feel it all around you? Not just the Middle East but the whole world beyond. Even here, in this, our – I mean your – country. Do you ever think, Sara, that you should be trying to do something, not just be part of the chorus on the sidelines? Instead, become an actor at the centre of the stage.'

'What is your play?'

'Who can predict that? You are an intelligent young woman.' He lowered his voice even further to a murmur, his lips almost touching her left ear. 'History will dictate that the rain of death on our people cannot go unavenged.'

She shifted in her seat, trying to edge away, but felt his body following hers. To her right, Maryam was engaged in a conversation across the table and almost pushing into her. She must disconnect, switch him off. 'You're talking rubbish, Kareem,' she whispered back, 'it's just boasting. Seeing yourself as some kind of prophet. You know as well as I do it's all an act. You even said it yourself.' She broke away. 'Time for me to leave.'

'No.' His loud whisper hissed it as an order. 'There is nothing to fear,' he continued, softening, 'I understand your feelings. Do you think I would ever want to frighten you?' His voice lowered again. 'You have meant more to me than anyone. I always see your face in my dreams.'

As once she'd felt love and then fear, now she felt a dulled contempt. She must leave before it turned to hatred. She turned away from him, fished in her bag, pulled out from her purse a five-pound note and an old receipt. Furtively, she scrawled a number on it. 'I'm so sorry,' she said, looking at her watch and rising. 'I've lost track of the time. I promised to be home for my father.' She waved the five-pound note. 'Can I—'

Kareem cut across her with a magisterial wave of the hand. 'Of course not. This is my evening.'

She threw him a short smile, replaced the note in her bag,

and turned back to embrace Maryam. 'Good luck,' she murmured, 'I hope everything works out well for you.' Her back to Kareem, she pushed the creased receipt into her hand, mumbling, 'If you ever need...' As Maryam took it, Sara saw bruising on her arms and wrists. She waved a hand at the other three men, looked past Kareem and walked as fast as she dared into the street, promising herself that, whatever else happened in her future life, Kareem Abdullah bin-Jilani would never come near her again.

'I want to find him,' she said.

'You just told me,' said Patrick, 'you left that night, wanting him never again to get near you.'

'Correct. This is me going to him. Don't put your own life on hold – that's what the surgeon said. He's right. What better purpose could there be right now? To track him down and hold him to account. For whatever it is he might have done.'

'Wherever he might be, we still need evidence of deeds done.'

'I want to see Isobel too. Confront her. She must know where he is.'

'No chance.'

'Who else then?'

'Has to be J.'

'Where is he?'

'I've no idea. But I can think of someone who will. We'll need to call by the office.'

The open-plan area was still hushed – Clovis and Rayah turning bleak faces and murmuring insipid hellos. There was no sign of Pamela; the door to Morahan's office remained shut. Patrick unlocked the Legal office door.

'I've brought the files in,' he said, 'we're going to show them to someone.'

'What?' murmured Sara.

He extracted a folder from his case, and headed for the door. 'Come with me.' He turned left and knocked on the adjoining door; it was unlocked and he entered without waiting for an answer.

A surprised face whipped round, lowering broad, grey-rimmed spectacles. 'Oh, the invasion of the Legals,' said Sylvia Labone without enthusiasm.

'Have you a moment, Sylvia?'

'My God, what a question,' she rasped.

'I've something to show you. But first I want to know something.' She examined him with an almost imperceptible show of interest. 'Why didn't you say? All these weeks and months you and I have been here, why didn't you say?'

'Don't give me riddles, Patrick.'

'That we'd met, of course. It came back to me in the night.'

'You must have been dreaming.'

'No. Not at all. Thames House. 2005. J had me in for a grilling. He went off to find a completely unnecessary cup of tea and you popped your head around the corner. I know, it's thirteen years ago, but it was you. I was sitting alone and you said something like, "Can I help?" I looked up at this long-skirted ex-hippy – well, not quite – her face lined with the experience of life, and I think I said something like, "I'm fine, thanks, just waiting for him, et cetera." You stared hard at me, said something and disappeared.'

'Did I really?' she mused, softening in a way Sara hadn't seen before. 'Did I really?'

'Yes, Sylvia, you did,' said Patrick. 'I've only just clocked. J wanted you to give me the once over, didn't he? The cup of tea was a feint.'

'J,' she said.

'What did you tell him?'

'I said I thought you were suitable.'

'Suitable for what?'

'Goodness, he'd never tell me that. I was just the archivist. When we had proper archives.'

'Keeper of the secrets.'

'So sad.' She looked at her computer mournfully. 'All kept in these machines now with their codes which any bright boy who can add two and two can enter. A real secret can only be held in the palm of a hand.'

Patrick dropped two slim folders on her desk. 'Put these in your hand.' Patrick sensed Sara's agitation. She was frowning, her eyes begging silent questions. As Sylvia repositioned her spectacles, extracted the Blackburn files and buried her face in them, he put a forefinger to his mouth and signalled a quiescent 'shush'.

'Hmmm. Unredacted. The real thing.' Sylvia spoke with little more than a murmur. 'How did you get these?'

'Do you have any friends called Sayyid, Sylvia? A nickname maybe. Even an alias.'

'If I did, I couldn't tell you. If I say I don't, you won't know whether to believe me.'

'I'll believe your answer, Sylvia,' said Sara. It was her first intervention.

'Sara Shah,' she hissed. 'Sara Shah. Do I remember?' Sylvia frowned at her, then shook her head. 'No. Distraction. You wanted an answer.'

'Sayyid,' prompted Sara.

'Sayyid. Sayyid.' The same mantra, the memory whirring – no fakery, thought Sara. 'Nothing. Nothing comes.'

'How deaf are your walls?' asked Patrick.

'Stone deaf. Deaf and dumb.'

'We need to see J.'

'I'm sure you do. As we all do.'

'I mean now.' He began to retrieve the files. 'I want him to see these. So we understand.'

'Don't make his life difficult.'

'If you tell me where he is, I promise I won't.'

She turned to Sara. 'I promise too.'

Sylvia leafed through a Rolodex file and stopped at an initial that was neither J, W nor T. Sara wondered what her code was – it certainly didn't delay finding the information she needed. She leant down, picked up a mobile phone from her handbag and dialled a number from the Rolodex rather than the phone's memory. It was answered immediately. Sylvia walked over to a window, turned her back and had a brief conversation out of their earshot. In what seemed no time at all, she was walking back – the call seemed too short to contain the information it needed to convey. She sat at her computer and entered a website – neither dared to peep over her shoulder as she searched.

She looked up. '11.37, St Pancras to Deal. He'll be waiting for you at the pier at 1.15. He said it's either now, in the hope that word of your arrival doesn't get out in time, or not at all. Now go, and we'll never speak of this again.'

Without a 'thank you', understanding it might not be appreciated, Sara and Patrick turned on their heels, exited, locked themselves inside the Legal office and walked over to their window.

'It worked,' said Patrick.

'You took one big risk there,' she replied. 'You still can't be sure she's on-side. I sometimes have the feeling she's watching us.'

'Me too. But not like that, I think. More the guardian angel.' He stared out of the window, confirming some distant truth.

'I've sensed it for a while. She hates them. But honestly, I didn't remember that encounter till just now. Even when I said it, I wasn't confident.'

'She remembered.'

'Oh yes, she certainly did. She doesn't forget. Or forgive.'

25

He stood alone halfway along the concrete pier. Patrick recognised him from the coat – the same brown corduroy jacket, fraying at the edges like the man wearing it. But as they neared him, there was nothing changed about the glint in the eye, illuminated against a dull blanket of grey cloud stretching down to a muddied, churning sea.

'No one's arrived yet,' said J, not bothering with a greeting. A man, thought Sara, who'd decided to act but not to prolong the action.

'Hello J,' said Patrick. 'Who are we expecting?'

'There won't be more than two of them, they won't have had time.'

'We can go inside somewhere. Less visible.'

'They'll know by now you're coming for a chat. No point in hiding that. At least with this infernal racket,' he gestured at the swell booming into the pier's supports, 'their recorders should be stuffed.'

'How are you so sure?'

'Don't be an arse, Patrick. Sylvia's phone, my phone, bugs in the office, you two in their sights...' He checked himself and turned to Sara. 'You're the new lawyer.'

'Yes, hello.'

'Well, hang on tight to that bloody scarf of yours, it gets windy out here. Right, what do you want?'

'We need to make a huddle—'

'For fuck's sake—'

'Against the wind. We've something to show you.'

Patrick fished the Blackburn files out of his case. J looked at them briefly. 'Where d'you get these?'

Patrick nodded to Sara to answer. 'They were delivered anonymously to Sir Francis Morahan. He passed them on to me. It appears he'd hired me so that a proper investigation could be done within the relevant Muslim communities, by someone they might trust.'

'Where did he get 'em?' J was gruff and curt; she took it as brevity, not discourtesy.

'He told me the source had identified himself only as Sayyid.'

'Male or female?'

'Sayyid?'

'It's only a name.'

'He didn't say.'

'Sara's initial investigations have added to the picture,' said Patrick. He described her encounter with Samir and the story of his incarceration and appearance before the Adviser. 'We've assumed both from that, and from your and my encounter in 2005, that this so-called Adviser was Kareem.'

'Correct,' said J.

'We need you to tell us what exactly Kareem was doing,' said Sara.

J looked over their shoulders to the shoreline and the white frontage of Deal with its strikingly asymmetrical roof lines. 'Christ, you don't ask much, do you?' A splutter turned into a hacking cough.

'Are you OK, J?' asked Patrick, seeing his cheeks go purple.

'None of your fucking business. Now where were we?' He conjured up a limpid smile and directed it towards Sara.

'What exactly was Kareem doing?' she asked.

J had a further glance around. 'Pay attention. You go first, Patrick. I'm only going to do this once. Wind back to our other modern terrorist enemy.'

'The IRA,' said Patrick.

'Yes. How did we beat them?'

'You tell me, J.'

'No. You try.'

'Information. Intelligence.'

'Correct. Where from?'

'Eavesdropping, watching, moles, touts.'

'Yes. What was the weakness the IRA had that our Islamist bomber brethren don't?'

'Pass.'

'It was this. Despite all the attempts at cell structures and separate brigades, as they liked to call them, the IRA was at heart a centralised organisation. They had a unitary command. It was called the Army Council.'

'Yes.'

'Question. What makes any such group paranoid and ultimately destroys it?'

'That it's been infiltrated, I guess.'

'Correct. Heard of Stakeknife?'

'Yes, there've been stories about it. Bad stories.'

'Idiot stories. I'll tell you how it started. In the late 1970s I...' J turned to Sara, catching her eye, 'yes, that's me, young lady... I was working with something called the Force Research Unit, FRU, in Belfast, when a Provo chappie walks in off the street one day. To cut a long story short, he says he's had a fall-out and wants to get his own back. Worst mistake they ever made to rile him. He pretends to eat humble pie, rises and rises, eventually becomes a senior cog in their internal security apparatus – it's charmingly known as the "Nutting Squad". Over the next decade, he's so successful in weeding out informers that he becomes its head. He's also chief vetter of potential recruits. The electrical circuit of intelligence. Vets, recruits, cleanses. He convinces the leadership the organisation is riddled with spies. No future operation is safe. Best pack our weapons bags. Start of so-called peace process. Geddit, Patrick?'

'Yes.'

'That was my plan for friend Kareem. We called it Operation Pitchfork. Get that too?'

'Mirror of Stakeknife?'

J spluttered again. 'Nearly. Pitchfork. Pitch for K. K for Kareem. Geddit now?'

'Yes, I get it. But you just said the Islamist threat wasn't unitary.'

'That was the whole bloody point. To make it like that.' J wheezed, searching for air. 'Kareem was perfect. His tendrils proliferated. So we offered him a job. To be our super-spy within British jihad. Like Stakeknife inside the IRA. From the end of 2005 till 2016 we had him in place. Tell me this. How many deaths were there from Islamist terror in the UK over that period? Just one. Right. That poor sod in Woolwich barracks. And what's happened since? London, Manchester, jihadists lying in wait all over the country, security services overwhelmed. But then...' There was a sudden gleam in his eye. 'Then... Al Qaeda, ISIS, recruiters, fighters – they all bought into it. Kareem was their rising, internal star – a man with drive, charisma and access to money. He succeeded. He built an internal security unit to expose their traitors and informers. In fact, he was vetting the likely lads for us and telling us who the bad guys were.'

'How could he convince them he was genuine?' asked Sara.

J turned from Patrick to her, as if to lecture the new girl in the class. 'By delivering them informers, of course. Touts, enemies within, traitors.'

'Delivering?'

'Yes.'

'Meaning?'

'For God's sake. Giving Imam Ali Baba the bad news that little Baba Ali has been working for the other side. Of course, he's not delivering any little Baba Ali's actually working for the other side – because that's our side, isn't it? And he's working for us.'

'Then who *is* he delivering to them?'

'Up to him. As long he's protecting ours.'

'Did he ever have to deliver any of "our" actual guys to maintain his credentials with them?'

'Come on, woman, don't expect me to answer that.'

'OK,' said Sara, not bridling. 'He "delivers" a little Baba Ali. What happens next?'

'That's between Kareem and his jihadi mates.'

'What if jihadi mate asks Kareem to get rid of little Baba Ali? Or Kareem decides that might be the thing to do. Mete out justice on the spot.'

'That's down to him. Nothing to do with HMG.'

'Though HMG gave him his contract,' said Sara. 'And his indemnities.'

'Yes,' said J. 'That was Isobel's call, not mine. But don't be so legalistic. Just a bit of paper.'

'I don't think so,' said Sara as quietly as she could against the shrieking wind.

J looked towards the shore again. 'I won't discuss that so don't waste time.'

'But you took one of the copies.'

'So you say.'

'Can I at least ask what you did with it?'

'No you fucking well can't. Move on,' growled J. 'But if you seriously think I'd ever have allowed my copy of that to see the light of day...' He allowed the thought to linger.

'OK,' continued Sara, 'the Blackburn files. Why are they significant?'

J chuckled hoarsely and spat into the sea. 'You must have worked that one out.'

Sara recalled what Morahan had been told by Sayyid. 'The inception? The tip of the iceberg?'

'Hooray. Yes – despite the silly words. Pull on the thread, find the ball of wool.' He stopped again to cough. 'It was the first op. You don't get any bloody rehearsals. Had to succeed.'

'Succeed?'

'Yes, prove his bona fides to both sides. Us, though we were sure of him. More importantly them. The jihadists. Expose an informer for them.'

'How did Blackburn end?'

'You don't need to know that.'

'OK, I'll put it another way. Was the contract a means that justified the ends?'

'Careful,' said J, 'you're on the cliff edge.' Sara kept silent, waiting for him. 'As far as I was concerned – and for as long as I was there – this was a legitimate intelligence operation which brought results.'

'What results?'

'One, we could concentrate on the genuinely bad boys at home, identified for us by Kareem. Two, he could give us the names of young warriors planning to head East for a slice of jihad. Names, departure dates and times – sometimes he even arranged their tickets – and therefore arrival times. Istanbul airport usually. Where there might be people to meet and greet. Like MIT.'

'MIT?' asked Sara. J rolled his eyes.

'Turkish intelligence,' interjected Patrick.

'Yes. Maybe other interested parties too. Nothing to do with HMG.'

'How many of these warriors were "disappeared"?' continued Sara.

'You should watch your grammar,' said J. 'It's another jurisdiction. I've no idea. That's if there were any.'

'You know there must have been. Didn't Kareem ever tell you?'

'Why on God's earth would I ask him?' This time, he made a 360-degree scan. 'Ten more minutes.'

'Did you know Maryam/Marion?' asked Sara.

'Knew of.'

'What was her role?'

'Ornamental. Kareem wanted her there. I doubt she saw much.'

'And after she left?'

'We kept an eye on her for a while. I understand she was unwell.'

'Do you know where she is?'

'That's enough on her.' His reply triggered a few seconds' break. Waves crashing around them, it was like boxers preparing for the final round.

'How long did you continue on Operation Pitchfork?' asked Sara.

'I retired – say again, I was retired – in 2011.' J raised a handkerchief to his mouth and spat into it. 'By then Isobel was pretty much running Kareem solo. Even though it was my idea. She'd brought in a new sidekick. Middle-ranker called John Donald. I understand he's now her new head of counter-terror.' Patrick momentarily froze, hunching his shoulders against the wind to cover up the shock. That was the name. 'John Donald'.

The man who'd greeted him so warmly outside his flat, aided by his muscled friend with karate skills.

'Did you stay in touch with Kareem?' continued Sara. Patrick relaxed; she and J were too locked in their quick-fire exchange to notice his reaction.

'Occasional calls maybe. Twice a year. Nothing of consequence. Just to check we were both on this earth.'

'Still in touch?' asked Patrick.

'No. No calls since 2016. No answer to my calls, that is.'

'Any whispers?'

'Nothing. Silence of the damned,' he rasped.

'What about after you retired?'

'You'll have to speak to Isobel.'

'Please, J,' interceded Patrick.

J turned slowly to Patrick, then stared at the sea beyond. The sky had darkened, a storm brewing in the channel. His own face seemed to cloud over in sympathy. 'Think about it,' he finally said. 'What's going on with our jihadist friends?'

'They're returning,' replied Sara.

'Good girl. Yes, the returners. Kareem has another important service to offer. The returners need vetting. Who's still loyal and wants to go on performing on the *Carry On Jihad* film set? Who's had enough? Who's seen the evil and wants to change sides? And who'd like to know the answers to all those questions? Obviously the string-pullers of terror. And… and…' He was leaning in towards both of them, his cheeks and lips livid.

'HMG,' said Patrick.

'Precisely. Particularly the *Carry On* Brothers, the future enemy within.'

'So that they can be monitored – or somehow got rid of?'

'Ask Isobel. Ask Kareem. If you can find him. Let me know if you do.' He began to walk towards the end of the pier; they fell in line either side of him. 'They've arrived.' Patrick and

Sara flicked looks behind. 'You won't see them, they're sat on a bench at the end of the pier. Nice-looking young couple. Not kissing and cuddling quite as much as one might expect on a lovers' day out to the seaside. Useless tradecraft these days, all done by bloody gizmo.'

'If I had the chance to ask Isobel and Kareem,' said Sara, refusing to allow his deflection, 'in an imaginary parallel world of truth not lies, what would they say?'

J stopped and rounded on her. 'I don't know what Kareem fucking well ended up doing. Or how many. In my time, there was precision. Afterwards, who knows? I was out, the brakes were off. Have you ever seen what the power over life and death does to people? I don't know what she was fucking well allowing him to do. I don't know if she even knew. Or wanted to know. He was her triumph. The woman who'd planted at the heart of British jihad the one truly successful mole we'd ever had. She was one step away from the top job, for Christ's sake, he was her ticket.'

'One last thing,' said Sara coolly.

'You're bloody right.'

'Kareem and Isobel. Were they lovers?'

He softened, looking at her with an astonishment that turned slowly to a gaunt smile. 'What on earth makes you ask that?'

'Because I think I understand him,' she replied. 'But I know nothing of her.'

J considered the question for a few seconds; she sensed him recalling images, faces, expressions, body language. 'If he fucked her – and if she was happy to be fucked by him, whether for trade advancement or personal pleasure – then I suspect we might all understand a great deal more.'

'But did they?' insisted Sara.

'How would I know? Put a camera into their bedrooms?'

'I'm surprised you didn't,' she said, unabashed.

Her cheek elicited a momentary grin. 'That's enough, lady lawyer. Now bugger off, both of you. And don't take a peep at the young couple.' With that, he stalked away, right to the end of the pier.

'Goodbye, J. And thank you,' said Patrick, not bothering to raise his voice. The brown-corduroyed figure was already well out of earshot, leaning over a railing and hawking into the gurgling sea.

'Do you ever feel someone's orchestrating this?' Sara asked.

'You're ahead of me again,' said Patrick.

Once past Ashford on the direct route to London, after Patrick walked up and down their coach, inspected the toilets each end and returned to his seat with a nod of the head, they'd begun to talk.

'It's like those clouds gathering over the sea,' said Sara. 'I sometimes think someone's whipping up a storm, pitching you and me into it, and then waiting for it to blow itself out. Don't you ever feel that?'

He smiled gently. 'To be honest, I don't. Must be lack of imagination.'

'It all starts with Sayyid. But who *is* Sayyid?'

'I guess we can shortlist – though I don't see it gets us anywhere.'

'Tell me.'

'Someone who's obtained a sample of unredacted MI5 files from two separate periods. Who had access to your dinner with Kareem and its transcript. Who's motivated by conscience and believes there's something rotten in the British secret state that the Morahan Inquiry offers a unique opportunity to investigate.'

'It may be a whistleblower we've never heard of and never will. But imagine,' she said, her eyes lighting up, wanting him to play her game, 'it's someone we know…'

'There are only two,' replied Patrick flatly. 'Aren't there?'

Her eyes dulled. 'You tell me.'

'J himself. And…'

'Sylvia. Now that I understand her.'

'Correct. Perhaps even working together.'

'Yes, perhaps.'

They fell into silence. As they emerged from the long tunnel cutting through the monotony of east London's suburbia, she stared out of the window at the curved concrete shapes of its 2012 Olympics. She thought of that triumphal event; then, however bristling with security it might have been, the city felt safe. No one believed they could be part of a crowd leaving stadiums with a suicide bomber in their midst about to blow himself up. For the four years that followed, Britain and Europe seemed a nation and a continent at relative peace. Then came Paris, Brussels, Manchester, London, political upheaval and burning tower blocks, not to mention refugees, mass drownings in the Mediterranean, that sense of a country and a world soured by menace.

She smelt the sea twisting beneath Deal pier's concrete legs, above them the parting image of J leaning over the end railing. She heard the smoker's cough and hoarse voice of Sylvia; and saw the outline of her back shaped in the window as she made that brief phone call to J.

'J's a sick man, isn't he?'

'Yes,' said Patrick. 'He was too angry when I asked him if he was OK. Too out of character. He was never angry before. Big-voiced, loud exclamations, fruity language. But never anger. This was his raging against the dying of the light.'

'And Sylvia?'

'Oh she's one of those smokers who'll live till she's a hundred. I said before she hates them. That's not quite right. It's pure, unvarnished contempt.'

'They got rid of her, didn't they? You're a single woman with decades of service and then they shaft you. What's left but revenge?'

Patrick didn't answer and now it was his turn to stare out. Sara watched him; that elegant clean-shaven profile and funnily squashed nose. She realised that she'd never asked him what he'd done with his copy of the contract. There had been just the three signed copies; his, J's, and Kareem's. It was a document that Sayyid had not produced. Because he was unable to or chose not to? A step too far or a hold-back for the final play?

'Patrick,' she murmured.

'Yes?' He turned, a slight smile of some distant memory playing around lips and perfectly white, straight teeth.

'You remember when you drove down to London to see your son's football night?'

'Ye-es.'

'And the match was cancelled.'

'Ever more mystifying, Sara.'

'It was late that night that Morahan went for his drive with Sayyid.'

'I don't have the chronology with me but I'll believe you.'

She summoned up the courage. 'You know something? Occasionally I've wondered if you happen to be "Sayyid". Or have a share in him.'

He looked at her in shock. 'Christ, Sara, how could you imagine that?'

'You were there. You had access. You knew – know – people.' She wished she'd held back. A question too many, a bridge too far. 'You're a good man too. A very good man. And I'd understand that you'd never have told me.'

He smiled. 'It's all right. I'm not that good a man. Though if I'd known when this all began what I know now... ' Her phone rang to rescue him.

She murmured the occasional 'yes', then covered the mouthpiece with her hand. 'It's the surgeon. He thinks they should operate. Now. He says his vital signs are declining and the only real solution is removing the haematoma.'

'What's the chances with the op?' asked Patrick.

She repeated the question into the phone and covered the mouthpiece again as she listened. 'He won't give me odds but feels if we don't he may slip away. It will be peaceful but it will be the end.'

'Then there's no choice, is there?'

She spoke into the mouthpiece. 'Go ahead. I'll be there soon after six to sign the permissions. Don't delay.'

She looked at Patrick, a plea in her eyes. 'If he dies on me, I'll kill him.'

26

She arrived at the hospital to find that he'd not yet gone in. Preparing the theatre, gathering the team for a hurriedly accelerated operation still took time. She realised his decline must have been sharp and unexpected. The ward sister said they'd be working through the night; she could stay in the family room if she wanted.

Her phone rang at 6.30 a.m., soon after *Fajr*.

'It's Azhar Mahmoud. I hope it's OK to call now.'

'Yes, of course.' She held her breath.

'We've completed the operation successfully.'

'Oh good.' She said it uncertainly, knowing there was more.

'By which I mean that we've reduced the haematoma and his vital signs are still functioning.'

'But that's not the end of the story.'

'No. But it's a start. He'll stay in intensive care and we'll make no attempt to disturb him for some time yet. I suggest you leave it till the afternoon before coming in.'

She phoned Patrick. 'They've operated and he's not dead,' she said brutally.

'That's good, isn't it?' he replied softly.

'I don't know what I'm putting him through.'

He sensed the tears she was repressing. 'You had no choice.'

'The surgeon said not to come back till the afternoon. Home doesn't feel too great right now, so I think I'll go to work.'

Patrick, his back to the door as she entered the Legal office, was staring out at the American Embassy. He turned.

'There's someone waiting to see us.'

'Where?'

'Here. In Pamela's office. A VIP.'

Sara followed him into the open-plan area towards the Secretary's office. Clovis, guarding its door, looked up at them, eyes flickering nervously. 'I'd better check.' He dialled an internal number, listened for a few seconds and put the phone down. 'You can go in.'

A tall, slender woman rose from one of four designer wood-backed chairs around the circular glass meeting table. She stuck out a thin, prominently veined forearm from a loose-fitting white blouse and offered a similarly lined hand to shake. 'Patrick, we've met.' The voice was oddly deep.

'Yes, Dame Isobel. Fourteen years ago, to be precise.'

'Just Isobel, please. And you must be Sara Shah.'

'Yes.'

'I should congratulate you on such a successful career. Meteoric, one might say.' Sara returned a formal smile. The beakiness was what struck her. A narrow, flat body – skeletal even, a reminder of Marion – wearing the loose-fitting blouse and black trousers to disguise it. A matching black jacket hung on the back of her chair. It was her nose more than anything – longish, with a distinct kink halfway down, sunken grey eyes behind contact lenses, thin lips, imperfect teeth she seemed anxious not to reveal, a hard chin but not out of proportion to her overall bone structure. It was possible that, as a younger woman, the emaciated angularity could have been attractive;

if so, that had worn off and she presented a forbidding figure, kept lean by an excess of nervous energy. Sara tried to picture her and Kareem standing together when they first encountered each other thirteen years ago, she some ten years older than him. He might have seen her as a challenge – a white-skinned woman in a position of secret power, a conquest in waiting.

They sat, Isobel on one side, Patrick and Sara opposite.

'This is not an official visit,' she began. 'I particularly didn't want to invite you to Thames House.' Patrick and Sara exchanged a glance, a silent acquiescence to let her make the running. 'If you would prefer that we go out of this office, perhaps for a coffee…'

'There appears to be coffee here,' said Patrick tersely, as the door opened to reveal Clovis bearing a tray.

'I realise this… this situation may seem odd.'

'Could I get one thing clear, Dame Isobel?' said Sara. She couldn't imagine calling this woman by her first name only. 'Unofficial or official, is this meeting on the record or off it?'

'I would like to give you some guidance which will save you both time and resources. But I must ask you to keep any information I provide to yourselves.'

'So this is a meeting that didn't happen,' said Patrick. 'A discussion that didn't take place.'

'Correct.'

'Are you intending to impart information involving potentially illegal activities?'

'No.'

'If you were to, there'd be an obligation on us to report it to the police.'

'Correct. "Secret" does not, and never can, mean "illegal". Those are the rules under which the Security Service operates.'

Patrick thought of the contract with Kareem. 'Sara?'

'I'm OK with this.'

'Thank you.' Isobel composed herself. 'I understand that you have become interested in the secret arrangements of which you are aware, Patrick, with Kareem bin-Jilani.'

'Could I inquire how you understand that?' asked Patrick.

'Yes,' she replied, now asserting herself. 'By legally authorised surveillance of a person suspected of a criminal act.'

'What criminal act?' asked Sara.

'A breach of the Official Secrets Act.'

'You've been bugging Walter Thompson,' said Patrick.

'You can't expect me to comment on that.'

'Nor can you expect either of us to comment on any part of ongoing investigations made within the remit of this Inquiry.'

'You make an inference about "remit" with which I might not necessarily agree,' said Dame Isobel, 'but that's not relevant to me being here.' Sara was beginning to see how this precise, careful, evenly modulated woman had unobtrusively risen to the top. 'To cut to the chase, there's something you need to know about Kareem.'

'About his activities?' asked Patrick.

'Allow me, Patrick. As you're aware, Kareem joined the staff of the Security Service in late 2005 under conditions which had to be kept secret. Over the coming decade, he performed services for the British nation for which its people would honour him if they were ever able to know. As the Islamist threat adapted, so too did Kareem. In the summer of 2016, in the role he was playing as an important figure in British Islamist circles, he travelled to Mosul in Iraq for a meeting with leaders of ISIL, DAESH, IS, whatever you like to call it. During that meeting he buttressed his trusted position with those leaders. He was also able to impart to us information of enormous potential future interest about their activities and habitats.'

She paused, turning to the tray of coffee and biscuits. 'Could

I have a cup, please, as someone has so considerately prepared it? I rarely talk as much as this.'

'Of course,' said Patrick. Sara suspected there was nothing genuine about the request. This was someone who understood how to play an audience; an unexpected talent belied by her appearance. Isobel poured a splash of milk into her cup and reached into her bag for a pack of sweeteners. She ejected one, dropped it in, slowly stirred, took a sip and resumed her story.

'On the morning of the 25th of July 2016, Kareem left Mosul in an unmarked car – a Mercedes SUV – driven by an ISIL driver and accompanied by an ISIL guard. What followed was, I'm afraid, a misunderstanding. Our American colleagues, unbeknown to us, had been tracking the man believed to be ISIL's second-in-command in Raqqa, who goes by the name of Mohammad Kalkani. This man had been previously identified as travelling in this particular car. When it was seen leaving Mosul, setting out west, an assumption was made that this key ISIL figure was heading for Raqqa in Syria. It's a journey that begins on the same exit road from Mosul as the route to the Turkish border point on the Syria frontier which Kareem was being taken to.' She paused, a sadness clouding her stark face. Though Patrick and Sara anticipated what was coming, they gave no reaction, allowing her to close the loop. 'The driver's face had been captured in reasonably high resolution. It confirmed that he was the ISIL leader's usual driver. Neither the passenger nor the guard had been caught on camera. After further confirmation of the car's identity, a decision was made to take it out with a missile from an MQ-9 Reaper drone. That operation was carried out to perfection.'

Though no tear was visible, she wiped both eyes with a handkerchief. The room fell silent, interrupted only by the muffled burst of a mechanical digger and distant shouts from workmen. Subconsciously attracted by them, Patrick walked over to a window and stared out. Sara stayed in her seat, watching Dame Isobel's moment of grief.

'I'm sorry,' Sara murmured, wanting Patrick not to hear.

Patrick rejoined them. 'If the Americans had taken out such a major target, they'd have announced it. At least let it be known.'

'They did,' said Isobel. 'I'm sure your excellent archivist,' she failed fully to curb the irony, 'will have the reports to hand.'

'They didn't correct the identity of the target.'

'What would have been the point? Owning up to the biggest intelligence own goal of the decade,' she said bitterly. 'I understood. Far better to claim the triumph and celebrate.'

'And when Kareem failed to return?'

'Oh, he'd hardly have been the first "jihadist" to venture into the war zone and go missing.'

'Quite,' said Patrick. 'Some of them by his own hand, as we understand it.'

'You're straying, Patrick,' she said icily. 'This is not the forum. I came here only to try to help you both,' she said, addressing herself to Sara.

She accepted the olive branch. 'We appreciate that.'

'I believe that Kareem was – became – a good person. It would be unfair to besmirch his reputation either in the public sessions of this Inquiry or in camera.' She paused and looked from one to the other. 'Particularly as he is no longer here to defend himself.'

Sara gave Patrick the slightest flick of the head. He understood and looked at his watch. 'I have another meeting, Dame Isobel, I hope you'll forgive me.' He rose and left the room. Neither Isobel nor Sara moved.

'Patrick has grown up,' said Isobel, relaxing.

Sara smiled at her. 'Have you really not seen him since… since…'

'No. As he said, nearly fourteen years. He was – how shall I put it? – more biddable then.'

'He knows that now. And he regrets it.'

'He shouldn't. What was done was right. It worked.'

Sara remembered J using similar words. She didn't challenge them – her aim was different. She allowed a moment and then, adopting a shy hesitancy, asked the question.

'Did you love him?'

Isobel, betraying surprise but not shock, hesitated not at all. 'Did you?'

Sara's brow creased; she hadn't expected it. 'I'd like to have seen him again. To have understood him. To hold him to account perhaps.'

'Would you?' replied Isobel, frowning. 'Would you really?'

'Yes, I believe so.'

'I'd never have thought that.'

Suddenly, impetuously almost, Isobel stood up, collected the black jacket from her chair and slid it on. The trouser suit enhanced her, a woman who had come to dominate a man's world. 'You're an interesting person, Sara,' she said sweeping through the door like a panther returning to a forest of obscuration.

Patrick was waiting in the Legal office. 'Well…' he began as she stepped in. He sprang up to shut the door behind her.

'Well indeed.' Sara was reflecting on this mysterious woman, keeper of secrets not just of the state but of her own life too. 'I think they were lovers. But I'm not so sure she was his victim. He may have finally bitten off more than he could chew.'

'You're on the right track – but only halfway there.' He spoke with rare certainty. 'Go the full circle. Follow the evidence, the chronology. Look for simultaneities.' He moved closer to her; she sensed him preparing an announcement that would shatter their preconceptions, so seminal that even the walls mustn't hear. 'Look, Sara, of course Isobel wasn't his victim, for God's sake, he was *her* bloody victim.'

'Explain.'

'The summer of 2016, Isobel Le Marchant is in final reach of her goal. Director General of MI5. Icing on the cake, she becomes a Dame. Route to the top – her brilliant handling of the operation which has made Britain safe. Imagine her peddling it. In the eleven years after 7/7, the Islamist threat in the UK is nullified, plots intercepted, arrests made, jihadists disappear to the Middle East never to return. But Kareem has served his purpose. She's arrived. And only she and he know what he's been doing to get her there. Maybe only he knows where the bodies are buried. The one potential loose cannon out there who can now threaten her. The skeleton in the cupboard. The darkness in the soul.'

'I'm listening.'

'That drone strike's not a cock-up or own goal. She's in on it. Knows precisely who's in that car. She's the one who's celebrating.'

'Is she capable of doing that? To a man she loved.'

'Come on,' he said, 'she's Director General of MI5. She's no softie. There's another angle. She knows jihad in the UK is changing. Lone wolves, single nutters, technology available to all. The Kareem gambit is out of time. Its success relies on there being networks, or parts of networks – however small – that can deliver him the so-called "traitors". Or the future "martyrs" to be vetted and tested. Kareem has no access to lone wolves. His usefulness is dwindling. She's squeezed him dry.' He hesitated, unsure how Sara was taking it. 'Maybe those long legs squeezed him dry too.'

'She has emotions,' protested Sara. 'I saw them. There were suppressed tears in her eyes.'

'Crocodile tears.'

'Even if you're right – even if she felt she had to do it – she still would have mourned him.'

'OK, maybe. But like the dramatist, we sometimes have to kill our darlings.'

He walked over to the window. A concrete lorry passed below, carrying the foundations for another addition to the jungle of affluence. 'It doesn't matter,' he said, eyes glazing over the sprawl of buildings growing, it seemed, photosynthetically towards the late-morning sun. 'How? Why? It really doesn't matter. She's the boss, he's dead and all we have are a few files we're told are the tip of an iceberg and an arrangement between the state and a probable socio or psychopath that I once signed my name to.'

She walked over to him. Only now did she fully see the guilt that had stuck. 'It's not your fault. You didn't have a choice.'

'We all have choices, Sara. They make us who we are.'

He turned back to the window, burying his own small darkness in the sprawling mass of humanity's energy. For a moment he regretted allowing her to see it; to witness his brutality in isolating evil. But truth was just that; pleasant and unpleasant, good and bad. False optimism – making the best of things – was the biggest lie of all.

Her phone rang. He turned as she listened, saying little more than the occasional 'yes'. Her eyes brightened, as if a cloud had scudded across a midday sky to reveal the sun at its zenith. She removed the phone from her ear, went and threw her arms around him, burying her head in his chest.

'It'll take time but he's out of danger.'

He wanted to tighten his arms around her but was stopped by a knock on the door. 'Who's that?' They broke away.

'Sylvia.'

'Come in.'

She entered, hardly seeming to notice them, carrying a

computer print-out of a newspaper page. She placed it on a desk and pointed to a three-paragraph article on the bottom right column. The headline was 'DROWNING VICTIM NAMED.' Below, it read:

> The body washed up on the shore of Walmer beach in the small hours of yesterday morning was named today as that of Walter Thompson, a former civil servant who retired five years ago to a seafront apartment in Deal. He lived alone with no known relatives. Police have appealed for any family members to contact them. Neighbours said Mr Thompson was a polite man who was always willing to pass the time of day. It is believed that he was in the advanced stages of lung cancer and police are not viewing his death as suspicious.

'I told you to keep him safe,' croaked Sylvia. They could see she'd been crying.

Sara put an arm round her. 'I'm so sorry, Sylvia.'

'He was a good man. And they crushed him.' She retrieved the page and, without a further word, left the office.

'Two deaths. One near death,' said Patrick.

'Which can all be explained away as accidents,' said Sara.

'No. It's too much. Happenstance, coincidence, enemy action. Kareem may be dead, but someone is still protecting him.' He searched Sara's eyes.

'We need evidence. Concrete evidence. Clues. Remnants. DNA. Bodies.'

'I'll go looking. But not you. Your father needs you. You can't risk yourself.'

'You already know what I'm going to say to that.' She glared at him. 'Just give me the rest of the day so I can see for myself that he's fine and sort the aunties' and cousins' visiting roster. Poor Dad, he doesn't know what's coming to him.'

Her brief smile turned to a grim ferocity. She grabbed her coat and bag, murmured 'I won't let whoever did this to him get away with it,' and shot out of the office.

One old man survives, another dies, thought Patrick. It had begun with the young men buried in the iceberg of unredacted documents – the executed, the disappeared, the tortured. But the chase had changed. Two deaths, one near death in the here and now. A secret killer still on the prowl, a foetid conspiracy still in play. To end it, they would have to find and destroy its still beating heart.

27

6 a.m. Sara slid into the passenger seat of the black Audi Patrick had hired.

The rest of the previous day, he'd prepared too. They'd agreed to involve Sylvia, no one else. Knowing their phones might be used to track their movements, he'd bought pay-as-you-go burner phones for the day – including one for Sylvia for any urgent communication. They left their own phones in Sara's house.

Leaving early, the journey should be doable in under four hours. That would allow nearly ten hours to search before nightfall.

'It always rains in Wales,' Patrick had said. 'Don't forget your wellies.' Each saw the other trying to make light of the trip, all the while thinking of the 'accidents' that had befallen others. J's drowning would never be legally provable as anything but an accident, Morahan's ugly end likewise. Tariq Shah's recovery and Sara's certainty that it was too professional an operation to have left evidence would deter police interest – unless her father remembered what had happened. It was better for him, and maybe her, if he didn't.

Each knew the trip was probably the last roll of the dice.

At traffic lights Patrick plugged in his iPod. The first track was Mendelssohn's 'O for the Wings of a Dove'.

'What's this?' she asked.

'I sang it as a chorister,' he said. 'Don't worry, this playlist is what they call eclectic. Next Led Zeppelin. Then the great Roy Orbison.' As the third track built to its crescendo of the repeating '*It's over*,' he tried to cheer her by joining in.

She listened, eyes alight. 'You really can sing. How do you reach those top notes?'

For a few seconds, he smiled with a joyful innocence, then darkened. 'I wish today was over.'

Beating the morning rush-hour, they were on the M4 within twenty-five minutes, past Bristol in good time, then saw signs leading to Abergavenny. The single-teated breast of the Sugar Loaf mountain came into view.

'The land of Mother Earth,' Sara said.

'These hills and mountains paint so many different pictures.' She inspected him; the trip was providing further glimpses into Patrick's soul. 'I once had to do a yomp here with that ridiculous school's corps. Masters acting out SAS fantasies, eager teenagers licking their boots. None of that could hide the magic of the place.'

Past Abergavenny and Crickhowell, the full spread of the Beacons lay ahead. 'Somewhere among that lot was Kareem's interrogation centre,' said Patrick. 'Let's hope Marion's mother's bearings stand the test of time.'

They rounded the town of Brecon and headed towards a fold of long-backed hills. After a few miles, they came to a narrow lane.

'I think that's the turning,' said Patrick. 'But let's climb first. See the whole vista from on high. Survey the battleground.' She felt him camouflaging his fear.

They wound their way up between long slabs of

mountainsides, scarred by ancient gullies where surging rivers once flowed. On the roadside, a leafless, stunted hawthorn tree leant to the east, the casualty of decades of buffeting from the west wind. The only spectators were sheep, the bare green of the hills dotted with a coppice or two on far ridges and the occasional deserted shepherd's hut. They reached the shoulder over which the next valley stretched, parked and walked up a few hundred yards to the nearest summit. Below them lay a steep fall into a valley which seemed to spread for ever into far vistas of England and Wales.

'The innocent hills of Britain,' said Patrick. He breathed deeply, puffing out his chest, and closed his eyes. 'Let's go.'

'Let me check in with the hospital first.'

He frowned. 'Do you have to?'

She narrowed her eyes. 'What's the problem?'

'Maybe I'm being paranoid – or overestimating their paranoia. But say they're monitoring the hospital exchange, they get the number of your burner phone.' He hesitated, then grinned. 'To hell with it, I *am* being paranoid. 'Course you should.'

A few minutes later, two miles down the lane they'd located, they came to a gate leading into a driveway and stopped. It led downhill to a square farmhouse of dark stone and mullioned windows.

'Too small,' said Sara.

'And too visible,' added Patrick.

'It should be more sunken. We need the solid gates to identify it. The buildings here all seem the same dark grey stone. Elizabeth Green said the end wall of the barn by the entrance gates was whitewashed. But lots of walls have had that done to them.'

'It could have peeled off.'

They returned to the car and crept along the lane. The

description on the map had brought them as far as they could, now it was for their eyes only.

'Stop!' She jerked round. 'Reverse about twenty yards.' He edged the car backwards. 'Here.' She leapt out and headed for what seemed to be a tangle of branches and creepers. He joined her and they tugged at clumps too set to shift, able only to peel them away branch by branch, strand by strand. The surface of a lichen-covered, dark green gate, some twelve feet high, became slowly visible. Sara turned right and walked a few yards up the lane, scraping away more creepers covering a stone wall. It was flecked with smears of old whitewash.

'It fits,' she cried out. 'What was it exactly Marion said… down in a dark valley… hills around…' She walked back towards Patrick. 'And that weird thing her mother mentioned she once said… when I smell the life inside me, I must leave the smell of death.'

'It may have been smells on the wind from an abattoir,' he said prosaically.

'No!' Sara protested. 'This is isolation. The sort of place you could yell and yell, day after day, month after month, and no one would ever hear you.' She thought of Marion slumped on her chair. 'A hell-hole to drive you crazy.'

'That gate's pretty solid,' he said. 'Any way round it?'

'That stone wall's just as tall and there's a long stretch of it – may not lead into the courtyard Sami described anyway.'

'I'll look left.' He walked in the opposite direction. 'The wall abuts an outbuilding.' He continued along a high hedge and stopped to feel through it. 'There's a wire fence behind the hedge. Doesn't help us.'

As he rejoined her, she was scratching at a rusting metal panel. 'Remnants of an entryphone. I reckon that proves it.' She stared at him, a challenge in her eyes. 'You lift.' She stood in front of the gate, arms stretched upwards.

'Sure?'

'No other way, is there?' He took her by the hips and pushed her up the gate, then she eased back to sit on his shoulders. 'Higher.' She sensed him hesitating. 'Get on with it, it's no time to be shy.' He pushed his hands beneath her buttocks, raising them while she used her own hands against the gate to steady herself. She bent one knee, flattening her heel on his shoulder, followed by the second. He managed to repress an oath as they dug sharply in.

She placed a hand on the top of the gate. 'Ow!' Her shriek echoed across the valley. 'I think I hit some old barbed wire.'

'Come down. This is no good.'

'It's all right. Just a nail. Don't move.'

Gingerly she felt for clean gaps between nails and wood splinters to place her hands, finding enough grip to push herself upwards while he raised his hands to hold her feet.

'I'm up. I can see over.'

'See what.'

'Buildings, weeds, a barn. It's a good size.'

'Can you jump?'

She looked down. 'Maybe. How do you get in?'

'Does the gate have a handle?'

'Yes, but looks as if there's a lock below.'

'I should have bought a f—' he stopped himself again, 'a rope.' He tried to think, then felt her feet rising from his hands as she hoicked herself onto the top of the gate. She leant forward, gave a little yelp, and disappeared from view. He heard a scrunch, followed by silence. 'My God,' he murmured. Further silence, then a rustle. 'Are you all right?'

He heard her voice. 'There's a keyhole. Look through it.' He did; her eye was lodged against the other side.

'You could have hurt yourself,' he said angrily. 'Badly.'

Her reply was a release of a latch. 'You push, I'll pull.'

After a few minutes of heaving they'd prised the gate several inches open. He took off his jacket, flung it in the car, and squeezed himself through. 'Just tell me what you'd have done if it had been locked.' She shrugged her shoulders. 'We'll shift the gate further open. Then I'll move the car off the lane.'

Sara looked around, admiring the accuracy of Sami's memory. Just as he'd described, the van would have twisted down the lane, and turned through the gates – before, presumably, he was bundled into the whitewashed stone building across the yard. Its door was ajar, hanging loose. She eased it open; it squealed with the shock of unfamiliar movement.

'Come,' she called to Patrick. Shafts of light from the door and high barred windows were enough to reveal the layout of stables.

'I guess once this would have been a significant farm,' said Patrick. He'd calmed, his tone more conciliatory. 'Big enough for visitors on horseback to need stabling. Their own horses too. Maybe a carriage.'

'Each stable door has newish fittings,' she said, 'presumably to take a padlock.'

'Horses don't need locks.'

'Sami's prison.' She pushed a stable door open – barred window above, concrete water basin, remnants of straw on the small square cobbles. 'And however many others too.'

'He said they shone light through the window at night, didn't he?' asked Patrick.

'Yes.'

'We can look behind later.'

She turned to him fiercely. 'So this is the place. What do we need to find?'

'At least one piece of incontrovertible physical evidence that criminal acts took place here. Probably kidnapping at minimum, murder at maximum.'

'So bones, fragments of clothing…'

'Blood stains… of sufficient quality for forensic testing.' His eyes roved over the stable, his nose wrinkling. 'And we have to act fast. We can't assume we'll have this place to ourselves all day. I did the best I could yesterday but they'll pick up a trail sometime. If the stables were the prison, let's start with those. Then be selective. I can't see the main house offering anything, the captives would never have been taken there.'

'There's what Sami called the big hall with the platform.'

'That must be the barn opposite the house. Let's look before searching the stables.'

They ran across the courtyard. The clouds they'd seen in the distance were floating over. The rectangular courtyard, sun reflecting from the farmhouse's windows, was transformed in no more than a moment to a menacing gloom. As she entered the barn, Sara jumped at something tickling her face and neck.

'Cobwebs,' said Patrick. He raised his arms and walked up and down, clearing thread after thread from wooden beams and corners.

'The platform's still there.' She imagined Kareem sitting in the centre like a Sultan on his dais, Maryam his consort on one side, the burly apparatchik on the other. The clouds erupted and what sounded like giant raindrops beat down on slate tiles sitting flush on the timber roof trusses.

'Creepy,' she whispered to Patrick.

The rain crashing onto the cobbles, each drop seeming to ricochet like a bullet before it settled, ceased as suddenly as it had started. Over a watery softness streams of sunlight decorated the courtyard with bright diagonal strings. They crossed back into the stables.

She heard a rustling in the far corner of a stable and crept toward it. She screamed. Patrick ran in to see her frozen, half-crouched, staring ahead. Coming alongside, he saw a giant rat, fattened on the detritus of the shed. It stared at them from the pink beads of its eyes, then scurried past their ankles.

'Eaters of flesh and blood,' he said. 'Destroyers of evidence.'

Hours later, between them they'd searched every stable and the connecting passage. Their prize was a single item, a pair of soiled, caked underpants buried beneath straw in a stable corner.

'You never know. There might be some blood traces,' said Patrick as they regrouped. He produced a cellophane bag and inserted the pants.

'When I spread the palms of my hands across those cold walls and harsh squares on the floors,' said Sara, 'it's blood I keep thinking of. That this was some kind of mini Lubyanka, now left to rot and hide its sins.'

'Imagination isn't evidence.'

'Sami was terrified here. He wasn't faking.'

'But he's alive.'

'Yes, he survived.'

Patrick checked his watch. 'Hell, it's nearly four.'

'Yes, I was thinking the same. I ought to check in with the hospital again.' She took her burner phone from a pocket. She quickly glanced again at the anonymous text that had arrived a couple of hours earlier while she was searching alone. This time, however much she knew the message wouldn't send, she checked her phone was on silent, hit reply and typed.

Who ARE you?

An instant reply. She jumped out of her skin.

Don't you know by now?

She turned her back to Patrick, thumbs gently tapping.

Just tell me it's you.

Seconds passed. Nothing.

Message sending failed.

'I can't get a signal,' she said, hiding her tension by fiddling with her phone. She disliked the lie and promised herself it would be the last.

He sighed. 'OK, we'll drive back up the hill till you get one. But be quick.' She was already marching down the drive, shaking with relief that he hadn't checked for a signal on his own phone.

Thirty minutes later, they were back.

'I overestimated,' said Patrick. 'Depending on the weather, we've got two or so hours of decent light left before the sun ducks behind the mountain. Maybe the stable was our best chance. But let's cover the ground – courtyards, drives, garden, perimeter. That's the one thing the underpants do confirm – if someone has tidied the place up, something else could have been missed.'

Beyond the house, they found a disused well. Patrick peered down; it seemed to descend for ever. 'You'd probably never see the bottom,' he said, 'even with the sun overhead.' He leant over, his head and long back disappearing. 'Anyway no need to chuck bodies down here. That's the trouble,' he said, pulling himself up and gazing at the hillside beyond, 'great expanses of green as far as the eye can see, some thick forests, lakes, reservoirs. Hiding bodies wouldn't be difficult if you had the will and the muscle.'

They were tramping around the perimeter fields as the sun ducked behind a ridge, their spirits sinking with the light. 'That's nearly it,' he said. 'One last look inside.' They walked back down the lane and slid back through the gateway. 'You said it earlier. It's not as if we found nothing.' He spread his arms towards the courtyard. 'We found the place itself.'

'Shush,' she whispered.

'What?'

She placed a forefinger on her lips and then pointed it towards the barn. He followed the line. 'Is that a light?'

'We can leave,' he murmured. 'Just turn round. Drive away.'

She shook her head, then nodded once, silently, and moved forward.

28

They crept across the courtyard. Nothing moved. Just an unexplained single bulb hanging from a beam at the near end of the barn.

'Looks like a security light on a timer,' whispered Patrick. 'There's some kind of watch over this place even if it's been left to rot.' The doors opened easily; they stepped inside, as if drawn to the light. The far end where the platform stood was dark. 'What was that?'

'What?'

They turned. The doors they'd come through had closed.

'Did you close them?' she asked.

Piercing lights from the barn's two front corners burst out, blinding them. Instinctively, they covered their eyes with their hands. A key turned noisily in a lock. They opened their eyes. Nothing. No movement. No sound.

Footsteps echoed from beyond the far wall, slowly growing louder and nearer. Three chairs had been placed in the middle of the illuminated platform. A door behind opened and a silhouetted figure entered, stepped onto the platform and walked to its front. Stepping into the pool of light, the figure stretched its hands out.

'You came here to hunt down the dead. Instead you find the living.' A deep male voice in a precise English accent.

Sara closed her eyes again, not wanting to believe it, however much she now knew it. She felt no panic, no jumping of the heart; instead a numbing confirmation of some huge deception.

'Hello, Kareem,' she said softly.

'Kareem was killed in a drone strike.'

'This isn't a game, Kareem,' said Patrick.

'Hello, Sara. Hello, Patrick.'

Patrick strode across the long barn's floor towards him. 'Please halt,' said Kareem with a show of quiet politeness.

A burly, roughly shaved man with coarsely brushed, thick grey hair, a large knife deliberately showing from his belt, appeared from nowhere to block Patrick's path. 'I believe, Patrick,' said Kareem, 'you were never introduced to Aaqil.' Sara, watching them, instinctively thought back to the unidentified person at the restaurant table. The only difference was the black hair now turned grey.

Kareem moved alongside the two men now facing each other and lowered his voice. 'Do not try anything, Patrick. He would cut you to pieces without a moment's thought – and with great pleasure.'

Kareem turned away; Aaqil nodded from Patrick to Sara and then to the chairs on the platform where he was heading.

'Come,' said Kareem, 'join me. I mean you no harm. You are my guests.' He directed them to two of the chairs and sat down in the third.

'How did you know, Kareem?' asked Patrick.

'Are you still as naive as you always were, Patrick? Did you not see that your movements yesterday were being observed? A man entering this world must learn how to look over his shoulder. Now, if you will allow me. You have come far with your investigation. But enough. It is over.'

'It's never over, Kareem,' said Sara.

Kareem smiled sweetly at her, as handsome as ever, hardly a crease in his face, the hair still thick and shining. He was clean-shaven, just as when she had first encountered him, and dressed in a dark grey business suit, white shirt and blue tie. For the identity he was now assuming his physical appearance had melted into West, not East.

'You are wrong, Sara,' he began. 'The story is finished. Although I prefer to use the word "narrative". You know much of it. An Arab boy from a rich family is sent to England to live and be educated. He begins to see a corrupted society, to meet people with other, better values. Now a man, he meets a beautiful girl called Sara with whom he could spend his life—'

'And rapes her.' She finished his sentence with a contempt that shocked Patrick.

'No!' It was a scream, a cry from the dark, a noise she could never have imagined him allowing to escape.

Kareem paused, taking a deep breath, uncrossing and recrossing his leg. 'There is no need for accusations, particularly false ones.' The voice had quietened – calmer, colder, more controlled than ever.

Sara, wanting to rebut him, bit her tongue as Aaqil, knife still displayed, moved into the lights. He carried a jug of water and two glasses. Glaring at her and giving an almost imperceptible shake of the head, he placed them on a side table between her and Patrick.

'I must apologize,' said Kareem, 'I am afraid we no longer have facilities here for tea.' He waved a hand at Aaqil who disappeared into the shadows. 'Perhaps I may now continue my narrative.

'One September day this man takes the girl for a ride on the Millennium Wheel. At the top, he imagines how beautiful, how deserved it would be if the Parliament he sees below could explode into the air. The girl fails to understand him.

335

'By a fateful coincidence, the next day real destruction happens – but in America, not the society and nation he has lived in and come to despise. He reads more, learns more, advances his own understanding. He flies to Pakistan where he talks to scholars and meets fighters. They tell him his role is not on the battlefield. He will be different, his task to radicalise and recruit. The Iraq war makes it easy.

'Then comes 7/7. There is nothing beautiful to him about it – not like 9/11. He sees flaws, but cannot desert the cause. He is picked up – illegally, though he does not complain – by MI5. His outlook changes, he agrees to switch sides.'

'Come on, Kareem,' said Patrick. He cast a glance to see if Aaqil was in hearing range. There was no sign of him. 'You had no bloody choice. You took the traitor's shilling.'

'How cynical, Patrick, you were never capable of real understanding. And please, your language. To continue... this man does his best for his new masters. But first, he must protect his bona fides with his old masters.'

'By appearing to expose and execute MI5 and police informers – and sometimes going beyond appearance,' said Sara. 'We want names.'

'Again please,' he said. 'His "handler" is a highly intelligent woman destined for the top. He admires her greatly and wants to help her. She gives him names on her list, he finds out what she needs to know and tells her.' He paused, looking down on them. 'I believe J has filled in these gaps for you.'

'How many were executed, Kareem?' said Patrick. 'How many were "disappeared"?'

'But then the woman he admires,' continued Kareem, ignoring him, 'is promoted to be head of her organisation. She will be too senior, too exposed, to continue their partnership. They agree an exit strategy. He is given a new identity and hopes

336

that, one day, he may return to be of service to her and her country. But for now he must be erased from the record.

'There is a coda. Two years later a short-sighted prime minister sets up an inquiry. A so-called whistleblower emerges. A sharp-brained female lawyer with a connection to this narrative is hired. She begins to poke her nose into dangerous areas. The threat is contained.'

'By the murder of two people and the attempted murder of another,' said Patrick.

Kareem shrugged. 'I am told your father had an accident, Sara. I am so sorry; I am sure no one intended it. I believe he is recovering well.'

'Where are the bodies, Kareem?' growled Patrick. 'For your own sanity and salvation, you need to tell us where the bodies are.'

'You are too impatient, Patrick. Please, have a sip of water, I repeat my regret that I cannot offer more.'

'Patrick's right,' said Sara, 'you'll never live with yourself unless you do. We can do a deal. You're the innocent party.'

'We have evidence,' said Patrick. 'Kidnapping, imprisonment, assault and battery, torture even.'

Kareem glared at them. 'What fools you are in danger of becoming. I believe you spoke to a young man called Sami.'

'Yes,' said Sara. She had been unsure till this moment, knowing her deduction was unprovable, whether to test it on him. 'He told me a part of his story.'

'Part? I understand he was most open with you.'

'I won't ask how you understand that. If you do, you will know he missed out the bit that really mattered. The last two hours. Why? Why was he so emphatic in telling me all about his friend Asif's life as a chef in Birmingham – when Asif's family said he disappeared twelve years ago. Why, Kareem, why? I've thought long and hard about it. Something happened, didn't it?'

'Do you really want to know the truth, Sara?'

'Test me.'

'Your little friend Sami was a police informer. A tout. A grass.'

'What?' She was stopped in her tracks. 'You're making this up.'

'I saved his life. In service of your country, of my employer, I declared his innocence.'

Patrick had been listening hard. 'Whose life did you take to save his, Kareem?'

Kareem, silent, shook his head, displaying a silent contempt.

'Was it Asif by any chance? The innocent young man you sacrificed to maintain your credibility.'

'Do not worry yourself, Patrick. Whether he is now dead or alive, that boy was a nothing.'

'That sounds like a confession to murder,' said Patrick.

Kareem slowly shook his head, his face forming a contemptuous smile. 'No, Patrick. No bodies. There never will be. We have moved on from the Irish days when an informer was left on the side of a lane with two bullets in his head for his loved ones to collect and grieve for.'

'How many more Samis, Kareem?' said Patrick. 'How many more Asifs?' He stood up, pulled out a sheet of paper from his jacket pocket and held it in front of Kareem's eyes. 'You may recognise this.'

Sara glanced at him, questions and fears in her eyes. Patrick had never mentioned he was bringing it; she had no idea. Had he had a sixth sense? Now that Kareem was in front of him, what card was he trying to play? To drum some sort of confession out of him?

'Of course,' replied Kareem. 'And I have kept my own copy.'

'The contract. My signature and yours. It truly was your licence to kill, wasn't it? I've lived in fear of it for twelve years,' said Patrick bitterly. 'But no longer. Tomorrow I will hand this original copy to the Secretariat of the Morahan Inquiry. If you at least acknowledge the existence of the contract, even if nothing more, your conscience can be clear.' He paused. 'And, though it will mean nothing to you, mine might finally feel clear too.'

At the mention of 'conscience', Kareem cast him a long, mirthful look of incomprehension. 'Morahan is dead, Patrick.'

'His Inquiry lives on. It's not over, it's unstoppable. This whole ghastly devil's bargain will be blown.'

'And you with it if you persist. But not me. For I am dead,' said Kareem with finality, allowing the silence of death to fall.

'Patrick?' murmured Sara.

'Yes, Sara.' Both men turned to her, a flicker of surprise in Kareem's eyes.

'When you were summoned to act as Kareem's solicitor – to represent him – you said he told you from the beginning that the police and MI5 had enough evidence to put him away for many years.'

'Yes, correct,' he said uncertainly, not knowing where she was heading. 'Kareem always knew that. So that was the choice – prison or join our side.'

'Did you ever examine that evidence?'

'There was no point. It was taken for granted and agreed by all sides before I arrived.'

'But what actually was the evidence?'

'Photographs, meetings where plots were hatched, transcripts.'

'I'll put it another way. Evidence that would be allowed in court – or that wasn't just hearsay.'

Patrick hesitated. 'I was never required to examine it. But I guess there would have been words he'd said publicly. Some of those transcripts might have been accepted. Evidence of conspiracy to commit terrorist acts, incitement to violence.'

'If you really think about it, did you ever see or know of evidence that would definitely convict him?'

'I guess not. But that was a given. J knew it, Isobel knew it. Kareem himself more than anyone seemed to know it was hopeless.'

'Yes, "seemed" to know.' She smiled at Patrick. 'It's OK, you were acting in accordance with your client's wishes.'

She turned to Kareem. 'You see, Kareem, it doesn't really hang together, your narrative, does it? None of it. From beginning to end. There's an alternative. Isn't there?'

29

'My dear Sara,' said Kareem with a regretful smile, 'if only, I often think. But always that streak of impulsiveness.' She said nothing; he couldn't resist the silent challenge. 'If you wish to display that streak now, who am I to stand in your way?' He looked at his watch. 'But be quick.'

Sara caught sight of Aaqil standing in the half-light below the platform, hand on knife. She turned to Kareem – he was gesturing at Aaqil to withdraw. She realised the sickening truth – Kareem was preening. She repressed a seething at his smugness, unable to believe that she'd once seen it as the superior knowledge and worldliness of a glamorous older man.

'Let us return to your trip to Islamabad,' she began calmly. 'You travel first class—'

'Of course,' he smirked.

'Ostentatiously you turn left into the plane while your fellow students turn right—'

'Hardly my fellows,' he said.

'Please allow me, as I have allowed you.'

'I only wish to give your alternative narrative every chance by correcting facts…'

'It's as if you are making a show. You stay in an expensive

hotel and are then whisked away. You change your travel plans, returning to England via a third country. A detour that could almost have been designed to attract attention. Once back, you take every visible step to raise your profile as a radical Islamist. You consort with future bombers, you act as a recruiting sergeant for jihad. 7/7 happens. You know full well you're under surveillance, that your phone must be bugged. Yet you start criticising 7/7 in front of the brothers. It was "inelegant", "wrong", you say – almost as if you *want* to be overheard. When you're picked up by the intelligence services, you neither protest your innocence nor point to the lack of evidence against you. Indeed, you appear to confirm it. Then, with hardly a struggle, you offer your services, ensuring you are bound into MI5 with a written contract that gives you a hold over it.' She paused. 'You say you want my account to be correct. Any inaccuracies so far?'

Kareem had sat impassively; now his face lit up with a manufactured grin and a short chuckle. 'It is an excellent "narrative". Please continue.'

'As you've done with other women, you seduce your handler, Isobel, now Dame Isobel, Le Marchant. You've put yourself at the very heart of the intelligence operation against Islamist terror. But who are you really, Kareem?'

'An interesting question, Sara. Who are any of us?'

'Let's turn it on its head. Perhaps it's not the jihadist leaders you must throw bones to, but your MI5 employers. And it is your real comrades, your real controllers – perhaps ultimately the man, or men, you met in Pakistan – that you are still working for. You calculate, plan, think long-term. Years, decades even. So yes, you throw the British security services some jihadist hotheads and idiots, none of them of real use to your cause. And you preserve the ones you believe capable of whatever final victory you have in mind. All the while you assure your MI5 handler, your lover, that they present no threat.' She rose from her chair and walked in front of his, her eyes over him. 'Correct?'

Kareem stayed in his chair, the smile still playing around his lips. 'You are a woman, Sara, I am a man. I will concede you one element of your narrative. Isobel. Dame Isobel. Even now, we see each other.' He paused and raised himself to whisper in her ear: 'I sometimes place my lips on her ageing bony cunt.' He relaxed back in his chair.

'I choose not to hear that,' said Sara. 'Then, in 2016, the game ends,' she resumed. 'The woman we speak of becomes her organisation's head. Largely because of the apparent success of your and her operation. You're signed off her books, killed by a drone strike. And you've achieved your ambition, of which she has never had a single inkling, so beyond her comprehension would it be. You have built your secret army for whatever plans you have in mind.'

Kareem looked again at his watch. 'Time passes. Is your amusing story nearly over?'

'Just the coda, as you've called it. Patrick and I have speculated about the identity of Morahan's source – the man, or perhaps woman, going by the name of Sayyid. Who is in possession of the documents Sayyid provided? We ran through names. We assumed it was a good person, exposing evil. But let us turn this too on its head. One other person would have possessed these files – given to him by his handler as he needed them for the role she believed he was playing. One person only knows why the dark-haired woman in the photograph, me, might be drawn to seek out the white-robed man seated on her right.'

She retreated to her seat, needing, from some indefinable urge, to restore distance between them.

'You, Kareem. You had those files.'

'But why, Sara?' The smile twisted itself into a pained puzzlement. 'Why would I wish to do that?'

'Boredom? Mischief-making? No, that's not you. The Morahan Inquiry, conducted thoroughly and scrupulously – as he wished it to be – presented a threat. Concealed within its mass of evidence might have been a route to the correct destination – and your exposure. So why not sow confusion? The wilderness of mirrors, as Morahan told me you called it in that strange conversation. Provide tit-bits of enticing, secret information to the Inquiry's chairman. And lead him to me – for whatever perverse satisfaction that's given you.'

'If this were so, Sara, might that not be a wonderful outcome? That you would see how I have served your country. Or should I say your "adopted" country.'

'I'm British, Kareem. Let me continue *my* narrative. British intelligence hires you to be its servant; and believes it will always be your master. But the reverse has happened. MI5, maybe MI6 too, teach you all their tricks – you become a super-agent, skilled and drilled, and you now deploy those tricks to defuse this potential threat to your ultimate ambitions. The Sayyid files are not the product of an idealistic whistleblower; they're planted by you to cause disruption. The death of Sir Francis Morahan is contrived by you, tailor-made so that conspiracy theorists can point the finger at an MI5 panic-stricken by the leakage of secret files and the possible consequences. Yes, MI5 is worried – perhaps it is they not you who threaten Patrick. But when an "accident" befalls my father as he intercepts an intruder, who is that?'

'I would never do anything to harm you, Sara,' said Kareem. 'I once told you that.'

'You already harmed me, Kareem. Finally, we come to J. It's a deliberate drowning. I remember what Morahan said to me. "I'm not a conspiracy theorist. I don't believe our intelligence services shoot people in the head or drop them out of helicopters, or out of boats with lead in their boots." Perhaps he was right. Perhaps MI5 doesn't. But there's someone who does – or whose henchmen do it for him. You, Kareem. You. And you end up the winner. The Inquiry is smothered. You're out of danger. You remain the hero whom your lover continues to parade as the saviour of the nation. You – and she, for her success suits you so well – emerge unscathed.'

She stopped, exhausted. Kareem's eyes bore in – despite herself, she felt that charge of seventeen years ago. 'Have you forgotten,' he said softly, 'surely not, the message you received on the night of July the 6th 2005? As you try now to harm me, how can you deny that I would never harm you?' Patrick glanced at Sara; her head was in her hands.

'Yes,' continued Kareem, 'you have nothing to say to that. But here you have much else to say. You are a clever woman, Sara. How much might we have achieved together? Even yet, you might understand me. So before I leave you to bide your time in this lonely place, I will, in return, tell you not yet a further narrative but a story. Having created your own fantasy, I hope you will enjoy it and appreciate its compatibility.'

This time he stood, circling the platform as he spoke, delivering his epilogue.

'Some years ago – let us say in the first half of the first decade of the twenty-first century – a young man arrives in the beautiful hilly country of Shangla in Pakistan. There he meets a very important person – a leader who, at that moment, is taking refuge in the mountains. In a year and a half's time, this leader will move to a large white-walled complex in the town of Abbottabad.

'After reaching the end of a rough track, the young man's car can go no further. He is escorted on foot deep into the mountains until he arrives at what seems little more than a shepherd's hut. It turns out to extend from a spacious cave. The leader he has come to meet is gentle, welcoming, softly spoken, unfailingly polite, wise, possessed of great learning, perhaps even divinity. He has been unwell but, in the mountain air, is recovering.'

Kareem stopped abruptly, tilting his head and listening. He checked his watch. Patrick glanced at Sara; she looked almost smug.

'Time rushes,' said Kareem, 'but I will finish my story. This leader offers his visitor tea and sits him down on a rug beside him. He tells him that he is a special person among those fighting to banish the corruption of the west. And he has a special mission. The way he will explain this mission is through a parable.

'"You are the fish swimming in the lake," the leader begins. "Fishermen try to catch you but they do not know what size or age you are. You understand they would like to know you better, to possess you, to eat you. One day, you will see a bait dangling above and then striking the surface of the water you are swimming in. You will bite at it. When the bait is stuck inside your mouth and the fishermen are trying to pull you onto shore, you pretend to fight. You fight for a well-judged number of minutes and then you surrender. You relax. Your body ceases to thrash around. In your floppiness, you allow the fishermen to bring you onto shore, store you in their canvas bag and take you to their home. The fishermen are hungry and will soon want to cook and eat you. This you will not resist. When they have tasted and chewed you, they will swallow you and you will descend into their stomachs. You reach their entrails and you will stay inside there for as long as it takes to poison and rot them. However many years that might be. And when they die, your glory will live on for ever."'

In the distance, emerging from the hum of the lights, Sara

began to make out a low rhythmic sound. And now, as Kareem talked of 'glory', its origin was unmistakable. A helicopter approaching. Patrick and Sara exchanged a quick look and turned back to Kareem. His expression was fixed, unreadable.

'A few more seconds, then I must leave you,' said Kareem. Despite the growing vibrations, he continued at the same measured pace. 'When the leader has finished his parable, he asks the man if he has understood its meaning. The visitor replies that he has. And when he returns to his country, the young man himself becomes a fisherman and distributes his fish to many important people throughout the land. Slowly they rise and rise within the highest institutions of government, business, industry and the state. They are the new fish. There are shoals of them. They are preparing.'

Kareem looked from Sara across to Patrick. 'It is an interesting story, is it not? It makes one think about the possibilities of the future world.' He turned back to Sara, moving closer. 'Before I slip away, Sara, I will tell you something,' he said softly but clearly. 'There will come a moment when you will finally understand me. And then you will appreciate what you have missed.'

'Stop, Kareem,' she hissed back. 'You have done your evil. Now leave me alone.'

Kareem rose, slowly shook his head once at her and strode towards the edge of the platform; Patrick ran round to intercept him. Aaqil was already there, knife in hand. They watched Kareem vanish into the darkness, followed by Aaqil and the sound of a door slamming.

'It's OK,' said Sara, the helicopter's din camouflaging her words. 'He's too late. Vanity. He had to finish. They'll get him.'

'What?'

'Shush. Later.'

Patrick leapt up and ran in the direction they'd left. A thick oak door was shut. He tried it. Locked, unmoveable. He went to the doors he and Sara had entered by. Locked.

'It's fine,' shouted Sara over the helicopter engines. 'They'll come and release us.'

'What?'

'I also texted Sylvia when we drove up the hill.' She grinned triumphantly. 'Until we found this place, I couldn't give her the co-ordinates. I asked her to send the local coppers round. Looks like she upgraded to choppers. Maybe she misread. Mind you, took longer than I'd have liked.'

'Why didn't you tell me?'

She paused, appearing to be picking her words carefully, all the time calculating how she would speak only truth and any sin would be of omission, not mendacity. 'Number one, I couldn't be sure Kareem would show up, though all my instincts were screaming it at me.'

'I thought we'd accepted he was dead. Just a question of cock-up or conspiracy.'

'Yes, we did. But after what you said, I kept going over it. Isobel somehow didn't make emotional sense. Her tears – you said they felt like crocodile tears at the time – seemed less and less convincing.'

'Sorry, I interrupted. There was a number two?'

'Yes, in case it didn't work out. Oh, and number three, you might have stopped me coming back.'

'You're bloody right I would have.' He wasn't smiling. 'OK, let's await the cavalry.' They sat down together on the edge of the platform. He put an arm round her.

She let him.

30

They waited.

The helicopter's roar vibrated the walls and floor of the barn; they huddled closer against its assault. Suddenly it changed pitch, screaming even louder, then gradually began to quieten.

'He's on his way. That thug with him, I hope,' said Patrick. 'Good riddance. What did you tell Sylvia?'

'To report it as kidnapping and false imprisonment,' said Sara.

'They've got him. Hope they don't forget us.'

He rose and switched on whatever further lights he could find. They waited, anticipating footsteps, then a shout, perhaps a beating down of the door.

Nothing. Only a drift into silence as the helicopter sounds ebbed away in the hills.

'I don't get it,' she said.

'And I don't like it,' he replied. He got up again and tried the door Kareem had left by. Still locked. He walked, agitation in his stride, to the second entrance.

'What the—' he began. He swivelled to her. 'This door's ajar.' He turned back and pushed. It swung easily open.

'Careful,' she said.

He poked his head out. As still as a windless lake. There was enough left of the gloaming to see across the courtyard and down the gravel driveway. He walked out, confirmed the picture and returned.

'Deserted,' he said. 'Not a soul. I didn't hear the locks being released.'

'Nor did I.'

'They, someone, must have done it under cover of the helicopter noise.'

'What's happened, Patrick?' Calm had deserted her. 'I don't understand what's happened.'

'You're sure you kept to the phone discipline.'

'Yes, I texted Sylvia from my burner to the one you got her. And told her to remember to use that one to phone the police.'

'She must be under even tighter surveillance than we thought.' He headed towards the door; she ran to catch up with him. Outside he stared up at the now moonlit sky. 'That helicopter was his cavalry, not ours.'

Eyes covering all angles, they headed towards the gates. The car was where he'd left it, apparently untouched. 'He'll be crowing now,' said Patrick, 'imagining how gulled we must feel.'

Driving back down the lane, neither wanted to start the conversation they had to have. Patrick's constant checking of the rear-view mirror allowed her an opening.

'Do you want to stop and go over the car?'

'What's the point? If the professionals are tracking, it'll be by satellite.'

'OK. Should we analyse what just happened? And what comes next.'

'Can we wait till we hit the motorway? These roads are making me twitchy.'

He started the same playlist they'd driven down to; this

time, she'd allow him to break the silence. Several tracks later, nearing the Severn Bridge, he finally did. 'So… You tell me. Which "narrative"? His or yours? And by the by, how long have you been thinking of it and deciding not to try it on me?'

'I'm sorry. I didn't even know I was going to do it. It was his arrogance. His certainty.' A riposte came to her. 'And *you* never told me you were bringing the contract.'

'No. No, I didn't.'

'Why?'

'I honestly don't know… some instinct, I guess. That, in its way, it was a weapon. A protection even.' He checked the rear-view mirror. 'Back to the narrative…'

'Neither. Both. I don't know. There *is* no certainty. It's all about power and manipulation. It goes back to what he is. Sociopath. Psychopath. Whatever.'

'Yes, we like to use those terms now to find explanations. But in his distorted way, he's brilliant. A genuine leader. The amoral mastermind who employs useful idiots. He said it himself. He wouldn't give a tuppenny damn about sacrificing any of them.' He hesitated. 'What was he saying about a text message, Sara?'

'I'm sorry.' She was subdued, not wanting to say but knowing she must. 'It's the one thing I couldn't tell you. Of course, he knew that. That's why he worked it in. It was hardly part of the story.'

'What happened?'

'It was the early morning of July the 7th. Two hours before 7/7. I had an anonymous text, it said something like, "don't use the buses or tubes in London today." I tried to hit reply, it wouldn't send. I assumed it was some kind of hoax. If I phoned the police, I thought I'd feel a fool. I talked myself out of doing anything. When I got to work, I suddenly thought I should at least do something. So I tried the Met confidential line.' She paused, feeling for a tissue in her bag. 'It was too late.'

He slowed down, switching to the inside lane, allowing himself a fleeting second to watch her. 'It's OK,' he said. 'Think about it. If you'd tried to report it – whoever you chose – how could it have made any difference? Not then. 7/7 came from a clear blue sky. They'd never have cleared the whole of central London transport on the back of a single imprecise text message. Let alone inside two hours. You didn't need to beat yourself up then. You don't now.'

'I felt guilty enough not to tell you, didn't I? To hold it back.'

'You've told me now.'

She felt an urge to complete the story. 'I tried to phone the number too. Just got a voice message saying it was unobtainable. Looking back, I guess he was using a burner phone and instantly dumped the SIM card.'

'Probably,' he replied. 'That's the only sure-fire way, now and then, to be anonymous on a mobile. Any other way's traceable.'

She frowned. 'How do you know that?'

'It came up when I was searching how Morahan's text to you could have disappeared.'

She relaxed – they were back in the present. 'That reminds me, I must lend Buttler my phone to sort that one out.'

'Are you sure you need to?' He paused. 'After what's happened today.'

'Yes,' she said firmly. 'I want the doubts gone.'

They fell into silence; the last secret between them was out.

Or so it seemed to him. She thought of telling him about the recent anonymous texts, but what was the point now? Particularly the last one she'd received seven hours ago in the stables:

Someone you want to see will meet you at the barn. You must vacate around 4 p.m. for thirty minutes to allow their arrival.

The real reason she'd lied about the phone signal, prompting the drive from the farm to find one.

Should, could she have shared it with Patrick? To find out the burner phone number Patrick had got her for this trip, they, whoever they now were, had either, as Kareem implied, tracked every one of Patrick's preparations for the trip or, as he'd feared, monitored her morning call to the hospital switchboard. The extent of the surveillance might have panicked him.

In addition, if she'd shown it to him without further explanation, he too perhaps would have realised it could only mean that Kareem was not dead but alive, wanting a final showdown with her. He would have insisted on pulling her out, putting his duty to protect her above all else, failing to understand that she could not – and would not – run away from it, nor from the opportunity to bring him to justice, however hopelessly that had turned out.

It was pointless too to tell him. She had a powerful sense that there would be no more anonymous texts. Even if it had begun with Kareem, she had come to wonder if there was an additional guiding hand. She might never know who that was. She must try not to think about it, it would achieve nothing.

The silence she was crowding with her internal arguments began to oppress her. 'What are we going to do about today?' she finally asked.

'He had some nerve, didn't he?' said Patrick. 'Why show at all? Why say what he did.'

She considered it for a while. 'It's partly his psyche. Maybe megalomania's what it really is. There had to be a showdown and he had to win. But I suspect there's a rationale too. His demonstration that whatever we know, whatever happened, we'll never be able to prove it. And he's right.'

'No. It's just as you say – we have the contract. Even if he escapes, it will expose what happened.'

'You're really going to lodge it with the Inquiry? Even though you're implicated?'

'Yes, Sara, I really am.'

'You should give me a copy for back-up if you're submitting the original.'

'I'll do it first thing.'

They lapsed into further silence. She wondered if she should argue; warn him that making it official Inquiry evidence could destroy his career. But she knew he must have factored that in and wouldn't change his mind. It was his right thing to do.

They passed a sign saying that Newbury Services were in a mile. 'I'm late for prayers. Can we stop?'

'Of course. I could do with a quick kip. Better than falling asleep at the wheel.'

The question had been building in his mind for days. As he turned off the motorway and into the car park, slowing to find the darkest possible space for a sleep as the exertions and tensions of the day subsided, he made the leap.

'Sara… I wanted to ask you something?'

'Oh?'

He looked shyly into her eyes. 'If I want to invite you out for a date, what do I have to do?'

'Well,' she said, eyes flashing back and allowing herself a satisfying delay, 'like other things in life, it seems, there are three phases. First, you have to wait till my father's well enough to understand your request. Second, he has to agree. Third, you have to agree he accompanies us as my chaperone. It's just the way we do things.'

'That's fine,' he said, the grin softening to the gentlest of smiles.

'It's OK, Patrick, I'm only joking. I've told you before – I'm a big girl now.'

He found a parking space and cut the engine. 'You know,

there may have been something else. All that stuff about wanting you to understand him. As if he needed your absolution. Or just your approval.' He paused. 'At least I might have that in common with him.'

'No. He was game-playing. You'd never do that.' She smiled, lightly cuffed him on the cheek, got out and shut the door.

He watched her heading inside. Despite the bizarre outcome of their journey, he felt a contentment he'd never believed he'd recapture. In fact, as he imagined her in her own small space, mouthing those words she found so calming, he began to feel a happiness greater than any he could remember. He restarted the playlist and lowered the volume to no more than the comforting embrace of long-loved sounds. He wound down his window a few inches to allow the night air of early summer to gently fan him, switched off the interior light, lay back in his seat and closed his eyes.

Twenty-five minutes later, she headed back towards the car, a skip in her stride and a gladness in her heart. Yes, he was fun – and gentle. Perhaps over-protective but she'd drum that out of him. It would be good to wipe the slate clean and spend more time with him, whatever disapproval she might face – though, she was somehow sure, not from her father. As for anything more, the stars above and the river of time below would decide.

She neared the car, hearing faint strains of Roy Orbison's soaring voice and thought back to Patrick singing along in the morning. She smiled.

She opened the door, slid in beside him, and sighed with a warming tiredness. She'd allow him a minute or two more in the darkness to sleep. Only faint echoes from the motorway services broke through the silence. Time to rouse him. 'I found a nice little spot,' she said. He didn't answer. 'Time to wake up and go, Patrick.' Still no answer.

She stretched out the back of a hand to stroke his cheek and nudge him – allow him an easy awakening. She felt an odd softness, some kind of liquid oozing through her fingers. She pushed her hand harder against his head; it seemed to drop, the flow of liquid to increase. She recoiled, felt for the internal light, switched it on and turned back to him.

'No… no… no,' she whispered, shuddering.

She closed her eyes for a second, then forced herself to open them. He was slumped, his neck and head propped on the right top of the seat back, wedged against the window. A livid, blackened oval hole disfigured his left temple and cheek, blood leeching from it. Pink and red fragments were scattered over his clothes and seat – bloodied flesh and bones. She felt her hands and looked down at her clothes. The blood was seeping over her and her seat too.

She leapt out of the car, repeatedly screaming 'Help!' in the darkness, and walked round to the driver's door, hoping that if she opened it, some miracle would show that most of him was intact. As she pulled it ajar, his body started to lean outwards. She pushed herself against him. In his right temple she saw another hole, smaller, neater, the entry point of death.

Still with her weight against him, she grabbed at his right arm, searching for the wrist, desperate to find a pulse. Nothing. His right hand, dangling by the door, was locked around a pistol's grip.

The song reached its end, the final note dying away. It was over.

There was no going back. No happy ending.

Sara knew that Patrick had not held or fired that gun. She also knew that she'd never be able to prove it.

She felt in the jacket pocket where he'd put back his copy of the contract. It was empty.

31

The phone call came just after 8 a.m. Even though she'd half expected it, Sara was still surprised at the speed and the voice on the line. She was invited to choose a meeting place – 'somewhere open that would suit us both' – and proposed the Temperance Fountain on the east tip of Clapham Common, a minute from the tube. With families and children all around, it felt safe territory.

She hadn't got home till 4 a.m. The response to her 999 call was fast and the police asked her to wait inside while they sealed the scene. Although it appeared to be a clear case of suicide, they said there would be a full forensic examination. As the hour was so late, the interviewing officer suggested a short, initial chat and asked her to attend Reading police station over the next day or two to make a full statement.

She'd given them bare, but truthful, bones: she and Patrick had been professional colleagues for just a few weeks; they were working together on a government inquiry and had visited Wales to interview a potential witness; Patrick's frame of mind had been good and cheerful; nothing during the day had, as far as she knew, affected his frame of mind; she wasn't aware of any present issues in his personal life though she didn't know him well; he'd told her he'd been divorced for a while and had a good relationship with his son; no, she did not know his next of kin; yes, she'd be happy to come back to Reading; no, she had no idea he had a gun and found it hard to believe.

A taxi to London was summoned – it cost her £110 at that time of night. On her arrival home she'd decided not to check Patrick's personal mobile, realising it could be seen as tampering with evidence. She switched on her own. In the inbox was a text from the pay-as-you-go phone Patrick had carried on the trip. She tried to remember the exact timings; it must have been sent around eight minutes before she'd returned to the car.

> Hi Sara, sorry that you'll be the one left with this mess. It's finally over for me. There's a sadness in my life that won't go away and I can't go on. You've been a great colleague, however briefly. Thanks for that. Patrick x

She read it and cried for longer than she could remember crying since she had been a child. A good – a very good – man had died, and had been beaten in the process. She understood that a part of her had died with him.

She went to the bathroom, showered, dried the tears and collapsed on her bed, not expecting sleep to come easily. Three thoughts kept revolving. How much he must have frightened them. How clever they'd been, particularly with that text. How she must stop herself feeling powerless. She set her alarm for 8 a.m.

Three hours later, she was sitting on a stone resting beneath one of the Temperance Fountain's four lion heads. She discarded her cardigan and lay it beside her – the day was hot.

Though she watched, she saw nothing till the tall, slim figure drew alongside, hovering over her – long linen trousers, a cream blouse, an elegant white hat with broad brow and large sunglasses.

'Hello, Sara.'

Sara stood. 'Hello, Dame Isobel.'

'As before, just Isobel. Also as before, this discussion is not happening.'

'Will it be the truth this time?'

'Would you mind if we walk? It won't take long. Perhaps towards the bandstand.'

They rose and walked silently until they were sufficiently alone.

'I'm very sorry about Patrick,' said Isobel.

'Are you?' said Sara. Her tone was flatter than the grass.

'Of course. He was a decent man and a good lawyer.'

'Decent man. So everyone says. When did you hear?'

'I heard the news around 6 a.m. I was deeply shocked.'

'Though not surprised.'

Isobel stopped in her tracks. 'Sara, I know you'll find it hard to trust me after what I told you about Kareem's death. That remains a necessary fiction – we must maintain it. But I have something important to tell you. At this very moment, Kareem – under his new name, of course – is being deported.'

'Deported?'

'Yes, returned, whether he likes it or not, to his home state.'

'Which is?'

'That need not concern you. Let's just say the Gulf.'

'Why?'

'For suspected breaches, in recent weeks, of the Official Secrets Act – which he signed up to on joining the staff of MI5.'

'You mean Sayyid.' Isobel stayed silent. 'Then you should be prosecuting him.'

'It's been decided that would not be in the public interest.'

'Don't you mean special interests,' said Sara.

'I understand your cynicism. It would never be provable in a court of law. The decision was taken rapidly and unanimously this morning, at the highest level.' Sara said nothing. 'I'd hoped you would feel reassured by this news,' continued Isobel.

'Wrong. The Morahan Inquiry has been cheated of its duty to examine a vital witness.'

'In that case, I must give you the fuller context. Please keep it to yourself.'

'I'm not willing to guarantee that. Not until I've heard you.'

'Should I trust in your good sense and your patriotism?' Sara looked straight into her eyes, giving nothing. 'I think I should,' said Isobel. 'I see an empty bench. Shall we sit?'

They spread themselves and Sara's cardigan to fill it.

'For a decade,' Isobel began, 'Operation Pitchfork was a success – vital to our security. Kareem performed services to this country, at great personal risk. He neither could, not would, ever be prosecuted. Back in 2016, in the weeks after my appointment as DG – but before I took it up – I continued to handle him. During those weeks I became worried by some aspects of his judgement and behaviour.'

'What aspects?'

'His character streaks of domination and manipulation were in danger of becoming overbearing. And potentially damaging. You may recall these from your own youthful experience.'

Sara felt her nakedness in the presence of this woman. 'Did he speak to you about me?'

'Yes, often. He was still bewitched by the thought of you. He told me everything. Or, perhaps, his side of it. He always seemed to want some kind of reckoning because you walked away. I told him that was a waste of his energy.'

'I was lucky to get away.'

'Perhaps you were. For me, it was different. He owed me. And though it was an exception for an agent handler, I decided to have a relationship with him if it kept him in play.' The trace of a smile showed in a squeezing of eyes and pursing of lips. 'I cleared it with the relevant people in the organisation, though not without initial difficulty.' The smile faded. 'To continue. Having created his death in the drone strike, I decided to keep Kareem within my sights and monitor him. His new identity allowed us to parachute him into two City directorships to occupy his mind. He was no longer on the Security Service staff or payroll though we were honouring his pension. Not that he needed the money – he spent half his time learning aerobatics.

'Then, though we succeeded in delaying it for a while, a naive government finally insisted on the foolish initiative that led to the Morahan Inquiry. Kareem saw a chance to become involved again in the manipulations he enjoyed. I'm still not fully clear on his motives. Perhaps they changed as events unfolded. He may have been angry with MI5, me included, for stopping Pitchfork, and wanting to make trouble – not much trouble, just enough to annoy us. He may have liked the idea of feeding the Inquiry in a way that would poison it. And he realised he might be able to use it to reach you.'

'But that was all so long ago.'

'As I said, he never forgot. Unfortunately, he was in possession of documents that we'd thought it necessary at the time to give him for Pitchfork—'

'He didn't need the restaurant photograph for that.'

'I apologise for that. When we made our arrangement with him, he asked for a print. As we'd already shown it to him as part of our evidence, there seemed no harm in it.'

'You actually gave him that photograph,' said Sara incredulously.

'Yes.'

'And the tape.'

'Yes.'

'What else did you give him?'

Isobel didn't answer. She checked to left and right; mothers, with eyes only for babies in prams and undisciplined toddlers, and joggers with earphones occasionally passed by. 'As well as documents, one or two of Kareem's team on Pitchfork had remained on his retinue. He paid for them.'

'Aaqil being one.'

'Yes.'

'Is he being deported?'

'No, he's a UK national. We'll deal with him. Without Kareem, he is, and has, nothing.' Isobel took a deep breath. 'What I'm trying to tell you, Sara, is that what has happened is the result of actions by a former agent who went rogue. I regret it.'

'What about the threat to Patrick outside his flat?'

'That was an exception. It was an intervention made with good intentions but it was unwise. I've reprimanded those responsible.'

'The watchers in my street. The injury to my father.'

Isobel frowned. 'I know nothing of those.'

'The helicopter arriving at the farm. Unless Kareem has his own air force.'

Isobel allowed the curl of a smile. 'By that time, too late I know, we were on top of Kareem's games. We were also aware of the plans Patrick had made for your trip to Wales. It was information acquired by legally authorised warrants. As was the monitoring device we planted in the barn.'

'You listened in?'

'We have a record – there are one or two inaudibles.' Sara remembered Kareem's disgusting whisper in her ear. He must have suspected. 'In fact, I contacted Kareem before your meeting with him in the barn—'

'Did you facilitate it?'

'By that time, we were in a position to take pre-emptive action. Without going into details, the answer is yes.'

Isobel stopped, as if she'd allowed herself to go too far. Sara frowned, hesitating, calculating whether to pursue it. 'Have you ever sent me any texts?'

Isobel screwed up her eyes in apparent astonishment. 'What?'

'Forget it,' said Sara. 'Why did you "facilitate" the meeting?'

'I felt it could be important to hear how he played it, what he'd feel provoked to say to you – and also ensure it couldn't go on too long. Pull him out in good time. Just in case it turned unpleasant.'

'Unpleasant?' Isobel stayed silent. 'And the call Sylvia Labone made to the local police?' continued Sara.

'As we ourselves were ensuring there were no safety issues at the barn, we intervened. It appears, I'm afraid, the one mistake was to return Kareem and his assistant—'

'Aaqil.'

'Yes… return them too quickly to their car. I'm not saying this is what happened, but Kareem and Aaqil would have had the know-how to plant a device in the car Patrick had hired. To be within close range as you turned into Reading services.'

Sara took her mobile phone out of her bag. She showed Isobel the text message sent from Patrick's pay-as-you-go. 'How did Kareem know my number?'

'Have you changed it since you gave Marion your number in the restaurant?'

Sara sighed. 'I suppose not. Phones yes, never the number.'

'You have an answer.' She looked up. The massive shape of an A380 was lumbering towards Heathrow. She waited for it to die down. 'It's easy for anyone who knows how, to find a phone number these days.'

'Why would Kareem want to kill Patrick?' asked Sara.

'Sara, we do have to wait for the police investigation,' replied Isobel gently. 'It could have been suicide.'

'He was killed. I know, you know. Even if it will never be proved.' Sara thought she saw Isobel unsettled. She moved closer. 'What are you thinking?' she said. 'Tell me – whatever it is.'

'If you must, Sara. If Kareem had detected you were becoming too close to Patrick, that inner rage might have boiled over.'

Sara felt an acute awareness of that part of herself destroyed along with Patrick. 'Am I safe from him?'

'Of course. He's being deported. Though I never felt he would physically harm you.'

'He already had.'

'If Kareem ever felt regret, that would be the only one.'

Sara allowed the idea to hang; she might once have believed he could feel sorrow or regret, but not now. 'Have you listened yet to the conversation in the barn?' she asked.

'Yes,' replied Isobel. 'At the time.'

Sara shook her head, understanding ever more the layers of deceit. 'So you heard his "parable" of the fish.'

'Yes. It was entirely in character. There is no evidence whatsoever for anything other than the first "narrative". When you related your own far-fetched fantasy – forgive me those words but they are accurate – of Kareem being some kind of long-term jihadist triple agent, I'm afraid he simply couldn't resist. It was too good an opportunity for one of his mind games – to agitate and scare you. We will, of course, go over all his contacts, decisions, actions, everything, however much we already know the answers. I can't guarantee that, even from outside the UK, he won't continue playing games with you. But his only weapon is his phone. He poses no threat to you or our nation.'

Sara saw a tiredness in the face opposite. Isobel must have started early and been on the go ever since, trying to fight the fire. Perhaps she was one of those mangled souls who slept for three hours a night and lived off nervous energy.

'The reason I have come here,' said Isobel, 'is in the hope that you will bear in mind the national interest and security when it comes to police and any other investigations of these recent, tragic events. We have dealt with the threat. Whatever evidence and accounts you yourself are in a position to give, neither they nor anything else will ever provide proof that any of these events were the result of illegal actions. Even to this day, I myself don't know for sure. The accident or suicide explanations are fully plausible. I may be traducing Kareem. Perhaps it was only mind games.'

'You know too much, Isobel, to allow yourself to believe that.'

'People overrate our omniscience.'

'What about the contract?' asked Sara.

'Contract?' Isobel's eyes widened with a second show of astonishment. It instantly made Sara question the first one.

'Please don't start lying now.'

The eyes narrowed. 'I understand what you're referring to. It is a matter of fact that there was no contract with MI5. Nothing was ever authorised from the top.'

'You were there. There was a signed and witnessed contract containing certain indemnities for Kareem.'

'We have to operate in a real world, Sara, to protect our nation. If Patrick and Kareem signed a piece of paper giving him some kind of assurances, Patrick, I'm sure, did it for the right reasons.'

'It was witnessed.'

'If so, not by anyone with official status.'

'It was an MI5 employee going under the name of Len Rogerson.'

'I'll check for you but I recall no one of that name in the security service.'

'And overseen by you.'

'No. That's not credible. If any such thing was ever told or hinted to you, either by Patrick or J, it's wrong. You should remember that they may have been saying things to protect themselves.'

'But it's convenient, isn't?' said Sara. 'All parties to the contract now gone. J and Patrick dead. Their contracts gone with them. Kareem out of the country. Just you left, Dame Isobel.'

'Sara, I understand your sadness. And your bitterness. And your mistrust. I hope in time they'll all begin to heal and pass. I've come here in good faith to give you the truth as I know it. I'm asking you to take it into account in your further actions. Enough has been said. I'll leave you in peace.'

Isobel rose and marched off, turning towards the road running alongside the south of the Common. As she reached the pavement, Sara watched a black saloon with tinted windows slow down and embrace her like a wraith gathered in to the shadows.

Was Dame Isobel a woman who, at cost to her own morality, was doing her best for her country? Or the most accomplished liar she'd ever met?

32

Three weeks later

Her father was practising 'oo's and 'ou's. The daily pattern of home visits from speech, physio and occupational therapists – young women with sunny smiles and breezy voices – was erasing the memory of the motionless figure on a hospital bed, invaded by needles and tubes. He slurred slightly and sometimes the right word refused to emerge from his mouth. But she could see the mind was functioning ever better. Soon she'd be able to leave him for long enough to allow a partial return to work.

That would not be to the Inquiry's office in Vauxhall. The day after the encounter with Isobel Le Marchant, Sara had been invited by Pamela Bailly for a chat about the future. It was a one-way conversation.

'I'm very sorry about everything that's happened,' Pamela had begun. 'Patrick's death is a tragedy. I now understand you've also been coping with misfortune at home. You should have told me; I'd have said take however long you need.'

'You didn't need to be troubled by it,' said Sara.

'A decision has been taken about the future of the Inquiry,' she continued briskly. 'Sir Roger Knell will be seeing things through in place of Sir Francis.'

'Sir Roger Knell?' said Sara, bemused. 'He was Permanent Secretary at the Home Office, wasn't he? He's parti pris with MI5.'

'Be that as it may,' said Pamela, 'the Secretary of State has made his decision. Furthermore, rather than proceed with hearings, Sir Roger will now oversee the writing of the Inquiry's report on the basis of submissions received.'

'You mean no more research, no more interviews. No examination of witnesses. No calling to account.'

'It is not for me to comment.'

'And no further role for me.'

Pamela offered a short smile. 'We will, of course, pay the final weeks of your contract. To be honest, Sara, if I were you, I'd feel pleased and relieved to be excused from any further responsibilities here and able to return to your own world.'

In the days since, Sara had asked herself what her own world now was. So far, she'd given the benefit of her doubts to Isobel. In her more detailed session with Reading police, she'd bided her time, truthfully answering questions limited by their unquestioned acceptance that Patrick's death was a suicide.

She looked across at her father, smiling at his attempts to flirt with the speech therapist. If, she sometimes thought, she hadn't had him and his recovery to devote herself to, she might have folded. Wasn't this all that really mattered – the happiness of loved ones and providing the support they needed?

Her phone rang. 'Yes?'

'Is that Miss Sara Shah?'

'Yes.' Half-recognising the voice and accent, she switched to alert.

'It is the father of Iqbal Jamal Wahab here, Ms Shah. You visited us in Blackburn.'

'Yes of course, Mr Wahab. I remember. It's good to hear from you.'

'Am I speaking privately to you?'

'Yes. Yes, you are.'

'We heard from Iqbal.'

'That's good, I'm so pleased.'

'It was just a text message to his brother. I think he allowed me to see it so I'd know Iqbal is alive. There was something odd. I thought I would ask you. Confidentially.'

'Of course.'

'It said something like this. "I need to stay away for a while. We're just waiting for the Adviser to tell us when. Could be months, could be years. Then it'll be done." I don't understand it. I'm wondering if you have come across anything like this in your research. Maybe you know what it means.'

Sara's heart was pounding. 'Did Iqbal leave any contact details?'

'No. I think it was a one-off phone of some kind.'

'And you have no other way of reaching him.'

'No.'

'Never mind. I'm afraid I haven't come across anything like this, Mr Wahab, but I'll look into it. Can I get back in touch if I find anything?'

'Yes, please do, Miss Shah. I will be most grateful. Just phone this number.'

'Thank you so much. I'll see what I can do.'

Heart racing, stomach churning, Sara grabbed a piece of paper and wrote down the words as verbatim as she could remember them.

'We're just waiting for the Adviser to tell us when. Could be months, could be years. Then it'll be done.'

It wasn't over.

If Isobel could be trusted, she should believe that, however circuitous the routing, it was a Kareem-contrived trick to show he could still play games with her. If so, she must report the call to Isobel. Perhaps that was the best thing, the right thing, to do.

Then, from nowhere, an idea struck her, a devastating flash that seemed to illuminate and solve all the contradictions and puzzles of the past weeks. One that would mean Isobel was the very last person she should inform.

What if Kareem – as with Marion, as so nearly with her – had succeeded not just in seducing Isobel Le Marchant and becoming her companion in bed, but in turning her? Converting her to his revolution. Joining him in his warped quest for revenge.

What if Dame Isobel Le Marchant, the Director General of the United Kingdom of Great Britain and Northern Ireland's Security Service, was the biggest fish in Kareem's shoals? It was the link that made sense of all the narratives. Whatever was done outside the law, the killings above all, sub-contracted to Kareem and his expertly trained sidekicks. The technology and surveillance – the warnings too, maybe even the 'burglary' at her home – ordered in-house by Isobel with all the wizardry at her beck and call. The perfect lethal combination.

Forget about the law of unintended consequences; try instead an alternative law of intended consequences. The Morahan Inquiry had been sunk. All dangerous witnesses and evidence of the contract destroyed. Dame Isobel and Kareem himself more secure than ever, safe from any further probing or investigation.

Judge events by their outcomes.

Had they planned it together from the outset? If so, not just the big picture but tiny details too could be explained. The tortuous methods Sayyid used for delivering information, designed to tantalise an ageing judge – a Kareem manipulation. The overnight change in Sami and the precision both of what he did say and what he didn't. The vile words about Isobel that Kareem whispered in the barn – a ploy to make any continuing relationship seem impossible. The anonymous texts – above all that last one to her at the farm, the one that had forced her last lie to Patrick.

How suckered she had been – not just by Kareem but, if she was right, by Isobel too. If only she had seen more clearly that it was not Patrick who needed to protect her, but she who needed to protect him, he might be alive now... even if their search would die.

For the first time since Patrick's death – perhaps in some kind of penance to him – Sara felt energised. Now that the idea had gripped her, and even if, at this point, she might be the only person in a position to understand it, she couldn't – and wouldn't – let it rest. Ludo Temple had been in touch, saying how much they looked forward 'after all this ghastly business' to having her back at Knightly Court. Yes, she'd go back, but there would be a condition. The Chambers must fund a full-time researcher to record and investigate all disappearances that could connect to Kareem and Operation Pitchfork. She herself must be allowed an agreed number of hours per week to work on the project. Somehow she knew Ludo would make his colleagues agree.

That was not enough. The Home Office, intelligence services, even Parliament's Intelligence and Security Committee would, she was sure, be deaf or compromised. Instead her approach must be that of a citizen in a free democracy – to trust in the law and hold to account a secret state which should not be allowed to sign contracts with evil.

She thought of those glinting eyes of DS Buttler, recalling that phone call from him a few days ago.

'Bob Buttler here, Ms Shah.'

'Oh?'

'Just to say I've got your phone back. The metadata does indeed show a text from Sir Francis's mobile was remotely deleted from it.' There'd been a pause on the line. 'I owe you an apology.'

'You don't, you were doing your job.'

'That's good of you to say.' Another pause. 'I heard about Mr Duke. A tragedy by all accounts.'

'Yes. It was.'

'Even if it's not a bad rule of thumb, I know the simple explanation's not always the right one, Ms Shah.'

'No,' she'd murmured. 'It isn't.'

'Well, as I said, I'm always here. Any time you want to talk. Anything I can do to help.'

Maybe she'd briefly been his target, but he wasn't a stupid man. Perhaps she would get back to him, make a further statement, do the same with the police at Reading. It would lay out all the background, including Sayyid and the documents, and all the facts, including the full account of the night of Morahan's death and the trip to Wales. She would even admit to her teenage entanglement with Kareem.

She would tell of his shoals of fish and the message sent by Iqbal Jamal Wahab.

The one thing she would not yet mention was her suspicion of Isobel; it would appear too far-fetched and undermine her. Facts were what mattered. She needed a good person to run with them; who, as she planted the seeds, would begin to see their growth. She needed someone with her to knock down doors – to reassemble the disappeared and track down the guilty. Someone both decent and good. Someone like Patrick Duke who would work with her to see that growth blossom into truth.

And then pray that if that truth turned out to be ugly and its consequences fearful, they would intercept it in time. In time...

33

2021
Wednesday 13 October
11.49 a.m.

He steps out of the lift at the 67th floor of the Shard onto the lower viewing platform, his ticket booked long in advance. An initial 360-degree sweep around reveals a bright autumnal view of London, blue sky, sun to the south nearly at its zenith, a few white vapours and streaks painted on the stratosphere but otherwise clear in every direction. Clarity. Not just of sight, but of mind. Clarity and finality.

He climbs onto the upper platform and the spectacle is enhanced. He looks down on the London Eye where, twenty years and thirty-three days ago, he lived a moment that, for him, will never die. Not only the leap of his imagination but the jump in his groin as he stood behind her, pressing, folding his arms around her belly, the violence of his imagination matching the violence of what he would like to do to her. Her pale olive skin, silky dark brown hair, smell of sweet sweat.

He waits.

Five minutes to go. They should almost be in sight, the two of them. He thinks of the woman on the ground, staring at her screens, her nerves jangling, checking over her shoulder to see if anyone notices. Years of preparation in the balance. But, as yet, there is nothing to suspect or to see. He takes up position at the north viewing platform and removes binoculars from a case. Below a barge floats along the river in slow motion; stick-like figures pass each other on Hungerford Bridge. Cars on the approaches to Tower Bridge are stationary and he sees the drawbridge rise. Beyond, an elegant, high double-masted, cream-painted yacht glides up river; he quickly calculates what point it will have reached in five minutes' time. Even his powerful lenses cannot individually pick out each pigeon on the steps of St Paul's, but he can see the cluster. They'll find a way of getting away; they always do.

The date, decided three years back, is a matter he wrestled with. The precise anniversary had a flaw – not merely the extra vigilance on the day but holiday season in the Palace of Westminster. He decided to wait. Allow no chance for lucky escapes, nor accusation of pointless gestures. Each generation might only have one chance. Twenty years and thirty-three days have passed; we have not gone away.

He sees the American A380, with its hundreds of passengers, on its south east-diagonal, about to make the ninety-degree turn for the north-eastern approach to Heathrow, leading it to the Thames. He takes a few strides to the right and scans the south-eastern path, the Middle East and the Indian sub-continent thousands of miles beyond. There, unmistakably, a second, equally packed A380 is heading towards him. He shuffles to and fro to compare the increasing sizes of these two enormous steel birds soaring ever nearer. Their progress is remarkably uniform. He wonders if any pair of eyes, apart from the woman at Drayton, is seeing anything unusual. He imagines being in the cockpit seat of the co-pilot in the second plane – the one who knows; the one in whose seat he himself craves to be; the one who, a few minutes before, will have secured the double-locked cockpit door, raised himself from his seat to walk behind the senior pilot beside him; the one who, stealthily, speedily, will then have placed an electric flex around the neck in front and pulled it hard and silently tight.

He imagines sitting in the other cockpit of the first A380 where the two American pilots will be admiring the approaching river and the Shard itself as their auto-pilot flies them over London's law courts towards Big Ben and the Houses of Parliament. Perhaps they are joking, making plans for the evening, preparing to put their hands up a hostess's skirt. The plane flies itself, as it has done thousands of times before, with an inhuman precision and flawless functionality – seven or so minutes to landing and an afternoon and evening of opportunity lie ahead.

In the second plane, the co-pilot may take a glance at the lolling head and lifeless eyes beside him. Theirs was only a professional relationship after all and the concentration with which he must now apply himself allows no time for pleasure or regrets. He has practised the manoeuvre over and over again on the computer program they built for him. He is one line of the equilateral triangle heading towards its intersection; the second plane is the other. But he is operating in the four dimensions of space and time; because in the final stages he will be pulling up sharply from a thousand feet below, he must be that edge in front to compensate for the extra distance created by the elevation. It is simply a matter of mathematics, a subject at which he always excelled and contributed to his double first from Queen Vic's. Curiously – he had not factored this in – at this very moment he can see its Gothic pinnacles down to the right. He takes the aircraft out of autopilot and assumes control. He sees the other plane across the river and above him. He eases right, off his correct Heathrow runway two path, to increase the angle of difference between them.

The man on the Shard platform watches it beginning to unfold. He admires the sheer beauty of these huge shapes floating ethereally towards their fate. Below the Speaker of the House of Commons bangs his gavel and shouts, 'Order! Order!' The Prime Minister rises. What will the questions be about? After all, today's world is a dull place, the threat of terror now seems to be over, the disposition of the nations of Europe is arranged to the mutual benefit of all, a more relaxed United States of America is living calmly with the rest of the world under its forty-sixth President. The first two decades of the twenty-first century may have been a troubled age but Planet Earth and those who inhabit her are set fair for a new age of optimism.

In London it is 12 midday. In New York and Washington it is five hours earlier, 7 a.m. The men and women rising innocently from their beds will soon hear the shock from three thousand miles across the Atlantic. And because lightning never strikes twice, they will little imagine their own shock to come.

A tall, wraith-like woman ranges alongside and brushes the back of her hand between his thighs.

'It's done,' he says.

'Yes,' she agrees, 'it's done.'

She melts silently away.

At this moment, Sara Shah is walking back from the Old Bailey to the Temple. She's been in court all morning, her mobile phone off. She desultorily switches it on; it's an uneventful day, an uneventful few weeks. She notices a text. It arrived three hours earlier, just before she went into court.

Stay clear of Westminster and Whitehall today.

No name. An unfamiliar number.

She is distracted by the noise of a huge jet overhead on its landing approach to Heathrow.

She looks up.

Acknowledgements

My thanks to those whose insight and expertise helped so much: Alan Ewers, Andrew Allberry, Jon Appleton, Sahina Bibi, Dorothy Byrne, Lily Capewell, Gavin Esler, Joanna Frank, Jamie Groves, Val Hudson, Nicky Kroll, Joanna Potts, Sarah Shaffi, Victor Temple, Laura Westbury, Robert Young. Thank you also to those who prefer not to be or cannot be named.

My agent, Julian Alexander, and HQ's inspiring leader, Lisa Milton, have offered constant encouragement. The gifted Ayisha Malik provided invaluable knowledge and understanding. Sue Carney of Ethos Forensics has become a splendidly ingenious, generous ally and new friend. An old friend, Paul Greengrass, demonstrated, with critical effect, his unparalleled creative generosity and the power of his big brain. Another big brain, my editor, Clio Cornish, has been terrific both for her critiques and her creative interventions.

Above all are those closest to home – so thank you, Helena and Olivia, and, above all, Penelope who, in addition to her great editing and narrative skills, is there in so many different ways.